P9-DFP-779

*Avon Books is proud to present
Elizabeth Boyle, an exciting voice in
romance, making her Avon Treasure
debut. Elizabeth's unforgettable stories
have already captured the hearts of
countless readers, and now this rising
star brings you her most compelling
love story yet . . .*

No Marriage of Convenience

Mason St. Clair, the new Earl of Ashlin, has
inherited a title for which there is no fortune, thanks to his older brother. Steeped in
debt, with three ungainly nieces to marry off,
Mason fears that he will have to wed a rich
heiress to save his family from ruin. Desperate for relief, Mason doesn't expect it to arrive in the breathtaking form of Madame
Fontaine, a woman of questionable reputation but irresistible allure, who glides into
his study. Though Riley's most certainly not
bridal material, she does suddenly seem to
be the solution to his troubles. In an impetuous—and inspired—act, Mason hires Riley
to transform his reluctant nieces into charming Originals . . . but never does he anticipate
that the seductive lessons of this temptress
would fill him with an unbridled passion.
And suddenly, his heart hungers for no marriage of convenience, but one of love . . .

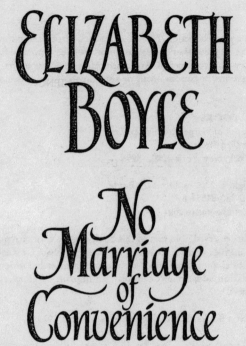

ELIZABETH BOYLE

No Marriage of Convenience

An Avon Romantic Treasure

AVON BOOKS
An Imprint of HarperCollinsPublishers

AVON BOOKS
An Imprint of HarperCollins*Publishers*
10 East 53rd Street
New York, New York 10022-5299

Copyright © 2000 by Elizabeth Boyle
ISBN: 0-380-81534-6
www.avonromance.com

First Avon Books paperback printing: September 2000

Avon Trademark Reg. U.S. Pat. Off. and in Other Countries, Marca Registrada, Hecho en U.S.A.
HarperCollins® is a trademark of HarperCollins Publishers Inc.

Printed in the U.S.A.

10 9 8 7 6 5 4 3 2

To my father, Denton Herlan,
the other storyteller in our family.
Thank you for teaching me
just how far you can stretch a fish story,
and then how to stretch it just a bit further.
All my love and deepest appreciation

—*Lizzie*

Prologue

London, 1772

"Mother, where are you sending me? You can't hide me away forever!"

The angry cries erupted outside the morning room where the Countess always took her breakfast. Summoning all the breeding and reserve of her noble forebears, the lady set down her teacup and awaited the next outburst. Even as she raised her napkin to her lips, her daughter Elise burst into the room. Two footmen followed the young woman, catching her arms and trying to pull her back into the hallway, their faces apologetic and fearful.

As well they should be, thought the Countess, *to allow such a scene in my house*.

Before she could chastise either of them, her scandal-ridden daughter shook herself free from her captors and continued her headlong rush toward the Countess.

"What are your plans now, Mother?" Elise cried, banging her fist down on the table and sending the delicate teacup clattering out of its saucer. "Commit me to Bedlam? I am a married woman with child, not some dockside whore riddled with pox!"

1

The Countess blanched at her daughter's vulgar outburst. Coughing discreetly, she waved the gawking maid and the ever-present butler out of the room. With a nod, she sent the footmen following as well. As the sound of their hurried steps died away, the Countess carefully set aside her napkin, reached for her gold-tipped cane, and rose from the table to face her only child.

A strained silence filled the room. The two women glared at each other, mirror images of stubborn determination.

Why couldn't she have borne a son? the Countess lamented. Though her husband's title and estates were entailed so they could pass to a daughter, Elise was not worthy to wear the noble name—not with her antics or her ill-fated connection.

The family's honor and decency had to be maintained, no matter the personal cost.

"Mother, I demand to know where you are sending me," Elise said, her scorn and contempt defining each word. "I'll have a say in my future. I'll not be treated like a child any longer."

Confronted again with this unrelenting defiance, the Countess lost any hold she'd claimed on her steely reserve and flew into a blind rage. Without even blinking, she slapped her daughter across the face as hard as she could.

The blow sent Elise reeling to her knees.

The Countess clenched her stinging hand at her side and continued to glare at her daughter.

From the floor, Elise looked up through the mass of dark hair that had tumbled loose in her fall and now fell about her head like a black shroud. "How dare you," she said. "I am with child!"

"I heard you the first time!" The Countess pounded her

cane on the polished floor. "Why not say it loud enough for even the scullery maids to hear?"

As Elise staggered to her feet, her chin lifted again in rebellion. "I'll say it loud enough for everyone in London to hear, once I am free of this house."

"Oh, don't worry. You're about to leave. But don't think for a minute you'll have the opportunity to make a greater fool of yourself." The Countess resumed her seat at the small table. Taking a deep breath, she steadied her shaking hands and poured herself another cup of tea.

Elise moved closer. "You truly mean to send me away from London?"

To the Countess's keen ears, it seemed her daughter's words held an anxious edge. She smiled inwardly at this first small victory in their battle over Elise's ill-advised elopement with Geoffrey Stoppard. Until fifteen years ago the Stoppards had been nothing but wool merchants, until they'd purchased a baronetcy in a pitiful attempt to raise their family above their common origins. Geoffrey, as a third son, had aimed at a higher lot in life than even his ambitious father could have imagined or purchased.

And Elise had offered him just that opportunity.

For as her husband, Geoffrey Stoppard not only would have gained control of her fortune, but the cursed letters of patent also entitled Elise's husband to take the rank left open by her father's death, the title of Earl.

The Countess shuddered at the unthinkable union of her daughter and some . . . some . . . conniving cit's son. Or worse, a cit's son taking her esteemed husband's title.

What would the *ton* have said about the sudden elevation of that odious man from commoner to one of the most respected titles in the peerage—all because she'd been unable to control her errant daughter?

At least she'd been able to prevent such a contemptible

situation—so far, though only through stealth and sheer bribery. The Countess had quelled all the rumors of Elise's springtime elopement, and even privately rejoiced when Stoppard and his arrogant ways had gotten him killed by brigands as the honeymoon couple returned from Scotland.

The entire episode could have been hushed up and forgotten, until this, she thought, glancing at the growing swell of Elise's normally flat stomach, this final reminder of Stoppard's rapacity and her daughter's reckless indiscretion.

"Where are you sending me, Mother?" Elise's insistent demand broke the Countess's reverie.

Selecting a roll, she buttered it with slow, precise strokes. "I intend to send you far enough away that this embarrassing situation will never be discovered."

Elise shuddered. "Why? Because Geoffrey didn't have all the titles and family connections you find so important? I don't care about any of that. I loved my husband. I'm proud to be carrying his child. At least now some part of him will continue on."

Anger narrowed the Countess's vision. "I doubt your precious Geoffrey would have appreciated such devotion, for he cared only for your money and the titles you brought to your marriage."

Her daughter's chin cocked upward again. "He cared not for those things. He would have loved me if I'd been a pauper. He told me so."

The Countess sniffed. "He said the same things to Lord Easton's daughter when he tried to elope with her last fall."

Elise blanched. "Cynthia?"

"Why yes, Lady Cynthia. Luckily her maid revealed their plans and Lord Easton was able to stop them before the idiotic girl ruined herself completely." She paused and glanced up at Elise. "Why, I thought you knew—nearly everyone does. But I can see by your face you didn't." The Countess glanced away, allowing her lie to sink into her daughter's love-besotted mind.

"What do I care what Geoffrey did before we were . . ." Elise struggled valiantly to defend her dead husband.

"Married?" her mother finished for her. "I wouldn't be so sure. There is no proof of a wedding, as you know, since you allowed it to be stolen along with all your belongings. And why would you want to claim it? Think, you foolish girl, what an alliance to that family would mean," the Countess said. "His father will step in as guardian to that bastard and take control of your inheritance. If something happened to that child, while the title would be safe, our holdings, our income, would pass to that wool merchant and his loathsome brood. No, it is better the entire episode is hidden away, better for you if this child is forgotten."

Elise shook her head. "Forget my child? Never." She drew herself up to her full height. "Geoffrey's child deserves a name, a home. Why should this babe bear the brunt of your anger because I married Geoffrey Stoppard?"

The Countess, refusing to speak, stared at her with icy regard.

"How can you deny your own grandchild?" Elise demanded.

"I will not acknowledge your unfortunate association with that impudent man, nor will I lend our good family name to his leavings," came the cold reply. "There is too much at stake."

"My child deserves a name."

The Countess raised her eyebrows at this continued defiance. Looking around the room she spied the wagging tail of her deceased husband's favorite hound lounging near the fireplace. "If you insist on giving your little bastard a name, call it Riley," she mocked, pointing her finger at the ugly old hound.

"After the dog?"

"Why not?" she told her daughter. "Without the protection of this family or that of a husband, you would be no better in the world than the whore you played to your perfidious lover. Riley is the best name your child could hope for."

Elise's hands folded over her stomach, as if to protect her babe from the nightmare unfolding around her. "You would have my child live as a . . ."

"A bastard," the Countess said coldly, dismissing any possible sentiment about the child her daughter carried.

Her grandchild.

Again, she took a deep breath. The child was none of her concern.

"I could marry someone else, pass this child off—" Elise said quietly.

The Countess shook her head. "You're too far gone for that. If you had come to me two months ago, it might have worked. I'm sure there are many who would take you even now, but I'll not endure the gossip come March when that babe arrives four months after a hasty marriage—nor will I risk any speculation by those Stoppards as to who the father may be."

The Countess reached for her cane and rose again. Pacing to the garden window, she glanced out at the cold November morning and frowned.

"So what will you do with me?" Elise finally whispered.

Drawing a deep breath, the Countess laid out her plan. "You will sail to France and bear this child in secret. Once it is all over, you can return and marry Tamlyn, as your father and I have planned since your birth. He's heir to his grandfather's dukedom. One day you'll be a duchess and all of this," she said, pointing a beringed finger at her daughter's stomach, "will be forgotten."

Elise shook her head at her mother's scheme, her gaze focused out the window as well. "No, there must be another way. I'll not abandon my child."

The Countess leaned forward. "You will agree to these arrangements, or you will find yourself in a French convent for the remainder of your days. I will live without a daughter rather than have you ruin this family's honored name."

"Even you wouldn't be so cruel to bury away your only child in some foreign convent."

The Countess arched a brow. "I would rather see everything pass to your father's cousin than allow you another opportunity to rain scandal down on this house. Give up this bastard and marry Tamlyn."

"My child is not a bastard. It has a father. My husband."

"Then where is he, Elise? Where is your proof of matrimony?" the Countess jeered. "I'll tell you where—stolen away, just like that conniving blackguard did with your virtue and reputation."

It wasn't without some regrets that she watched Elise's shoulders sag in defeat.

All is not lost yet, my child, her mother thought. *You can return and take your position as Tamlyn's wife and you'll rule society as I have.*

A famous beauty from the moment she'd stepped into the London social circuit at sixteen, Elise and her mysterious green eyes had been regaled by poets, her lithesome and flirtatious manners imitated by the highest born down to the parroting masses, and her company sought by every man from seventeen to seventy-nine.

Elise slowly turned her gaze from the window. The Countess watched her with a level stare, trying to discern any sign, some evidence that her daughter would make the right decision.

"What will it be?" the Countess asked, silently urging her to make the right choice. *Forget this child. Marry the Duke.*

"I'll go to France." Elise's green eyes burned with hatred. "But I will not give up this child. Nor will I marry Tamlyn."

The Countess instantly heard something underlying her daughter's terse words.

Hope. And a plan.

Well, she would nip any harebrained designs right here and now. "Don't think because you go to France you will have any opportunity to gain your freedom. You will be escorted by Edrich and his brothers, all of whom have been well paid and are not foolish enough to risk my wrath."

The Countess rose from the table, her cane in hand. "They will take you under guard to the ship, and then you will be locked in a room for the crossing. The Captain has been informed of your unfortunate tendency toward lunacy and is more than sympathetic to seeing you kept under lock and key. Your wiles, your pleas will go unheard, for you will neither see nor speak to anyone. In France, the abbess will not allow you to leave your cell until the child is born. And if you continue to refuse to marry Tamlyn, in the Abbey you will remain for the rest of your days. There will be no escape."

"Mercy, what will become of my child?" Elise said quietly, the words whispering of despair and loss.

The Countess thumped her cane down hard on the floor, driving away the bitterness of the last two months now wrenching at her heart. She wouldn't let imprudent sentimentality tear her from the course of action she'd chosen.

"That is no longer my problem," the Countess replied. "I wash my hands of you. You have done everything possible to ruin this family's name with your common behavior and theatrics more suited for the stage than my home. Your days of bringing disgrace to this house are over. If you do not come to your senses when this child is no longer an issue, then I will tell the world you died of a fever."

At the Countess's signal the footmen returned and caught Elise in their strong grasp.

"I shall escape you, Mother. And I will return," Elise cried out, as they dragged her from the morning room.

Though she did escape, she never returned to her mother's house.

But one day, Riley did.

Chapter 1

London, 1798

"**C**ousin Felicity, my brother had the business sense of a pelican," Mason St. Clair, the new Earl of Ashlin said, waving his hand over his littered desk. "Look at these. Bills for carriages. Bills for horses. I've looked in our stables. We have no horses. And we have no carriages. From what I can surmise, as quickly as Freddie bought these extravagances, he gambled them away."

Mason's announcement hardly seemed to upset his elderly relative, who sat primly on the settee in the corner of his study.

"Frederick always said life was just a dice toss away. Perhaps you should take up gambling." She nodded sagely, as if she'd recited gospel.

He picked up several sheets of paper and shook them at his cousin. "That's exactly what got us into this situation. That and Freddie's ill-advised investments. I never knew anyone who could throw so much money at such nonsense. Gold mines in Italy, Chinese inventions, and of all things, a theatre!" The Earl shook his head. "Only my brother would invest in some tawdry play on Brydge Street."

"Really, my dear, you shouldn't speak ill of the dead," she sniffled. A day never passed that Cousin Felicity didn't find something to cry about, especially when it came to Frederick. "My poor Caro and dear Frederick have only been . . . been . . . gone now . . ." Cousin Felicity faltered, unable to continue. With a shaky hand, she reached for her ever near lacy handkerchief and dramatically blew into it. She glanced up at him, her blue eyes misting, making her look frail beyond her fifty-odd years.

Mason sighed. "Yes, I know the last seven months have been terribly difficult for you and the girls. But weeping all the time does not solve the problems at hand. The bill collectors are becoming quite insistent, Cousin. If we don't find a way to satisfy some of the more pressing debts . . . we'll be out on the street."

"Pish posh, my boy," Cousin Felicity declared most decidedly, her bout of tears forgotten as she settled back into the elegant settee and reached for her embroidery. "You are the Earl of Ashlin. They wouldn't dare cast us out. Honorable debts are always overlooked." She leaned forward in a confidential manner. "Frederick informed me thusly whenever my dressmaker became rude or insistent about my account."

"I'm sorry to be the bearer of bad news, Cousin Felicity, but debts are never overlooked, honorable or not."

"But Frederick said—"

He held up his hand to stop her from spouting another litany of Frederickisms. Even Mason had his limits with the saintly accomplishments and nonsensical witticisms his cousin attributed daily to his deceased brother.

"Really, Mason, you always tended toward exaggeration as a child. I would have thought you'd have outgrown that by now. Our situation can hardly be as bad as you say."

"I don't see how it could be any worse."

"If that is the case, you could secure quite a tidy fortune by marrying Miss Pindar," she began deliberately. "She's just come out of mourning for her father, and from what I hear, she's exceedingly well off. Yes, that would be the perfect solution." She went back to selecting a thread.

Mason leaned over the mounds of paper and gave his cousin what he hoped was a censuring look.

Marry Miss Pindar?

He'd rather suffer transportation to Botany Bay. The girl embodied every vapid, silly pretension he detested. Besides, he'd never considered himself the marrying type, having been happy until now to live out a bachelor existence.

But if Cousin Felicity wanted to deal out marriage cards, he had one of his own.

"Cousin Felicity, why don't you marry Lord Chilton?"

Cousin Felicity turned a rosy shade at the mention of her twenty-year romance with the reluctant baron. "I wouldn't find that convenient right now." She took on a renewed interest in her silks.

Mason knew that what she was really saying was that she hadn't been asked. Not once in all these years. Oh, he hadn't meant to embarrass her about her hesitant beau, but he found it the only way to stop her from pushing this proposed marriage to the cloying and wealthy Miss Pindar. And with Cousin Felicity temporarily quieted, he could get back to the accounts at hand.

"My heavens," Cousin Felicity said, interrupting his tally of the greengrocer's bill. "Have you considered the girls' dowries? You could borrow against those accounts."

Mason shook his head. He should have known Cousin Felicity never gave up easily. "Frederick drained them years ago," he told her. "Even Caroline's dower lands are mortgaged to the rooftops."

Cousin Felicity looked aghast as the reality of their situation finally sank in. "Whatever shall we do?" True to form, the elderly lady finally gave way to a full bout of weeping. "Take my poor pin money. I also have some set aside. . . . It is yours, my dear boy. Take it with my best wishes," she said between sobs.

"No, please, Cousin Felicity," Mason said, getting up from the desk and sitting beside her. He couldn't take her small allowance, besides the fact that it probably wouldn't even begin to cover their bare necessities. But perhaps now she'd be willing to discuss the economies he'd been trying to explain to her earlier when she'd come into his study to badger him about firing their French chef. "You know how I feel about tears."

"But the girls . . ." she wailed. "How will they ever hope to find husbands without dowries?"

Mason groaned. Not this husband subject again. It was worse than discussing his order that she cease her weekly visits to the dressmaker.

"Oh, Mason, this is a disaster. I'll not say another word about the way you cast out dear Henri, for the girls must have husbands. I will forgo whatever necessities I must, for I've promised them all brilliant matches."

"Cousin Felicity, you should never have made them such a vow." He lowered his voice, and though he felt guilty saying it, he uttered the words both he and Cousin Felicity knew were true. "There isn't enough gold in all of England to entice a man to marry one of those girls."

She opened her mouth to protest, then just as quickly shut it.

While Frederick and Caro had held society in their thrall with their wit and grace, the likeable and handsome pair had passed none of their amiable traits on to their children.

Cousin Felicity glanced at the door, then back at Mason before she too lowered her voice. "Oh, I'll grant you they are a bit on the ungainly side, but that's just because Caro neglected their schooling." She sighed. "I don't like to gossip, but I always thought it scandalous that she wouldn't entertain the notion of seeing the girls brought out. I'm afraid Caro felt that having daughters out in society would call attention to the fact that she wasn't a newly arrived Original herself." Cousin Felicity picked at a loose thread on her needlework. "Certainly, with a bit of time and help, I think Louisa may show some real promise. And Beatrice and Margaret need only the right guidance to bring out their true talents."

Mason nearly laughed, too afraid to ask her what those talents were. Though he loved his nieces in spite of their faults, what his cousin proposed would take time and cost a great deal of money.

Two things they didn't have.

As Cousin Felicity offered up names of tutors and ideas for economies, Mason glanced over at the mountain of debts on his desk and considered his next course of action.

When he'd received Cousin Felicity's note seven months ago informing him of his brother's and sister-in-law's deaths in a yachting accident, he'd left his fellowship at Oxford fully intending to settle the family estates, see his nieces and cousin established comfortably, and then return to the college before the fall sessions started.

But since then he'd done nothing but try to unravel the tangled Ashlin estates. First working with the solicitors, and then enduring the visits by creditors.

The visits. Oh, how he dreaded them.

So sorry, my lord. If I could trouble you for just a moment, 'tis the matter of this debt.

I hate to speak of such things, my lord, but I was wondering when you could see to this bill.

Lately their creditors had become less polite and more to the point.

My lord, without some sort of consideration or payment, I'm afraid I'll have to . . .

Mason knew what they would have to do. His nieces and cousin wouldn't have anything left, even their shifts and stockings were part of unpaid accounts.

And up until a few weeks ago, he'd been inclined to let everything be taken away, sell whatever was left, and retreat back to Oxford. There he would make the best life he could for his family and forget he'd ever been made heir to the Ashlin legacy of debt and wastrel ways.

That was until, late one night, he'd stumbled across a tattered volume on his family history in the library upstairs. In his desire to separate himself from every tawdry thing his recent forebears represented, he'd never taken the time to realize his father and Frederick were nothing like their illustrious ancestors.

Ashlins had fought beside their kings in the Crusades and been consulted in matters of state during the reign of Henry Tudor. Ashlins had sailed as privateers under a grant by Good Queen Bess. Ashlins had helped Charles II regain his throne.

Instead of being known for gambling debts, endless strings of mistresses, and other dubious endeavors and scandals, the Ashlin name, Mason discovered, had once been associated with honor, their sacrifices for King and country revered. It was the reason the very square they lived on was named after them.

So in the faint light of dawn, as he'd finished the last

page of the heroic testimonial, Mason knew there was only one thing to do.

Keep the family from being mired any further in scandal and return the name of Ashlin to its place of honor.

A sharp rap at the door brought Mason out of his silent musings and stopped Cousin Felicity's prattling about potential husbands for the girls.

Looking up, he found Belton entering the study. The family butler for two generations, Belton remained the stalwart defender of the house. As a child, Mason had thought Belton old. Looking at the crusty butler today, he wagered the man to be in his seventies, an age when others were confined to their chairs complaining of gout. The only evidence that the butler had aged in the last twenty years was a smattering of gray hair at his temples.

"Yes, Belton, what is it?"

"My lord, there is a *person* who wishes to see you," the butler announced, a slight Scottish burr tingeing his words and giving away his Highland origins.

Mason knew when Belton's speech slipped from anything other than his normally upper crust London tones, it meant another bill collector had arrived. Belton possessed an unholy disdain for those in trade, and an even worse attitude toward those who expected their bills to be paid. And it always came out in his accent.

"Send him in," Mason said, rising to his feet and returning to his chair behind Frederick's imposing mahogany desk.

"As you wish, my lord." Belton nodded, then exited the room.

Mason turned to his cousin, who was getting up to leave. "Fleeing before the storm?"

"I have no wits for these matters, my boy. Truly it is

best if you handle these people." She began retrieving her discarded bits of silk and clippings.

Mason saw through her haste. "No, stay. I insist. It could be your dressmaker, after all."

When she ignored him further, continuing to gather her jumble of belongings with even greater speed, Mason realized he was on to something.

"Is that a new gown?" He didn't need to hear her answer, for her own guilty features convicted her on the spot. "I hope that went on Lord Chilton's account, and not mine."

Cousin Felicity opened her mouth to protest such a gross impropriety, but before she could utter a word, Belton admitted their unwanted guest. If Cousin Felicity had been gaping like a freshly hooked salmon, her mouth opened even further at the sight of a woman entering the study, a spectacle far more welcome than the weasel-eyed bill collector Mason had expected.

Suddenly realizing his lapse in manners, he bounded to his feet.

Though he knew his cousin was far too near-sighted to really see the woman, even a blind man would have had a hard time missing the vibrant green of the woman's gown or the rich glitter of silver embroidery decorating the fabric.

Having reviewed enough bills lately for women's clothing and toiletries, he knew the woman before him was a walking fortune. Her wide-brimmed straw hat, powdered and curled wig, and frothy silk gown alone would fetch enough gold to ward off the worst of his creditors.

Mason's gut tightened as his imagination suddenly envisioned just that, this creature stripped of her finery and standing before him clad in only her shift.

It wasn't that difficult to picture, as he glanced for a

lingering moment at her low-cut bodice where her full breasts threatened to spill out.

Eh gads, he was starting to think like Frederick.

So he tried to study her as a professor would, as a theory or hypothesis to ponder.

His classical training told him she had the figure of a Venus and the grace of a Diana. But mythology studies hadn't prepared him for the way his breath stopped in his throat.

Cousin Felicity's gasp brought his attention back up to the entrance of the room where, ducking through the door, a man with Eastern features followed the lady.

This additional guest wore a tall red silk turban, which only added to his great height and breadth. Stretched across his nearly bare, muscled chest he wore an open, richly embroidered tunic which fell to his knees and contrasted sharply with his wide-legged striped trousers. Tucked in a black leather belt circling the man's waist glittered a wicked Saracen blade.

Whatever untoward thoughts Mason had amassed about the lady, they cooled somewhat with one dark look from her protector. The man's features were unholy indeed, sharp boned and fierce, not unlike those of some of the infidel warriors Mason had read about in his studies of the Crusades. Like his twelfth-century predecessors, this man looked as though he would enjoy gutting everyone in the room just for the sword practice.

Mason glanced back at the woman, who'd stopped a few feet in front of his desk.

She inclined her head politely. Her perfume, an enticing concoction, wafted toward him.

Try as he could to discern her expression, he found most of her features were artfully hidden under the wide brim of her hat. He could see her face was made up, but where other women might use such devices to hide flaws, he could see her layers only attempted to hide the perfection beneath.

The powders and paints did little to conceal the fullness of her lips, the gentle curve of her cheeks and finally the mysterious languid pools of her green eyes as she stole a glance at him.

Before he could stutter out a greeting, she turned to her companion and held out her hand. The man bowed and with great precision and ceremony drew a familiar-looking blue packet of papers from within his tunic and handed them to his mistress.

Mason knew exactly what that meant. Those blue papers could only be one thing—warrants of collection.

He'd obviously underestimated the local creditors.

They'd taken to hiring women to dun their more recalcitrant debtors.

He was loath to confess it but he should be congratulating them. She was enough to entice a man to give her anything and everything he possessed.

Her companion came to stand behind her, his legs spread in a wide stance, his posture like a rod of iron, his arms crossed over his chest.

One hand, Mason noted, rested idly on the hilt of his blade. Apparently if she failed, her warrior friend added his own form of persuasion to the transaction.

He turned his attention back to the intriguing woman before him and tried to put on the blandest expression he could muster.

"Uh, will you have a seat?" he asked, waving at a chair. The lady smiled toward Cousin Felicity, who, Mason noted wryly, had reclaimed her place on the settee and was searching frantically through her embroidery basket.

More than likely looking for her spectacles, he wagered silently.

"Thank you," the lady murmured, as she perched on the edge of the chair.

Mason sat as well, relieved to have the support of Freddie's solid and expensive furniture.

She shifted slightly, and raised her head, the plumes in her hat fluttering back and forth above the brim as she revealed her emerald gaze to him.

A shade of green so clear, Mason knew he would never forget it.

Like the verdant blush of the Christ Church meadow on an April morning, like a—

He stopped himself from waxing any further into poetics. Why, he never indulged in such fanciful thoughts and he could only cringe at what had possessed him now—probably the last vestiges of Freddie's unwanted influence haunting the room.

Then again, perhaps he should have listened to Frederick a little more often. His brother would have known what to say . . .

Though that innate knowledge of witty forte, Mason reminded himself, was what had gotten the Ashlins in this predicament in the first place.

He resorted to cool indifference. "May I help you?"

The lady smiled, a winsome pretty gesture that almost unraveled Mason's resolve.

"Why, yes," she said. "Though I have a rather personal matter to discuss with you, my lord and you alone." She inclined her head ever so slightly toward Cousin Felicity.

A personal matter.

Those three words tossed all his musings aside in an icy dash of reality.

Oh, she was a bill collector, of a sort. More likely, she

had come for the rents owing on her town house and her unpaid millinery bills. Just like the others.

The angelic lady could be nothing less than another of his brother's mistresses. Yet even as he came to this logical conclusion, he still couldn't help shake the notion that there was something very different about this one, something almost too fine for the fickle vagaries of high priced prostitution.

"Whatever you have to say, can be said in front of me. There are no secrets in this house," Cousin Felicity piped in, as she continued searching for her spectacles.

Mason knew there was no evicting his cousin now. She might love a trip to the dressmaker's, but there was nothing like a good piece of gossip to make Cousin Felicity's day.

He nodded for the young woman to continue. Maybe it wouldn't hurt to enlighten his dewy-eyed cousin as to how her faultless Frederick dallied away the Ashlin fortune.

"It has come to my attention that there is a matter of an unpaid debt between us," the woman began.

Mason shook his head. "A debt? I certainly doubt that. We've never met."

"You are the Earl of Ashlin, are you not?"

He nodded, thinking her voice held a magical quality, drifting through the room like notes from Pan's flute, striking the chords of his unsettled soul.

Poetics again? Gad sakes!

He needed to get back to Oxford as soon as possible before he found himself composing bad sonnets and dressing himself like one of those self-styled idiotic Romantics.

She folded her hands in her lap and shifted once again, another delicate breeze of perfume floating toward him, creating havoc with his senses. He struggled to keep his mind on the matter at hand, but her fragrance did nothing except fuel his earlier musings of her clad only in a chemise.

And if she had been his brother's mistress, she'd probably spent most of her time in a lot less.

She let out a pretty little sigh. "I recently learned you are having . . . well, how does one put it? Some difficulties. So I've come to repay part of the money I owe you."

"*You owe me?*" Mason wasn't quite sure he had heard the woman correctly. He was either still asleep or going stark raving mad like the eighth Earl of Ashlin. As far as he knew, beautiful women didn't just arrive in one's study claiming to owe one money.

"Well, I cannot pay it back all at once, but I do have a partial payment." With an artful grace, she drew out a pouch from within her lace-trimmed décolletage and offered it to him.

Later Mason told himself that it was the lure of sudden wealth that made him bound to his feet and hastily walk around his desk toward her outstretched hand.

This Ashlin would never admit that what truly pulled him toward her was a wrenching desire to fill his senses with the closeness of her intoxicating scent. Nor would he admit how his fingers itched to hold the velvet purse still warm from its hiding spot between her perfectly shaped breasts.

But then, Mason was still working on this new family image, and honesty could come later.

"Thank you," he said, as he took the offered bounty. The bag weighed heavily in his hand, and from the feeling, he knew it contained good English gold.

Enough to give him some respite from Frederick's creditors, until out of the corner of his eye he saw Cousin Felicity furiously shaking her head.

She was right, he realized, it wasn't good to appear too

eager. He paused and chastised himself silently.

He had more business sense than that. At least he'd had a measure of it before this lady had entered his study.

What kind of man was he becoming, when he was willing to take money from his brother's ex-mistress?

Ignoring the enticing warmth in his hand and the mountain of notes behind him, Mason handed the pouch back to the woman.

"I can't accept this. Whatever *understanding* you had with my brother, it ended with his death. It is not my place to interfere with his liaisons," Mason stated, returning to the relative safety of his desk.

The woman looked first at him and then to his cousin. Confusion fluttered over her partially concealed features, and for a moment, Mason thought she was about to cry.

Lord, not more tears, he thought. Cousin Felicity's daily deluges were bad enough.

He couldn't have been more wrong.

"My lord, I think you are *very* mistaken." Her tone held an icy edge, her words firm. "I don't know anything about liaisons with your brother. The moment I learned of your difficulties, I came straightaway. This debt is one I fully intend to repay." Standing up, she walked over to the desk and deposited the pouch, as luck would have it, on top of the more pressing bills.

During her speech, Mason noticed something odd about her voice, something which had escaped him earlier. She spoke each word with deliberate diction. Hardly the purring tones of a mistress in search of a new source of income.

They sat in silence once again, until Cousin Felicity spoke up. "My dear girl, when was the last time you were with Lord Ashlin?"

Mason could have sworn Frederick's mistress blushed

like a virgin beneath her layers of powder at his cousin's indecent inquiry.

"My lady, I've never met Lord Ashlin. That is, until now." The woman smiled politely at Mason.

If she had never met Frederick, then she had never been his mistress . . . and if she'd never been his mistress that meant . . . Mason cleared his throat as he tried to brush aside his errant thoughts.

It meant nothing!

"If we have never met, and you never knew my brother, Freddie, I'm unsure how you can owe me money."

The lady opened her packet of papers, and pulled out a document. "Perhaps this will refresh your recollection."

Mason quickly scanned the paper, which she'd laid before him, recognizing the contract instantly.

A partnership agreement with R. Fontaine. Frederick had lent this woman an immeasurable sum to finance a new play at the Queen's Gate Theatre.

"You are the Fontaine mentioned here?" he asked.

"Yes," she replied. "Madame Fontaine, at your service."

Cousin Felicity, who'd finally found her spectacles, promptly dropped them at this introduction, groping about the floor in a very unladylike fashion until she'd located them at the Saracen's feet. Hastily, she shoved the lenses up on the bridge of her button nose and stared at the woman and her servant as if they were a pair of new curiosities bound for the Royal Zoo.

Mason tried to ignore his cousin's gaping and turned his attention back to his guest. "And you say *I* lent you this money?"

"Yes. Don't you remember? I know it may not seem a great amount to a man of your means and generosity, but the circumstances and conditions of the agreement must at least stand out."

Mason returned to his review of the document.

"Are you truly Madame Fontaine?" Cousin Felicity asked excitedly.

"Yes, my lady."

"And is that Hashim?"

The woman smiled again. "Yes, this is my servant, Hashim."

"You played Helen in *Love's Fancy*!" Cousin Felicity had gotten to her feet and stood before the woman, peering unabashedly into her face. "No wonder I didn't recognize you! You don't look anything in person like you do on stage—why it is amazing—you are even more beautiful than when you played Confite in *The Lost Minuet*. Mason, we're famous! Madame Fontaine is here! In our study. Is it true you slept with the Prince and his entire regiment of Guards in one evening?"

"Cousin Felicity!" Mason found himself shouting, as he jumped to his feet. "Where are your manners?"

Madame Fontaine glanced over her shoulder at her servant as if to give him a signal not to silence Cousin Felicity with one stroke of his deadly blade for her incredible tactlessness.

"I'm afraid that rumor is slightly exaggerated," the lady demurred.

His cousin appeared visibly disappointed.

"Felicity, apologize this instant to our guest," he told her.

"But you don't understand," Cousin Felicity said. She turned to Madame Fontaine, and began apologetically, "He's been in *Oxford*." She made it sound like he'd been living in some Hottentot village in the darkest reaches of Africa, instead of at the intellectual center of England. Before he could stop her, Felicity rushed over to the lady's servant. "Is it true your tongue was torn from your mouth by the Pasha of Cairo himself?"

For the first time since the man had entered the room, Mason detected a hint of emotion in Hashim's grim features. His obsidian eyes glittered with what could have only been described as amusement.

"Oh, is it true?" Cousin Felicity asked again.

Hashim opened his mouth and answered Cousin Felicity's question by allowing her a look past his lips.

For about two seconds Cousin Felicity peered into the giant man's mouth, then let out a bloodcurdling scream and promptly collapsed in a dead faint into Hashim's arms.

Mason fell back into his seat and wondered how his day could get any worse.

Madame Fontaine, or Riley, as her friends called her, fanned the prostrate woman with her handkerchief, praying the Earl's cousin would recover from her fright. Hashim had deposited his victim on a red velvet settee, while Lord Ashlin poured the lady a drink from the nearby tray of spirits.

As she continued her fanning, Riley hoped this little interlude distracted Lord Ashlin from looking too closely at the fine print on their contract.

That was exactly why she'd trussed herself up in this damned dress—to keep his lordship too busy to do anything other than ogle her—for it certainly wasn't comfortable being crammed into some infernal corset. And to make matters worse, she was sure she was going to catch her death with the amount of skin she had exposed.

But Aggie, her long-time partner, had assured her she looked divinely distracting.

All she knew was that it took a lot less to divert the

tradesmen to whom she owed money, so this costume should have guaranteed the Earl's attention would be beguiled into less of a financial direction.

He was an Ashlin, after all. Certainly not the dashing man about town Aggie had described, but then again, Aggie hadn't told her their former indulgent patron was dead.

She stole another glance at him. There was something different about this man—something Riley wasn't too sure of—a feeling that left her unsettled.

"Fashionable" was a description the man would never earn—for he wore his golden brown hair in an old-fashioned queue like some Colonial merchantman. His clothing, a dark coat and plain white shirt and cravat, befitted a local printer, not the Earl of Ashlin.

And as if all this wasn't enough to leave her wondering, the man wore spectacles.

Spectacles on an earl!

She would never have believed it.

Despite the fact that he looked more ready to lead them all in prayer or sell them his latest acquisition from some far off port, given his family's reputation, she would have thought he'd already have tossed her paperwork aside and begged to have a private audience with her.

Still, she mused, could she be so lucky that his cousin's fainting spell would distract him from returning to his sharp-eyed perusal of the contract?

"There, there, Cousin Felicity. Drink it slowly," Lord Ashlin advised his cousin. He slowly tipped the glass to the lady's lips.

The brandy worked immediately as Lord Ashlin's cousin caught a hold of the glass and tossed down the entire contents in one large gulp—a maneuver that would have made a sailor choke and sputter. Cousin Felicity however just sighed and laid back on the settee, her hand resting dramatically over her forehead.

Riley wondered if the lady had ever been on the stage.

"My sincerest apologies, my lord," Riley said, hoping to soothe the man. "Hashim is rather proud of his injury and delights in showing it off."

She shot a glare over the Earl's shoulder squarely at Hashim.

You needn't grin so much, you great fool.

Hashim's shoulders shrugged slightly. *Well, she asked for it.*

When would he learn that sheltered English ladies didn't usually see a mouth where a tongue had been cut out? Continuing to wave her handkerchief over the lady, she commented, "Why, she seems to be coming to quite nicely."

"Oh, my. Oh, my," Cousin Felicity said, her eyelashes fluttering over her wide brown eyes. She started to sit up, but Lord Ashlin stopped her.

"Careful, Cousin. You've had quite a shock."

"Oh, haven't I!" she said triumphantly, before falling back on the cushions again. "What a tale to tell. I've seen Hashim's mouth! With my very own eyes. Why I'll be the envy of all my friends. I'll be the toast for some time." She reached over and clasped Hashim's hand, drawing it to her ample bosom. "I will be forever in your debt, sir. Forever."

Hashim bowed his head slightly and tried to extract himself from her grasp, but it appeared Cousin Felicity was not about to let go of her newfound hero.

Riley's lips twitched with amusement at Hashim's obvious discomfort, until Lord Ashlin came to his rescue.

"Cousin Felicity, release Mr. Hashim."

The woman did, though with a great sigh of reluctance.

Hashim fled to his post behind Riley's chair. Following Hashim's example, Riley retook her seat, carefully posing herself to her best advantage, head tipped, chest up, and posture straight.

Back in an upright position, Cousin Felicity adjusted her spectacles. "Oh, Madame Fontaine, it is such an honor to have you in our house." The woman turned, her white lace cap fluttering. "Mason, Madame does not make social visits, so we must count ourselves very lucky indeed."

"Well this is hardly a social call, my lady," Riley explained to her. "However, on some of my business matters, I find a personal touch makes the transaction go so much more smoothly," she added, her statement directed with a smile and a demure nod at Lord Ashlin.

It was one of her better poses, one she'd used with great skill in *Romeo & Juliet*, yet the man seemed unaffected.

Cousin Felicity, meanwhile, continued peering at her as if she were on display. "Oh, I can see now why they call you 'Aphrodite's Envy.'" She turned to Lord Ashlin. "Wouldn't you agree, Mason? Isn't Madame Fontaine the most tempting woman who's ever graced the world?"

He looked very much like Hashim had just a few moments ago. "Yes, cousin. Madame Fontaine is tolerably pretty."

Tolerably pretty?

Riley didn't know if she should be insulted or wonder if Lord Ashlin needed new spectacles.

One called sallow-faced debutantes with large dowries and title-hunting mothers *tolerable*.

Pretty described whey-faced dairymaids fresh from the country.

Never once since she'd taken the London stage and been dubbed "Aphrodite's Envy" by the young bucks of London had anyone described her as "tolerably pretty."

Her vanity, now that she had grown used to being the recipient of sonnets and tokens of affection, found itself pricked at Lord Ashlin's vague praise.

Tolerably pretty, and from an Ashlin, no less! Rakes, reprobates, and wanton flatterers, the entire lot of them. And great patrons of the arts, well, rather actresses, opera singers, and ballet dancers.

What had happened to this one? Riley wondered.

He held the sharp look of a Lloyd's advisor, able to add a column of numbers in his sleep. After all, she only wanted to make a down payment on the money she owed him, not let on that he was due a lot more.

Money she didn't have.

And much to her growing irritation, he'd picked up precisely the page he'd just set aside moments before. As she watched him scan the document with an efficient gleam, her pulse raced. Perhaps after he threw them out into the streets, she and the company could stage a play dedicated to him—*The Curate and the Actress*.

It would do well in the country, she thought, as she watched with a sinking heart as one of his brows rose with an elegant arch and a smile curved at his lips.

Oh, she was in trouble. They'd be lucky if they had enough left over to stage a puppet show.

"Are you familiar with the conditions of this loan?" he asked.

Riley tipped her head back and smiled sweetly, hoping the look would succeed in dazzling him out of his current line of inquiry. To her annoyance, it didn't seem to distract him in the least.

A handsome nobleman impervious to her charms?

Oh, she was in more than trouble.

"Well, I think so . . ." she faltered, stalling for time. Maybe if she lifted the edge of her skirt a little and revealed a bit of ankle—goodness knows, that fair sight had kept the printer in abeyance for over four months.

But before she could put her plan into action, he frowned at her ever so slightly, rustled the papers with an important air, and spoke. "This contract shows that you owe me the opening night receipts from a fortnight ago."

Her hands curled into tight balls. "We've had some unforeseen difficulties which have prevented us from opening on time. I assure you, we will be in full production within a month. And then you shall have your money."

"What, and have you run up more bills in the meantime? No, that will never do." Lord Ashlin shook his head, sending one of his golden brown locks straying out of its mercantile and orderly queue—giving him a rakish air and lending her hope that he truly was an Ashlin, not some foundling foisted onto the estate to maintain the lineage, as she was starting to suspect.

"Besides," he continued, "with your payments overdue, that puts this loan in default. According to this paragraph here," he said, pointing to a subsection in small print, "I'm entitled to collect the total amount due immediately, with penalties."

"But I have no more cash, other than what I've brought," she replied too quickly.

This appeared to stop him for a moment, until he glanced over at the gold-filled pouch on his desk. "Then you'll have to find some other means of raising it. Perhaps your theatre company has props or costumes which can be sold?"

Riley looked down, pausing for a moment to prepare for the performance of her life. There was too much at stake here, and she'd do anything to save her theatre— from Lord Ashlin and the other problems which had plagued her these past months.

Searching her repertoire of characters, she glanced once more at Lord Ashlin and settled into what she hoped would be a role to touch even his stony heart.

Slowly raising a handkerchief, she dabbed at the corners of her eyes delicately, adding a small sniff and a quiver to her lips.

"I . . . I . . . I only meant my meager offering as a token of kindness for the immeasurable consideration your brother bestowed upon the arts. Think of his memory, my lord. This play, our production, is a memorial to him— his charity, his fine works, his dedication." She looked upward at the plaster ceiling, a pleading glance meant to evoke the most benevolent of emotions, while her fingers clutched her handkerchief to her breast. "Now I fear my gesture is lost on his successor and will be the ruin of my poor beloved company." She dropped her gaze to the wool rug, not daring to hope her speech had worked.

From the sobbing and sniffling across the room, his cousin had more than enjoyed the performance.

"Oh, Mason, you can't close Madame Fontaine's theatre," the woman wailed. "We would be shunned by everyone in London." She turned to Riley. "Madame Fontaine, please forgive my cousin. He's been at Oxford these many years and doesn't understand how things are done." She turned back to Lord Ashlin, shaking her finger as if he were a recalcitrant schoolboy. "What would people say? It just isn't done! Not at all."

"Cousin," he said, "Madame Fontaine owes us a great deal of money. Money better spent . . . well, say, on the girls. For all that finery and those lessons you think are so necessary for finding husbands."

"That much?" Cousin Felicity replied in awed tones.

He nodded back at her.

Cousin Felicity sighed. "Oh, how Freddie's dear girls

do need those lessons. If only they possessed a bit more deportment, knew when to use their sweet smiles, or how to do the latest dance steps. 'Tis a terrible shame. I know our girls could be the talk of the town, what with the proper instruction and all. Imagine it, Mason, they would be able to make their entrance into a room and all eyes would turn on them. Why, with the right teacher they would be the most tempting creatures, the envy of . . ." The lady's voice trailed off as her bespectacled gaze fluttered, then turned slowly toward Riley.

The weight of the woman's last words hung in the room, until not only the lady's gaze, but the Earl's as well, had swung in her direction.

Cousin Felicity, for Riley couldn't think of her as anything other than that, was beaming again as if Riley had just deposited the Crown jewels in their study, rather than an odd sum of coins.

Lord Ashlin, on the other hand, was shaking his head, his face a mask of disbelief, as if his cousin had just proposed stealing the royal treasures in broad daylight.

Riley shifted uncomfortably in her chair.

"It's perfect, Mason," Cousin Felicity announced. "She is perfect. There isn't a man in London who can resist her, and who better to bestow a measure of charm and grace on our dear girls?"

Mason's head shook faster. "You are not proposing that I . . . that I let *her* . . . ?"

"Proposing what?" Riley interrupted, having the strange notion she was about to agree with the prickly Earl.

"Oh, Madame Fontaine," Cousin Felicity bubbled. "You're about to render a service to our family that will be remembered for generations."

Chapter 2

“Riley, my love, whatever took you so long? While you were out dilly-dallying with our dear patron, I've been working my fingers to the bone." Agamemnon Bartholomew Morpheus Pettibone the Third held up his smooth white hands, which had never borne a callus, let alone a hangnail, in their sixty-some years of avoiding manual labor. "Ah, what you've missed! I've been inspired, divinely so."

Riley took a deep breath. Whenever Aggie uttered the words "divine" and "inspiration" in the same breath, disaster soon followed.

"I heard him speak to me. I vow he guided my hand as I wrote," Aggie called out from his dressing table. "What lines he gave me! 'Twas like he stood right where you are, dictating to me. Ah, to be guided by the great Bard's spirit." He smiled at the memory of it. "And you off and about on that fool's errand of yours, missing it as you did."

Not more revelations from Shakespeare! Riley counted to ten and stepped further into the apartment they shared above the Queen's Gate Theatre. From the discarded costumes and scattered drawings of sets and sheets of scripts,

34

Aggie was obviously going through a "character renewal," as he liked to call them.

Character chaos, Riley knew from experience.

Nor did it appear that her troop had completed their daily rehearsals, which Aggie had assured her he would direct in her absence. No, her friend was settled in front of his mirror, working on his makeup for his upcoming role as the humble woodcutter in their production of *The Envious Moon*.

Wrapped in a striped green silk dressing gown, a gift from an aging marchioness or some other rich elderly patroness Aggie had managed to bamboozle with his repertoire of false credentials, he was in the process of tucking his iron gray hair underneath a skullcap.

"Where is Nan?" she asked, looking about for their émigré maid.

"*Petite* Nanette?" He affected a phony French diction, all the while peering at his reflection in the mirror. "I fired her. Such an ineffective wench. No depth in her delivery. No *joie de vivre*. No presence. I'm starting to doubt she's French."

Riley groaned. "Aggie, she's a servant, not an actress." Aggie's dismissal would mean Nan had probably fled to her mother's cheap flat in St. George's Fields. Riley added to her list of things to do this afternoon a trip to Southwark, where she'd have to engage in a great deal of bribing to entice the greedy but efficient girl to return.

"We are better off without her!" he declared. "The inconsiderate chit refused to fix my tea before she left."

"Well, now that you've fired Nan, you'll have to fetch your own tea," she shot back.

At this comment, Aggie sniffed and began sorting the makeup items before him. "Whatever took you so long with our dear patron, Freddie? Now, there's someone with a presence, someone who knows how to make an entrance. If I've told him once, I've told him a thousand times, he'd make a fine actor."

Riley pulled off her hat and set it down on Aggie's dressing table covering his pots and paints. "Aggie," she said slowly. "When was the last time you saw your dear Freddie?"

Aggie tipped his head as he considered her question, looking her straight in the eye. Riley knew he was trying to gauge her mood and determine whether or not he could get away with lying.

"Why, it must have been two months ago—before he and his lovely wife went north for a shooting party." Aggie smiled and went back to studying his reflection in the mirror.

"Two months," she asked. "Are you positive?"

"Quite," he said, warming to his invented tale. "The dear pair invited me to join them—really, 'begged' would be a more apt account, but I explained quite patiently that I had my commitments here. Why? Is he still cross with me for declining?"

She shook her head. "He uttered not a word of it."

"That is because he is a gentleman. Ah, well, next time." Aggie reached under her hat for a bit of cloth to begin blending a new color into his already rouged features.

"Now that's the funny point about all this." She leaned over his shoulder and stared at his reflection in the mirror. "As it turns out, your dear Freddie is dead. Quite dead, and has been so for seven months!"

"Oh, my!" Aggie swallowed several times, his great Adam's apple bobbing up and down.

"Oh, my, indeed," she returned. This had been Aggie's responsibility—to keep tabs on their investor, to ensure he remained happy with their arrangements and see that the flow of Ashlin money moved in one direction—into the theatre's coffers.

"Seven months, you say?"

"Seven months."

"Oh, my. I don't see how I could have gotten that so wrong." He shifted in his seat under her cold gaze. "Now that you mention it, I do remember some such bit of gossip about the Earl of Ashlin and his wife being lost at sea." He snapped his fingers. "Yes, I remember—their boat overturned and they drowned. Don't know how I forgot. Quite tragic. Might even make a good play." He pushed aside her hat, selected a pot of yellow paint.

Riley frowned back at him. "*Tragic* would be a better word to describe *our* situation."

He dismissed her dire words with a wave. "What does it matter whether it is Freddie or his heir? Ashlin men are all reprobates and wastrels. And poor businessmen to boot. You probably had the new Earl kissing the hem of your gown and begging you to take more of his gold."

Kissing her hem, indeed! She pulled a chair up next to Aggie's table. "This Earl may have gained the title, but the rest of his Ashlin inheritance you seem to think is so assured appears to have skipped our new patron. This Lord Ashlin is no reprobate."

Though he certainly could be one, Riley thought. She could well imagine the stir he'd cause in his own box on opening night—decked in the latest fashions, his golden brown hair brushed back just so, and his piercing blue eyes scanning the audience.

Her play about a curate suddenly held a new dimension. The vicar with a past—he'd been a pirate before he'd taken his holy vows. A man filled with remorse, driven by his sins . . .

Perhaps that was the explanation behind the earl's

bookish manners. He'd been terribly wicked as a youth, and now he was paying for the sins of his misspent adolescence.

Somehow, Riley doubted it.

Instead, she filed the idea away. If they managed to keep the company afloat, they'd open the fall season with it. And dedicate it to the Earl.

"So I take your silence to mean the man did not fall at your feet, forgive you our debts, and beg for box seats next to Prinny's for opening night?" Aggie asked, his tone light and jesting, the notion of a man who hadn't done so, utterly unthinkable to him.

At this, Hashim made a snorting noise, as if even *he* felt the insult to his mistress.

Aggie turned slowly in his chair, looking first to Riley, then to Hashim, then back to Riley. "You mean he was impervious to *you*?"

"Yes. In fact, he hardly seemed to notice me." Riley got back up and paced carefully through the littered room.

The very notion was aggravating. She wasn't foolish enough to think it was her acting skills that were the reason for their theatre's success. No, their ticket sales were fueled by rumors of her past—making the men of London all that more anxious to unmask the mysterious Madame Fontaine.

So they kept purchasing subscriptions, watching her plays, and vying in countless ways for her attentions.

And Riley continued to refuse politely—though that didn't stop the arrogant louts from bragging about their exploits with her. She knew Cousin Felicity's story about her night with the Prince's regiment was only a small tale compared to some of the other grandiose exploits she'd heard bandied about.

She wondered if any of them realized she'd probably

be dead if she'd done half the things the *ton* attributed to her licentious and all too fictional life.

Aggie appeared to be considering the idea that this man hadn't fallen prey to her wiles, when suddenly his mouth curved into his famous sensual smile. "Perhaps I should have gone. Perhaps I would have had more influence with him. Perhaps a lady isn't his—"

Riley shook her head. "No, he would not have appreciated your charms either."

Of that she was positive.

While he might be outwardly bookish and scholarly, there was no doubt in her mind that Lord Ashlin was definitely a man who liked the attentions of a woman.

Just not hers.

Why it rankled her she couldn't be sure, for she'd never considered herself a great beauty. But tolerably pretty?

Why he was probably as blind as his cousin, she told herself. Yes, that was it, he was nearsighted and he was too rolled up to buy new spectacles.

But even that excuse didn't soothe her ruffled vanity.

"So what happened?" Aggie asked, interrupting her thoughts.

Riley continued to pace carefully about the littered apartment. "As we decided this morning, I tried to give him a down payment, as a goodwill gesture. To keep him appeased until we open. But the man would hear none of it. He was more concerned about keeping his papers straight and his harebrained cousin under control."

The mention of a cousin perked Aggie's more Lothario-like propensities. His hand drew up to rest over his heart. "I take it by harebrained, you mean this cousin is a lady?"

"Yes, Aggie, a lady cousin. And don't start getting any ideas." And while Aggie never went out of his way to seek female companionship, he was never one to turn down their fawning attentions or their riches, and often talked of making an advantageous and convenient marriage to secure his retirement.

An activity, Riley knew, that was going to get her friend into a lot of trouble one day with an aggrieved relative or an outraged son. She took the pot of paint out of his hand and passed him a different shade. "I doubt she has any money, at least, any for you."

At this Aggie appeared unconvinced.

Riley shook her finger at him. "If there was any money, I'm sure it's gone by now," she said, hoping to deter that mercantile look in Aggie's eyes. "She's a foolish, silly woman. When this Cousin Felicity laid eyes on Hashim, I thought she was going to have a fit of apoplexy."

Aggie leaned back in his chair. "Oh, let me guess. She wanted to see your friend's tongue."

"Of course she did." Everyone always wanted to see Hashim's tongue—or rather lack of one.

"Did he oblige her?"

Riley's brows rose. "What do you think?"

"Oh, how delicious!" Aggie beamed at Hashim. "Did she faint away? Scream? Beg for a second look? Oh my, why do I always miss the great scenes?"

Her patience thinning, Riley's hands went to her hips. "Aggie! What you missed was the fact that this new patron of ours has no intention of continuing to assist us. In fact, he rather expects this loan to be repaid."

Her declaration stopped Aggie's theatrics in a flash.

"Repay our debts?" He rose from his seat, coming eye to eye with her. "How decidedly vulgar of the man! Certainly you're joking? You're teasing me in my dotage. Repay our debts to Ashlin—that would take . . ."

She finished his lines for him. "Every last farthing we've got on hand. Then we'd have to scrap the sets and props, pawn the costumes and jewelry, and find a buyer for the furniture to come up with the rest."

Aggie plopped back down in his seat, and for the first time since Riley had met the man, he remained silent and dumbfounded.

But silence and Agamemnon were never an easy mix. "And you couldn't charm him out of this?"

"Well, in a manner of speaking, my charms have given us a reprieve. You could say Lord Ashlin and I reached an agreement."

The man's brows shot into an indignant V. "Why that villainous motley-minded pumpion! How dare he! I'll not stand for it. I'll call the miscreant out for blackmailing you into such a compromising situation. My innocent girl is not a bit of muslin to be handed *carte-blanche*!" He reached for his sword, a leftover stage prop from *Hamlet*, and swung it in a wide arc, scattering Riley and Hashim into the far corners. "I'll skewer the flap-mouthed jolthead for even suggesting the notion!"

Riley shook her head. "Aggie! Put that sword down."

Heedless of anything but his own voice, Aggie continued to prod and pummel their poor furniture, knocking the limbs off his imaginary foe, using every Shakespearean curse in his vast repertoire to decry the new Lord Ashlin.

"Aggie, that is quite enough!" Riley exclaimed. "Whatever are you ranting about?"

"Why, Lord Ashlin! How dare he use our debt as a means to force you into becoming his mistress."

"You old fool, I never said anything about becoming his mistress. The agreement is that I teach his nieces how to be more charming, like I am on stage. You know, appealing to men so they can find husbands—rich ones."

From his open-mouthed expression, Riley would have

thought the truth was more repugnant than her being compromised by the Earl.

"You agreed to do whaaaaat?" he sputtered.

"You heard me the first time. I'm to tutor his nieces."

"Hiring yourself out as a *tutor*?" He choked on the last word as if he'd drunk from Romeo's vial. "Why, it is unheard of! Sharing your talents outside the boards? With one of *them*?"

"Cry and wail all you want, but the deed is done and agreed upon," she told him.

Aggie immediately went into a new tirade about the sacred secrets of the stage being given to the audience.

She wasn't any more pleased with the idea of tutoring the Earl's nieces than Aggie, but what choice did she have?

Riley didn't want to consider four weeks in Lord Ashlin's proximity—she found the idea too unsettling. Try as she might to convince herself it was because of his obvious disapproval, she knew what it really was.

She found the Earl of Ashlin rather distracting.

While he found her—well, he'd said it plainly.

He found her *tolerably pretty*.

A pox and a bother. As if she cared what the likes of Lord Ashlin thought about her.

Riley pushed her fingers up beneath her wig and scratched at her scalp. The towering horsehair contraption always gave her a headache. Not that Aggie's diatribe wasn't contributing a fair share to the pounding between her temples.

She tipped her head toward him. "Help me out of this, would you please?"

"Oh, of course, my love." His great speech forgotten, Aggie sat down beside her and began unpinning the wig ever so gently, so as not to pull her own hair beneath it.

"Whyever does Lord Ashlin want you to tutor his nieces in acting?"

"Not acting. He wants me to prepare his nieces for the Marriage Mart. In exchange, he's willing not to foreclose."

Satisfied that all the pins were out, Aggie gently lifted the wig off her head and stared at her as if he hadn't heard her correctly.

"You teaching them—" His shoulders convulsed. He clutched the chaise for support as he bent over in laughter. "Oh, this is too delicious." He slumped over and continued to quake and howl until great streams of tears ran down his powdered cheeks. "Tell me, whatever possessed you to agree to such a ludicrous idea? I mean, you, of all people, teaching young girls the art of husband hunting."

"I hardly see the humor in all this. I saved our company from ruin. Besides, you're the one who likes to quote the *Observer*'s description of me all the time—'an enthralling and engaging lady who held the audience's enraptured attentions with her enticing and beguiling manners.' " Riley plucked at her lacy sleeves.

Of all the people to be thrilled for them, Aggie should be thanking the stars that she had snatched them once again off the steps of debtor's prison.

"Yes, they did say that, Riley my love. But that is when you act. Offstage is another matter."

"Obviously, I know something about attracting men."

"Harumph! That's a fine bit of nonsense if ever I heard any," he declared, flouncing back into his seat at his dressing table. "Everything you learned, you learned from me. You may attract them, but you repel them just as quickly. This entire idea is foolish."

Riley couldn't agree more, but she wasn't about to tell Aggie that. "Well, if you don't like it, you have no one to blame but yourself. You came up with all that flimflam about me being the incarnation of Aphrodite—whatever that means. And it was you who insisted on spreading those tales that I am the distant daughter of Cleopatra, rescued from a pasha's lascivious clutches and carried fevered and sickened through the desert by my faithful servant!" she said, nodding toward Hashim. "You've got the male half of London delirious to know my 'Eastern secrets' and the female half either secretly curious or appalled that I am allowed out in public."

Aggie made a failed attempt to look contrite. "That 'flimflam,' as you call it, has made our every production since *Anthony and Cleopatra* a sell-out!"

"That's fine now, but the Earl's addlepated cousin insisted that with tutoring from a *living goddess*—" Riley paused and shuddered. *Aphrodite's Envy, indeed!* "These girls would be betrothed before they made their debuts."

"And when are these little angels making their tender entrée into society?"

"The night we open."

Aggie looked as if he'd not only drunk from Romeo's vial of poison, but impaled himself on Juliet's dagger as well. "But that's only a month away and we've just started rehearsals."

Riley frowned at her best friend. "Don't you think I'm well aware of that? I told you we should never have borrowed so much money from one person."

"Well, who would have thought a vital young man like Freddie St. Clair would go and stick his spoon in the wall? Why, he and his charming wife were the toast of London. I remember the time they—" Aggie stopped himself in mid-sentence. "But that's it! These girls, they are Freddie and Caroline's, aren't they?"

"Well, I assume so."

"Don't you see, Riley? These girls can't be anything *but* gifted with charm and grace. You have nothing to fear. A bit of polish, a little practice with their fans, and you'll have them out the door and in front of a parson before this new Earl can swing a dead cat."

"Let's hope so." While Aggie's reasoning seemed sound, Riley wasn't so sure. She had a nagging suspicion the Earl of Ashlin had not only been impervious to her charms, but had also bested her in this business deal.

Really, if they were anything like their gregarious parents, why would they need her help?

A pox and a bother on the man! And this time she really meant it.

"And when are you supposed to start this charitable endeavor?" Aggie asked.

"Tomorrow."

"Oh, that won't do at all." Aggie rose from his chair, his head nearly brushing the ceiling. A tall man of stately bearing, his aristocratic features were the only inheritance he'd received from his noble father, a man who'd kept Aggie's opera-singing mother as a mistress through four children. Sometimes, when Aggie towered over his audience or whomever he was addressing, it was hard to remember that he was baseborn and grew up much like Riley had, in the back of a theatre.

"What about rehearsals?" he complained.

"You'll have to make do without me. I didn't have much of a choice. Lord Ashlin insisted. Either that, or he called in our note in full."

"There is more to this, Riley Eugenia Fontaine, than you are letting on." Aggie circled her. "You would never have bargained so lightly unless you had some ulterior motive."

"I haven't the vaguest notion what you mean," she said,

not about to give Aggie one hint at her unwanted fasci-
nation with the man. Riley rose from the chaise and
strolled over to her clothes press.

Opening it up she pulled out two gowns, reworked from
their production of *The Lost Princess*, and held them up
to Aggie, artfully changing the subject. "Whatever does
one wear to tutor young ladies?"

Sufficiently diverted, Aggie forgot his line of questioning, shaking his head at the midnight blue brocade and
smiling broadly at the rose chiffon in her left hand. Selecting a hat from the shelf, Aggie launched into a long
dissertation on the appropriate dress and attitude a teacher
must command.

Riley listened, only half interested, using the few moments to tally up the tasks she needed to complete before
her morning appointment at Ashlin Square.

One thing for certain, she needed more information
about Lord Ashlin. Something she could use if her lessons
with the girls failed.

"Aggie," she said, interrupting his one-sided argument
over the use of firm authority as a teacher or the use of
example. "Do you know anything about Freddie's
brother? This new Earl?"

He shook his head. "I can make some inquiries, if you
like."

Riley studied the pink silk again. "Tonight if you
could—and no cards—just gossip. When I go in tomorrow I do not want to be unprepared, as I was today."

"You are taking Hashim with you, aren't you?" Aggie
asked, his concern for her genuine. "I insist. I'll not have
you travelling about this city alone. Not after the last incident."

Riley shook her head. "I hardly think Hashim's presence is necessary. He takes great delight in scaring young

girls and I'll never get them prepared in time. Besides, I think the Earl found Hashim's presence rather disruptive," she said, thinking of the maid who'd fainted in the foyer when they'd made their exit from the study. "I'll go alone."

Aggie looked from Hashim back to Riley. "You mean the man doesn't know Hashim isn't just an ordinary servant but your bodyguard? You'll have to tell him you go nowhere without Hashim. If you don't, I will."

Riley looked up at the ceiling. "And how would you explain the need for Hashim's constant presence?"

"Though I'm loath to admit it and find it completely out of character, I'd say on this matter I'd tell the truth," Aggie declared. "Just explain to the Earl that someone is trying to kill you."

Chapter 3

~~~OO~~~

The next morning Mason stared out his study window onto Ashlin Square as a hackney delivered Madame Fontaine and her servant, Hashim, promptly at half past nine. He smiled to himself as he watched the woman bring her hand up to shield her eyes from the early spring sunshine.

Must seem quite an ungodly hour for a night creature such as yourself, he thought, wondering what time in the afternoon actresses usually stirred from their well-appointed lodgings.

Not that he'd ever been to an actress's apartment, but he could well imagine the place, having been presented by Freddie's last thespian mistress with the unpaid bills for the rich furnishings and costly bric-a-brac his brother had contributed to the lady's unholy den.

As he gazed down at Madame Fontaine and mentally tallied the expense of her latest outfit, he realized that not only opulent surroundings, but even more costly wardrobes appeared to be indispensable attributes for actresses.

Though today's gown, with its deceptively innocent hues of pink, was less ostentatious than yesterday's, the dress did little to hide her . . . how had one of the young bucks at the club phrased it last night?

Ah, yes, Mason recalled, *her devastating charms*.

And this was the woman he'd allowed Cousin Felicity to convince him would be the perfect tutor for his young nieces?

If he wanted them to grow up to be the worst kind of Cyprians!

What had he been thinking?

No, he corrected himself, he knew exactly what he'd been thinking with, glancing again at the glorious rise of her breasts and the seductive curve of her waist and hips as she sauntered toward the steps.

He'd like to hope the chiffon scarf draped over her bare shoulders was her concession to modesty, yet the fabric was so diaphanous that its original nod toward propriety had been lost as it did little to conceal her . . . how had the other member of his club put it?

Her arresting attributes.

Taking a deep breath, he tried to pull his gaze away, however he found it enticed and beckoned by the saucy white plumes on her hat as they undulated with her every sleek movement. Even her powdered and curled hair hinted of slumbering seductive captivity, lying as it did in a thick ringlet of deceptively controlled curls against the bare skin of her neck and throat, just waiting to be un-bound and freed by an anxious lover.

In one hot, fleeting moment, he saw himself with her, unfettered of his life of restraint, free to unwrap all her rich trappings one silken piece at a time, in a moonlit room furnished in red velvet and far from Mayfair . . . far from the responsibilities of . . .

Eh gads, what was he thinking? In shock, Mason took a deep breath and hastily stepped away from the window.

Those kinds of musings belonged to the likes of Frederick, and for that matter, their sire before them. And the three prior generations of Ashlins who'd built the family's reputation of being more than willing to tally up debts and vowels in the lusty pursuit of nightly encounters with opera singers . . . and actresses.

It was a wonder the title or any property remained.

No, Mason told himself sternly, he'd been smart to ignore Frederick's chiding remarks about the University's requirement that their professors live celibate lives. The strict regime had taught him how to remain focused on his studies, and now would help him stay the course while he restored the Ashlin name and fortunes.

That is as soon as he got rid of Madame Fontaine and her unwanted influence.

He glanced over at the window, and began considering his choice of words as he waited for Belton to announce her arrival.

Tucking his hands behind his back and pacing around his desk as if he faced a classroom of first-year students, he practiced his opening speech.

"Madame Fontaine, I find your reputation and manners inappropriate for an association with my nieces." Warming to his subject, he continued, "First and foremost, there is the way you dress. This outfit is a perfect example. It tests the very limits of decency."

His, mostly.

Mason ran a hand through his hair. Gads, if he didn't sound like the worst kind of stuffy antiquated prude.

Rather like old Cheswick who'd taught philosophy for over forty years at St. John's College. He'd railed at the younger teachers to live the very model of restrained, sober, and chaste lives.

Even as Mason tried to recall some of the man's more

poignant speeches, he then remembered Cheswick had recently been retired to Bath—and the reasons behind his mentor's sudden departure. After years of militant temperance, Cheswick had been discovered in his bachelor apartment utterly foxed, singing ribald songs and being bathed by two tempting French-born armfuls named Monique and Marie.

Perhaps Cheswick was not the best guide to call forth at a time like this.

Well, still, he told himself, there was nothing wrong with being a staid, respected man.

Not unless you want to spend your final days singing tawdry verses whilst they haul you away, a voice not unlike Frederick's niggled at the back of his thoughts.

Mason shook his head, trying to clear his mind.

Mayhap he should take Cousin Felicity's advice about finding a wife more seriously. Not some rich, artful minx, like Miss Pindar, but a quiet, moderate girl of good breeding who'd bring advantageous family connections to a marriage. They'd wed, have a passel of well-behaved children, and live out their lives in the relative tranquility of Sanborn Abbey, the Ashlin ancestral home.

Once there, he would see his nieces met only the best young men, and in time they too would be settled just as comfortably, not trussed up and fed to London's rakes like so many morsels.

Yet even as he envisioned this tidy scheme, a stray thought, a Frederickism at its worse, whispered in his ear.

Little brother, a mistress would be more fun.

"This is ridiculous. He'll find me out before the morning's over and everything will be lost." Riley turned and headed toward the departing hackney.

Hashim caught her by the back of the skirt before she

reached the street. He shook his head and nodded at the imposing front door of the Ashlin residence.

"Didn't you hear me? I said this is ridiculous. Past ridiculous—it borders on insane! I know nothing about being a lady."

He shook his head and laid his hand on his heart.

"Well, I know a little bit about being a lady," she conceded. "But not the kind of lady who lives in a house such as this or attends balls or whatever it is they do in these venerable piles of stone. The likes of what I know will certainly not please him."

Hashim shook his head, his eyes crinkling at the corners with good humor.

"Stop that right now," she scolded. Her friend and servant knew her too well. Then again, they'd been together for ten years, ever since she'd "bought" him from a slaver in Paris. There had been something about the man's regal stance and nobility, trapped as it was by circumstances that Riley had understood only too well. Having just made her entrée onto the Paris stage, she'd earned just enough money to buy him, and had promptly freed him the moment the papers had been signed.

But the giant had refused to take his emancipation. At least until the debt between them was paid.

She had considered it paid in full years ago, but Hashim just shook his head every time she broached the subject of his liberty.

Over her shoulder, he coughed and nodded toward the front door.

Riley took a deep breath and considered the information she'd had Aggie solicit during the night regarding their patron. "According to Aggie, the new Earl taught some kind of ancient history. Dreary battles, dead kings, lost causes." She grimaced. "No wonder he acts like an old vicar instead of an Ashlin."

Hashim's eyebrows rose.

"I just think he would look rather interesting if he didn't wear all that black," she commented. Teasingly she added, "If he's inclined toward history, we could offer him one of those Roman togas left over from *Anthony and Cleopatra*. That ought to give him a new appreciation of fashion."

Hashim didn't appear to find any humor in her idea, while Riley laughed at the image of the stodgy Oxford professor clad in only a linen sheet.

Until, that is, she thought of his bare legs and long arms, the breadth of his chest covered with only a thin, white cloth.

A heated blush rose on her cheeks as she realized he wouldn't look all that bad.

Whatever was she thinking? The early hour must be bringing on a fever. It was the only explanation.

Lord Ashlin, indeed!

Even more vexing, Hashim, she knew, liked the bookish earl. "How on earth do you think he can help us?"

He shrugged his shoulders and put his hands together as if he were praying.

"Faith? You have faith in him." Riley shook her head. "After one meeting you suddenly decide he is my savior. I'll never understand you. Or is it that you just like him because Aggie found out he's celibate? You two can start a club."

Eyebrows raised, Hashim pointed at her.

"Thank you for reminding me. But that is supposed to be a secret. How many tickets do you think we'd sell if everyone knew I was . . . well, you know what I mean." She looked up at the house.

For the life of her, Riley couldn't see how a bookish earl, who'd probably spent most of his life locked away in some dusty library, could do what the most skilled and, she noted with some pique, the most expensive Bow Street Runner had been unable to do—find out who was trying to harm her.

Not that she cared to consider the notion, but there was no denying that the problems at the theatre were not mere accidents, but actions directed at her. The scenery bar crashing onto the stage when she was practicing her soliloquy, the curtains catching fire when she was alone in the house, and this morning, a note.

Leve Englund whore or sufer.

She hadn't shown it to anyone—certainly not to Hashim, knowing the ugly missive would only send her loyal servant into a dark rage. He considered it his personal mission to keep her safe, and if he saw this latest threat, he'd probably stop sleeping and insist on watching over her twenty-four hours a day.

Still, why would someone want her gone—or worse, dead? None of it made any sense. So she'd stuffed the horrible bit of scratching in her reticule and decided to forget about it.

The Runner she'd hired intimated it was probably nothing more than a prankster or a rival theatre owner trying to get them to close down.

She told herself that was the best answer and set aside her niggling worries to concentrate on the task at hand— convincing their patron not to shut them down. She loved her theatre, and her company of players had become the family she'd never had. She'd be damned if she'd let some unseen coward take away her livelihood and the livelihood of so many other people.

Glancing up at Hashim, she saw that the giant's expression said what his mutilated tongue could not: *You'll never know without trying.*

Still, she felt a tremor of fear, worse than any stage fright she'd ever experienced. "What if—"

Riley's stalling tactics came to an abrupt halt as the door sprang open, and Cousin Felicity flew down the steps and onto the curb with all the subtlety of a fishwife.

"Oh, my dear, *dear* Madame Fontaine, and Mr. Hashim," she cried out, her curious stare lingering unabashedly over Hashim's closed lips as if she were weighing her own courage to request another peek into his mouth. Instead, she began a fluttering rush of words. "Why I can't tell you how delightful it is to have you, and I do mean *both* of you, here again at our humble residence." The woman barely took a breath as she caught Riley by the elbow and towed her up the steps.

"My best friend and dearest confidante, *Lady Delander*," Cousin Felicity said, emphasizing the woman's name as if to tell Riley how truly important this Lady Delander was, "will be pea-green when she learns of the veritable social revolution Lord Ashlin has undertaken by engaging your services. I would venture that you may find yourself no longer tromping about the planks, as they say in the theatre. Why, you'll be completely booked, and I do mean in complete and utter demand with only the best young ladies seeking to learn your . . . oh, how does one say it . . ." she spared a blush at Hashim, before she whispered into Riley's ear, "your Eastern secrets."

Eastern secrets? Eh gads, it was worse than she thought.

Riley took a deliberate step backward from the door,

but between Cousin Felicity's grip on one elbow and
Hashim's firm hold on the other, escape appeared impossible.

Aggie's favorite encouraging words peeled in her ears.
Fortitude, my love. Fortitude.

Glancing around the formidable Ashlin foyer, with its
grand marble staircase, dark oak trim, and yellow brocade
curtains, she tried to tell herself it wasn't so different from
the lobby of their theatre.

Well, without the marble. And the Ashlin house didn't
smell of spilled wine and forgotten chestnuts.

"Once I tell our little secret to Lady Delander—"

"We won't be telling anyone about Madame Fontaine,
Cousin Felicity," Lord Ashlin announced from the door
of his study.

His interruption startled Riley, not only with the firm
order underlying his words, but with the deep tones that
rustled up her spine, leaving her both breathless and filled
with a strange anticipation.

Pox and bother, she silently cursed. He had the ability
to set her at odds with just the sound of his voice. Riley
could well imagine the Earl using his rich baritone to coax
a woman into something less benign than just keeping his
secrets.

Thank goodness he found her barely tolerable, as evidenced by his glowering expression. She didn't even want
to consider what she would be willing to do for this
man . . .

"But, Mason—"

"Not one word, Cousin," he told the lady, his sharp
intent unwavering.

Riley could see a room full of students snap to attention
under such a command.

From the far-reaching frown on Cousin Felicity's face,

the lady did not appear willing to give up just yet. "Oh, Mason, not even Lady Delander? I've had *such* a vexing time trying to outdo her since her niece became betrothed to Lord Penford." She turned to Riley. "You'd think the lady had arranged the marriage herself, to hear her tell the story. And hear it I do, every time I dine with her." She turned her imploring wide, blue-eyed gaze on Lord Ashlin.

He shook his head. "Madame Fontaine and I have several matters to discuss before this situation continues any further."

"Fuss and bother, my boy, you are the worst scold and toady. One would think you a foundling and not an Ashlin to be so strict!" She hurried up a few steps further. "Well, at least I'll be able to sit in on the girls' lessons and pick up a thing or two. Mayhap you'll have four brides from Ashlin Square this Season." She blushed and turned around on the stairs, looking up and down the steps. "Oh, where was I going?"

Riley, realizing very quickly that since their last meeting Lord Ashlin had changed his mind and was about to cancel their agreement, prompted the lady without hesitation. "The girls?"

Cousin Felicity's mouth curved into a wide smile. "The girls! Of course. I'll have your students downstairs in the wink of an eye." She bustled upward without another glance back.

"Cousin Felicity!" Mason protested, but the lady ignored him.

He let out a deep sigh, one Riley wagered did not bode well for her, as it was followed by Lord Ashlin turning his critical gaze on her. There was something new about the stern set of his jaw that hadn't been there yesterday—a disapproving severity Riley found more appropriate for a military man than an Oxford don.

He'd obviously found out who she was, or at least who the London gossips thought she was. And now he meant to dismiss her and scrap her theatre to pay his debts.

Then where would she be? Or Aggie? Or Hashim?

She straightened her hat, then smoothed her skirts, calming herself from reproaching him outright for this about-face. Not that she hadn't fully expected it.

Well, she knew a thing or two about bargaining with men and his lordship was a man, even for all that drivel about his supposed celibacy.

A celibate Ashlin? Utter nonsense!

She tipped her head and glanced up at him shyly. "Is there something wrong, my lord?" she asked in the most dulcet voice she could muster. "I daresay you look unwell this morning. Perhaps you need a tonic or a good rest in the country."

Stall, she thought. *Find a way to keep him from discharging you outright.* For if there was one thing of which Riley was certain, she needed him.

Probably more than he needed her.

In her favor, she'd beaten more wily opponents than some owl-eyed earl. And she'd had all night to dream up every argument in the book.

She soon discovered, so had Lord Ashlin.

"Madame Fontaine, I believe I've made a terrible mis—" He glanced over her shoulder and she turned as well to see not only the footmen gaping at them, but a good portion of the household staff peering from doorways and alcoves.

Riley couldn't tell who was garnering more attention, her or Hashim. The gruesome Turk wore his most sinister glare, a ferocious look he loved using to frighten young women or intimidate her more insistent suitors.

She chose to smile graciously at her audience, a gesture that seemed to annoy the Earl even further.

"Belton!" Lord Ashlin all but shouted. "Do we pay these people to gawk and gape?"

The instant the butler stepped from the serving door, the other servants ducked belowstairs or hustled off to whatever duties they were so evidently neglecting.

Lord Ashlin nodded at his butler and returned his cold gaze to her. "Madame, as I was saying, I would like a word with you. In private." He directed this last order squarely at Hashim.

She turned to her self-appointed protector. "If you don't mind?"

Hashim eyed Lord Ashlin with a quick head-to-toe appraisal and then nodded his approval for her to continue with Lord Ashlin alone. As Riley followed the Earl into his study, Hashim took his post near the door, assuming his usual stance, his arms folded across his chest, one hand resting lightly on the hilt of his jeweled scimitar.

Riley found herself puzzled by the man leading her into his study. Lord Ashlin moved with a fluid, athletic grace, hinting of a well-developed physique beneath his plainly cut black coat and breeches.

Obviously there was more to the professor than just books and exams . . .

She took the seat he offered her. His desk had been cleared of the unpaid receipts and notes, and she would have said something, if Lord Ashlin hadn't spoken first.

"Madame Fontaine," he began, "I have made some inquiries regarding your credentials in preparing my nieces for their debuts—"

"And you find me extremely overqualified," she interrupted, having anticipated this first argument. She would have wagered her share of the theatre on just what he'd learned, subjects they probably did not cover at the university.

At least not in the classrooms.

School is about to begin, my lord, she thought, as she scooted her chair a little closer to the wide and imposing oak desk between them.

"Well, your qualifications are certainly . . ." he paused, as if struggling to find the right word.

Riley took advantage of his discomfort and filled in for him. "I think the word you are looking for is 'perfect.' I know you probably think such a task is beneath my considerable *forte*, and I certainly agree with you." She held up her hand to stave off what appeared to be a counter-assault, and he politely let her proceed.

Luckily, Riley suffered no such boundaries as the confines of good manners. She went on unabashedly.

"My lord, I find myself completely indebted to you and your family for your generosity and foresight in supporting our latest production. Therefore I can suffer no artistic vanity over assisting you in such a delightful task." Riley drew a quick breath and continued before he had a chance to forget his manners and interrupt. "My goodness, when I told my fellow players at the Queen's Gate about your largesse, the entire company asked, nay, I must tell the truth here, *demanded* that our opening night production be dedicated to you, our dearest patron."

Lord Ashlin looked anything but honored.

Riley gritted her teeth and fluttered her lashes, hoping the sincerity she'd practiced all night cloaked her words with the measure of truth they lacked.

"I can see from your expression you think we should continue our tradition of bestowing the opening night honors on the Prince." She nodded thoughtfully. "After all, he will be there, and with you beside him in the Ashlin box, it may be uncomfortable. I assure you, I will smooth the social waters over with regard to Prinny." She leaned over the desk, tipped her head so she glanced shyly up from beneath the brim of her hat, and said in her most confidential tones, "The Prince and I are quite close."

As she let her little white lie slip, she realized her mistake by the sharp look in his eyes.

If she thought he'd looked stern before, his face now took on the qualities of granite as he leveled his gaze at her.

"And it is just that 'closeness' with men that I wish to discuss," he said, jumping in even as she struggled to think of some way of smoothing over her disastrous improvisation.

"My nieces," he continued, "are sheltered, innocent girls, and I would like them to stay that way—at least until they find themselves married. What my cousin has proposed, using you to enhance their social graces, seemed to be a good idea at first—"

"And it still—" Riley stopped in mid-sentence as she watched one of Lord Ashlin's eyebrows arch wickedly, the meaning clear.

The Earl cleared his throat. "My brother and sister-in-law took great care in seeing Beatrice, Margaret, and Louisa gently reared so someday they'd take their rightful place in society." He leaned forward. "And as their guardian, I will not risk their reputations by allowing them to associate with a woman of your character."

Of her character?

Why the stuffy, priggish, puritanical . . .

Riley abandoned her original course of flattery and decided to try a different approach. "My lord, I can see you have given this careful thought, but let me be honest with you. The Season is about to begin and London will start filling with young girls out to find eligible husbands."

"And what has that to do with retaining your services?"

"Why, everything," she told him. "While your nieces may be accomplished and beautiful," at this she paused and smiled, knowing full well if they were real beauties he wouldn't have hired her in the first place, "they need something to set them apart. Qualities that will allow them to stand out amidst the crowd. To make them Originals."

"Whatever guidance they require," he said slowly, "I'm sure my Cousin Felicity will do the job quite admirably."

"Are we talking about the Cousin Felicity I met, or do you have another?" she asked, hoping to lighten the mood. When he looked neither amused nor appreciative of her observation, she went back to honesty. "Tell me, has your Cousin Felicity ever caught a man's attention and held it long enough to get him to propose marriage?"

His silence answered her question.

"Well, I have. So many times I've lost count. With your cousin's directions, your nieces will be lucky if they get invited to dance."

Finally, he looked as if he might be considering her arguments.

She continued in a mad rush. "Given your current financial crisis, the girls will have a tremendous disadvantage against the vast number of young ladies with dowries. Substantial dowries, I might add. I can tell you want the very best for your nieces, and that is admirable, but a dowry is essential in making an advantageous marriage. To secure their futures your nieces will need more than any well-meant advice your Cousin Felicity can give them."

"Your suggestions are sensible, Madame; however, I've already made other plans to secure my nieces' futures."

While he sounded sure, Riley swore she detected a hint

of doubt to his conviction. "Overnight, my lord? I am intrigued," she said, settling comfortably into her chair. "Do tell."

He rose from his seat, his hands going behind his back. Pacing a couple of steps, he finally announced, "I plan to wed."

It was Riley's turn to raise her eyebrows in amazement. Part of her didn't like the idea of Lord Ashlin married, especially not to some simpering miss, but then she realized this was nothing more than a bluff.

It had to be.

"So quickly?" she asked. "Who is the lucky lady?"

He frowned at her. "I'd prefer not to say until the banns are read."

So, you don't have anyone in mind, she thought.

Lord Ashlin turned and paced a few more haphazard steps. "Once I am married, I believe we shall all retire to the Ashlin estates in the country."

To escape the worst of your creditors, Riley would have loved to add.

"And from there I will be able to find suitable husbands for my nieces. Men who can appreciate their gentle natures and quiet manners."

At this, Riley bit her tongue to keep from asking if what he truly meant were old, doddering fools who hadn't been to town in so long, their favorite hunting hounds were starting to look comely.

Listening to his own words, Mason wondered if anyone would have believed them. The bemused look flitting across Madame Fontaine's features said quite plainly she'd found his future plans as amusing and likely as the latest *on-dit*.

Well, they had sounded perfectly rational not fifteen minutes earlier.

Oh, who was he kidding—he needed cash, not a wife.

And his nieces were . . . well, he didn't want to consider how much money it would take to entice a man to marry even one of them, at least not until they received the polish Cousin Felicity was convinced this woman could offer.

Damnation, he needed her and her theatre. If what he'd heard last night at his club was true and her productions played to standing-room-only crowds, Frederick's investment could return more than enough dividends to pay off the worst of his creditors.

Mason couldn't help but feel the sting of irony in all of it. Freddie and the two earls before him had squandered the family fortunes on actresses and their ilk, and now it seemed the very path of the Ashlins' self-destruction may also be their salvation—but it was akin to lying down with the enemy.

And the last thing he needed to be thinking about was lying down anywhere near Madame Fontaine—the images of a red plush apartment still murmuring in the back of his imagination.

"My lord, your plans sound so promising," she began, rising from her seat, "that I hate even to make the new offer my partners asked me to extend on their behalf."

Before he could stop himself, he repeated, "A new offer?"

"Why, yes," she said, sounding as hopeful as he felt. "My partners authorized me to extend a new proposal in the unlikely event you'd made 'other plans.' But you sound like you're well on your way to solving your difficulties, so I am loath to waste your time." She sighed prettily and smiled at him.

The kind of smile that would make a man forget every vow he'd ever made. Forget his pride, forget his plans.

Forget he was a new kind of Ashlin.

But it didn't let him forget he owed his soul to every debt collector in London.

Taking a deep breath, he nodded for her to continue.

"As you well know, you are entitled to a percentage of our receipts. My partners and I are willing to double that percentage to allow your debt to be repaid in half the time. And by the end of production you will have more than tripled your brother's investment."

Mason didn't speak at first. As it turned out, his shock and inability to utter a response to her offer worked well to his advantage. She continued quickly, heaping additional enticements onto her already unbelievable proposition.

"I know you have doubts about my qualifications and I promise you I won't teach your nieces anything but the most ladylike of manners and grace," she said in a hasty rush. "In fact, I am so positive that I can enhance your nieces' chances in the Marriage Mart that I'm willing to wager they'll be betrothed within a week of opening night. If not, I'll throw in my five percent of the first three weeks' receipts." Madame Fontaine stuck out her hand. "So, my lord, do we still have a deal?"

Before Mason could strike what he was sure was a deal with the devil, his eldest niece, Beatrice, burst into the study. She skidded to a dead halt in the middle of the room.

Looking back over her shoulder toward the still swinging door, she shouted at her youngest sister, "Lud, Louisa. 'Tis true. You have to take back calling Cousin Felicity a senile old hag. Uncle really does have some Haymarket bird in Father's study."

Mason stared at his eldest niece and saw what Madame Fontaine probably saw—a coltish and fair-haired girl of twenty and some odd years.

Then, to his horror, his middle niece, Margaret, barreled into the room with all the energy of a pack of hounds and half the grace.

Not having noticed her sister frozen in the middle of the room, nineteen-year-old Maggie plowed into Bea, sending her flying toward the settee and in the process tearing a large patch out of Bea's already well-worn skirt.

"Lawks and the devil," Bea cursed, with all the native inflection of a wharfside rat. She held out her ruined gown for her sister's inspection. "Mags, can't you enter a room for once and not act like a drunken sailor?"

Mags promptly burst into a loud cacophony of tears, turning her already ruddy face into a mottled mess. "I didn't see you, Bea," the girl sobbed. "I'm sorry."

"Well, you are as blind as you are stupid," her sister continued, adding a string of curses that would have made a battle-hardened marine blush.

"Uh, hum," a third voice coughed.

Mason glanced up to find Louisa, his youngest niece, in the doorway, her toe tapping impatiently because no one had noticed her.

All of seventeen, Louisa stood poised, not unlike how her mother used to make her own dramatic entrances. But where Caro had been bright and glowing, Louisa's look was one of utter disdain. With the stalking precision of a military officer and none of her mother's sleek elegance, she tromped over the still prone Bea, giving Madame Fontaine a wide berth, as if their guest carried the plague.

The girl turned her haughty features toward him.

"My God, Uncle. Whatever is this vile whore doing in our house?" she said, pointing at Madame Fontaine.

He looked for only a second at his nieces and saw his future—one that featured this ill-mannered, uncivilized trio as a permanent fixture in his household for the remainder of his days.

I love my nieces, I love my nieces, he chanted like some strange Eastern prayer, hoping to convince himself, but the truth be told, they were the three most unappealing harridans who'd ever graced the face of the earth.

In that bleak moment his frantic gaze fell on Madame Fontaine and the contrast became only too clear.

The devil had never looked so much like an angel.

Before she could withdraw her hand, he grabbed it like a lifeline and sealed their bargain with an enthusiastic shake.

Chapter 4

Riley could only stare down at the Earl's firm hand locked in an unholy promise with hers and ask, what had she gotten herself into?

She glanced up and found his sharp blue gaze cutting through her, piercing and demanding—and, she noted, with just a touch of desperation.

Eh, gads, she realized. *He truly expects me to marry off these appalling minxes!* And minxes, she knew, was the only polite way of describing the St. Clair sisters.

While the Earl might be convinced she could save the day, or maybe he wasn't, but she didn't doubt he saw her as his last hope. Oh, she had an ominous feeling that her future could be summed up quite concisely in a few lines from Macbeth,

> *Double, double, toil and trouble,*
> *Fire burn and caldron bubble.*

And this unhappy trio, like their Shakespearean counterparts, appeared quite capable of brewing more than a potful of mischief.

Oh, the girls were pretty enough, and with a bit of cooperation on their part, she'd see their wretched manners ground away until they sparkled like a trio of diamonds.

No, it wasn't that part of the deal that had her panicked.

It was the Earl of Ashlin and the look she spied behind his innocuous spectacles. For a moment she saw beyond the Oxford professor and spied a man she found disarmingly handsome.

And as his fingers continued to envelope hers, binding her to him, she realized she'd made a deal that went far beyond lessons in manners.

That was the devilish part.

Something told her that this Ashlin, for all his scholarly airs and orderly pretensions, had inherited his fair share of his family's legendary charm.

Charm to which even the fabled Aphrodite would have found herself susceptible.

She struggled to pull her hand free and extract herself from this fool's bargain, even as the strength underlying his touch crept up her arm and toward her sheltered heart.

She'd never met a man who hadn't immediately fallen to her feet and declared his undying devotion, and perhaps that was what vexed her about this one.

It made no sense whatsoever. How could some bespectacled, badly dressed, and ill-mannered nobleman pique her curiosity so, when at the same time, he made her feel so ungainly, so ill favored, so wretchedly inadequate with only one dismissive phrase?

Tolerably pretty, indeed!

Well, she wasn't about to fall prey to any foolish, misplaced sentiments. Not her. Not one wit . . . She'd seen too many actresses fall in love with the wrong man, or rather, nobleman.

Oh, they were kind enough—when it suited them. Even generous—when it suited them. But when they were done with their actress *du jour*, they moved on, never looking back or making amends for the broken heart they left in their selfish wake.

Well, this was one nobleman who wasn't about to leave her heart on the wayside.

So, with a deep breath and a wrenching pull, she freed herself from his grasp.

Brushing her hand against her skirt, she told herself that was enough to break his spell.

Yes, she could do this. Keep her promise. It wouldn't be so hard. She just had to avoid touching him.

Mason watched the lady brushing her hand over her skirt and wondered how long he'd been clasping it like a moonstruck fool.

He probably should feel a bit guilty about having been less than forthcoming about the girls' state of neglect.

The last thing he needed now was for her to flee or point out his dishonesty, so he tried to sound encouraging. "I think this will work to our mutual benefit, Madame. My nieces are eager to be wed."

"Uncle!" Beatrice exclaimed, "we want no such thing." She cast a scathing glance toward Cousin Felicity, who'd quietly sneaked into the room.

Mason could only wonder what this outburst was all about. Cousin Felicity had assured him the girls wanted husbands, and surely they must see for themselves they were ill fitted to undertake such a task.

Besides, he was only trying to help.

"If you think, Uncle, that we are going to take lessons from some petticoat merchant, you are sadly mistaken," Louisa announced. "Mother would be appalled, and I am sure my father would call you out for the sheer insult of having *that* kind of woman in *our* house. Not to mention," she said, jerking her thumb toward Hashim, who'd entered the room behind Cousin Felicity, "this heathen she's brought along. Why, I won't be surprised if the watch finds us all with our throats slit and the silver missing before the day is out."

She nodded to her elder siblings, and the threesome stuck their noses in the air and marched toward the door in sisterly unity. Their protest would have had some meaning if Maggie hadn't tripped with her second step and bumped into Bea, who promptly lit into her sister with a litany of curses.

Louisa grabbed their arms and started to drag them from the room before they lent more damage to her cause.

Mason resisted the urge to berate his lot in life to the heavens.

For there was no doubt in his mind that if he let his nieces loose on society in their current state, they would write a chapter in the family history that twenty generations of Ashlins would be unable to repair.

Even worse was the rigid line of Madame Fontaine's posture. Louisa's insulting comments hadn't sat well with the actress, and for that matter, they hadn't gone over that well with him.

Freddie and Caro had been dead for all these months, and it was high time he put his foot down and made his own rules as to who was welcome in the house.

Madame Fontaine may be everything the girls and popular gossip claimed she was, but she was also a guest in *his* house, and as such, she would be given the due consideration that status conferred to a lady.

Louisa had yet to cease her very vocal tirade as to her uncle's mismanagement of their lives. "I can't believe, Uncle, that you would think we need this . . . this . . . *whor—*"

"Enough!" Mason said, his booming order shaking his

errant nieces out of their circus antics and bringing them
to shocked attention.

Even Cousin Felicity, he noticed, usually a whirl of
perpetual motion and worries, froze in place at his uncom-
mon outburst.

"But—" Louisa started again.

"I said enough!" And he meant it. If he was going to
restore the family name, he'd have to start by taking control of his household. He looked over at the girls, teetering
as they were between righting Maggie and trying to flee
from this unexpected wrath. "Margaret, stand up straight
and don't move."

"How dare you," Beatrice said, coming to the defense
of her sister. "Louisa has every right to call that woman
a—"

Mason swung his gaze squarely on his eldest niece.
"Beatrice, one more foul word from your lips and you
shall spend the rest of your life in a convent so silent the
only sound you'll ever hear is your own heart beating until
the day you die."

Even Madame Fontaine took a step back from him at
this point.

The only one who seemed unfazed by his uncharacteristic outburst was the lady's servant, Hashim. The imposing man stood in the corner, grinning like an idiot. When
he noticed Mason's gaze on him, the man didn't blanch
but nodded for him to continue, as if he approved of the
Earl's finally having come to the defense of his mistress.

Mason had always had control of his classrooms, so a
household of women shouldn't be that much more difficult, he told himself, folding his hands behind his back
and striking his most severe pose—the one he used on
errant first-year students.

"Now that I have your attention, you will each listen to

me. I have retained Madame Fontaine's services to assist you for the upcoming Season. All three of you will come out this year."

Bea's mouth opened—to protest, he assumed—but he cocked a brow and waited for her to speak as if he dared her to utter a word of contradiction.

Obviously he hadn't lost his touch, for her lips remained gaping like a fish for a few moments and then snapped shut—either having realized her remarks were futile or fear of that convent had made an indelible impression.

"As I was saying, Madame Fontaine will start your lessons today."

"Today!" all of them protested.

He glanced over at Hashim, whose grin seemed to say, *Put your foot down.*

"Yes, today. And from the behavior I have witnessed this morning, it isn't a minute too soon."

His firm stance was greeted with glum expressions but no further verbal protests.

Mason took a deep breath, feeling for the first time since Freddie's death in command of his own destiny. He paced, taking a few tentative steps and then stronger strides around the corner of his desk.

"Uncle, if I may ask a question?" The inquiry came from Louisa, which didn't surprise him, given her daring, but it was her soft tones and sweet smile that startled him.

"Yes?"

"I understand that you have hired Madame Fontaine with the best of intentions," she said, smiling both at him and the lady in question. "But what if someone discovers her presence here? Discovers that you've hired a . . ."

"Common strumpet?" Bea offered, an equally sweet smile pasted on her face.

Louisa shot an annoyed glance at her sister, and then finished her own inquiry with a little more polite phrasing. "A lady, shall we say, of questionable qualifications to instruct us. Think how such a thing might be interpreted." She shuddered delicately.

If Mason hadn't lived with his nieces for all these months he might have been moved by Louisa's demure protest, but he was past falling for their tricks.

Besides, the solution to her argument was quite simple. "No one will know about Madame Fontaine's engagement in our house, because we will not breathe a word of it to anyone."

"But the servants," Bea protested.

"I will instruct Belton to advise them that if they want to stay employed, they will keep this information confidential."

Not that they had that many servants as it was. The only ones who'd remained had done so only out of loyalty to the family. "Not one word, or there will be no Season for any of you, no invitations to balls, or vouchers to Almack's," he told his nieces again.

"*Almack's*," Maggie whispered in reverent tones. "Do you really think we might get vouchers?"

Mason smiled at his niece, hopeful that perhaps at least one of them would see they had something to gain from Madame's tutelage. "You will have to prove to the patronesses that you are worthy of gaining vouchers. From what your Cousin Felicity tells me, it can be quite difficult."

"Not for us," Louisa avowed. Her arms crossed over her chest. "Why, our mother was welcome everywhere. There is no reason to believe . . ." she paused and glanced at her sisters. "That at least one of us will be given vouchers."

"But there are no guarantees," Mason told her, "that any of you will be given such a rare distinction if *one* of you disgraces the family." He let the impact of his words sink in.

The girls glanced at each other, obviously measuring their siblings' social faults. From the trio of frowns which followed, they hadn't liked the way their estimations tallied up.

"So, do I have your word?" he asked.

They nodded, albeit reluctantly, and then their glances swung toward Cousin Felicity.

Mason understood the aim of their concern. "This was your idea, Cousin. What do you have to say? Can you refrain from sharing any mention of Madame Fontaine's presence in our home with your acquaintances?"

Cousin Felicity pursed her lips. Her worried brow told everyone in the room they were asking a high price of her.

"Not even your dressmaker," Mason added.

"But Mason, not even Lady—" she started, the lace on her cap all aflutter.

"—No, Cousin. No one. This must be a secret."

The poor woman looked as if they had asked her to attend a court levee in last year's gown.

Madame Fontaine stepped forward, laying a gentle hand on his cousin's arm. "Consider my poor servant's fate. While I don't know for certain, there were rumors in Paris that his tongue was torn from his mouth after he let some rather confidential information slip." Madame Fontaine sighed. "It is never prudent to be indiscriminate."

Mason nearly laughed as Cousin Felicity gulped and turned slightly to glance at Hashim, who stood in the corner glowering at his mistress.

She shrugged ever so slightly at her servant, as if to say, *Sorry, my friend.*

Hashim's glower did not soften, but his stance eased just a bit, giving one the distinct impression his reply was, *We will discuss it later.*

"Well, what say you, Cousin Felicity? It seems you hold the girls' future in your hands," he said.

At this she let out a little sigh of defeat. "If you insist, Mason. While you might not believe it, many of my friends consider me to be the cornerstone of discretion."

At this, Bea let out the most unladylike snort.

All gazes swung over at her.

"What?" she asked.

Mason shook his head. Madame Fontaine surely had her work cut out for her.

Folding his hands behind his back, he wondered at their apparent acceptance. He should have known better than to think his nieces would give up so easily.

Louisa spoke again. "All this is well and good, if we keep quiet, but what about *her*?" She pointed at Madame Fontaine as one might an unknown carcass at the side of the road. "And *him*," she continued, tipping her nose over her shoulder in Hashim's direction. "They don't exactly fit into the usual crowd parading about Ashlin Square. Someone is bound to notice them coming and going, especially done up like that." She paused. "In case you haven't met all our neighbors, Uncle, believe me when I tell you there isn't a one who possesses Cousin Felicity's 'cornerstone on discretion.' " She smiled at the elderly lady as if she meant her comment as a compliment.

While he didn't like Louisa's tone, he had to agree with her assessment.

Madame Fontaine stood out, but perhaps with a change

of gown and a subtler hairstyle, she might blend into the comings and goings of the Square.

But Hashim? Mason doubted there was any way to disguise the giant Saracen.

He decided to address one problem at a time. "My niece has a point, Madame. Tomorrow, I would ask that you arrive promptly at seven—"

"Seven!" came the shocked chorus.

He noted wryly that even Madame Fontaine had added her voice to this objection.

"Yes, seven. A very wise Colonial once said something about how the early bird gets the worm. We have no time to lose, since the Season starts in less than a month." He stood firm and when he heard no more complaints beyond a muttered curse coming from Bea's corner, he took a deep breath. "So I would ask, Madame, that when you arrive tomorrow morning, you come dressed more appropriately for your station as a tutor to gently bred young ladies."

The arch of her neatly shaped brow was her only contradiction to his order. And he knew it wasn't about the time of day or her manner of dress.

She probably was wondering where he was going to find the gently bred young ladies.

"As you wish, my lord," she said.

There, that settled everything, he thought. He'd set order to his house, once and for all. In a few weeks the girls would go out into good society, find well-mannered husbands, and move on with their lives so he could continue with hers.

Mason shook his head.

No, he meant, continue with *his* life. Not *hers*.

For a moment, Mason closed his eyes to the swell of her breasts threatening to spill out from the low décolletage of her gown, to the rounded curves of her hips, and the teasing, billowing sway of the feathers in her hat which seemed to beckon a man to come closer.

Merciful heavens, what had he wrought on himself, inviting her into his house for a month?

Hopefully, stripped of her finery, she wouldn't be such a temptation to his Ashlin heart.

Yes, he told himself. *She is probably quite plain beneath all that artifice.*

Or so he prayed.

"Uncle, are you listening?" Bea's insistent question pierced his wayward thoughts.

"Yes? What is it?" He straightened and tried to appear attentive.

"I was saying, you can dress this fancy piece of yours in sackcloth, but what about *him*? Infidels are about as common on Ashlin Square as a snowfall in hel—"

"Yes, Beatrice. I think we all get your point." Mason turned toward Madame Fontaine. "My niece is quite right. Your servant must remain behind."

Hashim growled at this change of events, the guttural sound bringing a frightened squeak from Cousin Felicity.

Madame Fontaine placed a placating hand on her servant's forearm. "I'm afraid the decision is not mine to make, my lord," she said politely. "Hashim comes and goes as he pleases. And it pleases him to escort me when I venture out."

He studied her for a moment. He swore he heard a catch in her voice—that she wasn't quite telling the truth. Then again, perhaps like the rest of the pampered London felines, Madame Fontaine was used to getting her way. Well, this time she would have to make an exception to that tradition.

Straightening his shoulders, Mason said, "Your servant

will just have to change his mind. If he arrives with you, it will only invite untoward speculation. Either he stays behind, or you had best bring the balance of your debt with you tomorrow."

The lady shot a glance over her shoulder at Hashim, a look that seemed to say, *Leave off. I'll fix this later.*

While he might not like her smug assurance that she could reprimand his order so easily, he had to admire her skill at handling her intimidating escort.

She turned back and tipped her head in acquiescence.

Mason acknowledged her gesture with a nod of his own. "There. Now everything is in order." He turned to his nieces. "Your lessons will commence immediately. Please show Madame to the Green Salon." He waved his dismissal to them, and settled back into his chair, opening the drawer to his right and pulling out his accursed account book.

When he glanced up, he realized they were still all standing there staring at him, each with her own censorious gaze.

"Aren't you going to sit in?" Madame Fontaine asked. "You had mentioned, my lord, that you were considering entering the Marriage Mart yourself, and perhaps a little polish might speed along your endeavors in that field."

"Uncle get married?" Louisa gasped. After a few seconds of stunned silence, she and her sisters burst out laughing.

He shot a disparaging glare at them, but it was of no use. The trio was lost in their mirth.

"What is so funny?" he asked.

"Oh, Uncle," Maggie said between giggles. "You are too old to find a wife."

He frowned. "I hardly think one-and-thirty is considered old."

This brought on another round of hilarity, and much to his annoyance, even Madame Fontaine shared the girls' amusement at this notion, for the woman shook with barely controlled tremors of laughter.

When she caught him staring at her, she brought her hand to her mouth and coughed.

"There now!" she said, her sharp tone bringing a quick end to the girls' giggles. "Your uncle is *tolerable* enough, and not *that* old. There is no need to think there isn't *some* woman in town or even beyond—" she paused as if she were considering if that was enough territory for his search, before she finished by saying, "—who *might* consider his offer quite an honor."

Her patronizing smile and tone grated at what little vanity he possessed.

Why, the woman made it sound like he were some old, lecherous cad whose only matrimonial hope was a three-eyed spinster whose last Season could be counted in decades, not years!

But in addition to her smile, there was a hint of challenge in her green eyes. A subtle dare for him to stay in her company.

That is if he'd hazard to run the risk.

Dammit if she hadn't been sent to test his mettle.

All too much.

Reminding himself that Ashlins no longer rose to such bait, he bowed to her and nodded. "Thank you for your kind estimation, Madame. Perhaps I will drop in on your lessons another time. For now, I suggest you take advantage of what little time you do have by retiring to the Green Salon. My mother's pianoforte is in there, and the room is sparsely furnished so it has enough space to move about. Cousin Felicity will assist you if you have any other needs." Bowing politely, he fled his study before there could be any further protests or comments.

Mason knew from his long years studying history that at times honor could be found only in a well-timed retreat from one's folly. And he had certainly found his as he beat a hasty departure. Though his flight came up short when he ran into Belton in the main foyer.

"Sir," Belton said, the single word tolling through the room like a warning bell. "Lady Delander is coming up the steps. What should I do with your other *guests*?"

"Lady Delander?" Mason cringed. An advertisement on the front page of the morning paper wouldn't do the job of spreading the news of Madame Fontaine's presence in their house that Lady Delander could do in a few short hours.

And to add insult to injury, her services were free.

"Oh, dear," Cousin Felicity said, as she fluttered over to Mason's side. "I forgot about her."

"Forgot what?" Mason asked.

"I asked her to call this morning."

"Cousin Felicity!"

"Well, that was before you uttered that dreadful edict, Mason. How was I to know you were going to snatch away my greatest triumph?" Cousin Felicity started to retrieve her handkerchief.

The bell at the door jangled loudly, rattling all of them to attention.

"Should I deny her entrance, sir?" Belton looked as if sending the gossipy Lady Delander packing would have been his own personal form of triumph.

"Oh, you can't do that!" Cousin Felicity protested. "Josephine counts half the patronesses as her closest friends. Snub her and we'll never see a single voucher for Almack's."

The bell tolled again, this time with decided impatience.

"We must let her in," Cousin Felicity whispered, "or she'll—"

His cousin didn't need to finish her statement because the lady in question did it for her.

The door to the Ashlin house started to open, but Belton was quicker and pushed it shut, throwing the latch to bar her entrance.

"Well, I never!" Lady Delander's protest came through the heavy panel as if she were standing in the foyer. "Felicity? Where is everyone?" she called out, followed by a sharp rapping that could only be from her cane. "This is most impertinent! Where is Belton?" A pause followed, which they soon discovered was only the lady catching her breath, for she quickly recovered and started her verbal assault anew. "It's that infidel I saw this morning. He must be in there murdering them all! Come out at once, or I will call for the guard and have them break in the door."

Mason looked around and saw his worst nightmare— the most scandalous actress in London and her Saracen bodyguard in his house while the most notorious gossip stood on his front steps trying to scale his home like a reenactment of the Norman conquest.

"Everyone, out of here!" he ordered, as Lady Delander had obviously called her footman to break down the barred door.

Beatrice caught Hashim by the elbow and propelled him into the open servant's doorway, and then fled through the portal, as if the hounds of hell had been let loose in Ashlin Square.

Meanwhile, Louisa caught Maggie by the hand and hauled her ungainly sister up the stairs, the pair fleeing in much the same frantic manner as Bea.

Mason didn't blame them—Lady Delander was probably mentioned somewhere in some obscure ancient text as one of the lost servants of the underworld.

Belton still held the door against the invaders, but he was losing ground fast.

Outside, Lady Delander continued to urge her footman onward. "Not a moment to lose, Peter! There are lives at stake."

With only seconds to spare, Mason caught hold of his last guest, and while it wasn't the kindest course of action, he tossed her into the nearest closet.

Slamming the door shut, he turned to Cousin Felicity. "Not a word, Cousin. Not one word." He started to wave to Belton to let the intruders in, just as the door to the closet popped back open.

"I will not—" Madame began to protest.

Mason had few choices left. With the front door about to give way, he realized he needed to silence Madame Fontaine immediately.

Later on, when he looked back at all the choices he could have made, he could only wonder why he chose that one.

It hadn't been the most honorable, or decent, or respectable decision.

It had been a Freddie–inspired impulse at its worst.

But it worked—it quieted Madame Fontaine—yet it also started an entirely new set of problems.

For even as the front door sprang open with Lady Delander leading the charge, Mason caught the protesting Madame Fontaine in his arms and plunged them both into the front closet. And once inside, he did the most Ashlin thing he'd ever done in his life.

He'd kissed the lady into silence . . . and discovered why his ancestors had left a trail of debt from Covent Garden to Vauxhall.

Chapter 5

〜〜✦〇✦〜〜

"I will not be—" Riley started to protest as the Earl crashed into the closet with her, enveloping her in his resourceful embrace.

His lips closed over hers, catching her unawares in a kiss.

This was no stage buss, no hasty, snatched affair from an overly attentive admirer.

His lips held hers under a masterful spell.

In a whisper and sigh, she found herself lost. The chaos in the foyer faded to a distant hum, until all she knew was the warmth of his body, the spicy scent of his shaving soap, and the taste of his lips.

How could it be that in an instant this unpolished man of letters, this stern, puritanical professor disappeared and in his place stood a rake of the first order, a man who knew how to hold a woman and tease her senses until they tingled with new life?

Even worse, she found herself answering his kiss with a need she never realized had been missing from her life.

So much for her promise to herself not to touch him, as she rose up on her toes to get even closer to him. Her arms wound around his neck as she melted against his chest. Her mouth opened further and he deepened the kiss until a cry, a strident peel like a battle-ax being sharpened for war, wrenched them apart.

"Lady Felicity, what is the meaning of this?" a shrill voice she assumed to be Lady Delander's cried out again.

"Shhh—" Lord Ashlin whispered into her ear.

As if she could say anything right now. She still couldn't catch her breath, let alone calm her pounding heart, which she was sure could be heard from the attic to the cellar.

"I will have an answer," Lady Delander demanded. "What is the meaning of all this?"

"Meaning of what?" Cousin Felicity replied.

"The door! Belton barred the door to me."

Too bad they couldn't have kept it that way, Riley found herself wishing. Wishing she had the courage to turn her face up and coax the Earl into kissing her one more time.

Oh, whatever was she thinking? This is what became of associating with nobility—it made one . . . well, hardly noble! She should be outraged. She should be indignant.

And she should certainly not be wishing for another kiss.

Out in the foyer, Cousin Felicity laughed. "Belton? Did you bar Lady Delander from the house?"

"No, Madame, I would never presume to question your or Lord Ashlin's choice of guests."

Belton's sarcasm sounded as if it were aimed directly at her.

"I tell you I was barred from your house," Lady Delander continued. "That door was shut in my face." This was followed by a great huff and sigh, like the wheeze of bagpipes.

"Odious woman," Mason muttered under his breath.

Riley heartily agreed. While she had yet to lay her eyes on the estimable lady, she could well envision her, having seen her kind in their private boxes, whispering and pointing their fans at the moral decay around them, and then delighting in sharing the latest *on-dits* and scandalous bits with anyone willing to listen.

"Oh, that door," Cousin Felicity was saying. "I'm afraid it sticks. Whenever it rains. Terribly inconvenient. I've been after Lord Ashlin to fix it, but does he listen to me?"

"Sticks when it rains?" Lady Delander's voice sounded incredulous. "Lady Felicity, it is not raining."

"Oh, so it isn't. Well, that's why it must have opened." In her own nonsensical way, Cousin Felicity was doing a good job of distracting their unwanted guest, but not for long.

Lady Delander, Riley quickly realized, was, if anything, persistent.

"Oh, never mind about the door," she said to Cousin Felicity. "I distinctly saw an infidel entering your house earlier, and in the company of a woman whose dress was, shall we say, less than respectable."

"Less than respectable?" Riley whispered. "Why, I'll have that woman know this gown is the height of—"

Her protests were cut off again with another kiss, this one just as swift and shocking as the first—melting her very heart.

His hand pressed at the small of her back, pulling her closer to him.

Oh, how dare he, she wanted to cry out, if only her body wasn't having the most disgraceful reaction. Her fingers gripped his shoulders and she pressed herself closer if only to feel all of him.

What the devil was she doing, throwing herself at him

like the worst type of Cyprian he already suspected her of being?

She broke away, their gazes meeting briefly in the meager light slipping in around the door.

There she saw a hunger that both frightened her and left her wanting to fill that deep void.

He put a single finger to her lips. "Shhh." His touch burned her skin as much as his lips had moments earlier. "Don't say a word."

All she could do was nod. Do anything he asked rather than break the spell between them.

"I tell you, I saw the most heinous heathen entering this house!" Lady Delander said.

"A heathen in Ashlin Square?" Cousin Felicity's words echoed with disbelief. She lowered her voice, though not enough so it wasn't heard through the closed door of their closet. "Josephine, have you been putting sherry in your tea again?"

"I certainly have not!" the lady protested. "I know what I saw. And I saw an infidel entering this house with the most wicked-looking sword. 'Tis a wonder you haven't had your throat slit. I told my son to summon the watch immediately."

Mason groaned. "Not the watch."

"Oh, dear! He didn't, did he?" Cousin Felicity was asking.

"Summon the watch?" Lady Delander said. "No, he refused. Said it probably had to do with another of Lord Ashlin's odd university studies and never to mind. But you know me, Felicity. I shan't stay still while my friends are in danger. So I summoned all my courage and came over here to see to you myself."

"A regular Lady Macbeth out there," Riley whispered. "Can't leave well enough alone." She changed the inflection in her voice to mimic Lady Delander. "*Out, damned spot.*"

Lord Ashlin's eyes widened with amazement, and then his mouth twitched with uncharacteristic humor.

Riley would have sworn such a smile on this man wasn't possible, and even worse, it lent him that spark of disarmingly handsome charm she'd witnessed earlier.

"Josephine, where would I be without a good friend like you?" Cousin Felicity was asking. "But there was no need. Come to think of it, I do believe Lord Ashlin was visiting with some fellow just back from some savage place or another. And in the most outlandish garb."

"Well, you should implore him not to associate with such people. This is Ashlin Square, not the democratic rabble of Oxford."

"How right you are. I assure you, I will pass on your sentiments the moment he returns. But in the meantime, you should come upstairs and we'll have our tea," Cousin Felicity said. "I have the most engaging news about Miss Pindar and my dear Mason."

"You mean . . ."

The ladies' voices trailed off, their footsteps passing overhead as the gossiping pair ascended the steps. As soon as the door to Cousin Felicity's salon closed, Belton opened the door to the closet.

There, much to the stalwart man's horror, he found the master of the house with an actress in his arms, kissing the woman in a most indecent fashion.

In his forty years of service at Ashlin House, the poor butler was loath to admit it wasn't the first time that closet had been used thusly by the lord of the house.

Mason realized only too late that the door was wide open, and his momentary lapse of honor was now being witnessed by not only Belton, but a gawking housemaid and footman.

He immediately set Madame Fontaine aside, probably a little too abruptly, because the woman faltered and swayed as if she'd consumed a decanter of port, while those damnable feathers in her hat winked and swayed at him like a trio of conspirators.

And as her gaze focused on Belton and the other servants, her cheeks pinked to a bright shade, as if she'd never been so embarrassed in her life.

Then again, he knew how she felt—and after he'd just spent the morning telling Belton how he was going to return the house to order and regain his seat at Merton College, then he'd gone and done this . . . this unpardonable act. This giant step backward in the Ashlin family evolution.

"Well, yes, there now, everything seems in order . . ." Mason muttered, stepping out of the closet as if nothing were out of the ordinary. If only he felt that way—instead of his blood raging with a new fire—a veritable Ashlin blaze of impropriety. He straightened his jacket and took another few steps into the foyer. "I see Lady Delander has been dispatched upstairs without any further incident. Good work, Belton. If you would call a hackney and locate Mr. Hashim, we will see our guests away before there are any other difficulties."

Now that was the way to handle the situation, he thought, as Belton sent a footman for the cab, leaving him only one person left to be dealt with—the lady herself.

For once he wished he had Freddie's experience in these matters. His brother would have known the right witty words to set them both laughing and call an end to this uncomfortable awkwardness.

While he considered what to say, dismissing half a

dozen or so dry comments, she bustled right past him.

Then she let out a pretty sigh and went to work straightening her dress and bonnet, finishing her toilet with a quick pat to her hair.

"You needn't worry," he said. "You look quite tolerable."

Her brows arched. "Tolerable? Is that what I am?" She turned her back to him, her foot tapping impatiently.

Bother! Now he'd gone and insulted her. And he hadn't the slightest clue why. "What I meant was, that you appear as if nothing happened. It wasn't as if anything did. Quite the opposite, wouldn't you say?" He added a laugh, hoping she'd see the humor in the situation though he wasn't too sure that it was amusing in the least.

Not when what he really wanted to do was to catch her up in his arms again and continue where he'd left off.

Oh, yes, he told himself. *That would solve everything.*

She glanced over her shoulder. "I would suppose, given your familial inclinations, assignations in the front closet are quite commonplace. I'll have you know, they are not in mine."

"They aren't in mine, either," he said, drawing himself up. "This . . . this . . . display was a complete aberration."

"Now I am an 'aberration?' " Her nose went up in the air.

Oh, the devil take it, he thought. That wasn't what he'd meant at all.

What had he meant?

He certainly couldn't tell her the truth—that her kiss had been like nothing he'd ever experienced. That to hold her in his arms was like being able to contain quicksilver—something elusive, vital and filled with fire. That when he brought his lips to hers all he could hear were the haunting lines of John Donne.

Come live with me and be my love,
And we will some new pleasures prove.

How was he supposed to tell her that in one kiss, he'd inherited everything he'd disavowed? That having tasted her lips, the memory of her kiss would haunt his mind, his soul?

"Well?" she was asking.

He glanced up. "What?"

Her eyes widened and she tipped her head, as if prompting him that the next line was his.

He shrugged, for he hadn't the vaguest idea what one did in these circumstances.

"Aren't you going to apologize?" she finally asked.

Apologize? Apparently an expression of regret was expected in these situations. Not that he regretted kissing her.

Well, yes he did, he tried to tell himself. It had muddled everything. Still, if an apology was the thing needed to set the situation to rights, apologize he must. He smiled at her, thankful that one of them had experience in this area. He didn't think it was quite necessary, but then again, society's rules had baffled him on more than one instance.

He put his hands behind his back, rocking on his heels. "Madame, I offer my sincerest regrets and apology for my lack of restraint a few moments ago. Kissing you was an inexcusable act and completely without merit."

There, he thought. That ought to solve everything.

Her face pinked again, but this time it wasn't from embarrassment. Why the lady looked quite capable of murder.

"Why, you arrogant, doltish, mangy, shallow-hearted—"

Mason was only too glad to see Belton and Hashim arrive in the foyer, for he had a feeling she was merely winding up for the real insults.

"—Ashlin!" she finished.

Apparently, being an Ashlin was the worst thing she could come up with. Well, considering his family's reputation, it was probably the worst thing one could cast up.

"Hashim," she said. "We are leaving."

Snatching up her skirt, she turned in a swish of silk and stomped toward the front door like Cleopatra.

"No, not the front door," he said.

Her royal procession of two came to an abrupt halt. Slowly she turned to him, one brow cocked in a questioning arch.

"Someone might see you, Madame," Belton finished for him.

"I can see how that would be a tragedy to *your* reputation," she said.

Mason flinched.

"This way, Madame," Belton said, nodding toward the servant's door. "There is a carriage waiting in the mews."

"My lord," she said stiffly, nodding to Mason.

He bowed back. As he rose, Mason didn't miss the puzzled glance Hashim shot in his direction, as if the man were trying to figure out what had happened between them in the little time since Lady Delander's arrival.

"Tomorrow then," Mason called after her. "At seven."

"Yes, my lord," she replied. "We'll be here at seven."

He cleared his throat. "We?"

"We," she said firmly. "Hashim and I."

Shaking his head, Mason replied, "I thought we agreed that Mr. Hashim would not be accompanying you."

"I've changed my mind," she told him. "Hashim's services will be indispensable to the girls' first lesson."

He eyed the silent Turk. He was almost afraid to ask the question. "And what lesson would that be?"

She smiled ever so politely. "Why, how to protect themselves from the unwanted and untoward advances of the lascivious popinjays they are likely to meet among *your* set." She turned to Belton. "My carriage awaits me. Lead on, sir."

Mason would have wagered that a more righteous and indignant departure than that performed by Madame Fontaine had ever been seen in a London house or onstage.

In fashionable London, the Ashlin house wasn't the only one receiving unwelcome guests, as a rap at the door by a servant brought a frown to the Marquess of Cariston's features. "What?"

"Milord, that person is here again."

"Is anyone about, Sanders?"

"No, milord."

Snapping the paper closed, his lordship waved at the servant. "Show him in. And make sure no one sees him."

Getting up from his favorite chair, he poured himself a drink and tossed it back in one gulp. *It must be rare news indeed to warrant the likes of Nutley coming to the house in broad daylight.*

And the Marquess knew exactly who was responsible for this unwanted interruption.

Damn her. Damn her to hell, he thought, pouring himself a second measure of brandy. The woman would be the death of him.

His fingers tightened around the glass.

Not if she . . .

His murderous thoughts trailed off as his visitor strolled into the room.

"Nutley," he said, nodding at a hard chair in the corner,

well suited for someone of this man's baseborn station.

Anyone looking at the tall, handsome guest entering into the Marquess's private room would never guess that he had been born and raised in the slums of Seven Dials, for he had all the noble characteristics of an heir to the loftiest of titles.

Dressed in the height of fashion, his lean patrician nose, dark, rakish hair, and athletic build gave little evidence to the man known in London's worst stews as "the Crusher"—a nickname earned for his ability to wring a man's neck with one hand.

But Nutley hadn't been destined for the dark horrors of an early death at Tyburn, like so many of his lowly peers. With his incredible good looks, and fashionable manners and speech picked up from his prostitute mother's better clients, he passed, for the most part, as a gentleman—and spent his days working for them doing the odd jobs and rather unsavory tasks a true gentleman would never lower himself to undertake.

That, his lordship told himself, was what would always separate the likes of Nutley from the upper class.

Nutley's gaze flicked over at the hard chair in the corner he'd been offered. He took the more comfortable chair in front of the fire, and glanced up at his host, as if challenging him to say anything.

And though Lord Cariston seethed inside, this nobleman, the son of an aristocratic line that went back to the victors at Hastings, was too much of a coward to provoke a man as dangerous as Nutley.

So rather than see his own neck snapped like a goose at Christmas, Lord Cariston soothed his vanity by pouring himself another drink and not offering one to his guest.

The subtle snub would have to do for now.

"I don't recall sending for you, Nutley."

"Forgive me, your lordship, for coming here without an invitation." For all Nutley's villainy, he was a polite devil. "It's just that I got some news about her that I thought you should hear."

Lord Cariston nodded for him to continue.

"She's taken a protector."

The words sank in slowly, like the fine brandy he'd consumed. But the fire it kindled inside him had nothing to do with pleasure, for if she had sought help within the *ton*, then it would be only a matter of time before she . . .

"Who?" he whispered, afraid to hear the answer.

At this Nutley laughed, a rarity indeed, but a telling one, for it momentarily reassured his lordship that perhaps all was not lost. "The Earl of Ashlin."

Settling back in his chair, Cariston wished he could share in Nutley's good humor.

"What the devil is she doing with him?"

"I'm working on that."

"Not good enough," Cariston snapped, forgetting his earlier fears of the man seated across from him.

Nutley glanced up. "No need to get into a dander. I can handle this. From what I hear, this Ashlin is a milksop."

"If you had handled this correctly from the start, we wouldn't be having this discussion."

Instead of showing anger, Nutley shrugged. "You're the one who wanted her run out of business. If we'd done it my way from the start, she wouldn't be around bothering you now."

The look of disgust on Nutley's face reminded the Marquess of an expression his own father had often worn—one that said they both doubted he had the stomach to do what was necessary.

Getting up from his chair, Lord Cariston poured himself another drink and swallowed it down. The evil warmth gave him the final bit of courage he needed to take this very necessary, but distasteful, next step. To order her demise.

He stared at the almost empty decanter, the amber liquid hypnotic in its warmth.

Demise. Now, there was a word that gave a man comfort when he had such business.

"Well, what do you want me to do?" Nutley asked.

"Get rid of her. But it must look like an accident."

Nutley rose. "Accidents are my specialty. But it would be more fun to play with her a bit."

"No!" he barked. "And hire the job out. I won't have this connected to you, and in the rare likelihood, to me. I cannot be associated with her." For a moment, his liquor-induced bravado outweighed his usual cowardice. "If any of this goes awry, I won't pay."

Nutley laughed, crossing the room until he stood nose to nose with him. "You'll pay, gov'ner. Or the fine people around town will be mourning a second unexplainable accident." Nutley's gaze narrowed and he stared at him until Lord Cariston blinked. "That's more like it," Nutley told him. He picked up a glass and helped himself to a drink. "So what about this earl of hers?"

"Move quickly, and keep him well out of it."

"Shouldn't be so hard. I'll do it first thing tomorrow," Nutley said. "But I don't see what you're worried about, this man is hardly a bloke to be concerned about, from what I hear."

If it had been the previous Earl of Ashlin they were discussing, he might have been cheered enough to offer Nutley a second drink with which to toast their shared good fortune. But he saw nothing to celebrate.

Mason St. Clair, the Earl of Ashlin, was no fool, and if anyone could solve the mystery of Riley Fontaine, it was the man determined to be the first saint of Ashlin.

Chapter 6

"**D**amnation, here comes Del," Mason muttered early the next morning, as he watched Lord Delander round the square on his best horse, leading an equally well-blooded mount for Mason. Unlike his mother, Del was an amiable sort, loyal to his friends, though unfortunately, not what Cousin Felicity would call a "cornerstone of discretion."

Del liked to share a good story.

"Belton, is that clock wound?" he asked, pacing back across the foyer and stopping in front of the tall, ornate clock that Caro had picked up in Italy on her wedding trip. Standing eye to eye with the gold filigree hands, he could only hope the time was wrong. "It can't be half past seven."

Belton's bushy white eyebrows rose just ever so slightly, an indication that the Earl's statements bordered on impertinence.

"Yes, well, I suppose it is correct," Mason said hastily, not wanting to offend his servant.

"It would seem, my lord," Belton said, "that Lord Delander is early."

Mason shook his head at this calamity. Del being early meant his rakish friend had been up all night and had yet to seek his bed—or had sought it someplace other than his own house. And he'd now expect an invitation to breakfast.

"I clearly told her punctuality was essential for discretion, and now . . ." Mason stopped himself from going any further as he caught a glance of Belton's expression, a strained look which clearly said that the butler thought Mason's partnership with the notorious lady was sheer folly.

Belton's unholy disdain for those in trade came second only to his utter contempt of the theatre.

Oh, the butler would never tell his employer a person was inappropriate, but Belton had a way about him that never left any doubt in one's mind exactly what the uncompromising man thought.

"Well, she's late," Mason repeated.

"She is an *actress*, my lord," Belton shook his head as if his simple statement told the real truth.

"Exactly," Mason muttered. "Unreliable and flighty. And not just actresses, Belton—all women. Is it any wonder I chose the academic life? And as soon as I am rid of my nieces," he said with a nod toward the stairwell, down which came echoing their shrill voices as they argued like a trio of fishwives over the possession of a bonnet, "and rid of Freddie's debts, I am returning to my books and studies and the peaceful life I once enjoyed at Oxford."

He paced back across the foyer and stopped before the window to survey the square. Though the only other occupant about appeared to be a young maid returning from an errand for her mistress, that didn't ease his apprehensions.

Del was even now dismounting and looking around for the lad to come and take the reins.

And any moment, Madame Fontaine's carriage would

come rolling into the square and his risky partnership with the most notorious woman in London would become public knowledge, compliments of Del.

It had seemed so easy yesterday—to tell her that he would seek his bride, make a marriage of convenience. And yet he'd gone out last night, determined to find his countess, attending party after party, looking over the heiresses and gaining the proper introductions to well-to-do widows, yet these all too respectable ladies of the *ton* left him wondering if he could live his life without the passion he'd experienced in Madame Fontaine's arms.

If only he hadn't kissed her. It had made a muddle of all his plans.

"My lord," Belton said. "You'd best intercept him. Now."

Mason had little choice but to go out and get Del away from the house as quickly as possible.

Before opening the door, he told Belton, "When Madame arrives, escort her up to the Green Salon and see that the girls join her immediately. Then don't admit any visitors—not a soul—until I return." Taking his hat from the butler and snatching up his riding crop from the stand by the doorway, Mason strode out the door and bounded down the steps, colliding with the maid he'd seen earlier.

He caught her before he sent her careening back down the steps, righting her and saying, "Excuse me, miss." It was easy to see how he'd overlooked her, for her drab little cloak left her all but blended into the stones and paving.

"It's perfectly all right, my lord," she murmured as he hurried past. "I suppose I deserve to be bowled over when I am so late."

Her response barely registered in his mind, for he was

already down the steps and shaking Del's hand when her words and soft voice finally took root.

So late.

He swung around and found himself gaping at the maid who suddenly wasn't as colorless as he'd first thought.

Nor was she a maid.

It appeared Madame Fontaine had taken his order to prune her feathers back in her own defiant style. Oh, yes, she wore the usual ugly, shapeless cloak one saw maids and ladies' companions bundled in—but atop her head sat another cheeky hat. Though not her usual monstrosity of ribbons and plumage, this jaunty little chapeau with its swans down trim, green bow, and two feathers was not the modest headcovering one expected to see on a tutor to young ladies.

Did the woman ever go out without wearing feathers? he wondered, eyeing the two small plumes dancing in wild abandon atop her bonnet.

Not only were those damnable feathers laughing at him, but when she turned, her cloak fell open, revealing an elegant day dress of soft green, cut just low enough to give her audience a stunning view of the curves and generous bosom he knew only too well lurked beneath.

But it was her face which held his rapt attention. Scrubbed clean of the makeup and artifice that normally masked her features, her face shone through as fresh and demure as that of the greenest country lass.

The skin once hidden by paint appeared almost luminescent, graced as it was with a soft pink hue and a delicate rose at her lips. To his amazement there was even a teasing hint of freckles across the bridge of her nose, like the faint light of summer stars when they first appear in the twilight sky.

Madame Fontaine with freckles? His world turned upside down at such an ordinary notion.

Gads, this delicate seraph couldn't be the nefarious woman who'd invaded his home yesterday. He swallowed hard. No, this girl looked exactly like the unknown English miss he'd told her he intended to wed.

"My lord," she whispered. "I said I was most sorry about arriving late. Is there something else wrong? My bonnet? This gown?"

Wrong? Hardly. She rivaled the first flowers of spring, the dew on a summer's morning, the . . .

As if she sensed his amazement, her hand rose modestly to her face.

"What, or rather who, have you been hiding from me, St. Clair?" Del interrupted, trying to edge Mason aside.

Mason planted his feet squarely to the pavement and stood his ground. While he had been silently waxing poetic once again about this woman who was more surely the Helen to destroy his Troy than an Aphrodite to inspire his sudden perchance for lovesick odes, he'd forgotten Del stood close at hand.

"You'll have to excuse the Saint, his manners are atrocious," Del said. "And no wonder he's standing there like a regular nodcock, an enchanting creature such as yourself would make any man a philistine." He grinned and shoved the dangling reins into Mason's hands, then smoothly sidestepped him and caught her by the elbow. "Allister Balfour, Viscount Delander at your service, my dear. And you are?"

"Charmed," she replied, taking his hand off her elbow and returning it to him.

Del laughed. "As I am, most decidedly." He turned to Mason. "You've been holding out on me, Saint. A veritable angel in your midst. Am I to assume you've taken a bride?"

Mason saw nothing but the impending disaster before him, or he wouldn't have been so quick to utter, "No, the lady is not my wife." Once it had been said, he realized his mistake as Del's eyes lit with delight.

"Even better," his friend replied. Del's lurid gaze swung quickly back to her. "Then you can rest assured that I will court you, my dearest angel, quite shamefully without having to worry about being called out by my friend here. Wasted in Oxford he's been. Just wasted. Best shot in town. I remember when we were just lads out at Sanborn Abbey—"

"Del," Mason interrupted. "This is not the time."

Del nodded. "Of course not. Why would I want to charm a lady with your exploits when I am positive she would much rather be listening to mine." The man laughed again, and much to Mason's chagrin, Madame Fontaine joined in, her infectious good humor bubbling up like champagne on the tongue.

She'd never smiled like that around him—not that he'd given her any chance—still, she didn't have to look at Del as if his every word were laden with gold.

Worse than that, her good spirits only fueled Del's advances along. "Now, let me see," he began. "I never forget a lovely face, and yours is not only delightful, but very familiar. Have we met?"

Before she could answer, Mason jumped in. "I doubt it, Del. The lady is newly arrived from the country."

He had to give Riley credit, the only indication she gave to this lie was a slight shift of her brow.

"The country? No, I don't think so, I've seen you elsewhere. Here in town and recently, if I recall." Del took her hand again, and this time gave no indication that he was going to let go until he gained some answers. "Were you at Lady Twyer's musicale last week?"

Then, before Mason could come up with a likely explanation, Cousin Felicity hustled out the front door, a dervish awhirl in muslin and lace.

His dire threat that she would no longer be allowed to attend the theatre or opera—two of her favorite places to gather gossip—if she let even a hint of Madame Fontaine's presence in their house fall past her lips, was obviously foremost in her mind. She looked absolutely stricken at the sight of Lord Delander bent over Madame Fontaine's hand.

"Oh, there you are," Cousin Felicity said. "I've been sick with worry." She caught Madame's free arm and tugged her loose of Del's overly cordial clutches.

"My lady, good morning to you," Lord Delander said, nodding to Cousin Felicity. "Perhaps you can tell me who your lovely visitor is?"

"She's . . . she's . . ." Cousin Felicity glanced from Lord Delander to Mason and finally to Madame Fontaine, all the while her lashes beating wildly behind her thick glasses.

Del's head cocked to one side, obviously smelling something afoot. "Well, do the two of you know this enchanting creature, or don't you?"

Cousin Felicity gulped. "Of course we know her, my lord." She glanced again at Mason.

He helped her along. "I was just explaining to Lord Delander that the lady is newly arrived from the country."

"The country?" Cousin Felicity repeated. "Oh, yes," she said, her face brightening with a smile. "Why, Lord Delander, of course, she's just arrived from the country."

"I don't believe either of you, for I swear I have seen this lady before." The Viscount scratched his head and then grinned. "Now I remember where I have seen you, you vexing little mystery. And you can't deny it now, for I have found you out." He grinned at an open-mouthed Cousin Felicity and a stunned Mason. "I know exactly where I've seen you. At the theatre! That delightful little one on Brydge Street."

Ignoring the look of apoplexy marring Lord Ashlin's handsome face, Riley smiled brightly at the Viscount. After Lord Ashlin's abominable treatment yesterday, she would show the pompous scholar a thing or two about how a gentleman treats a lady. She wouldn't even go over his outlandish kiss—for she'd spent too much time last night recalling every moment. No, she had more reason than that to be angry with him.

Why, he'd tricked and deceived her most wickedly about his abominable nieces. He'd even had the audacity to call them gently bred.

Rabid badgers possessed better manners. And, she imagined, would be more amenable to training.

Then there was his insistence that she appear in an appropriate costume, and appear she had, albeit a little late, and not exactly to his specifications, but she'd had her own reasons there.

Why, she'd spent the better part of the night reworking a piece of curtain from one of their less popular plays into this cloak so she was appropriately covered.

However, the gown underneath was another matter. She'd be damned if he ever called her tolerably pretty again.

And she'd obviously gone too far with her decision to wear her newest spring gown, for all he could do was glower at her.

It was his insistence on her change of wardrobe that

was the very reason why she was late—she'd had a terrible time hailing a hackney, even with Hashim's assistance. In her usual costume, the drivers lined up to carry her, but covered up like someone's spinster governess, they drove by with nary a glance.

Now he wanted her to act like some country fool? Oh, she'd give him an innocent miss, one his overly attentive friend wouldn't forget for quite some time.

"Oh, my lord," she said in a sweet, breathy voice to the Viscount. "I don't see how that could be possible. I have never been to the theatre."

For good measure she let her lashes flutter and dropped her chin in a demure gesture. With a shy glance through her downcast lashes, she could see the man was taken in by her performance.

Obviously he hadn't seen her role as the virtuous and upstanding young girl in *Wayside Maid*.

Lord Delander shook his head. "No, you must be joking. I know I've seen you before and I've a good memory for these things. It was the theatre, I know it was."

Riley sighed. "I don't see how. My esteemed guardian always told me that a theatre is filled with the worst kind of reprobates and not a place for the innocent of mind. And out of respect to his worthy opinions, I make it a point to heed his sage advice."

Of course, Aggie usually finished his description of the typical London audience with a long, happy sigh and a breathy "God bless every one of them," but Lord Delander didn't need to know that.

"Yes, yes," Cousin Felicity chimed in. "How could she have been to the theatre if she's newly arrived from the country? You are simply mistaken, Lord Delander." The lady let out an impatient breath as if that settled the matter, and took Riley by the arm. "Come along, my dear. The girls are so delighted you are finally back from your stroll." She turned to Lord Delander. "Have you ever heard of anything so quaint—taking the morning air, in London no less, and without a proper escort."

"Oh dear! Was that wrong of me?" Riley gasped.

"Country ways," Cousin Felicity said in an aside to Lord Delander, shaking her head with a solemn, understanding nod.

The Viscount rallied to her defense. "Never fear, my dearest lady. Your reputation is safe with me. And whenever you wish to venture out, I would be honored to see to your escort personally."

Beaming at the man, Riley said, "Oh, my lord, how kind you are. How gentlemanly. My guardian warned me to beware of the men in London, for they will take the most egregious advantage of innocent ladies before one can ever utter a word of protest." She smiled at the Earl and hoped her words hit the mark, fair and true. "How refreshing to be in the company of someone who truly cares about a lady's most sterling possession, her reputation."

Certainly she was overplaying the scene, but she did like the way her speech was leaving Lord Ashlin shuddering like a veritable volcano.

With all that said, Cousin Felicity tried to take Riley in tow, toward the sanctuary of the house, but Lord Delander wasn't about to give up yet.

He cleared his throat. "I never make mistakes when it comes to a charming face. And yours, Miss . . ." He paused again looking for either Lord Ashlin or Cousin Felicity to fill him in on her identity, but when both of them remained stubbornly silent, Lord Delander continued. "Well, yes, I say your face is remarkably familiar." He peered intently at her until a light of recognition went off in his eyes. "That's it! Now I've put it together." He caught her chin and tipped her face up. "Oh, yes, I see it now. You look exactly like that actress down there." He let go of her and turned to Lord Ashlin. "What the devil is her name?" He snapped his fingers several times. "What I am asking you for? That would be like asking a Chinaman for directions to Carlton House. If you hadn't been off hiding at Oxford all these years, you would know the things that are truly important. Oh, whatever is her name?"

"Madame Fontaine?" Cousin Felicity suggested, smiling at Lord Ashlin and Riley as if she had just helped the situation.

Lord Delander slapped his knee, a smile splitting his handsome face. "That's it. Madame Fontaine! Your guest here is the spitting image of that actress."

Riley glanced over at Lord Ashlin, who'd gone grayer than a two-day-old corpse. She felt compelled to salvage this disaster, even though a small wicked part of her liked watching the Earl twist a bit in a wind of his own making.

"An actress? You think I look like an actress?" She let her eyes widen in horror. Then, calling on what was described by the reviewer at the *Observer* as her "pithy and compelling use of emotion," she let a small tear run down her cheek.

It stopped, as if on cue, halfway down.

Turning to Mason, she said, adding a sad little sniff to every other word, "I am so mortified that I . . ." Her bottom lip trembled as if she didn't dare finish without dissolving into a fit of tears. "If you turn me out, Lord Ashlin, I'll understand. I would be forever mortified if your other friends came to the same conclusion. Think of those dear *faultless* girls upstairs and what an association, even an erroneous one, would mean to their sterling, innocent reputations."

She reached for Cousin Felicity to steady herself, holding out her hand for the handkerchief the lady always had at the ready. While Riley considered that she was probably laying it on a little thick, to the point where even Aggie would be cringing, she rather liked the way her speech now had Lord Ashlin nearly ready to erupt.

Served him right. Kissing her, indeed, and then having the audacity to dismiss her as if it had meant nothing. Well, it had meant something to her.

Even if it was the last thing she wanted.

Taking to her role as protector of their country relative's virtue, Cousin Felicity glared at Lord Delander, and at the same time, patted Riley's hand with all the sincere worry of a kindly aunt. "There, there, the Viscount never meant to slight your character." The lady looked up. "A character above reproach, I might add."

Riley glanced over at the lady and shot her a warning glance. There was overplaying a role, and then there was overplaying . . .

"Oh, well, I didn't mean to imply . . . I just meant . . ." Lord Delander stammered. "Oh, bother. The resemblance isn't that convincing. Just a bit around the edges. And I meant it as the veriest of compliments. Truly I did. Please, no more tears."

Riley steadied her quivering lip and shot him a brave look. After a hesitant glance toward Cousin Felicity, she even dared a small, shy smile.

"So you accept my deepest apologies, Miss . . . ?" he said, once again taking her hand and bringing her fingers to his lips.

"Yes, of course, my lord," she offered demurely, while at the same time attempting to retrieve her hand with a practiced twist and yank.

The maneuver failed on such a well-studied rake as

Lord Delander. He held onto her gloved fingers with all the determination of a man fatally smitten. "Now you must tell me your name, and no more deceptions. And I will know where you are staying so I may call on you and your guardian," he persisted.

"I'm . . . I'm . . ." Riley struggled for the right lines to redirect the man's attentions, when Cousin Felicity came up with her own nonsensical solution to the problem.

And added an entirely new dimension to it.

"Why she is staying with us," the lady said.

"With you?" Lord Delander turned slightly, shooting Lord Ashlin a questioning glance.

"Oh, yes," Cousin Felicity continued in her own bubbling fashion. "Staying with us. Where else would *family* stay?"

"Family?" At this Lord Delander grinned. "Another cousin, I presume?"

Riley glanced at the Earl, who appeared too stunned even to speak. Why didn't he do something—like silence his errant cousin before she made matters worse?

"Yes, yes, our dear Cousin . . ." the lady hestitated.

"Cousin . . . ?" Lord Delander asked.

"Riley," she told him, realizing there was no other way than to toss him a bit of a line to chew on.

Lord Ashlin glanced over at her. "Riley?"

"Yes, Riley," she told him, knowing now why the traveling companies always said to avoid Oxford. These professors hadn't a bit of improvisation in their soul.

Well, perhaps in kissing . . .

"Yes," Lord Ashlin said, finishing the introduction as if he were announcing a hanging. "Miss Riley St. Clair."

Lord Delander didn't look all that convinced, but he was too much of a gentleman to make an issue of it. "Delighted to meet you, *Cousin Riley*," he teased, finally releasing her hand. "And your esteemed guardian? Is he staying at Ashlin House as well?"

"Still in the country!" Cousin Felicity interjected. "And our poor cousin without any other living relatives to look after her *interests*."

Her *interests*?

Even Riley, with all her training and years of practice, felt her mouth drop open and her jaw gape at this outrageous lie.

Cousin Felicity made her sound like some sort of heiress—a conclusion Lord Delander had obviously reached from the knowing glance he shot in Lord Ashlin's direction.

"How commendable of you, old boy," Lord Delander commented. "A regular saint, to take in another *poor* relation."

The man grinned at Riley like she stood before him holding a dowry of Spanish treasure, while Lord Ashlin gazed heavenward—probably praying to be struck down.

Which wasn't so far from the truth.

She let Cousin Felicity lead her up the stairs only too happy to flee from the Earl and his friend before the bird-witted lady decided to invent a family history to go along with her newfound fortune.

If Mason had thought for a moment that a powder keg of disaster could be averted when Del and Madame Fontaine had arrived at that same time, Cousin Felicity had seen to bringing not only the fuse, but a lighted torch as well.

And all his plans would continue to go up in smoke if he didn't separate his rakish friend from his newfound "cousin."

Damnation, could his life become any more entangled?

"Come now, Del," he said. "Our ride?"

"Ah, yes, our ride," the Viscount replied, gazing at Riley's departing figure. They mounted up and turned their horses away from the house. "Your cousin, you say."

"Yes." Mason wondered if he could legally lock Cousin Felicity away as mad.

Del straightened in his saddle. "So are you thinking of courting her?"

"Courting who?"

"Your Cousin Riley, of course."

"Certainly not!" Mason told him. Gads, all he needed now was a rumor about town that he was about to marry his cousin. Not when he needed to find a real bride.

Del shrugged. "No need to get into a state. Here I've been worried sick over all the rumors about you being rolled up, and now I find you've got an heiress tucked under your roof. Doesn't take a degree from Oxford to put two and two together."

"There are no twos to put together. My country cousin is neither rich nor in the market for a husband," Mason told him.

Laughing, Del turned toward the park. "There isn't a single woman in London who isn't in search of a husband."

"I assure you, my cousin is not."

"I think you doth protest too much," Del said, waving his hand with a dismissive gesture. "I can see very clearly you mean to steer me away, but it won't work. You've let the devil out of the bottle now. And I have every intention of uncovering exactly what it is you don't want me to find out about her."

Mason sighed. "Del, you're making a big mistake."

"How so? Felicity said quite clearly the girl has *interests*. We both know what that means."

"Cousin Felicity? You're staking your future on Cousin

Felicity's blithering? In all the years you've been acquainted with her, has she ever known what she is talking about?"

"Well, not especially," Del conceded. "But remember, you are speaking to someone who has known *you* all your life, oh sainted one. And I have to assume your cousin must be scandalously rich for you to be so protective."

"Del—Riley is not rich. Quite the contrary. And I'm warning you . . ." Mason should have known better than to fend Del off with a reproach, for the words of caution only served to fuel his friend's unwitting resolve.

"Harangue me all you like, for I've no mind to ruin the girl or get into any mischief. You may not believe this, but the moment I saw your cousin, I felt something very special."

"Oh, I believe that," Mason muttered. He felt only too much around his new cousin.

"Her air of innocence, her beauty, that wealth of gently bred qualities have all inspired me."

"Inspired?" Mason didn't like the sound of that at all. He knew damn well what Riley inspired in him.

"Yes," Del said, a little too enthusiastically for Mason's comfort. "The moment I saw your cousin I knew it was time to start my nursery."

"Your wh-a-a-t?"

"My nursery. You heard me the first time. I think that cousin of yours will make a first-rate mistress for Delander Hall. Exactly the respectable chit to please my mother and plump up my pockets if my suspicions about her purse are correct."

"Your mother?" Mason knew he shouldn't have asked the heavens how his day could get any worse. "You can't be serious. I doubt very seriously your mother will find Riley acceptable."

"My mother will find your cousin extraordinary."

More than you know, Mason thought. "I think you ought to consider your choice of bride a little more carefully before you start introducing her to your mother."

"Are you daft? Riley is perfect. Odd name, that, but a rose by any other name, as they say." He leaned back in his saddle, his eyes closing. "She is like a breath of fresh air. Wherever did you find her?"

"I didn't find her. She found me," Mason said quite truthfully.

"I swear you Ashlins have the damndest luck. But not this time. I intend to steal your little heiress right out from beneath you." He waggled his eyebrows suggestively, then laughed hilariously at his own jest.

Mason chuckled, but not for the same reason. He could well imagine what the Dowager would do if her son married an actress.

As they rounded the corner and were about to enter the park, Mason spied Hashim walking toward them.

He had told Riley not to bring her outlandish escort, and now here he was, parading onto Ashlin Square for all to see.

As they passed, Hashim made no acknowledgment toward them.

"Look at the fierce creature, Saint," Del commented once they were well past the imposing man. "I say, you should consider reporting him to the watch. Can't have the likes of that wandering 'bout frightening the citizenry. He's probably the same fellow my mother was clamoring on about yesterday. Ever since that actress arrived in London a few years back with her Saracen, now all the ladies want one. They've become a plague. And if my mother looks out the window and sees him passing by, she'll be atop the house. She'll insist I move back in." He shuddered as if that would be a fate worse than death.

Mason smiled to himself. Del may well consider death a welcome fate if his mother found out he was courting the woman the male half of London called Aphrodite's Envy.

Chapter 7

～ ❧❧ ～

Mason returned from his ride an hour or so later, determined to put Madame Fontaine—no, he corrected himself, Riley, on notice.

He'd had a hell of a time getting rid of Del, who'd lounged about looking for an invitation to see more of Riley. But Mason had ignored his friend and even now took the front steps two at a time, ticking off her demerits, while Del rode away with a determined look on his face that said only too clearly that this was not the last they'd seen of the Viscount.

Mason didn't know what irritated him more—the matter of her tardiness, her overly appealing appearance, or her flirtatious manners.

Why, she was a veritable lodestone of charisma, and he wanted her to put a stop to it immediately.

He'd spent most of his ride, between listening to Del come up with names for his and Riley's children, preparing his own future for the impossible lady.

First, she was under no circumstances to see or speak with Lord Delander. She was to avoid him at all costs.

Second, there was the matter of her servant. He'd told her quite plainly she was to leave him behind. And yet here he had been this morning, walking along Ashlin Square as if he owned the place.

"Belton," he called out, stripping off his riding gloves and stuffing them into his hat.

The butler came around the corner. "Yes, my lord?"

Mason handed off his cloak and hat, and said, "Send Madame Fontaine to my study. Immediately."

He was three steps away when he heard Belton's reply.

"Madame has already left."

Mason turned around. "Left? What do you mean, left?"

"She and that infidel departed about a half hour ago."

"Whatever for?"

Belton shot a withering glance up the staircase, where Mason caught a fleeting glance of muslin as a guilty-looking trio fled the impending storm.

"Did Madame Fontaine say anything before she left?"

Belton shifted. "I'm afraid it was in French, sir. And rather unrepeatable even in the translation."

Mason could well imagine. He let out an exasperated sigh and continued into his office, Belton following in his wake.

There on his desk awaited his correspondence and accounts, which he was now an hour overdue to begin. His daily schedule lay in shambles.

"Should I ring for your morning tea, my lord?"

At least something of his routine could be salvaged. "Yes. And send for my nieces. Tell them to be in my office in five minutes, no more, no less."

"Yes, my lord," Belton said, remaining in place.

"Is there something else?" Mason asked.

Belton held up a reticule. "Madame Fontaine left this behind."

Mason waved his hand at the thing. "You can return it to her tomorrow."

"If she comes—" Belton said under his breath.

"Yes, well, I imagine Madame Fontaine is made of sterner stuff than what those harridans of ours can dish out." If he thought that was the end of it, Mason was quite mistaken. Belton remained in front of his desk like a sentry.

An unwanted one.

"Belton! Why are you hovering?" Mason had never seen the butler so out of sorts. "What is it, man?"

Belton cleared his throat. "When I was retrieving the lady's reticule, a note fell out." He reached into his pocket and pulled out a tattered piece of paper, placing the scrap on Mason's desk.

"Belton, the contents of Madame Fontaine's reticule are hardly any of our business, and I cannot believe you would stoop to—" he stopped short of saying "snoop through her belongings" when his gaze fell on the crudely lettered missive.

Leve Englund whore or sufer.

"Well, at least they spelled 'whore' correctly," he remarked.

He picked it up and looked at it more closely. It wasn't written in a woman's hand, the letters were far too clumsy. For some reason, he suspected Riley's writing would be like that of the lady herself, full of passion and curves, not this ignorant scrawl.

So what the devil was going on? he wondered. It made no sense, unless . . . He dismissed the notion as ridiculous.

Someone threatening Riley?

The note suddenly felt as cold as death in his hands, and he hastily stuffed it back into her reticule.

That was a mistake. For as he opened the brown velvet

bag, he caught a hint of her perfume. His body knew that scent, knew it only too well, and all his instincts clamored for him to protect her.

He dismissed that errant notion outright. The lady was hardly his, or his concern, but certainly he knew what needed to be done—he should return her reticule and get to the bottom of this mystery. He had an investment to protect.

Yes, an investment. That gave an entirely respectable reason for him to rush down to Covent Garden—that Ashlin den of sin and iniquity.

Well, he was a new kind of Ashlin, impervious to the allurements found there.

Even Madame Fontaine's, he resolved.

An hour later, his nieces left his study. He'd listened to their claims of no wrongdoing, but he hadn't believed a word of it. They were a little too insistent. So he'd sent them off with an admonishment that their days would begin by helping Mrs. McConneghy in the kitchen if their next lesson didn't fare better.

On his way out to his awaiting carriage, he cringed at the sound of Cousin Felicity bustling up behind him in a flutter of lace. "Oh, Mason, you are a dear to call a carriage for me," she said, moving past him and climbing into the conveyance without a second glance back.

"Cousin, this carriage is for me. I have some business to attend to," he told her, peering inside as she settled in.

"You can drop me off, for I have a little shopping to do," she said, patting the seat beside her.

"Cousin, I told you, no more unnecessary expenditures."

She shook her head. "Dear boy, none of my expenditures are unnecessary. Besides, you are going to see Riley and return her reticule, aren't you?"

He shot a glance in her direction. Were there no secrets in his house?

"Yes," he said, unwilling to go any further into the business.

"Then you can drop me off on the way," she said, settling deeper into the seat.

Mason knew there was little hope of evicting her now, so he climbed in, and he gave the driver directions. With a lurch and a pull, the carriage was off.

"Dreadful business," she said quite lightly. "Mason, I do hope you discover what this 'leve Englund' nonsense is about."

His gaze spun around. "You read it?"

"Well, of course. I was there when Belton went through—" She stopped short of completely condemning their butler. Instead, she finished by saying, "We needed to know who the reticule belonged to, so Belton thought it best to open it."

It was the flimsiest excuse he had ever heard. Cousin Felicity made it sound as if leftover lady's reticules were a common occurrence at Ashlin House.

"Whyever would anyone want our dear Riley gone?"

"I haven't the vaguest idea, Cousin. I am sure it is nothing more than some type of theatrical lark." He hoped that was the case, but something about the note told him there was more to it. "Now, where may I drop you?"

She smiled. "Oh, I'll just tag along to the theatre, if you don't mind."

"I do," he told her. "If this is some type of threat against Madame Fontaine, I don't want you mixed up in it."

Cousin Felicity straightened her shoulders. "I am quite able to take care of myself. Look at how I handled Lord

Delander this morning—I diverted him most efficiently with my story about Riley."

"You certainly did that," Mason said, "but you made things more of a muddle by intimating that she is rich."

"Isn't she?" Cousin Felicity's gaze lit with hope.

Shaking his head, he told her, "No, cousin, she isn't."

"That's a dreadful shame, for if she were, then you could marry her."

Mason sputtered and choked.

Pounding him on the back, she continued, "She is quite a lovely girl and would make a beautiful bride."

Given the way his cousin tended to mix things up, Mason knew he had to make his next point very clear. "Cousin Felicity, I cannot marry Riley."

"Whyever not?"

"For one thing, she's an actress," he said, still too stunned by his cousin's suggestion to offer the million other reasons as to why he couldn't take Riley as his wife.

Cousin Felicity sighed, as if the entire world had gone mad.

They drove along, rolling into the crowded streets of Covent Garden, drawing closer to the Queen's Gate.

He glanced out his window to get his bearings when he happened to spy Riley walking down the street.

Rather, he spotted those damnable plumes—undulating their way above the crowd with their haremlike movements—announcing her impending arrival with their voluptuous dance.

In contrast, the lady below the feathers moved with an elegant grace that made her seem as if she were entering a ball rather than walking down the litter-strewn street. As passersby spoke to her or called out a greeting, she inclined her head with nothing less than a royal nod, a gesture so regal that it left him almost believing the rumors that she had descended from the very Pharaohs of Egypt.

Lost in the reverie of such a notion, he didn't see the two men approaching her until it was too late to call out a warning.

The evil shining out from their beady gazes as they closed in on her from either side betrayed their injurious intent.

Helpless to intervene through the throng separating them, he could only watch as one of them threw a hand over her mouth, while the other caught her arms and they dragged her into a narrow alley in the wink of an eye.

As the greasy hand clapped over Riley's mouth and nose, she gasped for air and her eyes began to water from the foul stench of her attacker. Before she could react, a second attacker caught her arms and pinned them to her sides. Her assailants quickly dragged her off the street and into the alley before anyone noticed her misfortune.

"Yer a right pretty one, ain't ye?" the first man whispered in her ear. "Well, ye won't be so nice when we get done with ye."

To her horror, he drew out a long knife that even in the dark of the alley flashed with a deadly glint. "Oh, this isn't the worst of it, my pretty," he told her. "I've me other blade that I intend to use as well."

" 'E said no sport, Clyde," his companion complained. "No sport with 'er, if ye know what's good for ye."

"I'll have my sport for the measly coins 'e's givin' us for this job. Not likely as anyone will be listenin' to 'er when we git done," Clyde said, his foul breath wafting over her with a malodor akin to a cesspool on an August afternoon. "I don't intend to leave 'er breathin' or talkin'."

Riley kicked and struggled, making every attempt she could to escape as they continued to pull her deeper and deeper into the alley. The more she fought, the harder they cuffed and kicked her to keep her moving along.

She should have heeded the warning in the note. Let Hashim escort her on her errands, rather than sneaking out without him. Done a thousand different things . . . but now it seemed her unknown enemy would truly see her dead.

But who? And why?

"If ye think a little sport is in order, I say we do it before we cut 'er all up," the second man said, loosening his grip to fumble with the rope that held up his trousers.

In that instant, she freed a hand. Exactly as Hashim had taught her, she balled her fingers into a tight fist and swung with all her might at the one called Clyde, while her foot came up and down on the boot of the other.

As they howled in pain at her sudden attack, she bolted for the street.

But Clyde was too quick for her. "Ye little bitch," he cursed, catching her by the arm before she could take a second step and swinging her into the wall, the back of her head snapping against the bricks, leaving her stunned and slumping to the ground in a daze of stars. "Ye're a dead one now."

She closed her eyes and started to count her final moments . . . regrets flooded her mind, but the most outstanding one was Lord Ashlin.

If only she'd been able to do more than just kiss him. To discover for herself whether there lurked an unrepentant rake behind his starched demeanor, or whether the few moments in his arms had been exactly what he'd said they'd been—an aberration.

Now, she would never know. Yet as she braced herself for Clyde's murderous blow, she heard a sudden commotion pounding down the alley toward them. She wiped at her eyes, but the stars still dancing there obscured her vision.

"What the—" Clyde said, as a flash of silver seemed to light the entire alleyway, an avenging angel rescuing her from her plight.

Hashim! He'd come looking for her. He'd heard the commotion and found her.

Clyde's piteous scream pierced the afternoon clamor of the streets.

"Leave off," the second man whined, his feet pedaling against the cobbles in desperate flight. "We meant no 'arm."

"Liar," she sputtered.

"She's the liar," Clyde spat back. "Invited us back 'ere for a little fun and then tried to rob us."

"I tend to believe the lady," a smooth male voice responded.

Her head jerked in that direction. Her rescuer spoke. So if it wasn't Hashim, who could it be?

"Are you well, Riley?" the man asked. "Can you get away?"

The voice—she recognized it, though she was certainly dreaming.

Lord Ashlin? Here in Covent Garden?

She shook her aching head, trying to clear her vision of its blurry haze. All she could make out was a figure clad in black swooping past her, blade in hand, chasing down the two henchmen who had threatened her life.

It was like a scene from her play.

Act Three, Scene Two. Aveline is rescued from the pirates by Geoffroi.

"Oh, my God," she muttered. She was dead and this was her hell—she was trapped in her own play with Lord Ashlin in the lead. As she felt herself slipping further into the darkness of unconsciousness, she tried to claw her way back.

Even she'd admit her plays were poor art, but to spend eternity in one was enough to make her fight for her life.

Before she could struggle to her feet, she was swept up into a strong pair of arms and cradled in their masculine security. Her champion, her Geoffroi.

"You're safe now," a deep, soothing voice said too tenderly to be Lord Ashlin. "Your assailants are well away."

She tried to open her eyes, but the lids were too heavy, and her head ached so that it made saying her lines back impossible, so instead, she raised her head as best she could and placed her lips on his.

The moment they touched her heart did a queer little flip-flop. His touch seemed gentle, and startled, and hungry.

Very hungry.

The kiss deepened and she poured her relief into her response. She was alive, so very alive, and this kiss seemed to show her just how much she would have missed.

"Geoffroi, my dearest Geoffroi," Madame Fontaine mumbled in his arms.

Mason thanked his good fortune that she was not asking for another kiss, for certainly he was being tested. Riley's sweet lips clung to his with a tenderness and trust he'd never experienced.

One that called on him to be there for her every time she needed rescuing.

Still, it was one thing to kiss a woman, but quite another when she kissed you calling out another man's name.

He struggled along with her limp form in his arms, her eyes shut, her features pale. She wasn't bleeding, he knew that much, but she was dazed from the experience.

"Geoffroi," she murmured.

He glanced down at his beautiful burden. Who the devil was this Geoffroi?

A lover, perhaps? Probably some *émigré comte* or *duc* who'd offered her his charm, and fine manners, and carte blanche.

Great, he thought. He'd risked his life to save her and her lover would get the credit.

Mason brushed aside the niggling jealousy that rushed out of nowhere. What did he care if Madame Fontaine had a lover? Or a legion of them, as gossip liked to favor her with? He certainly hadn't rushed to her aid to gain her favor, he'd just been on the corner when she'd needed him.

Well, not him, exactly.

He supposed it could have been anyone, but it had just happened to be him.

And now that he'd rescued her, what the devil did he do with her? To his right he noticed a side door into the theatre. Nudging it open, he carried her down the short hallway, until it opened up into the orchestra pit.

On the stage above him, the rehearsal stumbled to a halt, the actors gaping at the sight of their mistress being carried in by a complete stranger.

For a moment a deadly silence held the room, until an older man wearing a loose shirt and black trousers stepped forward. "Great devils of misfortune," he cried out in a booming baritone. "What have you done to my dearest girl?"

At this cue, the other actors and stagehands surged forward.

Mason held his ground, relieved to see Hashim at the

edge of the hue and cry. At least there was one friendly face in the crowd.

Perhaps not overly friendly, for Hashim's murderous expression mirrored that of the rest of the company.

"Set her down, you villain, you knave, you heinous bounder!" the older man continued to rant. "And we shall deal with you as we would any other pestilence who would dare mar our Riley, our blessed muse, our virtuous queen."

Mason shook his head. "You have this all wrong. She was attacked. I came to her aid," he told them. Nodding over his shoulder at the door, he explained, "There were two men. They stole her off the street. I stopped them and brought her here."

"A likely tale to cover your misdeeds!" the man who seemed to be the rallying point cried out.

Even more unnerving, Mason watched Hashim draw his sword. The theatre company parted immediately and gave the furious Saracen a wide berth.

Hashim stalked forward until he towered over Mason. The man glanced down at Riley's inert form and then his piercing black gaze bore into Mason's.

"She took a blow to the head, but doesn't seem to be hurt anywhere else," Mason told him quickly. "I thought it best to bring her here rather than chase them down and leave her alone."

Hashim nodded and then raced to the alley after her attackers.

" 'And if you wrong us, shall we not revenge?' " the older man quoted after Hashim's departing figure. He turned back to Mason. "There you, what are you waiting for? Bring her up here." He turned to a man dressed like a pirate and another in a white shirt and breeches and said, "Daniel, Roderick, bring that chaise over." He turned back to Mason. "Well? What are you waiting for?" The man sighed. "If that walking Persian carpet of ours thought you had anything to do with this, we wouldn't be talking, but mopping the spot where you are standing. Now, bring her up here, gently."

Relieved by this about-face, Mason followed the man's directions, carrying Riley up the side steps and onto the stage, and over to the chaise the other actors had brought forward.

Gently he laid her down. Kneeling, he smoothed her hair back from her face. She was so pale, and at the same time, so startlingly beautiful. Her lips trembled for a moment and he recalled how it felt to have them pressed to his.

Why the devil would anyone want to harm her?

The company crowded around, the older man taking her other hand and patting it with great display. "Riley, sweet Riley, speak to me. Tell us what fiend did this to you."

Her lashes fluttered open and she turned toward Mason. "Geoffroi, Geoffroi, you came for me," she said, before her eyes closed once again.

"Huzzah!" the man beside him cried out. "That's my Riley. Even in her distress, she remembers her lines. You there, Hortense, go fetch that wretched Nanette and tell her to bring down a basin of cold water and a cloth for her mistress."

Mason was still stuck on the first part of the man's speech. "Her lines?" he asked. "This Geoffroi is part of a play?"

"Well, yes. Our new play. Who else would he be?" He blew out an impatient breath.

"Then this Geoffroi is not her . . . her . . . ?"

The man's eyes widened at the implication of Mason's faltering question. "Her paramour?" His surprise was now replaced by a twinkle glinting in his sharp gaze.

Mason nodded, to which everyone in the company started to laugh. He didn't know what he had said that warranted such hilarity, but he had the odd feeling the joke was on him.

"Oh, you are a rare one," the actor said. He wiped at the tears streaming from his eyes. "Geoffroi is the hero from our new production. And this girl you brought in so gallantly is the leading lady of Covent Garden. Perhaps you have heard of her by her stage name, Madame Fontaine." He paused for a moment, studying him, his gaze taking a none-so-approving glance at Mason's poor jacket and cravat. "There now, I see you have heard of her. You'll have quite a tale with which to regale your country neighbors." He caught Mason by the arm and dragged him upward. "Now I must thank you for helping our dearest girl. If you are in town again anytime soon, do stop by the theatre and I will see about securing you a ticket to one of our performances. Our compliments. Just ask for me, Mr. Pettibone."

"But . . . but . . ." Mason protested as he found himself being expertly evicted from Riley's side. "I insist on staying and seeing that she is well."

The man glanced over his shoulder. "Never you worry. Look there, she is opening her eyes as we speak. Right as rain, our Riley. Now off with you, Mr. . . . Mr.—"

"St. Clair," Mason told him, all the while finding himself being guided further and further from Riley's side.

"Ah, a St. Clair, like our noble patron, the Earl of Ashlin. Perhaps you are related."

"Aggie, you great oaf," said the lady herself.

Mason turned around to find her up on one elbow, her other hand rubbing the back of her head.

She let out a great sigh. "That man you are about to toss out of here so indelicately *is* the Earl of Ashlin."

Chapter 8

Before Riley could make any further introductions, the door to the theatre burst open and to her surprise, Cousin Felicity came blustering down the main aisle.

"Murder! There is a murder being committed!" the lady cried, her handkerchief waving this way and that.

"Cousin," Lord Ashlin said, taking the elderly lady into his arms. "All is well. There has been no murder. I was able to come to Riley's aid."

"No murder?" Cousin Felicity's lashes blinked several times.

"No murder," he told her again.

"Oh, bother," the lady said. "And it would have made such a glorious tale." She spied Nanette coming in with the cloth and basin and called over to her. "Miss, have a care. Bring that here straightaway. My head is all a flutter."

Nanette glanced over at her mistress and Riley nodded for her to take the items over to Cousin Felicity, who had now sunk into a theatre seat and was fanning herself with more show than Aggie at a sold-out performance.

Riley got up, a little unsteady on her feet, and smiled

to her colleagues. The last thing she needed was for them to witness any discussion with Lord Ashlin or his less than discreet cousin, so she waved them away and said, "Perhaps we've had enough practice for the day. I'll see everyone in their places tomorrow at eleven."

The actors and hands dispersed, mumbling about the events and shooting curious glances at the Earl.

"Cousin, those were meant for Riley," Lord Ashlin admonished his relative, as she laid the cold compress on her head.

Cousin Felicity glanced up. "She looks well enough. Not even a scratch. You did well, Mason. Leaping from the carriage like that, and drawing out that wicked-looking—"

"—There, there," he told her, stopping her account of the events. "All is well now."

"You sound as if you have suffered a terrible shock, my dear lady," Aggie said, leaving Riley's side so quickly, she nearly faltered. He was down the stage steps and up the aisle to Cousin Felicity's side in the blink of an eye. "Allow me to be of assistance and comfort," he said, taking the compress from her, dipping it into the cold water, and wringing it out. With great flourish and care, he replaced it on her brow and bestowed his best smile upon her. "If I may be so presumptuous, I am Agamemnon Bartholomew Morpheus Pettibone the Third, Master of the Finer Dramatic Arts, at your service." He reached over, caught her fingers, and brought them to his lips. "I would be delighted if you, dear lady, would call me Aggie."

Cousin Felicity tittered and cooed. "Oh, Mr. Pettibone, I couldn't! It wouldn't be proper."

Riley moved to the edge of the stage and watched this sideshow with a bemused smile. If Aggie thought Cousin Felicity another of his dim-witted old widows to weasel out of her pin money, he was going to be sorely disappointed.

Still, she knew she had best put a stop to it before it went too far. As she started for the steps, Lord Ashlin immediately came forward to offer her his arm.

"You appear a bit unsteady, Madame," he said, helping her down from the stage.

As her hand touched his sleeve, the muscled strength beneath the wool surprised her once again. What was a professor doing with arms that could sweep a woman to safety?

"It *was* you," she said, wishing her voice didn't sound so astonished. It was probably rather insulting to a gentleman not to consider him capable of such an act.

"I did very little," he said. "Dumb luck, really. Your assailants frightened easily—fortunately for me."

She struggled to remember the events and reconcile the blurry images in her mind with the unassuming man before her. He'd had a sword, or she'd imagined one, which seemed more likely.

Lord Ashlin, with a sword at the ready?

Preposterous.

Perhaps she thought she'd seen the blade because she'd thought he was Geoffroi, and when she'd thought him the hero in the play, then she'd . . .

Oh, dear goodness. She'd kissed him!

"Oh, my," she murmured, her fingers going to her lips, her cheeks growing hot. "I didn't really, did I?"

He glanced down at her. "If you mean kiss me, well, yes, you did."

The man needn't sound so put out by it. She had been delirious after all. Besides, had her kiss been that offensive?

She straightened up and decided to restore a bit of decorum to their relationship—for her sake.

"My lord, I thank you for coming to my rescue." He had led her away from the others, so she added quietly, "I don't go about kissing men as a rule. A momentary lapse in my confused state. I mean, I thought you were—" She snapped her mouth shut before she said anything more to make the situation worse.

Oh, bother. Here she was trying to make less of what had happened, and she was only making it worse. Why did this man leave her so tongue-tied?

"An aberration?" he suggested.

"Yes. That's it. And I can assure you it won't happen again."

He nodded. "I think that would be the best course of action."

Still trying to reconcile the conflicting images of her rescuer in her mind, she asked, "Whatever were you doing in that alley?"

"I'd come to see you."

Riley took a step back. "Why?"

"To discuss Lord Delander."

"Who?" she asked.

"The man you met this morning. Outside my house."

"Oh, him." She'd all but forgotten about the young Viscount.

"Yes, him." Lord Ashlin shifted. "Apparently you made quite an impression."

Aggie must have been eavesdropping, for he piped right up. "My Riley, make an impression? Of course she did. She's a sensation wherever she goes."

Lord Ashlin did not look pleased at that description. "That is exactly our problem. Lord Delander nearly recognized you."

"Oh, Mason, I helped you there," Cousin Felicity interjected. She turned to Aggie. "I was quite brilliant."

"I am sure you were," Cousin Felicity's new champion declared.

Lord Ashlin's response was an arched brow that said only too clearly that her help, then and now, was not necessary.

"While I agree that Cousin Felicity's assistance wasn't the most discreet," Riley said, rising to the lady's defense, "it seemed to stop him from making any further inquiries."

"Quite the contrary," he said. "Del intends to wed you."

"I sincerely doubt Lord Delander wants to make me his bride," Riley said, trying to lighten the Earl's mood. "The man just met me."

Lord Ashlin shook his head. "You don't know Del. He has come to the conclusion that you would make a perfect wife. Especially with the generous dowry Cousin Felicity so graciously granted you."

That, she conceded, was a problem, but she assured him, "I have been proposed to before and nothing has come of it. I will refuse him and that will end it."

"Yes, that would be the simple solution, if Del was the sort to take no for an answer." Lord Ashlin folded his hands behind his back. Riley had the distinct impression that he must have cast an imposing shadow over his students. He continued his lecture by saying, "I've known Del all my life. When he sets his sights on something, he is single-minded until he possesses it. He once saw a horse at Tattersall's, and he would not—"

"Lord Ashlin," she interrupted. "I am not a horse. Nor am I a plaything to be passed around. If this Lord Delander is such a close friend, perhaps you should consider telling him the truth and be done with the matter."

At this, Cousin Felicity intervened. "Oh, no! That

would never work. Lord Delander is not known for his discretion."

Riley would wager that if Cousin Felicity dared call a man indiscreet, the situation was probably as bad as Lord Ashlin was saying. "Then I will just have to avoid him."

"I doubt you'll be able to. Especially since he is planning on sending his mother over to call."

"Lady Delander?" Riley shuddered. She had no desire to meet the harridan who'd stormed Ashlin House yesterday.

"And if Del is considering you as a potential bride," Lord Ashlin said, continuing his lecture, "the old girl will examine you with a fine-tooth comb and she won't be looking for your better qualities. Especially if she sees you coming and going at odd hours."

"And then the cat will be out of the bag," Aggie commented.

The four of them stood silently, considering their options.

Riley came to a rather alarming one. "You mean to call off our agreement. You dishonorable—"

He held up his hand and she stopped before she got to some of her better insults.

"Yes, that was the conclusion I came to at first," he said. "That is, until I found this." He reached inside his pocket and pulled out a bit of paper. "Can you explain it?"

She opened the note for a second, saw what it was, and crumpled it closed into her fist. How the devil had he gotten his hands on . . . then she remembered. "My reticule!"

"You left it at the house."

"But how did you find this?" she asked, holding up the scrap. "That note was inside and private."

"It's not what you think," he protested. "When Belton found your purse, the note fell out—"

Fell out, she just bet.

"—And when he saw the contents, he brought it to my attention."

"What note, Riley?" Aggie asked, coming forward. "What is he talking about?"

She crushed the horrid threat in her hand, not wanting to show it to her partner, not wanting to believe the ugly truth that her encounter in the alley had only confirmed.

Someone wanted her dead.

"Nothing, Aggie," she told him. "A bit of dialogue I wrote down for a future play."

The skepticism in the Earl's expression mirrored Aggie's. Obviously, they both found her explanation lacking.

"Give it to me," Aggie told her, holding out his hand.

Riley clenched the note tighter. She didn't want to involve any of them in this.

"Oh, I can tell you what it says, Mr. Pettibone," Cousin Felicity blurted out.

Riley turned an accusing gaze at Lord Ashlin. Had he let his entire house view the contents of her reticule?

He shrugged. "She got ahold of it before I got home."

Much to Riley's dismay, Cousin Felicity gave her rendition of the contents just as Hashim returned. His furious expression said two things—that he hadn't caught her assailants, and that her deception regarding this latest threat on her life was inexcusable.

Lord Ashlin turned to her, his voice low and rumbling with emotion. "How long has this been going on?"

"It isn't any of your concern," she told him.

"It is now." Lord Ashlin made an impatient noise in the back of his throat.

Aggie stepped forward. "I think you should tell him."

She shook her head.

Lord Ashlin turned to Hashim. "Then I will get the story from him."

"My lord, he can't talk," she said, for once relieved of Hashim's silence.

"Yes, but I can." And with that, Lord Ashlin began to speak in a language she'd never heard. But apparently Hashim had, for his eyes lit up at the sound of what must have been his native tongue, and through nods and shakes of his head and holding up his fingers, in no time the Earl had the entire story.

"What did he say, Mason?" Cousin Felicity demanded when they finished their odd conversation with a bow to each other.

"He said that the lady is in grave danger, and that every day she spends here puts her life in greater jeopardy." He turned to Riley. "Would you say that is a fair account?"

She nodded, shooting an angry glance at Hashim, who stood shoulder to shoulder with the Earl, his arms crossed over his bare chest, utterly ignoring her.

The turncoat!

Cousin Felicity pulled out her handkerchief, worrying the poor thing between her fingers. "Then there is only one thing to be done."

"And what is that, Cousin?" he asked.

Riley was sure she wasn't going to like the answer.

"This dear girl must move in to Ashlin House so we may keep her safe."

Shooting a glance at Lord Ashlin, she thought for sure his face would reflect the same shock she felt at such an outrageous suggestion.

But the man's jaw set in a line of grim determination. "For once, Cousin, you and I are of the same mind."

*   *   *

Riley's head still spun at the speed with which her move to Ashlin House had taken place. Once the Earl had set his mind to changing her residence, there was no countermanding the man's order.

Not that she'd had any help from Aggie or Hashim. Both had firmly set their feet in Lord Ashlin's camp and refused to surrender to her arguments that the move was unnecessary.

She didn't want the Earl's protection, and she certainly didn't want to be living under the same roof as this enigmatic man who found her tolerable . . . especially when she found him . . . well, she didn't know how she found him.

Vexing, most decidedly. And when he'd kissed her . . .

She shook her head. The last thing she needed to be doing was thinking about the Earl's kisses.

But there were other matters that needed to be settled, her attendance at rehearsals for one thing. Gaining the girls' acceptance for another. Especially since they hadn't taken her temporary arrival in their midst very well.

Leaving her room, Riley made her way downstairs in search of Lord Ashlin. When she reached the entrance foyer, she froze at the sight of the man Belton was escorting out.

As the door closed, she asked the butler, "What was *he* doing here?"

The man gave her his usual pained expression, as if talking to her was truly beneath his station. "You know that person?"

"Yes," she said. "What was he doing here?"

"Why does it not surprise me that he is acquainted with you?" he muttered more to himself as he turned away and started down the hall.

"Fine," she muttered, her temper rising at the man's imperious treatment. "I'll just ask *Mason*." This brought the butler to a halt. He slowly turned around and stared at her.

She winked at the crusty old Scot and bustled past him toward the Earl's study. "I'm sure *Mason* will tell me everything."

She glanced over her shoulder and watched the butler's mouth fall open at her familiar use of Lord Ashlin's Christian name, a freedom she had no right to, but let the butler determine that on his own. It would probably put his overly tight drawers in a knot for the rest of the day.

Continuing down the hall, she threw open the door to Lord Ashlin's study without even knocking. He and Hashim were at his desk, going over some paperwork.

"What was my Runner doing here?" she asked.

"Hashim brought him here, but if I were you, I wouldn't worry about him any longer," Lord Ashlin said. "I just relieved him of his duties."

Riley's ill-humor flared into a hot temper. "You did what?"

"The man is incompetent. I sent him packing." Lord Ashlin went back to his list, while Riley stood there, her foot tapping out a staccato beat. "Was there something else you wanted?"

She ignored him and turned to Hashim. "You let him do this? You went behind my back and let him do this. How could you?"

The pair gave her no regard.

"Do you have everything you need?" Lord Ashlin asked him.

Hashim nodded, then bowed slightly to Lord Ashlin and left the room, as if she weren't even there.

"What have you done to him?" she asked Lord Ashlin. "You've turned him against me."

"Hardly," he told her, gathering up his papers and placing them in a drawer out of sight. "Mr. Hashim is very concerned about your welfare, as am I. We've decided to work together to bring this matter to a speedy resolution."

A speechless Saracen and an Oxford professor! They thought they could do what a professional Runner had been unable to do.

Riley closed her eyes and counted silently to ten. "This is none of your concern," she protested, even though she could see her words were falling on deaf ears.

"I disagree. As long as you live in my house, you are under my protection and my concern." He straightened and folded his hands behind his back, looking every inch the professor rather than the protector.

His protection. Did he even know what that meant? Certainly he had saved her once, but even he had admitted it had been more accident than skill.

What if the next men her unknown enemy sent weren't as cowardly as Clyde and his inept partner?

She glanced over at the Earl. The steely gleam in his determined gaze told her he was going to remain resistant to her every argument.

She decided to try another angle. "You can't afford this."

"Actually, by firing that nitwit you were wasting money on, I am saving you a healthy purse." He smiled at her, as if daring her to try another charge. "With more money in your coffers, you should be able to repay me that much quicker."

Riley crossed her arms over her chest.

Damn the man. How dare he turn this into a joke, when his life may be at stake! Hashim she didn't worry about overly much, for she had seen him on more than one occasion defend them in the rougher corners of Covent Garden—but Lord Ashlin?

What experience did he have in these matters?

"You can either stand there in a temper," he told her, "or you can help us. While Hashim is a valuable partner, I think you hold the key to why someone would want you dead."

She stared at him in disbelief. "Are you suggesting I know who is doing this?"

"Yes. Though you may not realize it."

That was the most ludicrous notion she had ever heard.

Lord Ashlin sat back down at his desk. Pulling out several sheaves of paper and catching up his pen, he asked, "Who do you think is trying to harm you?"

"If I knew the answer to that, I would have told the watch and been done with all this a year ago when it started."

Lord Ashlin scratched down a note.

She leaned over the desk. "What are you writing?"

"That this all began a year ago. Sometimes the obvious clue to something is in the smallest of details."

She shook her head. "Anything else then, Lord Runner?"

Lord Ashlin took off his spectacles and wiped them clean. "Yes. Sit down, this may take a while."

She groaned, but could see no other way around it. If she was to keep an eye on him, then she would have to cooperate with him. "Ask away."

An hour passed as he grilled her on every detail of each incident, on her competitors, on her company. "Is there anyone at the Queen's Gate who might have a grudge against you?" he asked.

She shook her head. "No."

"Has anyone left the theatre company who might have feelings of animosity toward you or the others?"

"No," she said. "The only person who's left is Miss

Gilden. She played some bit parts and sang occasionally, but she could hardly be the mastermind behind any of this."

Lord Ashlin still took down her name. "How is that?"

"She's not overly bright. Rather featherbrained."

"That could just be her disguise."

Riley laughed at the notion. "Lord Hobson's youngest son proposed to her."

"Oh, I see," Lord Ashlin said.

"No, you don't," Riley told him. "She refused him and his thirty thousand a year to marry his valet."

Lord Ashlin scratched that name off his list. "Anyone new to the theatre?"

Riley scratched her chin. "Daniel—he plays secondary characters. I doubt he would have anything to do with this, for he came to us only a few months ago and before that was with a travelling group for several years. The only other new person is Mr. Northard. He's come around several times in the last year looking for work, but we didn't need him. Then, when we decided to stage our current play, we gave him a chance. He's rather good, though a bit haughty."

"Do you know anything else about the man?"

She shook her head. "No. But he's cast as the lead, Geoffroi, so he hardly has reason to see the play close. He'd lose his stage debut."

Sitting back in his chair, Lord Ashlin ran a hand through his hair, studying the notes before him.

Riley leaned back as well. She couldn't even remember why she'd come down in the first place. She knew one thing—if Lord Ashlin did find whoever was threatening her, all he had to do was tie the hapless fellow to this chair and start questioning him.

The poor bloke would be begging for transportation to Botany Bay in a matter of minutes.

Really, the only other times she'd felt this exhausted were after dress rehearsals.

Rehearsal.

That was what she had wanted to ask him. She cleared her parched throat. "If the play is to open on time, I will need to attend rehearsals."

"What?" he said, looking up from his notes.

"Rehearsals. I will need to go down to the theatre to practice if we are to open on schedule."

"Of course you will not," he told her. "That would leave you unprotected, and I haven't the time to traipse back and forth to Covent Garden every day." He held up his hand to stave off her next argument. "Neither does Hashim. He has other matters he will be working on from now on."

Riley did her best to hold her temper in check. She was unused to having her life and freedom controlled by another, and she didn't like it one whit. "You'll never see your investment returned, for without practice the play will never open."

"Hmmm." He seemed to be weighing other options. Then he nodded. "Practice here."

"Here?" she asked, wondering if he had any idea what he was suggesting.

"Yes, here. The ballroom should be sufficiently large enough."

Riley smiled. It would serve him right. And she couldn't help but wonder at Belton's reaction when the entire troupe arrived on his sacred steps. For that alone she decided not to protest his unconventional solution, and she rose to leave.

"Um, one moment," he said, ticking off one or two

things from his notes and then glancing up.

If she didn't know better, she'd say he looked embarrassed. "Yes?" What more could he ask?

"What about a former . . . a former . . ." Lord Ashlin's question trailed off as he struggled to find the right words.

"A former what?" she asked, weary of all the questions.

The Earl shifted in his seat. "You know what I mean."

"No, I don't know—" she started to say, and then stopped.

A former lover.

"Yes," he said, obviously seeing the pink heat on her cheeks. "A former."

How could she tell him about such an intimate aspect of her life? Besides, she doubted he'd believe the truth.

"This is important," he insisted. "Someone you cast aside. Perhaps left for another? Mr. Pettibone said you hadn't anyone at present, but maybe a past . . . uh, paramour might feel he has reason to exact revenge."

Gads, he obviously thought her quite the lightskirt. Then again, she hadn't done anything to dispel that notion. "No. There are none."

"Someone from Paris, perhaps?"

She shook her head. "No. There isn't anyone."

He took off his spectacles and studied her. "Riley, being shy in front of Del is one thing, but I know who you are. I know about your past. I am only trying to help. While it is obvious you have some regrets, you must tell me the truth and not hide behind this misplaced shame."

Why of all the patronizing, arrogant assumptions . . .

"I have nothing to be ashamed of," she told him.

"Of course not," he said. "You can't help your past."

Riley's temper sprang life. "You pompous, arrogant—"

"—You needn't get into such a state," he said. "I may

have been in Oxford all these years, but believe me, nothing you divulge within these walls will shock me. My father's and Freddie's misdeeds made sure of that."

She threw up her hands and groaned. "That is what I am trying to tell you. There is nothing to divulge."

"Riley, I made some inquiries about you, after you first came here. The betting books at White's are filled with your exploits. Every young rake in town has a story to tell about you." He picked up his pen and poised it over his list. "Why not just give me the names."

Riley did that by standing before him in silence.

"This isn't helping," he told her. "Just tell me their names."

"Fine!" she said. "You want names, then I shall give you names. Prinny? Is that a good one? The Dukes of Kent, Cumberland, Sussex, and . . ." She snapped her fingers several times. "Oh, dear, I always forget that freckled one. Oh, yes! Cambridge. Now after that successful entrée into good society, I believe I had a brief liaison with an entire company of Horse Guards—just the men, not the horses." She smiled at him, then scratched her chin, considering who else to add to her mythical list. "Ah yes, and there was the week I spent with Lord—"

"Enough!" Lord Ashlin said, tossing aside his pen. "I am trying to compile a serious account of your past and this ridiculous oration is not helping matters."

"But you didn't want to hear the truth," she said. "When I told you there are no names to give, you did not believe me. For you see, Lord Ashlin, I have never had a lover."

He shook his head. "That is impossible. I heard from—"

"—You heard gossip and speculation," she said. "Do you believe everything said about your brother? From what I heard, I doubt he ever slept."

"Frederick's accounts have been rather exaggerated," he conceded.

"Then, Lord Ashlin," she said, "you have two choices. Believe that I have made love to every man in London, or that I have never had a lover. Which will it be? For only one is true."

Mason had been mistaken when he'd told Riley that nothing she confided to him would shock him.

Madame Fontaine had never had a lover? Unbelievable!

He was still trying to make sense of her preposterous confession when he returned home from his investigations several hours later and was met at the door by a grim-faced Belton.

"My lord," the butler said, in that ominous grave tone of his. "He has gotten into the house."

Mason groaned, for he knew exactly who Belton was talking about. *Del*.

Damn his persistent hide. He'd been by earlier in the afternoon, flowers in hand, demanding an audience with Riley, but Mason had flat out refused him entrance to the house.

Now it appeared the Viscount had managed another way to storm the Ashlin gates.

"Where is he?"

"The Green Salon," Belton told him. "Miss Felicity has ordered tea brought round. Should I hold it off, or send it in?"

"Is Madame in there?"

Belton just cocked a brow in answer.

Of course she was. "Send it in," Mason said. "Perhaps our poor fare will starve him out of here, since threats don't seem to work."

"As you say, my lord."

Mason marched toward the salon, still pondering Riley's confession that she hadn't any former lovers.

How could that be true? He'd heard the talk at White's, as well as at half a dozen other places. He tried to tell himself she was lying, that she had something to hide, but her pretty blushes and stammered confession hinted that perhaps the lady was telling the truth.

Or a damned good actress.

Then again, he considered all the gossip he'd heard about Freddie's exploits—most of which he knew was utter rubbish. If that was true for Freddie, there was no reason to believe it couldn't be true for the woman known as Aphrodite's Envy.

So what did he really care whether she'd had no lovers or made love to half the *ton*? It wasn't any of his business. His only concern should be getting Del out of his house and away from Riley. And then he needed to uncover who was trying to kill her. And find husbands for his nieces. And his own bride. And then he would worry about his finances.

He let out a frustrated sigh.

When had his life turned into this circus?

Oh, he knew. The moment he'd let Riley Fontaine in. The woman was a damnable distraction and overly bothersome.

But little brother, he could hear Freddie saying, *when was the last time you had this much fun?*

In the salon, Cousin Felicity sat before the small table, just starting to pour the tea the maid had brought in. Louisa sat half reclined on a settee in the corner, thumbing through a fashion magazine. Bea stood by the window watching the square, while Maggie sat on the long sofa beside Del.

Riley, he noted, had chosen the narrow, straight-backed chair well away from the Viscount. She looked as if she were sitting before the bench at Newgate instead of having tea.

She spared him only the briefest of glances, as if she found his presence as troublesome as she had hours before when she'd stormed out of his study.

He didn't see what she need be so miffed about—he'd only been trying to help her, not embarrass her.

"Mason!" Cousin Felicity called out. "How delightful that you can join us. I was just telling everyone about a disturbing item in the paper, the Duke of Walford's heir is missing, and they propose to drag the river. I was just getting to the good part when Lord Delander arrived. He insisted we continue our break from our lessons with a bit of tea and some cakes he brought over."

Del grinned at the girls, though none of them returned his infectious smile. "Lessons? Female secrets on how to catch us poor unsuspecting men in the parson's mousetrap, eh, Bea? Perhaps Mason and I can help—besides, we might be able to use some help in finding brides." Del grinned at Riley with what was apparently his best rakish endeavor, but she wasn't looking at him, so his efforts were wasted. "Come now," he said to Riley. "What lessons would you recommend to your cousin?"

Riley demurred. "That would depend on what type of bride he seeks."

Mason shifted in his seat as all eyes turned to him.

"Oh, yes, Uncle," Maggie said, with the first show of spirit he'd seen since entering the room. "What sort of bride are you looking for?"

"Rich," Del suggested.

Louisa nodded in agreement.

"Pretty," Del added, rising to his feet and warming to

his subject. "And not too young, I would think. I can't see your uncle with some simpering miss just out of the schoolroom." He paced around the room. "She can't be one of these silly creatures you find everywhere. She'd bore him beyond redemption." Del scratched his chin. "But how to find her?"

"She sounds like that mincing and prancing Dahlia Pindar," Beatrice said.

"Exactly!" Del told her. "There is a perfect heiress for your uncle. Rich and respectable."

"And a regular ninny-hammer," Bea added. "I think she could get lost in a closet."

Mason should have known that Riley would eventually extract her own form of revenge as she took this moment to turn to him and ask, "And why haven't you swept this veritable paragon off her feet and made her your countess, *Cousin*?"

With everyone watching him, their expectant gazes awaiting his answer, Mason shrugged. "It's a little more complicated than that."

Much to his chagrin, Del leapt into the fray. "Then Miss St. Clair," he said to Riley, "you should expand your charm school to include your cousin here, for it seems he needs a bit of prodding if he has any hope of making the illustrious Miss Pindar his bride. We can both help him."

"Such a fanciful notion, Lord Delander," Riley told him. "I had no idea you were such a romantic."

"I am whatever you wish, my dear lady."

Mason groaned at this flattering gallantry.

"You see," Del said, pointing an accusing finger at him. "You haven't the slightest idea how to talk to a lady."

"And what about you, Lord Delander?" Maggie asked. "What do *you* seek in a bride?"

At this Del came to a stumbling halt. "Only one thing."

He paused dramatically. "She must be able to beat my mother at piquet." He turned to Riley. "Of course, you play, don't you?"

Riley shook her head.

"Bother that, but it's fairly easy to learn. You'll master it in no time when we are—"

"Del," Mason interrupted. "How did you find your way in?"

"What? Give away the location of my secret tunnel so you can fill it in? Add vats of boiling oil to the attic windows?" His friend pointed at a large rent in his breeches and the scuffs in his usually immaculate boots. "But since you ask, I waged my assault on this prison of yours by climbing the garden wall."

Mason smiled. "It looks like the wall won."

Del laughed. "It did. Sneaky tactics, letting the mortar get into such a state of disrepair that the least bit of weight and it sends one toppling over in a hail of bricks."

"You don't look all that much worse for the experience," Mason told him, accepting the cup of tea Cousin Felicity offered.

"I'll mend," he said woefully. "My only thanks is that your garden is in an equal state of snarl. Those thorny monsters out there someone once called roses broke my fall." To prove his point, he plucked a wicked-looking thorn from his jacket.

"Lord Delander, are you sure you aren't hurt?"

This tender inquiry, much to everyone's surprise, came from Bea, who had relinquished her place at the window and now stood beside Del. When she realized all eyes were now on her, she frowned. "Well, that wall is an embarrassment. Lord Delander is lucky his throat wasn't slit in that wretched tangle."

"Huzzah!" Lord Delander said. "I have recruited Beatrice to my side."

At this passionate declaration, Beatrice blushed.

Lord Ashlin took a second glance at his eldest niece.

Bea, blushing? What the devil was that all about?

"What side would that be?" Louisa inquired from her solitary post in the corner, sparing a sly glance at Bea. There was an undercurrent to her question Mason didn't understand, but he made a note to himself to inquire after it later.

Del glanced over his shoulder at Louisa. "I would have thought by now your uncle would have informed all of you of my intentions."

"What intentions?" Maggie asked, offering him the plate of cakes and spilling half of them in the process.

Del smiled at the girl and wiped the crumbs off his pants. "Those toward your cousin, of course."

Riley's gaze rolled heavenward.

"Who?" Louisa asked. "Cousin Felicity?"

Del laughed, as did an uneasy Cousin Felicity. "Louisa, you are a sharp one." He turned to Riley. "My mother always said that one would come to a bad end—watch out for her."

"How is your mother, my lord?" Louisa asked, in tones that sounded as if she hoped the report would be dire.

"Admirable," he told her. "The old dragon is in alt today." He grinned at Riley. "Especially since I told her of my intentions to wed your dearest Cousin Riley."

Bea sprayed the tea she had been sipping across the room. "Marry *her*?"

Maggie bounded from the sofa and pounded her sister's back. In between thumps, she glared at Riley.

"As soon as she says yes," he told the wide-eyed sisters.

Riley turned to him and smiled. "My lord, your offer

is most kind, but I cannot possibly marry you."

"You can't?" the sisters asked in unison.

"Of course not," she told them. "My first obligation is to you three. The Viscount's offer is generous and kind, but overly optimistic—I would never marry a man I barely knew."

"Then I shall just have to remedy that," Del told her. "Tonight you shall accompany my mother and me to Mrs. Evans's musicale. It promises to be a terribly dull affair, I grant you, especially since your cousin will be there, but it will afford you plenty of time to hear all about me from my mother."

"Now that *does* sound dull," Louisa muttered.

Mason ignored his niece, and told his friend, "I am afraid my cousin's time is taken up with assisting the girls with the preparations for their Season."

Del laughed. "You three? Out for the Season. Now, there's a lark." He started to laugh, but was the only one in the room who found any humor in the situation.

Riley turned to the Viscount and said in a chilling tone, "And why do you say that?"

"Well, there was the time Bea called the Duchess of Harleton a harl—" he began, then faltered when his statement was met with stone-faced resistance. He tried again. "Or when Maggie stumbled in front of Lord Jeremy's prized hunter at the park and sent the skittish creature racing, and Lord Jeremy left on his a—"

Again his jest faded away as it fell on deaf ears. "Oh, bother," he finally said, turning back to Beatrice. "Come there, Bea. You were more fun before you decided to grow up. Remember the larks we used to have? The time your uncle and I taught you to ride at Sanborn Abbey the summer we were home from school? You were just a bit of muslin, but every time you fell off you used that phrase you'd learned from the footmen, and then—"

"Oh, you . . . you . . . big nodcock," she stammered, then ran from the room, her cheeks flaming.

"Whatever did I say?" Del asked Maggie.

She rose as well. "Bea's right. You're a regular nodcock." She went to follow her sister, though as she passed in front of Del, she trod heavily on his foot.

The Viscount yelped in pain, but Maggie didn't even bother to spare him so much as an apologetic glance in her race toward the door.

For once, Mason doubted that accident could be blamed on his niece's clumsiness.

With a great sigh of resignation, Louisa rose, too. "My regards to your mother," she tossed over her shoulder as she sauntered past the puzzled Viscount.

"Oh dear," Cousin Felicity said, frowning at the girls' sudden departure.

Mason noted that the only one who didn't look upset was Riley.

Perched on her chair, she stared in the direction Beatrice had fled, a calculated smile on her face.

Chapter 9

Riley had watched from the library window as Mason and Cousin Felicity strolled down the steps and out toward the waiting carriage.

She could see a young lady inside the elegant barouche, and wondered if this was the infamous Miss Pindar.

Oh, bother, if only she could . . .

Stopping herself short of making that impossible wish, Riley returned to the papers and work she'd brought to the library. Just because she'd left the theatre didn't mean she could neglect her duties.

But in the warm comfort of the library, Riley soon found her eyes more often shut than open.

What would a little bit of a nap hurt? she thought, curling up on the thick carpet before the fireplace and drifting off into sleep without another thought—until she started to dream.

She was lost in the warrens beyond Covent Garden. She ran and ran until she could barely catch her breath, calling for Lord Ashlin, for anyone to help her . . .

Footsteps clattered from the murky shadows and she knew she had to keep moving—keep ahead of them . . .

As she turned a dark corner, Clyde and his filthy grasp

caught and pulled her into his loathsome embrace.

"Yer a dead one now," he whispered into her ear.

Riley awoke with a start, her breath coming in ragged gasps, her eyes blinking at the unfamiliar surroundings. Where was she? Then she remembered what was real and what was a dream.

Though it hadn't all been a dream. Clyde was only too real, and still out there, somewhere in the darkness.

She wrapped her arms around herself to ward off the shivers that were not entirely from a chill. The candles had burned low, and she rose quickly, lighting more to illuminate the darkness and chase away her demons.

Even as she lit the last one she could find, she heard the sound of someone creeping up the stairs, the poorly maintained steps of Ashlin House groaning and complaining with the person's every move.

She opened her mouth to cry out, but closed it just as fast. Her gaze flew over the room, looking for a place to hide, but there was little in the way of cubby holes to provide cover. But she did see one thing that gave her some measure of comfort—a heavy fire iron leaning against the grate.

She crept as silently as she could to her newfound weapon and snatched it up. Weighing it in her hand, she knew she'd only have one chance to stop her assailant.

And it was a chance she couldn't waste.

Mason returned home just after one from Mrs. Evans's musicale. The house was dark except for the library, where it appeared someone was still up.

Riley.

She was hard at work on her future, and he'd spent the night hard at work on his . . .

Unlocking the door, he let himself in. He'd instructed

Belton not to wait up for him. The man had enough duties at his age, and sitting up all night didn't have to be one of them. He was relieved to see the stalwart butler had taken his orders to heart and was nowhere in sight.

Now Mason would seek his own respite—exhausted and weary from the music and chatter that had filled the Evanses' ballroom to an overflow.

A crushing success he'd heard someone call the evening—a crushing bore, he thought a more apt description.

One young lady after another had come forward to delight the audience with her musical skill, or lack thereof. Miss Pindar had been singled out for her performance on the pianoforte and had been asked to play a second time.

The girl had beamed at Mason the entire time, as if to say, *I would make the most perfect Countess.*

And she was right, she would, but she wasn't . . .

He stopped himself right there. He had generations of Ashlins, not even counting his nieces, to whom he owed a duty to see the family name restored to some level of respectability.

Freddie was probably even now chuckling over his brother's moral dilemma.

Climbing the stairs toward his chamber, he stopped on the first floor; at his feet a sliver of light illuminated a narrow path to the library door.

It beckoned him, teased him to follow its shadowed course.

Go on, little brother, he swore he could hear Freddie whisper. *She's waiting for you.*

As tempting as that notion might be, he straightened his resolve and turned the corner to the next floor when the door burst open, and the light from within opened its arms to envelop and blind him.

"Oh, my lord," he heard Riley say, " 'tis you."

Then, as his eyes adjusted to the light, he saw her and marveled at the ethereal sight before him. Silhouetted as she was, she looked like an ancient warrior queen in her simple muslin gown, her fierce weapon held aloft. Her breathing was erratic, her chest fluttering up and down, her breasts straining against the low neckline. Her hair, the color of wheat, resplendent in its shimmering warmth, was bound in a single loose braid falling nearly to her waist. At the hem of her gown, her bare toes peeked out.

Boadicea never looked so fierce or so beautiful. Nor had she, Mason knew, ever carried a fire iron.

"Do you know how to use that?" he asked.

She glanced up at her improvised weapon. "If I get the first strike, I do."

Despite her warning, he stepped closer. "Remind me to have my arrival announced from here on out," he teased, using one finger to push the iron down from her armed stance. He was so close he could almost feel her trembling.

He'd done this—frightened her with his untimely arrival. While he could tell himself it was his duty as a gentleman to offer his protection, he also found that being this close to her all he wanted to do was fold her into his arms and promise her that she'd never know another moment of fear.

A promise he'd seal with a burning kiss.

"My apologies," she said, turning away hastily, as if she could read his errant thoughts. "I heard someone about, and I . . . well, I didn't expect you back so early, and I thought . . ."

"I'm sorry to have startled you. Where is Hashim?" Mason had only gone out because Hashim had promised to stay by Riley's side until his return.

As if on cue, the man rose up out of the shadows like a phoenix.

Mason nodded to him, marveling at his stealth. "Go to bed, sir. I shall guard our lady well," he told him in Persian.

Hashim bowed and took to the stairs.

Riley leaned out the door, watching her servant's departure. "What did you say to him?"

"That, Madame," he said, "is between Hashim and me."

"Harumph." She blew out an impatient breath, and stomped back into the library, the fire iron still at her side.

Mason couldn't help himself. He followed her, hypnotized by the saucy sway of her hips. He tried to reason with himself that he had given his word to Hashim that he would watch her, but he doubted that included eyeing her form.

Or the line of thoughts that came to mind with each seductive movement she made.

Did the woman know how she affected him? He hoped not.

Riley put the iron back into the holder next to the fireplace, then settled down cross-legged on the floor, where apparently she'd been working. Scattered pages, account books, and bills formed a semi-circle of litter around her.

Along with a pair of stockings and two red garters.

"How do you work in all that clutter?" Mason asked, his gaze lingering over her discarded undergarments. Why didn't it surprise him the lady wore red satin garters?

"Quite well, thank you," she snapped, gathering her unmentionables up and hiding them beneath her papers. "If you must know—I prefer to work in my corset and petticoat, but decided, for propriety's sake, only to relinquish some lesser items. It won't happen again."

Mason hoped not. He could well imagine the sight that

would have greeted him if she'd donned, or rather un-donned, her usual coverings.

The idea of her in red garters was bad enough.

After a few moments, she took a deep breath and sighed. "I'm sorry, my lord. I'm quite out of sorts to-night."

For good reason—she'd had a hell of a day and his untimely arrival had probably frightened her thoroughly.

"I'm sorry if I startled you," he said.

She made an indifferent shrug, so he decided not to pursue the matter. At least, not right away. Besides, she was probably still angry over his earlier interview.

The interview where she'd claimed she'd never had a lover.

How could that be? The woman's every move spoke of sensual promise. Her damned penchant for feathers, her rich tangle of hair, her luminous skin.

And those green eyes . . . every time he looked into them he found himself waxing between poetics and some-thing all too Ashlin.

His gaze meandered back to the hint of red satin peek-ing out from beneath her papers.

Red satin garters? And she claimed not to have had any lovers?

"Uh-hum," she coughed, her gaze flitting toward the door in an unabashed hint.

He decided not to take it.

Removing his jacket, he joined her on the floor, stretch-ing his legs out in front of him, toes up against the grate where the coals glowed with a cozy warmth. "What is all this?"

"Revisions, schedules, blocking notes, orders for all the items we need for costumes and to finish the sets." Her

tone bordered on curt, and with a not-so-subtle message—
leave.

But he didn't want to—leave, that is. After the senseless
din of Mrs. Evans's, the quiet disorder of Riley's world
called to him like a lone flute.

"I have quite a bit to do," she said, hinting once more,
this time with a glance and a pointed shrug toward the
door.

He continued to ignore her. "And you've chosen to do
it all at once?"

At this, she finally smiled. "You wretched man," she
said. "Here I am, trying to stay mad at you, but you won't
let me." She reached over and playfully squeezed his arm.

After an evening of being treated to every artful wile
Miss Pindar possessed, Riley's guileless touch startled him
with its innocence.

Yet at the same time, her touch ignited his imagination,
already smoldering at the idea of red satin. Of what it
would be like to gather her into his arms ... his fingers
pushing aside her skirt, while his hand moved upward until he touched that fiery satin, warm from her skin and
beguiling to the senses ...

"I suppose now I must apologize," she said.

"Whatever for?" he asked, wondering if it was he who
should be apologizing, and profusely, for his wayward de-
lirium.

Maybe staying hadn't been the best idea.

"For my behavior earlier, when you told me you had
fired my Runner. I was ungrateful and acted most unbe-
comingly."

"You are never unbecoming," he told her, wishing for
once the woman could look dowdy and plain, like the
young misses who had flocked to his side this evening.

And not as if she'd just tumbled out of bed.

"I think you look quite tolerable," he joked.

She snorted at his compliment. "I can see you are working on your charm. And here I thought I would have to give you lessons. Did this hidden talent serve you well this evening? Are you betrothed?" she teased back.

Mason shuddered. "I think not."

She glanced away, and he couldn't tell what she was thinking. Finally she asked, "Was Miss Pindar there?"

"I don't recall," he lied. For some reason he didn't like discussing his suit for Miss Pindar's hand with Riley.

She smiled. "Your cousin has high hopes you will find favor with the young lady. According to Cousin Felicity, Miss Pindar is quite plump in the pockets."

"Yes, she is that," Mason said. What he didn't add was that he found the lady cloying and pretentious, and as Bea had said, a ninny-hammer.

Riley continued sorting through her papers. "Was she in the carriage that picked you up?"

Mason glanced over at her. Riley had watched him leave?

"No, that was Lord Chilton's daughter."

She wrinkled her nose. "Lord Chilton? I keep hearing his name—who is he?"

"Cousin Felicity's beau."

Riley's mouth fell open. "Cousin Felicity has a beau?"

"Yes," he said. "She and Lord Chilton have been seeing each other for nearly twenty years."

"Twenty years? Oh, you jest," she said, waving her hand at him again, but this time not touching him.

Mason shook his head. "On the subject of Cousin Felicity's marital prospects, I never jest. Freddie teased her quite mercilessly about the situation. Offering monthly to call Chilton out if the old boy didn't marry her posthaste.

Ask her about him and she has a thousand excuses for why they are still as yet unattached." He paused. "The truth is, I think she finds the entire arrangement embarrassing."

"Then why hasn't he married her?"

Mason shrugged. "He's a Chilton. They are terrible about making up their minds. The story is that it took him twenty years to propose to his first wife, so the joke is that Cousin Felicity can't be that much further away from getting her trip to the parson."

"The poor dear," Riley said. "How humiliating. There must be some way to get Lord Chilton to propose."

"If you can do that, you'd more than repay your debt to the family. I think Lord Chilton holds off so he doesn't have to pay her modiste bill."

Now Riley laughed. "She does love her clothes."

"Yes, she does," he agreed. "And I have the bills to prove it."

They both laughed at this.

"I see you've changed some other habits as well," she said, nodding at his evening clothes. "You've lost some of your *predictable* severity."

He didn't know if he liked being described as predictable. "One of Freddie's that I had reworked," he said, plucking at the sleeve. "My brother left closets of suits that had never been worn. I saw no point in having new ones made. Much to the horror of his tailor, I had these recut to fit me."

"We do that in the theatre all the time. I think I've worn this gown in nine different productions. The poor fabric is getting terribly thin just from all the sewing." Riley shrugged. "I know it isn't fashionable, but I have a terrible time throwing anything out. That, and we never seem to have enough money to buy new costumes."

Mason laughed. "Then we can be quite unfashionable together." He reached over and picked up one of her papers. "What is this?"

She reached over to take it out of his hands, and when she did, their fingers touched ever so briefly.

But it was enough. Enough to drive him to venture a gaze into her eyes and wish that so many things in his life were different.

That he could follow his passions like his ancestors had so many times—for now he understood why they could let their desires get in the way of good sense.

For a moment, he swore he saw the same fire of recognition in her eyes—until she tugged the paper away from him and snapped, "Nothing of any importance, my lord."

"Mason," he corrected, in the face of her sudden vehemence. He couldn't remember the last time anyone had snapped at him like that. Few people ever spoke their mind to him anymore, and certainly not since he'd gained his title. "I would like it if you called me Mason."

She glanced up. "What?"

"I think if you are going to bark at me like that, you might as well use my Christian name," he said.

"I'm sorry if I got a bit high-handed," she said. "Aggie says I have an artistic temperament."

"That would be a polite way of describing it," Mason told her.

"I would hardly call it a temper."

"No, you're right there," he agreed. "Temper would hardly begin to describe it."

She glanced over at him. "Oh, you are teasing me, my lord." She buried the paper into the pile with the rest of her collection of scraps and scribblings.

"Mason," he repeated.

"Huh?"

"Call me Mason."

She shook her head. "I don't think I can."

He sat up straight. "Whyever not?"

"Well, look at you," she said, waving her hand at him as if that was answer enough.

"And what is wrong with me?"

"Nothing," she said.

For some strange reason, he sensed her answer went beyond this discussion. And even more odd, that idea pleased him.

She sighed. "You're an earl. It would hardly be proper for me to call you by your Christian name."

"But we're related now," he said.

"Only in Cousin Felicity's estimation," she said. "And that is hardly a recommendation."

"What if it is my wish," he said.

"Your wish or your command?" she asked.

He was glad to see the twinkle back in her eyes. "If I must, I command it. But I would rather that you gave it freely."

"Now you sound like Geoffroi, the hero in our play," she said. She arose from the floor. Taking a step back, she made a low curtsey, worthy of a presentation at court. "If my lord commands it, then I, just the mere daughter of a woodcutter must humbly comply."

He nodded in acceptance of her tribute. "Are you?" he asked.

"Am I what?"

"The daughter of a woodcutter."

She laughed, but there didn't seem to be much humor in her voice this time. "No. It is just my role in our play.

When you said that about commands, it just reminded me of the play, and then I answered from the third act." She shrugged. "Rather silly, I suppose."

He shook his head. "Not at all."

Their gazes locked, and Mason felt once again the pull that left him aching to be closer to her.

She looked away first. "I also wanted to thank you."

"What for?" he said.

"For saving my life. I would have died if you hadn't come along." She bit her lip, a shy, sweet gesture.

He rose from the floor. "How would the heroine in your play have thanked her hero?" he asked, once again surprised by the light teasing tone in his voice. He was sounding more and more like Freddie with each passing minute.

Her eyes sparkled. "The heroine would be overwrought, beside herself with love and appreciation."

"And what would she say?"

"She wouldn't say anything," Riley told him, edging a bit closer to him. "She'd just go to him. And then she'd—"

He looked down at her, standing almost within his grasp. He knew he shouldn't, but there was a magic in the air leading him astray, a siren's call. "And she'd—?"

Riley blushed. "She'd kiss him."

Once again that impetuous Ashlin nature took over. All of a sudden he found himself catching her in his arms and pulling her close. She didn't fight him or protest, just looked up at him with those mysterious green eyes of hers—so innocent and so filled with fire.

He lowered his mouth to hers and kissed her, reawakening the fire that had started the first time he'd done this.

For a while they just kissed in the silence of the library, with the low crackle of the fire the only other sound, that is, except for the soft sighs that escaped her lips as he pulled her closer.

His fingers caught the ribbon binding her braid and gently plucked it free so her hair fell loose. She shook her head, sending her hair tumbling over her shoulders in a wild tangle. Her eyes were now hooded in a sultry gaze as she watched him.

His siren, his Boadicea, his Aphrodite. She inflamed him with this madness, this sickness, this curse of being an Ashlin.

"I thought you professors praticed celibacy," she teased.

He leaned back and smiled at her. "I have, that is, until you came into my life."

"Oh, go on," she said. "You expect me to belive that?"

He let go of her and straightened his shoulders. "Yes, because it is the truth. I took my teaching vows very seriously—even after I inherited the title, for I thought then that I would still be able to return to Oxford."

"But that was months ago. You mean to say you haven't . . . well, what I mean is, in all this time, you haven't . . ."

"Taken a mistress?" he finished for her. Mason laughed. "Even if I could afford one, I wouldn't. I've never viewed sex the way my brother or father did. I always assumed that it should occur between two people who love each other and who stand on that commitment as a lifelong vow." He shrugged. "Rather old-fashioned and foolish, I suppose."

Riley shook her head. "Not at all." She slanted a shy glance at him. "But with all that said, why are you kissing me? Practice?"

Mason was asking himself the same question. What the devil was he doing, kissing Riley?

"I know," she said, waving her hand at him before he

could articulate an excuse, even a poor one. "This is an aberration."

"It's not that," he said, wondering how he could explain the way Riley made him feel, and how impossible it all was.

She backed away from him and headed toward the door.

He caught her by the arm. "Don't leave, Riley. Not yet." He heard a small sigh slip from her lips.

"I am sorry, milord. You must think me the worst type of Cyprian. But I am not. This was an aberration, and I promise you it won't happen again."

As he watched her flee from the room, he realized she was wrong on both counts.

He didn't think of her as a lightskirt, nor was the evening an aberration.

It was, he suspected, only the beginning.

As he started after her, he heard the crackle of parchment underfoot. Looking down, he realized she'd left her papers. Gathering up the pages, he was about to put them in a stack for her when one of the lines in the text caught his eye.

My Lord Ashlin, your kindness will always be remembered by our family. It was a line for a character named Aveline.

Obviously this was the play his brother's money had been squandered to finance—and from which Riley intended to pay them back.

Apparently, financing a play also gave a patron the added benefit of having a character named after him.

No wonder Freddie had given Riley so much money. The idea of being immortalized as a romantic hero would have been far too much of a temptation for his vain and frivolous brother to pass up.

Suddenly it occurred to him that he'd never asked what the play was about—something rather important, he gauged, considering his family's future rested in these words.

Since he doubted Riley would want to see any more of him this night, after his second blunder into her private affairs, he caught up the loose pages, out of order as they were, and settled down in the comfortable high-backed chair near the fireplace to decipher the story.

None of it made sense at first, considering most of it had annotations and deletions and cross-references to other scenes. Obviously the play Riley seemed so confident about was still a work in progress.

Something she had neglected to tell him.

From what he could tell, the heroine, "poor, lost Aveline," was being forced to marry the "despicable and aged Lord Tamworth," while at the same time she pined for her lost love, the "beloved and faithful Geoffroi."

"Romantic drivel," he muttered, after scanning the first few pages.

But as he continued to piece together the story, he found himself caught up in Aveline's adventure. So much so that when he got to the next to the last page where Aveline was making a long declaration to her beloved, he found himself clinging to her every word. Especially when it appeared she was about to confess the truth amongst all the play's deceptions.

I am not the woodcutter's daughter; in truth I am—

Mason flipped the page to find the answer, but realized the one he held was the last. His gaze quickly scanned the room to see if there were any more pages to be had. As he was about to give up, he spied a bit of white sticking out from beneath the secretary that sat on the other side of the room.

He sprang from his chair, crossing the room quickly, and dropped to his hands and knees, reaching and stretching for the last elusive piece of the puzzle.

Finally his fingers were able to draw the page into his greedy grasp, but much to his ire, the page was nothing more than the cover sheet to the script.

Still, the words emblazoned across it took him by surprise.

The Envious Moon—A Dramatic Comedy Presented by the Players of the Queen's Gate Theatre . . . by R. Fontaine.

Riley? Riley had written this play?

Mason sat back on his heels, holding the page up to the light to see if he had read it correctly.

Even on the second glance, and a third, just to make sure his eyes weren't deceiving him, her name remained as the author.

Mason shook his head.

This woman he'd assumed to be no more than another spoiled pampered London feline, this renowned mistress to King and country, not only lived in the attic of her tumbledown theatre, wore reworked clothing until it was threadbare, and managed her company of misfits through long hours of hard work—but she also managed to write her own plays.

As he looked down at the notes scribbled in the margins and the crossed out and cross-referenced lines covering the pages, he realized how little he'd truly known of the woman he'd asked to move into his house and into his family's lives.

And even more startling was how much he wanted to know her.

*　　*　　*

In the wee hours of the morning, Del sauntered into his mother's sitting room. He strode across the floor to where she sat at a small table opposite his uncle, the Duke of Everton, playing piquet.

"Hello, Mother," he said, leaning over her shoulder and giving her a sloppy buss on the cheek. "Winning?"

"Of course," she snapped, pointing at the pile of coins before her.

Del knew his mother cheated, but had never `dared broach the subject. Besides, she was always happiest when she was beating some hapless player at her favorite card game.

"Your Grace," he said, bowing to his respected relative.

"Delander," his uncle said, laying down his cards. "Your mother was just telling me you've decided to get married. About time."

Del grinned. "And to a veritable angel, as fair as a rose in the morning, as innocent as a—" He couldn't think of anything innocent enough, so he finished by saying, "Well, you get my meaning."

"That's all very well, Allister," his mother snapped, obviously unhappy about having her winning hand interrupted, "but your uncle and I are having quite a time placing the girl. You say she is a relative of Lord Ashlin's?"

"Yes. Miss Riley St. Clair. She's just come in from the country."

"Whereabouts?" his uncle asked.

Del shrugged. "I never thought to ask."

This didn't please the Dowager in the least. "I don't see how this girl is connected to them. Can you, George?" she asked her brother.

The Duke shook his head. "Never heard of her before and I thought I knew all the St. Clair relations, though they are a strange lot—has anyone ever determined how Lady Felicity fits in?"

"That nitwit?" the Dowager said. "She's no more a St. Clair than Biggers is my twin sister," she said, nodding at her long-suffering abigail who sat nodding by the fireplace. "She's a Dalrymple, related through their mother's side. And a distant one at that. But we weren't discussing her, we are talking about this Riley person. I find it quite vexing that her connection isn't all that clear. Mark my words, I will not sanction any marriage, Allister, until we have this straightened out."

"Then why not do it yourself, Mother?" Del suggested, taking a cake from the plate. "Why not call on the lady yourself? Tomorrow. I promise you will be as enchanted as I am—and you won't care a whit about where she fits in on the St. Clair family tree. She's a veritable paragon of virtue."

"Harumph!" the lady said. "We'll see about that."

"I think I might join you, Josephine," the Duke said. "It's been a long time since I met a paragon."

Chapter 10

Mason arose the next morning at the same time he always did, and went about his daily rituals with the same precision which had always regulated his adult life.

He dipped his hands into the washbowl and splashed the icy water over his face and stubbled chin.

Order . . . rules . . . discipline, he told himself, as he reached for his shaving soap and razor, were the distinctions of an honorable and civilized gentleman.

Kissing actresses was not.

In the light of day, last night appeared as a startling lapse of judgment. Therefore, he intended to put some principles back into his life immediately. First thing, he'd make it clear to Riley that they, as adults, should be able to maintain a proper relationship.

How hard could that be? he asked himself.

Having finished shaving, he got dressed and went downstairs to his breakfast, which he always took at nine. Halfway down the stairs, he recalled a line from Riley's play, the words dancing like a Freddie-ism through his righteous demeanor.

For life, dear Aveline, is a constant delight, an unend-

ing surprise, if only you take the chances offered.

The line held a tempting appeal. Not unlike Riley herself. Well, perhaps he might take some chances—that is, as soon as he'd gotten his life and family in order.

Mason realized later he should have known better than to tempt fate by lapsing, albeit minutely, into his brother's way of thinking.

Even as he came down the stairs the aroma of coffee tantalized his nose, something so beyond the realm of their frugal economies, he came to an abrupt halt.

"Cousin Felicity," he muttered under his breath. This was her way of getting back at him for his firing their French chef and hiring Mrs. McConneghy in his place. The stout Scottish woman might not know how to glaze an ostrich, but she did know how to squeeze their meager budget to feed the entire household—a budget which didn't include coffee.

"My lord," Belton said, coming out of the servant's doorway. "I need to discuss a matter of—"

"—Not now," Mason told him.

"But my lord, I must speak to you about certain persons," Belton said, following in Mason's angry wake.

Having come down to the ground floor and nearly upon the dining room, more rich aromas wafted toward him. Mason inhaled the forbidden bounty. "Is that bacon *and* sausages I smell?"

Belton sighed. "Yes, my lord."

From within the dining room, it sounded as if a celebration were taking place rather than his usual quiet morning repast with the paper. Above the din, he heard Cousin Felicity happily nattering on about the prior evening's gossip.

"Allow me, my lord," Belton said, pushing open the door.

Isn't this what you just wished for, little brother? Freddie's voice chided him. *An opportunity to try something new.*

"Not if it beggars us," he muttered back.

Belton's white brows shot up. "Pardon, my lord?"

"Nothing, Belton." Mason set his jaw and entered the dining room just as the clock on the mantel struck nine.

Everyone in the room, save him, burst into laughter. At the table, Cousin Felicity extended her hand to none other than Riley's partner Aggie and said, "I told you, Mr. Pettibone. At precisely nine o'clock his lordship would enter, so I have won our wager. Lord Ashlin is the most predictable man in all of London."

Predictable? Mason bristled at her tone. She made him sound like some stodgy don. It didn't help that Riley had said the exact same thing about his clothes last night.

"I am hardly predictable, Cousin," he said.

He didn't like the way his pronouncement was met with ringing feminine laughter from his usual lie-a-bed nieces.

"Uncle Mason," Beatrice said, between choking bouts of laughter, "You make Belton look slipshod."

Her sisters joined in adding their giggles to the clamor.

"He arises at quarter past eight every morning," Louisa began telling Mr. Pettibone. "Not on the hour or half past, but precisely quarter past eight."

Beatrice nodded. "Breakfast and his paper at nine."

Maggie joined into the chorus. "Accounts at ten."

"House report from Belton at half past eleven."

"Consult with Mrs. McConneghy at noon."

"Leave the house at quarter 'til one," Maggie said.

"To avoid the creditors who arrive at two," Bea added in a whispered aside.

"What you do, Uncle," Maggie said, "from then until you return at four is a mystery to us."

Bea nodded. "Four-thirty we take tea in Mother's parlor and you tell us how bad the accounts you reviewed at ten are and how we can no longer waste money on unnecessary expenditures."

Louisa leaned across the table and said in a loud whisper to Mr. Pettibone, "Can you explain to our Uncle that there are no unnecessary expenditures?"

Egads, when they laid his days out like that, he sounded worse than predictable. Like one of those old scholars at Merton College who the young students used to set their pocket watches by each day as they doddered across the greens at the appointed hours like the hands on a clock.

Well, he was certainly nothing like that. Yes, he kept a daily regiment, though it was hardly the rigid schedule they described. More of an ordered series of events, a daily means of conducting oneself that kept the chaos they brought to his life at bay.

Cousin Felicity turned to Mr. Pettibone. "He isn't at all like his brother. Freddie was such a gadabout, and so impulsive."

"Then I see you take after the late Earl, my dear lady," Mr. Pettibone said, his voice a mixture of Irish charm and something else Mason couldn't quite put a finger on. "For I find you the most unpredictable and enchanting woman in all of London."

Mason stared in shock as Cousin Felicity's cheeks turned the most rosy shade of pink.

What had come over the women in this house? First Bea, now Cousin Felicity.

The aging rogue kissed her fingers again. "I swear your youthful face reminds me of my beloved and long departed Rosalinde. It breaks my heart, it does." He let go of her hand with a dramatic sigh, and gazed for a moment longer than was proper into her worshipful gaze.

"Uh, hum." Mason cleared his throat. Schedule or not, whatever nonsense was going on between Cousin Felicity and this Mr. Pettibone needed to be put to a halt. He made a note to discuss these irregularities with Riley between his morning meeting with Belton and the cook.

"Cousin, as I was about to say when I came in—"

"—Oh, Mason, why aren't you eating?" Cousin Felicity waved at the plates of food. "Your breakfast is growing cold, and you know how you prefer it hot."

He took a deep breath. Did his cousin have to make him sound like some old man? He could well imagine what Riley would add to his cousin's description. Thankfully, she wasn't in the room.

"I will not eat one bite of any of this," he said, unwilling to step into the room and give any credence to this outrageous display. "I will have an explanation as to the meaning of this."

"It is only breakfast, Mason," she replied. "It's been so long since we had a decent one it's no wonder you don't recognize it. Sit down and have a cup of coffee. You can't imagine how wonderful it is after all these months of *economies*."

She said the word as if it were as bitter as the mug of chocolate she was also savoring.

Chocolate and coffee? Had they all gone mad?

He'd be at his books until well past his meeting with Belton to get this straightened out, and then the rest of his day would be spent trying to make up his sched—

Mason halted that self-incriminating line of thought.

Cousin Felicity continued buttering her toast. "Mason is quite strict about matters of *economy*," she told Mr. Pettibone.

It was the kind of response Freddie would have made.

Still, he had to admit the smell of coffee, a luxury they

could ill afford, as well as a nice plate of almond rolls
lent a heavenly and enticing aroma to the room.

He took another deep breath and reminded himself of
his earlier resolve—this is what happened when one allowed temptation into one's midst.

And he included actresses on that list.

Cousin Felicity drew in a deep breath. "Heavenly," she
uttered. "Why, I can't remember the last time we had such
a breakfast!" She reached for one of the rolls.

Even as her fingers touched the illicit bounty, Mason
said, "Cousin, not one bite. They all go back. The coffee,
the rolls, all of it. I said we would have economies in this
household, and we will have them whether you like it or
not."

"But Mason—" Cousin Felicity protested, disregarding
his order and taking a roll. "I didn't purchase any of this."

"Then who is responsible for these extravagances?" he
asked.

"Let me guess," a voice behind him said.

He turned to find Riley standing just behind him, and
alongside her, Hashim. She nodded slightly and then continued into the room as if she were the lady of the house.

Hashim followed, taking his place behind her chair.

He didn't have to wonder long how much she'd heard
of his cousin and nieces' discussion as to his habits as if
he were some dithering dowager, for she motioned for him
to take his place and said, "Please, Lord Ashlin, have
breakfast. I would hate to be the cause of your schedule
becoming undermined."

Her appearance this morning was a far cry from her
tousled gown and missing stockings of last night. In place
of his warrior queen walked a modest, demure lady, her
hair simply dressed, and wearing a quaint muslin gown
that one would expect on a visiting country cousin. Albeit

one with a Saracen bodyguard trailing after her.

After Hashim poured her coffee, Riley turned to her partner. "Aggie, whatever are you doing here? My note said rehearsals were not to begin until eleven."

"Wait until then to see that you were settled in? I think not! Besides, I had an epiphany regarding the second act around midnight, so I had to come see you straightaway—though I got a bit sidetracked on my way here."

Riley groaned. "How much did you lose?"

Mason shot her a sideways glance.

"How much, Aggie?" Riley repeated.

"I am insulted, my love," the man replied. "I won. Quite handily. And since it is altogether rude to arrive empty handed when one is flush, I thought to repay our esteemed patron for his kindness in extending to you his protection. A poor fare, this," he said, waving his hand over the laden table, "but well fought and won by the turn of a card." He glanced over at Mason, who still stood in the doorway. "Do you gamble, my lord?"

"No," Mason told him.

Aggie shook his head. "Are you sure you are an Ashlin?"

"Aggie!" Riley said.

Mr. Pettibone turned his disbelieving features back to Riley. "Can we be sure?"

At this Riley groaned. "Yes, I'm quite positive."

He shot her an aggrieved look. "I ask only because the man confesses a displeasure for cards, and that, my lord, is a keen loss, for you have the look of a worthy opponent."

"I prefer not to gamble with a fortune I do not possess," Mason told him. Not with some measure of reluctance, he finally took his seat at the breakfast table. He nodded to

Aggie. "I, uh, thank you for sharing your own winnings with my family."

Aggie rose and made an elegant bow. "At your service always, my lord." He passed Mason the plate of almond rolls. "How could I doubt your parentage, sir? For now I see the elegant cast of the Ashlin brow and the sharp wit of your intellect. I would have known you were Freddie's brother anywhere. If I'd seen you in the bazaars of Baghdad or the far reaches of that dark continent, Africa, I would have known you, sir, to be an Ashlin."

That, Mason knew, was laying it on more than a little thick, but before he could respond, Cousin Felicity said, "Mr. Pettibone—"

"—Agamemnon, my dear Miss Felicity. Please call me Agamemnon."

"Agamemnon," she tittered. "Have you been to those places?"

He settled back into the chair beside her. "What places?"

"Baghdad or Africa?" Cousin Felicity's eyes shone with excitement.

"Baghdad and Africa," he sighed. "Such places of wonder! Excitement and danger at every turn."

Riley choked on her chocolate, and when all eyes turned on her, she raised her napkin to her lips and coughed.

"So you have been there?" Cousin Felicity persisted.

"Well, been there? Actually, no," the man said. "But the stories I can tell you, the stories I have heard, would lead you to believe that I have been there."

The lady sighed with delight. "And I have never even been to Kent."

"No!" Aggie said. "Why, I'd have sworn with your continental flair and sense of style I'd seen you gracing the courts of Louis or Charles or Catherine."

"Oh, Agamemnon," Cousin Felicity said. "Really? Truly?"

"You would be their glittering star. Why, the courts of Europe—" the man began to say, looking as if he was about to tell the largest tale ever cast up in the Ashlin dining room.

And Mason knew for a fact that Freddie had spun some large ones.

"Aggie," Riley interrupted, "you said something about the second act?"

Effectively diverted, the man stopped his unlikely dissertation and went on to another subject close to his heart. "Ah yes! The second act. I was borne away on pure inspiration."

"The second act?" Mason interrupted, feeling quite the stranger at his own table. "What did you change?"

"That terrible scene with the woodcutter and Geoffroi. My inspiration came while I was playing piquet—"

Riley cringed. "You weren't playing *piquet*?"

Mason didn't miss the accusation in her voice, and wondered if perhaps the Queen's Gate's financial woes weren't a problem of covering her partner's gambling losses, rather than the mysterious accidents she'd claimed.

It certainly made more sense, he reasoned, and resolved to look into it immediately.

"Riley, such an unpardonable use of brows. You'll be wrinkled as Hortense before the year is out if you continue in that manner." Aggie turned back to Cousin Felicity. "Now, where was I?"

Mason doubted Mr. Pettibone would approve of the face Riley was currently making.

"The crowned heads of Europe," the lady urged him.

"No, I think you were saying something about the second act," Mason interrupted. "You had a moment of inspiration after a game of piquet."

"Ah, yes, my excellent round of piquet. I was playing with the dullest of company, one man especially. Lord Childs? No, that isn't it." Mr. Pettibone scratched his chin. "Lord Chelden? Such a tiresome old fool. 'Tis any wonder I remember that much of the fellow's name. Not that he is in the least important, other than the fact that his purse supported this fine repast. Better to fill our stomachs, I say, than collecting moths in his tight pockets." He tipped his cup in mock salute to their unnamed benefactor. "As I was saying, this Chipper bloke was blithering on, and I suddenly realized that the second act needs a bit of comedy, something to break the strain of having to listen to that tiresome Geoffroi lament at great length about his lost Aveline."

Riley had finished her breakfast and was carefully folding her napkin. "Aggie, I don't think this is the time to discuss changes to the script. Besides, I think the second act is fine the way it is."

"But Riley, my love," he said between bites, "I tell you, the second act needs some comedy."

She shook her head.

Mason recalled what he'd read of that part of the play and weighed in with his opinion. "I think Mr. Pettibone is correct. The scene with Geoffroi is overly long. Did you have something in mind?" he asked Aggie.

Riley shot him a scathing look. "How would you know? You haven't even read it."

Now it was Mason's turn to have the upper hand. "That is where you are wrong. After you left me in the library last night, I discovered your copy and read it."

All eyes turned on the pair, and Mason realized that

perhaps he shouldn't have been so quick to let everyone know about their meeting in the library. "We were discussing the content and breadth of Madame Fontaine's lessons, if you must know."

Beatrice snorted.

"That seems nothing out of the ordinary," Cousin Felicity rushed to add. "But I do wish you hadn't left so early last night, Mason. Miss Pindar was in quite a state over your disappearance. She wanted to send for the watch, for she thought something might have happened to you." Cousin Felicity turned to Riley. "I fear the girl is quite smitten."

Smitten with the idea of being a countess, and leaving her cit origins far behind, Mason thought.

"You must be more considerate of Miss Pindar," Cousin Felicity scolded.

"Miss Pindar, eh?" Del inquired from the doorway. "You certainly didn't waste any time on that one."

Without an invitation, Del strolled into the room and settled comfortably into the open seat next to Bea, which also happened to be directly across from Riley. He held out a bouquet of violets and offered them to her. "Of course, with your cousin otherwise occupied with Miss Pindar, that would leave you unescorted and in need of a protector, oh fairest flower of my heart."

Riley accepted the flowers, but only nodded her appreciation.

Mason couldn't say that he was surprised to see his friend arrive so early in the morning—but for now, he had to get him out of the house before someone slipped up. "Nice to see you, Del, but don't you have business at Tattersall's this morning?"

Del shook his head. "Sent my agent after that fine bit of cattle." He turned to Bea. "A real handful. The kind of beast you'd appreciate. I'll let you take him for a turn in the park next week, if you'd like."

"Perhaps we should ride down there and take a look," Mason offered, hoping the bait of a ride would induce Del to leave. "In case the animal isn't what it seemed the other day."

Mason's efforts were lost on Cousin Felicity.

"Why, Mason, you never go riding on Thursdays and you haven't had a bite to eat," she admonished. "And after Mr. Pettibone went to all the trouble of playing piquet last night so you could have almond rolls this morning. The least you could do is show some appreciation." She then turned to Del. "Oh, where are my manners, Lord Delander? You must share in our good fortune, so kindly provided by our good friend, Mr. Pettibone."

Del happily took the plate Cousin Felicity proceeded to heap with food for him. "Piquet, eh, Mr. Pettibone? I've been known to play a hand or two. Perhaps we could find a game later."

"No!" Riley said, startling nearly everyone at the table with her outburst. She took a deep breath and then offered Lord Delander a small smile. "I mean, not today, my lord. Mr. Pettibone has pressing matters which won't allow any time for idleness."

"Some other day, then," Del offered. Between bites, he kept glancing over at Mr. Pettibone. "You look vaguely familiar, sir. Have we met?"

"Well, since you asked," Mr. Pettibone began, "I am known in many circles, but most recently—"

"—He's been in the country," Riley interjected.

"The country?" Mr. Pettibone shook his head most decisively. "Riley, that is most unkind of you. I haven't played the country since I was a green lad cast—"

"—Casting around the Continent on your Grand Tour,"

Mason said, struggling to save the conversation, let alone the entire morning.

"Ah, yes, my tour of Europe. All the great houses welcomed me." Mr. Pettibone sat back, his hands crossing over his chest. "I remember once in Vienna, I had the lead in—"

"In a story that is best not repeated in front of a young audience," Riley warned him, tipping her head toward Del and not the girls. "Didn't you just mention that you had some very pressing *business* matters to attend to this morning?"

Mr. Pettibone frowned but obviously took the hint, rising from his seat. "Yes, I believe I did. Well, as they say in the City, business never waits, does it, gentlemen?"

"Never does," Del lamented. "Pressing matters of business, eh? That must be it. We've talked investments over papers and port at White's or Brooks's, haven't we?"

"I doubt it," Riley said, jumping in before her partner had a chance to open his mouth. "Lord Delander, Mr. Pettibone is just arrived from the country. He's . . . he's . . ."

She looked to Mason to fill in, but for the life of him he couldn't think of a logical occupation for the old Corinthian.

As luck would have it, Bea did. "Mr. Pettibone is Riley's guardian."

Guardian? Mason swung around and stared at his niece. He didn't know whether to congratulate her for her brilliance or cringe.

"Yes, my guardian," Riley said. "And as my guardian, you had best go see to those matters so they all go on schedule."

Mr. Pettibone smiled at her. "You are a girl for regiment

and order." He glanced over at Mason. "You two would make quite a pair of martinets."

With this said, a red-faced Riley led Aggie out of the dining room, propelling him toward the door. "Aggie, I told you not to call on me before eleven," she whispered, once they'd gained the front foyer.

"You would make me wait? To visit my best girl?" Aggie scoffed at the very notion. "Besides, I was worried sick about you. It was too quiet last night in my room without that walking Persian carpet of yours snoring away in his corner."

"Aggie! You promised to take rooms elsewhere," she scolded. She lowered her voice. "You know it is too dangerous for you to stay at the theatre. Especially alone."

"Danger," he said, stabbing his hand at the imaginary foe as if he held a silver blade. "I am immune to danger."

"You are not immune to any such thing. Now, please take the room at the Pen and Pig, as we discussed."

"If you insist." He scuffed his boot at the carpet like a small child caught stealing tarts.

"I insist," she told him.

The door to the dining room swung open and Cousin Felicity came out, her head held like a duchess. "Mr. Pettibone, you will be coming by later to check on your dear ward, won't you?" She nodded her head back at the dining room and smiled, as if she were doing an excellent job perpetuating this latest lie to surface in the Ashlin House. She leaned forward and whispered, "I mean, once your practice is complete, you should have plenty of time to take tea with us, say half past four?" She held out her hand to him.

Aggie, the eager gallant, stepped forward. "I would be honored to—*oof*," he gasped, as Riley wedged her elbow into his stomach and stepped between him and his unwitting victim.

"I'm afraid, Cousin Felicity," Riley told the lady, "Aggie will be unable to stay for tea, as he has theatre responsibilities that will keep him occupied for the entire afternoon." She smiled at her. "Would you mind terribly seeing the girls upstairs for their lessons? You have such a way with them. I know with you in charge, they won't get lost like they did yesterday."

"Oh, certainly," Cousin Felicity said. She leaned around Riley. "Until our next meeting, Agamemnon." She tittered and waved her handkerchief at him, before retreating to the dining room to fetch the girls.

Riley paused for a moment. "What is this great flirtation with the Earl's cousin all about? I tell you, the woman hasn't a crown to her name. She's as poor as the rest of this lot. You'll not be getting any silk robes or specially blended snuff out of her."

Aggie tapped his nose. "This is never wrong. If it smells money, then she's got a king's ransom hidden somewhere. And if she hasn't, then I'm not a direct descendant of . . ."

"Kings and queens," she said, repeating his favorite line about his alleged noble heritage. "Yes, I know. And you aren't, and she hasn't got any."

He shook his head. "I've never been wrong, not when it comes to money. And I am just the man to help the dear lady find her lost riches and spend them."

"You mean cheat her out of them."

"Cheat? Riley, you wound me. I fear my heart is broken."

"You have no heart, you old fraud. The only reason you like women such as Cousin Felicity is that they are easier to part from their money than your usual paramours."

"Not always," he said, patting his breast pocket where she knew he always kept a deck of cards.

"Oh, and speaking of that, no more piquet," she told him. "One of these days it is going to be your downfall."

He grinned, hardly the penitent reaction she wanted. "Shot in the act, perhaps," he suggested. "Pistols at dawn. I've always wanted to do a dueling scene."

"Yes, I'm sure you have, but when gentlemen duel in the park they use real pistols, which fire rather fatal lead bullets."

He frowned. "How vulgar. Someone might get hurt."

It was her turn to shake her head. "That is why I don't want you playing any more card games, you wretched cheat."

"Tsk, tsk. You are a scold this morning. I can see the rarified air of Ashlin Square hasn't done anything to improve your sense of fun." He caught her chin with his fingers and turned her face so he could study her. "There is something different about you, though. Give me a minute and I'll have it."

Riley blanched. If her night in the library with Mason remained so evident on her face, she had no doubts why—every moment seemed emblazoned in her memory.

She'd lain awake for hours recounting every detail and trying to tell herself she wasn't listening for his footsteps. She'd retraced how he'd looked at her, every nuance of his voice, the touch of his lips to hers. And then this morning, she'd glanced half a dozen times in his direction, trying to see some hint, some idea that last night hadn't been an "aberration," yet he was back to business as usual, as if nothing had happened.

Oh, a pox and bother on the man! If that was what he wanted, then that was just fine with her.

Kissing the Earl, indeed! What had she been thinking?

Much to her relief, before Aggie could weasel the details out of her, Belton arrived.

"Belton!" She rushed over to the stony-faced butler, who looked as if he'd like nothing more than to pitch them both out on the streets. "Could you please show Mr. Pettibone up to the ballroom? We will be practicing up there later this morning."

Belton peered down his nose at Aggie.

Always irrepressible, Aggie accepted Belton's less than favorable scrutiny with his most winning smile. "Does he bite?" he asked her.

"Not unless provoked," she told him.

"Might be fun to find out what that would take." Aggie winked at Belton. "Never mind, Button, I'll find the ballroom myself."

Belton sputtered and choked as if he was going to have apoplexy. "That man is . . ."

"Incorrigible." Riley thumped the mortified butler on the back. "There, there, Belton. Everyone grows to love Aggie. Even you one day."

"A cold one it will be indeed, Madame. A very cold one," he finally managed to say.

Having washed her hands of one problem, she started back toward the dining room when her next one, Lord Delander, came hurrying out, nearly colliding with her.

He glanced around the foyer and then out the window. "Oh, dash it! I'd hoped to catch your guardian."

Mason was close on the Viscount's heels. From behind Del he frantically shook his head, mouthing an emphatic "No!"

Riley certainly didn't need to be told that.

Catching Lord Delander by the arm, Riley anchored the Viscount in place. "He was rather late for an appointment, my lord, so he took off at an amazing clip. Surely you wouldn't want to hold him up any further?"

"No, I can't say that would be polite," the man said, his gaze still scanning the street outside. "Perhaps you can give me the direction to where he is staying so I may call on him there."

She shook her head. "I'm afraid he didn't say. Perhaps next time he is in town. I will pass your regards on to him."

"I thought to give him more than my regards. I meant to speak of him of my suit."

"What suit?" she asked, hoping her question sounded both demure and sincere.

"For your hand." Del grinned at her. "You are an admirable girl to be so shy and reluctant, but I'm sure once I've spoken to your guardian, he'll waste no time convincing you that I am the better man." He shook a significant look over his shoulder at Mason. "Mr. Pettibone seems a right sensible fellow. Good taste in fashion as well. Such a dramatic air to him. When next you see him, could you also get the name of his tailor?"

"I'm sure that can be arranged," Riley demurred, wondering what Lord Delander would think of Jane Gunn, their one-armed seamstress.

"Brilliant!" he said. "Now, Mason muttered something about lessons you must conduct this morning, so afterward I insist you accompany me on a ride in the park in my new carriage."

"I hardly see how that is possible," Riley told him. "I haven't the time."

Lord Delander remained undaunted. "Perhaps I can help with these lessons—say as a potential suitor for the girls to practice their wiles on."

"That would be so kind of you, Lord Delander," Beatrice said in a soft feminine voice that left everyone staring at her.

"See? I have one vote already," Lord Delander said, glancing over at the flushed Beatrice as if he didn't recognize her.

Even Riley was taken aback, but she recovered quickly.

So it was true. Beatrice was in love with the Viscount. Now if she could just move the young man's affections in that direction . . .

"You're still here, Lord Delander?" Cousin Felicity asked, as she herded her charges through the crowded foyer. "Off with you, so we can start our day." She waved to the girls, who trailed after her like convicts on their way to Newgate. As she passed by, Beatrice pushed a deliberate wedge between Lord Delander and Riley.

Much to her chagrin, Riley found herself crowded up against Mason. He put his hand on her shoulder to steady her and his touch burned through her daygown.

Her back and legs pressed into his, and they molded together as they had last night, but this time in front of the entire household.

Her cheeks must be flaming, she thought, for her entire body seemed heated.

The moment the girls passed, she stepped out of his shadow. "Excuse me," she murmured.

"Quite all right," he replied just as quietly.

She dared a glance over her shoulder to see if their shared touch had ruffled his composure as it had hers. But much to her chagrin, he stood stoically behind her, his features revealing nothing but that of a hint of impatience behind his scholarly spectacles. Nowhere in sight was the devil-may-care rake who'd so audaciously taken her into his arms and kissed her senseless.

Riley ground her teeth together. What was she becoming when the merest touch from this man turned her into a puddle of distraction?

"Well dash it," Lord Delander complained, as Mason showed him toward the door. "I won't be deterred from my quest, Miss Riley. I shall rescue you from this prison."

As Belton closed the door behind the persistent Viscount, Riley started to dart up the stairs behind the girls.

"Madame," Mason called out. "If I could have but a moment of your time."

Madame. Riley cringed. So they were back to that . . .

Steeling herself for another lecture on circumstances that were hardly her fault, she turned around on the stairs and marched back to the last step before the foyer.

As the pair argued about the problems presented by Del, Cousin Felicity and Aggie stood overhead on the balcony.

"They make a lovely couple," Cousin Felicity mused.

"Sound like a pair of old married people down there," Aggie said with a shudder. "I fear your cousin and my dear girl are more alike than either of them would care to admit."

"I just hope they will figure it out before it is too late."

Chapter 11

"**O**h, Mason," Cousin Felicity wailed as she burst into his study. "I had nothing to do with this! Nothing!"

The total of the long column of numbers he had almost finished tallying slipped away, fleeing his mind as if frightened away by Cousin Felicity's histrionics.

He buried his face in his hands and shook his head. This was what he got for thinking he could take control of his life.

"Oh, Mason," she wailed. "This is a disaster."

He sighed. Now what?

Cousin Felicity rushed to his side, handkerchief in hand. "What could I do?" she whispered. She glanced at the door, her fingers plucking at the linen square. "*She* came to call. I couldn't have Belton send *her* away—especially since she came with *him*, and now what are we to do with *them*?"

Mason was afraid to ask. "Who came, Cousin?"

"Lord Ashlin," an imperious voice called from the foyer below. "Where are your manners? One does not keep a lady of my advanced age idling about one's foyer like some tradesman."

Mason cringed at each strident note.

Cousin Felicity had been right to act as if the French were landing. For if the French rabble ever dared cross the Channel and storm the British shores, England had one thing not even they would dare cross.

Lady Delander.

"What is that dreadful noise?" Lady Delander complained, looking up at the ceiling as if the very plaster offended her.

"Dancing lessons," Mason said, offering the most plausible answer to cover for the rehearsal taking place in the ballroom overhead. "The girls are practicing for their upcoming Season."

"What are they wearing?" she asked, frowning overhead. "Clogs?"

Mason laughed for a few seconds, but when no one else joined in, he stopped, wondering how his day could get any worse.

Not only was he entertaining Lady Delander, but also her brother, the Duke of Everton—while abovestairs the entire house shook with what he assumed was the pirate battle from the third act.

Mason had tried his best to steer his guests to Cousin Felicity's parlor, which was on the other side of the house and as far from the Queen's Gate players as he could get them without entertaining them in the cellar, but Del's mother had been adamant about being taken to the best room in the house.

"Besides," Lady Delander had said, as she'd led the way to the Green Salon, "I always envied your mother this room. It has such a lovely view of her garden."

Once everyone had been ensconced in the salon, Cousin Felicity had ordered refreshments brought around, while

Mason sent Belton to notify "Cousin Riley" of their visitors.

Upstairs the racket continued unabated, as several large claps of homemade thunder reverberated through the ceiling.

The Dowager jumped in her seat. "Gracious heavens! What heathen ritual are they dancing up there?"

Mason glanced at Cousin Felicity, who suggested, "Perhaps the pianoforte is out of tune."

"Best you see that instrument repaired, my lord," Lady Delander said. "Those girls will be deaf before the week is out. I say that instrument should be silenced immediately."

As if in answer to Lady Delander's edict, the ballroom stilled, the rehearsal coming to a sudden halt.

Mason breathed a sigh of relief. Obviously Belton had reached Riley and informed her of the impending disaster they were facing.

"There was quite a parade of unusual people through the Square and into your house this morning, Lord Ashlin," Lady Delander commented.

"We're having some work done around the house," Mason replied.

"Rather odd workers," she sniffed. "It looked like a veritable circus."

"We've also retained some tutors for the girls," Cousin Felicity filled in when Lady Delander continued to look suspicious. "The fashions of these French dancing masters." Cousin Felicity rolled her gaze upwards as if she didn't know what the world was coming to.

"Hmm," Lady Delander mused, eyeing them both carefully before she said, "Wherever is this cousin of yours, Lord Ashlin? When I was a young girl, I would never have been so rude as to keep callers waiting for hours on end."

Mason forced a smile on his face. "I can't imagine what is delaying her."

"You said she would be expecting me," Lady Delander directed this complaint at her son, whose lovesick gaze remained fixed on the doorway. "I am unused to waiting for anyone."

"Now Josephine," the Duke said to his sister. "Leave off on the poor girl. She may be nervous about meeting you."

Lady Delander straightened. "Nervous about meeting *me*? Ridiculous! Whatever has the girl to worry about?"

"Being eaten alive," Mason muttered under his breath.

"Mother," Del said, "I am sure Riley wants to make the best impression possible. After all, you'll be her mother-in-law."

"We'll see about that!" the old girl snapped. "Lord Ashlin, my brother and I were trying to figure this out yesterday, and I found it most vexing. However is this young lady related to you?"

"Uh, she's . . . well, it's . . . it's complicated," he said. He momentarily dashed around his family tree trying to find a logical branch from which to pluck Riley and one with which the Dowager might not be familiar. "Do you recall my grandfather's youngest brother?"

"Henry?" she asked. "That scamp. Ran off with Lord Middlewood's daughter. A poor match if ever there was one. But you can't tell me this Riley is related through that line—your great uncle and his wife had only daughters, and they never married. Inherited their looks and temperament from those uppity Middlewoods." The lady nodded, as if that was enough said about that unfortunate connection.

"Did I say youngest brother?" Mason corrected, cursing

the Dowager for her steel-trap memory and intimate knowledge of the *ton*. "I meant next-to-youngest brother."

"Who, John?" The Dowager smiled. "Now there was a dashing man. I remember seeing him once at a ball in his regimentals. A major or a lieutenant-colonel? Do ycu remember him, George?"

"Barely," the Duke replied. "Went overseas. Don't think he ever came home."

Mason sighed with relief. "Yes, that's right. He never came home. Riley is descended from Major St. Clair's line."

The Dowager's eyes narrowed, like those of a ferret after a rat. "Indeed. Most peculiar indeed that no one knew of her until now."

Much to Mason's fear, Cousin Felicity started filling in the holes in his newly invented family history. "Major St. Clair died quite tragically."

Lady Delander turned her skeptical gaze on Cousin Felicity.

"Yes, quite tragic," his cousin continued in a nervous rush. Then, to his horror, she launched into a long dissertation about their far-flung cousins, complete with tales of snakebite, lost babies, and feats of heroism not even Shakespeare would have dared pen.

"Now this is where I can't go on," Cousin Felicity was saying, tears beginning to stream down her cheeks.

Mason prayed she wouldn't.

She did.

"When I think of what happened next, it wrenches my heart so." Her hands clutched over her breast, her gaze heavenward, Cousin Felicity looked like Mrs. Siddons ready for a dramatic demise. She'd obviously been taking more than just social lessons from Riley. "Oh, the tragedy of it."

"What happened?" The Dowager snapped.

"The St. Clair curse!" Cousin Felicity declared. "The same one which took my dearest Freddie and Caro—also sent the dreadful fever that claimed our dearest Riley's mother and father when she was just a babe."

"The St. Clair curse, indeed!" the Dowager scoffed. "I never heard such nonsense."

Mason had to agree—but if there was one, he wished it would take him right there and then so he didn't have to witness another moment of Cousin Felicity's theatrics.

The show, however, was just beginning. Cousin Felicity had the audacity to look completely affronted at the Dowager's mockery. "Can you explain Freddie and Caro's unfortunate deaths?" she demanded. "The untimely demise of Riley's parents *and* her grandparents?"

Well, the Dowager couldn't, and her open mouth clapped shut with a decided snap.

"When I think of that poor motherless girl—" Cousin Felicity's bottom lip quivered. "Being raised by those bloodthirsty natives and not knowing she had any family, I just weep."

Mason wanted to as well. He just hoped the rest of the room realized Cousin Felicity's bloodthirsty natives would never have come from the Indian subcontinent.

Cousin Felicity obviously didn't know or care, for she was sniffing and sobbing as if the entire family was about to fall prey to this mythical hex.

"There, there," Mason told her, reaching over and patting her hand. "Our newfound cousin is quite safe and sound now. You needn't continue like this."

Please don't continue, he silently begged.

"She's a blessing to our family," Cousin Felicity told the Dowager between exaggerated sniffs.

Del rushed to confirm Cousin Felicity's convictions. "An angel to behold," he began. "From the first moment I saw her, I knew—"

"—Oh, enough, Allister," his mother snapped. "You've been nattering on about this girl so that I expect her to be able to walk across the Thames, what with all her heavenly merits and blessed virtues. Though I must say, promptness is one asset that seems to have passed her by." The irritation and impatience in the Dowager's voice rose with each word.

As Mason was about to try and make further amends, the doors to the salon swung open and in walked Riley.

Not just Riley—but Riley of the East. The lost daughter of the St. Clairs. He could almost hear the Delhi snake charmers playing their flutes as she entered the room.

Though she looked English enough in her simple yellow muslin, she'd draped over her shoulders a shawl woven in the Eastern style. Her magnificent hair, which last night had tumbled down over his fingers, tempting him to undress her further, was now for the most part, covered with a modest white turban, from which dangled what appeared to be a small ruby.

Beneath the hem of her gown peeked a pair of Oriental slippers the likes of which no one had probably ever dared wear in front of the Dowager.

"Cousin," she said softly to Mason, making a pretty curtsey, and then a salaam to their guests, just as Hashim might have. "My deepest apologies to you and your guests for my delay. I'm afraid I was quite unfit to appear before such distinguished company and had to make the *appropriate* changes." She blushed and hung her head with demure shame.

"That is quite all right," Mason told her, wondering at

this transformation that left her looking exactly like the waif in Cousin Felicity's tale.

Cousin Felicity's unlikely tale.

Then he glanced over at the family's newest bard and caught her winking at Riley, who in turn inclined her head so slightly the movement was discernible only to her partner-in-crime.

Mason did a double-take at his zany cousin and equally troublesome *faux* cousin.

The two of them had cooked up this entire script.

Then as if on cue, Riley turned to Belton and held out her hand.

The poor aggrieved butler sighed, then produced a small bouquet of flowers.

Riley took them up as if they were gilt, instead of the poor scroungings they looked to be and carried them over to the Dowager.

"Part of the reason I am late is that I was trying to finish these," she said, holding out the flowers to the Dowager. "Cousin Felicity confided that you and Lord Ashlin's mother shared a love of flowers." She fluttered her hand at the window which gave way to the tangled mess that was once the Ashlin garden. "I thought you might appreciate a small remembrance of the blossoms she tended. I believe these roses are quite rare."

As she held out her offering, Mason saw the hand holding it was bandaged.

So apparently had the Dowager. "What is wrong with your hand?"

"Nothing," Riley said, hiding it behind her back.

"What have you done to yourself?" This time, not waiting for an answer, Lady Delander reached out and caught Riley's arm, pulling it forward and peering down at the wrapping covering her fingers.

Riley sighed. "I fear I am unused to English gardens," she told the Dowager. "I got caught by the thorns while I was trying to pick your flowers."

"Wicked patch of them out there," Del said, rubbing his shoulder where he had fallen the day before.

The Dowager stared down at the roses and other pickings in the bouquet. "Well, I never," she announced, as she looked from Riley's hand to the collection of roses beneath her imperious nose.

Mason and everyone else watched the formidable matron, awaiting her verdict.

"Well, I've never been so touched." She sniffed a couple of times and then, much to Mason's amazement, a flurry of tears fell down the stony cheeks of the dragon of Ashlin Square.

Mason wouldn't have believed the sight if he hadn't witnessed it first hand. Riley had made another conquest. He was beginning to think there wasn't a heart in London she couldn't win.

Just so long as it wasn't his.

Cousin Felicity fished out another handkerchief and handed it to the lady. "Our Riley is such a thoughtful, kind girl. And so brave in her distress."

Lady Delander nodded as if she didn't trust herself to respond.

"Mother, are you all right?" Del asked.

"Of course I am," she snapped at him, shoving the thorny bouquet into his arms and turning toward Riley, her waspish features immediately softening. "Roses. You picked me a bouquet of roses. You sweet child." Lady Delander glanced back at Del and frowned. "Not even my own son is capable of such kindness."

"I'm just so sorry I was unable to complete my task,"

Riley said, heaping on the regret and adding a sorrowful expression to her downcast features. "There are ever so many lovely blooms out there, but after my mishap, I grew too timid to attempt to reach them."

"I would only be too happy to—" Del began to say, rising to his feet and reaching out to take Riley's hand.

"Oh, do shut up, Allister," Lady Delander told him, slapping away his outstretched hand. "Go sit over there. Next to Lord Ashlin," she bade him, as if he were a lad of six, instead of twenty-and-six. "And you," she said to Riley, "shall sit next to me."

Mason watched, wondering if he wasn't dreaming, as Lady Delander, the arbiter of fashion and manners, settled the most notorious woman in London down next to her and began fawning over her as if she were a Princess Royal.

"Now we must get you vouchers, my dear," Lady Delander began. "And invitations to the right social events. Lord Ashlin, whatever were you thinking last night in not bringing your cousin to Mrs. Evans's musicale?"

"Well, I . . . I just didn't think she . . ." he began.

The Dowager shook her finger at him. "Oh, don't bother with your excuses. I know exactly what you were about last night and why you came alone." She turned to Riley. "Men! When you are my age, you'll know all their tricks." The Dowager snorted. "Look at Lord Ashlin, sitting over there playing quite the innocent, when he spent the entire evening wooing Miss Pindar."

Miss Pindar? Riley glanced over at Mason, trying to buoy the sinking feeling in her heart.

Why should she care if he'd spent his evening looking for a wife? He'd made his intentions to enter the Marriage Mart very clear.

So why had he lied to her and told her differently? Not that it really mattered to her.

Oh, but it did, much to her chagrin.

"You'd best not dally, Lord Ashlin," Lady Delander lectured. "With Miss Pindar's fortune, someone will carry her off to Gretna right under your nose if you don't offer for her immediately."

Mason mumbled something polite, but it wasn't the denial Riley longed to hear. If only he'd tell the nosy old hen he had no desire to wed the impossibly rich and probably beautiful Miss Pindar.

"Though I must admit," Lady Delander said, continuing her speech as if it were being delivered to the House of Lords, "I usually don't condone marrying into the merchant class—it's unseemly. But in Miss Pindar's case, I would make an exception."

Riley wondered what virtues the estimable Miss Pindar possessed to make even Lady Delander drop her rigid standards.

"Besides," Lady Delander was saying, "I think you make a handsome couple. Almost as handsome a couple as Allister and your dear cousin."

At first Riley was still too irritated over the lady's revelation to register her comment, but then it sank in. Had the lady just referred to her and Lord Delander as a couple?

Eh, gads! She and Cousin Felicity's plan had gone far better than they had hoped. They had thought that their story of her being orphaned and raised by Hindu natives might pique the Dowager's interest in her, but exclude her as unfit material for a daughter-in-law.

Obviously the bouquet idea had been too much.

Aggie always said she liked to overplay the second act.

Now she had not only to remain in the woman's good graces, but extricate herself from a marriage she didn't want.

Before she could even come up with an inkling of how to do this, the Dowager started planning Riley's upcoming Season.

"—It is imperative that you meet everyone. The vouchers I'll secure tomorrow, and you'll need to accompany me on my Tuesday and Thursday calls so I can introduce you to all the right hostesses. And don't accept any invitations without my approval."

At this boon, Riley shook her head. "I fear I cannot accept your kindness."

"Whyever not?" the lady snapped, momentarily reverting to her usual crusty self.

"Because I am not here in London for my own cares, but to help my cousins prepare for their Season. I fear I haven't the time for my own *pleasures*."

She hoped Mason knew that comment was meant more for him than for their company.

Miss Pindar, indeed! Well, if he wanted someone to kiss, he could just take his pleasure with his eligible, rich nonpareil.

"Stuff and bother, girl," Lady Delander declared. "I will have my way on this."

Riley smiled and shook her head. "I was raised with the understanding that one repays one's good fortune before seeking one's own happiness. And Lord Ashlin has bestowed upon me a safe haven in these perilous times."

"Utter nonsense," Lady Delander said. She stared at Riley for a moment and then added a "harumph." When Riley shook her head again, the lady's thick frown creased even deeper into her florid face. "Well, you are a determined thing, so we will just see that Lord Ashlin's nieces are presented posthaste." The lady turned to her brother. "George, have your secretary send around a new invitation to your masquerade for Lord Ashlin, and include his nieces and dear cousin here."

Riley drew a quick breath. The Everton masquerade? She'd never hoped to see the girls invited there. Riley knew, from the reports of it that filled the papers every year, it was considered the opening gala to the Season.

The invitations were very select, and a young lady invited to it was assured of being invited everywhere in the weeks to follow.

"We accept your kind invitation," Riley said quickly.

"On the contrary, Cousin," Mason said. "I am afraid we must decline."

"Decline! Are you mad?" the Dowager asked.

For once, Riley agreed with Lady Delander.

"Mason, refusing the Everton masquerade just isn't done," Cousin Felicity told him, smiling at the Duke and nudging Mason with her knee.

"Yes," Riley added. "If the Duke is so kind as to extend invitations at this late date, we would be remiss to refuse."

Mason shook his head. "I am afraid we must."

She knew only too well that stubborn set to his jaw. That same face of stone had been the one that wouldn't listen to her protests of moving out of the theatre. But this time, Riley couldn't see one good reason for Mason's refusal. The Everton masquerade would ensure the girls' success.

Then it hit her: he didn't want *her* there.

He didn't want to be responsible for allowing the notorious Aphrodite to be mixing with the *ton*, or even perhaps rubbing shoulders with his cherished and chaste Miss Pindar.

Her jealousy got the better of her. "Won't Miss Pindar be there, Your Grace?" she asked.

Lord Delander's uncle nodded. "Yes, Miss Pindar and her mother are on the guest list and will most decidedly be there."

Riley smiled as pleasantly as she could muster. If Miss Pindar was going to be there, then so was she.

If Mason intended to marry this woman, then Riley wanted to take her measure—see what the *ton* considered the perfect young lady. She told herself it was research to aid in her lessons for the girls. Yes, just research.

Ignoring Mason's glower, she smiled at the Duke and for a moment Del's uncle's gaze lingered on Riley longer than made her feel comfortable.

Questions, confusion, and then shock flickered in his eyes as he studied her.

But before she could make heads or tails of whether the Duke had recognized her, Riley was distracted by another inquiry from the Dowager.

"How many of them are there?" she asked Riley.

"How many what?" Riley asked.

"Well, sisters. How many girls did Caro and Freddie have?"

"Three," she told her.

"Harumph," the woman snorted, and turned her glare on Mason, as if this vast number of nieces was somehow his doing. "No wonder Caro and that rapscallion brother of yours kept them hidden away at Sanborn Abbey. 'Twould beggar any man to have three girls out in society—let alone considering your own poor finances." She shook her head. "No wonder you're after Miss Pindar's hand."

"I am hardly pursuing Miss Pindar," Mason protested,

though to Riley's ears his efforts sounded half-hearted at best.

"So you say," Lady Delander sniffed.

Once again, Riley found herself in the vexing position of agreeing with the old dragon.

Chapter 12

❦❦❦

"You can't decline the Duke's invitation," Riley said, following doggedly at Mason's heels as he retreated to his study. Now that Lady Delander and her entourage had left, she was free to speak her mind. "Think of what this could mean for the girls!"

He spun around so quickly that she slammed right into his chest—that muscled wall of Ashlin strength Riley had no right to covet—not since Lady Delander had all but spilled the beans over his courtship with Miss Dahlia Pindar.

Still, she couldn't help but put her hands upon his jacket to steady herself. Her fingers retraced the path they'd taken last night and her imagination only too happily recalled where that course had taken them.

She looked up and saw in his eyes a hint of the same fire she'd tasted last night.

"How can you refuse?" she repeated, not sure she was asking the same question.

"I must," he said, not sounding all that convincing. He looked down at her and for a moment she thought he was going to . . .

Gads, couldn't she think of anything but kissing when she was around him?

She pushed off from him and steadied herself, her hands finally coming to rest on her hips. A pox and bother on his distracting hide.

"I am refusing the Duke's invitation because of the girls," he said, his gaze going over her shoulder to the stairwell behind them.

Riley glanced in that direction as well and saw the last flash of muslin as the girls hurried out of sight.

"Come in here," he said, hauling her by the elbow into his study and closing the door behind them. "Don't you see they can't attend?"

She yanked herself free of his grasp. "Not when what you mean to say is that *I* can't attend. Well if my presence is so offensive, then I will decline the Duke's invitation and you take the girls."

He raked his fingers through his hair. "Not want you there? Whatever gave you that foolish notion? I would well imagine that if you went you'd set the entire establishment on their collective ears."

Riley turned a shocked and suspicious gaze on him. Had he just given her a compliment?

Just then he took off his spectacles and began wiping them clean. As he glanced at her, she saw the rake, not the scholar, and wondered which man she preferred.

Both, she realized. Both intrigued her; both mystified her.

"I imagine," he said, "if you worked the same magic on the *ton* as you did today on Lady Delander, you'd steal the heart of every man between the ages of fourteen and ninety-four."

Riley resisted the urge to preen under his high praise. Hadn't she heard such flattering words before from so many others? Yet it tugged at her heart that Mason thought her so beguiling and left her wanting to ask but one question: would that collection of stolen hearts include his?

Setting aside that foolish desire, she redirected their conversation back to the real matter at hand. "At least consider taking the girls," she urged him.

Mason shuddered. "How can I trust that they will behave? Lord help me, they are hellions. Can you say your lessons are helping?"

Lessons? she wanted to ask. What lessons? Lessons with the girls consisted of two hours of them hurling insults at her while she resisted hurling a candlestick back at them. Still the Everton masquerade would ensure their success—and get her off the hook with Mason, if only she could get them to see that as well.

"What if they did behave?" she offered.

"Would you stake your reputation on Bea making it through an evening without consigning something or someone to hell?"

Riley laughed. "I haven't a reputation to worry about."

"Consider yourself lucky in that regard." He glanced at her again, that odd look on his face as if he were puzzling some knotty dilemma. "A reputation can be a hindrance to live by."

She wondered at this odd confession as he strode over to his desk. A mountain of notes covered the top. Riley heard a quiet, desperate sigh slip from him as he eyed the very plain evidence of his financial distress.

"So will you accept?" Riley asked.

He shook his head. "I can't. Just don't tell the girls about the Duke's invitation. I can well imagine the anarchy I'd have in this house if they found out I refused them the perfect entrée into society."

*   *   *

Upstairs in the room directly over their uncle's study, Bea and Maggie strained to get their ears closer to the crack in the floorboards. They'd spent nearly an hour like this in the room next to the salon struggling and waiting to hear Lady Delander make mincemeat of Madame Fontaine.

Much to their chagrin, the lady had been entranced.

How would they ever be rid of their unwanted tutor if she continued to make conquests right and left? Including their uncle.

"What is he saying?" Louisa demanded.

Bea waved her off. "Shut up," she whispered. "I can't hear a thing with you yapping away."

"Then let me listen," she said. Dropping to the floor, Louisa also stuck her ear to the opening in the glistening hardwood. "Sounds like a bunch of gibberish."

"Shhh," Maggie hissed. "He's deciding whether or not we get to go."

All three girls held their breath.

When they heard their uncle's final verdict, they lifted their heads from the floor and stared at each other, eye to eye.

Bea uttered a salty phrase that only went that much further to confirm everything their uncle had just said.

Riley decided a serious attempt at teaching the girls was in order. If she was to get herself out of Mason's control, she needed to see these girls take the Everton masquerade by storm—but she hadn't any idea how to reach the trio of miscreants.

She still thought she'd have better luck dressing up a bunch of badgers and passing them off as the late Earl's daughters.

With Mason out for the afternoon, Riley girded herself for battle. But instead of the usual feisty and impertinent students she'd been expecting, the trio listened listlessly to her discussion on the use of a fan and how to make a stylish entrance.

Running out of ideas, she resorted to reading from the little book Aggie had slipped into her reticule before she'd moved out of the theatre.

"A lady always appears in society," she read aloud, "with a modest demeanor and a calm, serene countenance, leaving all who bear witness to her aspect no doubt that she is a vessel of purity." Riley paused in her recitation and flipped over the book to see who had written this drivel.

A Graceful Distinction, the title proclaimed. By an unnamed "lady of grace and upstanding character."

"Bloody hell, what the devil does that mean?" Bea asked.

For once, Riley found the girl's bellicose outburst a welcome change from the unnerving quiet that had ruled the afternoon.

"It means you might as well consign yourself to a long spinsterhood raising cats in some moldy cottage, dear sister," Louisa purred from her seat in the corner. The little minx went back to paging through her fashion magazine.

"I know what it means," Maggie suggested.

Bea snorted, "As if."

"Yes, Maggie, what does it mean?" Riley urged the girl to answer, hopeful that this uncharacteristic assistance was a sign that one of the sisters perhaps was even listening to her.

"It means Beatrice hasn't a chance of ever becoming Lady Delander." Maggie and Louisa both laughed.

Beatrice, however, flew from her post by the window

and lit into her sister like a sailor in a tavern brawl.

Riley stared open-mouthed at this unbelievable display.

"You take that back, you clumsy little bi—" Bea swore, as she caught Maggie around the neck with her arm and pinned her to the floor.

"Lady Delander, Lady Delander," Maggie chanted unrepentantly, fighting back like a wildcat.

Closing her eyes, Riley counted to ten. Suddenly a life of putting on puppet shows at country fairs and sheep sales for crowds of gaping yokels didn't look so bad after all.

"Do something," Riley ordered Louisa.

The girl set aside her magazine and sighed. Not bothering to rise from her chaise, Louisa spared a glance at her sisters. "Bea, you'd better make sure there is room for two in that cottage of yours." When this didn't do anything but incite the fighting sisters further, Louisa shrugged.

Riley ground her teeth. Standing beside the girls, she stomped her foot. "Stop this," she told them. "Immediately."

"Not until she takes it back," Bea shot back. She continued to shake and rattle her sister.

"You'd better listen to the next Lady Delander," Maggie taunted, elbowing Bea in the stomach.

Riley looked around the room and spotted the large vase of flowers Lord Delander had left for her the day before. Snatching it up, she upended it above Bea and Maggie, sending a shower of water and roses over the pair.

They fell apart, sputtering and cursing.

Well, mostly Bea. "Why, you—"

Riley held the vase at hand. "Don't tempt me, Lady Beatrice. I would be more than happy to dash this over your spoilt, impertinent head."

"You can't call her that," Maggie said, rising to her sister's defense. "How dare you! You aren't even a lady."

The ludicrous irony of Maggie's indignation left Riley speechless. Then all she could do was laugh. Laugh until she sat down to steady herself and wipe the tears from her eyes.

Even Louisa got up from her perch and joined her sisters to stare at their unwanted teacher. "I believe she's gone mad."

Finally Riley got to a point where she could speak again. "Mad? It's a wonder I haven't been carted away, after spending the last few afternoons with you three. Look at you!" She pointed at the large mirror over the fireplace which reflected most of the room. "Take a good look and tell me if you can see any ladies in there." She got up and stood behind them. "And don't count Cousin Felicity."

The girls glowered back at her.

"Exactly my point. How old are you, Bea? Twenty, I'd guess. And how old will the other girls be for their first Season?"

Bea's jaw worked back and forth. "Sixteen," she finally mumbled.

"Yes, sixteen." Riley handed her and Maggie towels from the tea tray. "And how have you spent the past four years improving yourself so as to stand out amongst them? Very ineffectively, as evidenced by this vulgar brawl. Personally, I doubt your skill in cursing and bear baiting will get you into Almack's.

"What are you going to do when your uncle gets married?" she asked them, realizing she finally had their attention. "Even now he is looking for a bride. How happy do you think the new mistress of this house is going to be at having you three underfoot, caterwauling and bickering all the time?"

"But this is our home," Maggie protested.

"It won't be for long," Riley told her.

"She's right," Cousin Felicity said, rising from her chair and coming to their side. "Gracious sakes, there's no guarantee the next Lady Ashlin will be as generous." The lady pulled out her handkerchief and dabbed her eyes. "If it hadn't been for your grandmother taking me in, I don't know where I would have gone."

"But Uncle would never—" Louisa started to say.

"You don't know that," Cousin Felicity told her. "It may not be his decision. When a man marries, the house becomes his wife's domain. And consider this: your uncle will not be making the love match your parents shared. He must wed for money, and that could bring any kind of lady into our midst."

Maggie gulped. "Oh, my. Dahlia and her mother."

Bea flopped down on the sofa. "We're in for it."

"Not necessarily," Riley told them. "While your uncle is out hunting for a bride, you can find husbands. You aren't trapped in this house. Only if you let yourselves be."

Louisa shook her head. "There isn't a chance of that happening. Not now, what with Uncle refusing the Duke's invitation."

"Louisa!" Bea said.

"You know about the masquerade?" Riley asked, circling the trio.

Maggie shuffled her feet. "We might have heard something of it in passing."

Bea punched her tattletale sister in the arm.

Riley sighed, but decided not to pursue the subject of eavesdropping until another time.

"Madame is right," Louisa said. "Look at us. We haven't anything but our mourning that fits—and black is hardly a good color on any of us."

Nodding in agreement, Bea added, "A Season is expensive. That's why we never got ours in the first place." Her sisters turned and looked at her. She shrugged. "I heard Mother and Father discussing it. They had to choose between their pursuits and bringing us out. So they kept us out at Sanborn Abbey."

Riley glanced over at Cousin Felicity, who nodded silently at this comment.

"So I suppose it is useless even to bother," Maggie said, the bitterness in her young voice piercing Riley's heart.

"I hardly think so," Riley told them. "Look at me. I've been proposed to hundreds of times, by many eligible and likely young men. I'm hardly the perfect prospect for a bride, so there is hope for anyone if I can interest a man."

"Yes, that is all well and good, but we can hardly go out in these," Bea said, holding out her waterlogged skirt. The hemline rose above her ankles and it appeared to have been mended—and badly, at that—several times. "This was my best dress. Without clothes, I haven't a chance of catching Del's—" Bea's mouth snapped shut for a moment. "Anyone's attention," she finished hastily.

Riley smiled and took her by the hand. Really, when she wasn't swearing and cursing, Beatrice had a nice voice, as well as a pretty smile. Perhaps there was hope for her yet.

Bea let out a long sigh. "Oh, go ahead. You can laugh at me, just like Louisa and Maggie. I suppose I deserve it. Cousin Felicity always says we will reap what we sow. Well, you can say I'm harvesting a bumper crop." She turned her back to Riley.

"Bea, I have no plans of laughing at you." And while

the chances of Beatrice, with her outrageous manners and her rather colorful choice of language, catching the Viscount's eye might be slim, maybe the girl still had a chance.

Bea swung around and demanded, "Why didn't you accept his offer to go for a ride in the park?"

"Because I didn't want to go," Riley told her.

Bea's eyes narrowed. "Why not? You like him, don't you? Is that it—you're playing hard to get like you were telling us yesterday? Being unattainable and distant, so he tries harder to win your affections?"

Riley didn't know what stunned her more, Bea's vehemence, or the fact that obviously through all her sullen faces and bored airs, she'd actually been listening to Riley's lessons. "As unlikely as you may find it, Lord Delander won't marry me, as I have no intention of accepting his proposal."

At this, Bea cocked her head. "You don't?"

"No," Riley said. "I don't love him."

The girl appeared to be considering the idea, though her expression still said she couldn't fathom the idea of anyone not being in love with the Viscount. Slowly she asked, "If you don't love him, do you think he could love someone else?"

Riley smiled, trying to sound as if she believed her words. "Yes, I think Lord Delander's heart could be swayed in the right direction—with a little work."

With a lot of work and a miracle, she thought.

Beatrice obviously had come to the same conclusion. "You can say that because you're an actress. You can be anyone you want to be, play any role. I'm just me and I'll never be anyone else."

You can be anyone you want to be, play any role . . .

Riley sat back in her seat, Bea's words echoing through

her thoughts. She knew she was gaping at the girl and looked probably as foolish as she felt.

Play any role . . .

She'd been trying to teach the girls to be something she knew nothing about, when in actuality she should be teaching what she did know more than plenty about—acting.

Riley bounded to her feet. "Beatrice, you are a genius." She towed her up from the sofa and strode into the middle of the room.

"She might be a genius, but she can't go out in these clothes," Louisa complained, holding out her own black skirt. "We look like ravens!"

"Leave the clothes to me," Riley said, something Mason had said last night, giving root to another idea.

Louisa muttered something back, what Riley didn't hear, but obviously Beatrice had, for she slugged her sister in the arm.

"Ouch," Louisa complained, rubbing her arm. "What was that for?"

"Oh, hold your tongue," Beatrice told her.

Without, Riley noted, the addition of any colorful phrases.

"I think it is time we tried a different direction with our lessons." With the rapt attention of all eyes on her, Riley announced, "I think it is time I shared with you my Eastern secrets."

Riley, Cousin Felicity, and the St. Clair sisters spent the rest of the afternoon plotting their new roles—ones that would take the *ton* by storm.

As it neared half past four, Cousin Felicity went downstairs to see to their tea, while Riley and the girls finished up their "lessons."

"Don't worry about your uncle or your costumes," Riley told them. "Leave that all up to me."

As the clock struck the appointed hour, they went downstairs. At the bottom of the steps, Beatrice drew to a stop. Riley knew why. A conversation from the parlor rose through the usually quiet house.

"My dearest Felicity," an all too familiar voice said, charm rolling off every word. "I spent the day in anxious anticipation of returning to the shadow of your lovely countenance. It is a blessing to find you in such fine spirits."

Aggie! She should have known the old scalawag wouldn't stay away. Not when he suspected there was ready money at hand.

"Mr. Pettibone is back," Beatrice said, hurrying toward the room.

"I wonder if he won any more money at piquet," Maggie said. "I would love lemon tarts for tea."

He had better not have spent the afternoon playing cards, Riley thought.

"Agamemnon," Cousin Felicity said through a tittering veil of giggles. "You make me feel like a schoolgirl again."

"A time not that long ago, one would think to gaze upon your flawless face," he replied.

Riley set her jaw. She wondered what Cousin Felicity would think of her flattering suitor when she heard him uttering the exact same line in the play they were currently practicing.

Resolved to put an end to this fruitless flirtation once and for all, she followed the girls into the parlor, where Aggie was ensconced on the settee like a prince, with Cousin Felicity practically in his lap. He had her hand to his lips and was cooing another line from *The Envious Moon* about her eyes and the stars.

Riley made a note to herself to cut that scene from Act Three immediately. She'd never be able to listen to it again without having this nightmare image of Aggie and Cousin Felicity in her mind.

"Aggie!" Riley said. "What are you doing here?"

"I came for tea, dear girl," he told her. "Don't you remember? Your kind hostess invited me."

She took a deep breath. "And I recall uninviting you."

Aggie turned to Cousin Felicity. "You must forgive my dear ward. As a foundling, she missed the gentle ministrations of a mother, and I have been all she's had to guide her in the ways of society."

Maggie's eyes grew wide. "Riley, you were a foundling?"

Riley flinched.

"Who was a foundling?" Mason asked from behind her.

Riley didn't dare turn around. His words caressed her skin as if he were touching her again. How tragic had she become when even the sound of his voice made her blush?

"Riley was," Louisa told him. The girl caught her hand and tugged her down onto the sofa next to her. "Where did they find you? Do you have any idea who your parents are? You could be royalty and not even know it." The wide-eyed girl sat back, staring at Riley with new respect.

"Louisa," Mason said. "That is quite enough. As far as anyone is concerned, Riley is a distant relation who lost her parents at a young age."

"Actually, Louisa isn't too far from the truth," Aggie told them, oblivious to her embarrassment. "For Riley is the daughter of—"

"Aggie!" Riley jumped to her feet. "That is quite

enough." Even as she made this outburst, Riley realized she'd only made the situation worse.

Now every face in the room held a curious gaze focused directly at her. They all wanted Aggie's revelation finished.

And it was the last thing she wanted.

Lord Ashlin turned and stared at her. But if she expected disappointment or condemnation, it didn't show on his face. Instead, he smiled in encouragement. "If only we could all escape the sins of the father."

"Exactly!" Aggie said. "I've told her time and again, she is not to blame for her mother selling her."

"She sold you?" Maggie's lip trembled. "Oh, Riley, how sad."

Cousin Felicity obviously agreed for she was already swiping at tears. "The story sounds like one of your plays," she said between sniffs. "The lost heiress found by a prince and brought home in triumph."

Aggie snapped his fingers. "I have told her the same thing time and again," he said. "She tries to deny it, but every play she writes tells her tragic story."

"You write your plays?" This question came from Beatrice.

"Yes," Riley told her, happy for the change of subject. "I write a new one for the spring and fall seasons."

"Oh, Riley," Louisa said. "What if your mother saw your play and realized the error of her ways? I can see it now—she'd come backstage, her eyes filled with tears, pleading with you to forgive her for making such a terrible mistake."

As much as she denied it to Aggie and anyone else who pointed out the common theme to her plays, she had secretly hoped that one day the woman who'd given her life would see the error of her ways and return to apologize

220   ELIZABETH BOYLE

and make amends for all the pain and lost years.

It was the last fantasy of her childhood—a lonely time spent in poverty and doubt . . . and dreams.

Mason pulled at his chin. "Do you know who your parents are?"

Riley shook her head. "All I know is that my mother was an English lady, but her family name, I never knew. To me, she was just 'mama.' "

The memories of that fleeting time came rushing forward.

Mama practicing her lines for the theatre. Playing with the laces and rich fabrics of her costumes. Flowers from admirers filling their small apartment with their rich scents.

They were happy times, blissful images, yet they were ever tarnished by her final memory of her mother.

Of the beautiful lady bidding her good-bye one frosty fall morning, before she boarded a carriage and left Riley behind . . . forever.

"You don't know anything else?" he asked. "Nothing about where she came from or a name that could give a clue as to her identity."

Riley looked away. "No. I was only five when she left."

Mason got up. "That's something. Your age. What year were you born?"

"What has that got to do with anything?" Riley asked.

"Well, to find her. To find your family. Aren't you the least bit curious?"

"No!" she lied. "Why would I care about them? They obviously didn't want me."

"Tell him," Aggie urged her. "You've spent the last seven years doing everything but placing an advertisement in the *Times* trying to find her. Let him help you."

"No," she repeated. What did it matter if they found out she was the illegitimate daughter of the King himself—the fact remained she'd been born on the wrong side of the blanket and would never be . . . good enough to be considered a suitable bride.

"But what if—" Beatrice started to say.

"Leave off," Mason told her. "If Riley doesn't want to find her family, that is her choice, and we must respect her privacy."

"But—" Louisa added, until her uncle turned a swift glance in her direction. Louisa closed her open mouth and sighed.

The room filled with an uneasy silence.

There, her sad story had put everyone in a downcast mood, Riley thought. And it had all started with Aggie and his indiscriminate tongue.

The unrepentant devil didn't seem to notice. "Didn't you say something about having tea?" he asked Cousin Felicity.

"Oh, how terrible of me to forget," she said. She started to rise to go retrieve the tray Belton had left on the small sideboard, but Aggie raised his hand to stop her.

"My fair Felicity, I couldn't have you lower yourself to such a task. Please allow me."

Riley took a page from Beatrice and snorted. This was a first. She'd never seen Aggie lift a finger to serve anything, unless it was to lift someone's wallet or a pilfered playing card.

Her partner sighed dramatically. "You must excuse my ward. She has always been a challenge."

"I am not your ward," Riley told him, as he crossed the room to fetch the tea service.

He shook his head. "Such are the trials of the generous of spirit."

Out in the hall the bell at the door jangled, and Riley glanced over at Mason, who had the same look of alarm. "Lord Delander?" she whispered.

Mason shook his head. "No. There is a horse auction this afternoon, and he was determined to obtain a pair of bays that he's had his eye on. I can't imagine who it is."

As Riley considered the worst option—Lady Delander making another surprise call—Bea solved the mystery quite handily.

"Cousin Felicity," the girl whispered. "Are you forgetting what day it is?"

"What do I care what day it is," she said, waving her handkerchief at Bea, her adoring gaze fixed on Aggie.

"But Cousin, it is Thursday," Maggie said, jerking her thumb at the clock. "And it is half past four."

Riley watched Mason's eyes grow wide, and then a smug smile spread across his face. "Oh, this ought to be interesting," he muttered.

Riley leaned toward him. "What is going to be interesting?"

"It's Thursday," he said, as if Riley should know the significance of the day.

"And?" Riley asked.

Mason leaned over and whispered, "On Thursdays, Lord Chilton always comes for tea."

Riley smiled. Perhaps there was justice in the world.

The arrival of Lord Chilton may provide Aggie the chance to realize his fondest wish. Before the day was out, her partner may just find himself in the duel he'd always longed for.

And Riley felt like offering her services as second to see the deed done correctly.

Second to Lord Chilton, that is.

*   *   *

If Mason thought that his usual afternoon tea would return some semblance of order to his house, he should have known by now that time spent in Riley's company was anything but conducive to routine.

Even in this common enough setting, she stirred his heart, brightening the salon with her smile and shimmering green eyes.

And it wasn't just her looks which gave him pause anymore—it was the lady herself. While Mason couldn't shake his dismay at the notion of a five-year-old Riley being sold like a piece of chattel, he found himself even more amazed and filled with awestruck admiration for the woman who'd risen above her circumstances with raw determination to become so filled with grace and poise.

Those were lessons, Mason realized, they could all gain from her.

How could he have ever considered her an unfit companion to his nieces?

Even her rapscallion partner, Mr. Pettibone, added a measure of levity that he realized now had been missing from their lives for far too long. And now it would be interesting to see if Lord Chilton found Aggie's presence in their midst as amusing.

"You've started without me, Lady Felicity," Lord Chilton said, an indignant flush rising on his cheeks. The man blustered into the room and took his place on the sofa next to Cousin Felicity, as he had done every Thursday for more years than Mason could recall.

Despite the baron's reluctance toward marriage, Mason still found Lord Chilton to be a decent and generally kind fellow. And most importantly, Mason knew Cousin Felicity was deeply fond of him.

But today the normally placid man looked about ready to burst with agitation.

"Whatever is wrong, my lord?" Cousin Felicity asked. Even after all these years, the pair maintained a formality that bordered on quaint.

"I was robbed!" Lord Chilton announced.

"Robbed? Oh my!" Cousin Felicity said. "Were you hurt?"

"Was it a highwayman?" Louisa asked.

"Or a real devil of a cove?" Bea grinned at the very idea.

Lord Chilton held up his hands. "No, no, no," he told them. "I am fine. But my adversary was a rare bounder, I tell you. I've spent the day trying to find this cheating fellow and set things right."

"What happened?" Mason asked, hoping Chilton would get to the point.

"I was cheated out of a fortune, I tell you," the Baron repeated. "It happened last night while I was playing piquet. I was tricked by some aging popinjay masquerading as a gentleman."

He heard Riley cough, and when he glanced over, she looked like she was bracing herself for a disaster.

At this opportune moment, Mr. Pettibone chose to turn around from the tea service and announce, "Piquet? Did someone say piquet?"

Lord Chilton's face immediately went from its usually florid color to a deep shade of red that suggested the man was about to suffer a fit of apoplexy. He jumped to his feet and turned toward Aggie. "*You!* What are *you* doing here?"

"Having tea with my dearest Felicity." With that said, Aggie set the tray down in front of the lady and settled himself back onto the sofa in the spot that had just been vacated by Lord Chilton.

The Baron huffed and sputtered for several seconds before he recovered his voice. "What is the meaning of this ... this ... affront? Someone call the guard. Call Bow Street. Call for the watch." With his finger pointed at Mr. Pettibone's nose, he declared, "This man is a criminal."

"A criminal? How dare you make such an unfounded accusation," Cousin Felicity snapped at her long-time suitor. "Mr. Pettibone is a welcome guest in this house. Now, sit down, my lord, before I call the watch to take you away."

Turning to Mason, Lord Chilton said, "I ask you, sir, as a gentleman to remove this scurrilous pestilence from your house."

Mason looked over at Riley, who sat with her face buried in her hands, as if she wished she were miles away from this scene.

And he'd been the one hoping for a bit of levity in their lives. But this? Before he could form a polite answer, Cousin Felicity launched a mighty defense for her newfound champion.

"Lord Chilton, if you cannot keep a civil tongue in your head, I will ask you to leave." She paused for a moment and then continued. "Mr. Pettibone is a guest in this house, and more important, he is *my* guest. If you do not like the company here, I would suggest you leave." With that, Cousin Felicity folded her arms over her bosom and turned her petite nose up in the air.

"And leave you in the clutches of this ne'er-do-well?" Lord Chilton sputtered. "Certainly not, my good lady."

"A ne'er-do-well?" Mr. Pettibone stepped to the forefront. "Who are you calling a ne'er-do-well? I'll have you know I am the direct descendant of—"

Before Mason could get to his feet, Riley jumped into the fray.

"—Aggie," she interrupted, placing herself between the two combatants. "This is neither the time nor the place to recount your lineage, as fine and noble as it may be." With her hands on her hips, she scolded Felicity's suitors further. "I would remind you both that there are young ladies present and I would be loath to acquaint their innocent minds with a scene that may verge on inappropriate."

Mr. Pettibone let out a great sigh, then straightened his coat. "How right you are, my dear," he said. He turned to Cousin Felicity. "Rather than challenge your allegiance to this . . . this . . . man, my dear lady, I will make my *adieux*." Aggie bowed to her and then to the girls, before he made an exit worthy of his forty years on the stage.

Just then Bea started to cough uncontrollably. Waving off Cousin Felicity's offer of tea, she rose from her seat, sputtering out an "Excuse me" as she hurried out of the room.

With the door closed behind her, Bea hustled after their departing guest. "Mr. Pettibone," she whispered. "Mr. Pettibone."

Her quarry turned around in the empty foyer. When he spotted her, he made an elaborate bow. "Lady Beatrice."

She rushed to his side. "Oh, Mr. Pettibone, is it true? Are you truly a sharpster at piquet?"

"My dear girl, where have you heard such lies, such deceptions, such falsehoods?"

Bea bit her lip. Perhaps she had gone too far this time. "It's just that Lord Chilton never loses at cards, and to have beaten him—well, you must have . . ."

Mr. Pettibone's gaze turned flinty hard and Bea thought for sure she had overstepped her bounds, but just as quickly, a twinkle appeared in those same eyes.

"Lady Beatrice, you are not a woman to mince words, so let us be honest with each other." He lowered his voice. "Will you promise not to say a word to Riley?"

She nodded.

"Good girl. Riley's got a heart made of gold, but she's a stickler about card games." He leaned closer. "If you must have the truth, then here it is: I cheated Lord Chilton out of every farthing I won from him last night and then some."

She knew she should be shocked, but the words were like a magic balm to her heart. "Oh, Mr. Pettibone, that is glorious news."

He laughed a bit and then scratched his head. "Well, that is hardly how most people would describe my rather abominable misdeed, but I am glad you find it so intriguing. Now tell me, why do you want to know?"

Bea took a deep breath and then let her story spill out in a hurried rush, and ended it with one breathless question.

"Oh, Mr. Pettibone, can you teach me to cheat at piquet?"

The man grinned from ear to ear. "For such a noble cause, I would be honored."

Chapter 13

⌢⌢⌢

The Dowager Countess of Marlowe sat in her morning room as she had nearly every morning for forty-five years, breakfasting on tea and toast. The only change to this regime had been the addition in recent years of a bit of preserves to her breakfast menu.

There were, after all, many more things she regretted about her life and the choices she had made than the late addition of preserves to her morning repast.

Out in the hall, the bell rattled on its hanger, announcing the arrival of a caller.

She sniffed at this breech of etiquette, since it was hardly the hour to make calls, let alone to leave a card. Yet in spite of her love of rules and order, she was glad for the interruption and the possibility of a guest.

Her maid entered the room. "Ma'am, there is a gentleman to see you. He is most insistent." The girl took a step back, as if waiting for an ensuing explosion.

The Countess felt a tinge of guilt. Was she truly such an old dragon that she left everyone quaking in his boots? The idea both pleased and annoyed her. "Don't leave me guessing, Regina. Who is it at this hour?"

"The Duke of Everton."

The Countess shook her head, not sure she'd heard the girl right. "Who?"

"The Duke of Everton, my lady." The girl fidgeted for a moment.

Why would Everton be making a social call after all these years? "Well, don't just stand there, see him in!" the Countess snapped.

Regina retreated quickly, and moments later showed the Duke into the room.

The Countess rose and made a regal curtsey at his entrance. "Your Grace," she said. "This is indeed an honor."

"My lady, you look as well as ever," he said.

"And you've always been a gracious liar." She waved her hand at an empty seat at her breakfast table and nodded to Regina to bring another setting. With the Duke seated and a cup of tea poured, she waved the girl to leave and waited until the door closed behind her.

"I have never been one to waste words or time, my lady, so I will get to the point straightaway. Why did Elise go to France?"

Elise.

No one had mentioned her daughter's name in years. Most had forgotten she'd ever existed—which was fine for the most part with the Countess.

"Madame, I don't mean to bring you distress, but I will have the answer I've waited twenty-six years to hear."

She took a tentative sip of her tea, trying to find a way to evade Everton. But the man was a duke and unused to being denied answers.

"You know why Elise went to France. She wanted to visit one of my husband's cousins. And I saw nothing wrong in sending her before she accepted your hand." She didn't look him in the eye, rather picked up her spoon and stirred another lump of sugar into her tea.

"That, Madame, is a lie." He paused for a moment, then rose from his seat and began to pace around the room. With his back to her, he said in a melancholy voice, "I loved Elise. I know she never cared for me that way, but I loved her all the same. And while you've done your best to see that she is forgotten by society, I never have. Not her smile, nor the way she walked, nor her green eyes. I loved her then, I love her still. You owe me the truth."

A chill spread down the lady's spine. He knew. Somehow he knew.

He turned around, and the Countess's heart began to thrum with a wild cadence.

The Duke leaned over the table and stared directly at her. "But I will ask you one more time. Why did Elise go to France?"

Clamping her lips shut, the lady could only shake her head. She couldn't betray her daughter's shame. She hadn't then, she wouldn't now.

He nodded. "I thought so." He paced a few more steps and stopped before the garden door, staring out at the early roses blooming in their ordered rows. "Well, if you refuse to speak, then let's discuss something else. Are you coming to my masquerade?"

The Countess shook her head. "You know I don't go out anymore."

"I had hoped you would make an exception this year. There is a young woman I would like you to meet."

An uneasy silence grew between them, until finally the Countess asked, "What do I care for these young chits they pass off as ladies? 'Tis part of why I don't go out much. I can't stand to see their simpering, mincing manners."

"I think you might make an exception in this case." He turned and faced her, his gaze intent.

"And why is that?" she snapped, more than a little unnerved at this entire interview.

"Because she is Elise's daughter."

The noise in the house grew more raucous with each passing minute.

Mason glanced up from his desk. What the devil was that woman concocting now? A week in his house and she'd created a new form of chaos every single day.

And the girls! She'd wrought a miracle with the girls. He'd heard Beatrice curse only twice in the last three days, and moreover, she'd apologized profusely for each slip. Maggie hadn't broken anything in the past twenty-four hours, and Louisa had even offered to help Cousin Felicity with her mending.

Louisa sewing?

He was starting to think Riley had made a bargain with the devil and found him new nieces.

Still, that didn't excuse this constant tromping overhead. He was trying to save his family from ruin, and she was making it impossible for him to concentrate. Not that close attention would change matters. His creditors were pressing for payment to the point that he couldn't put them off any longer. Even the promise of the play's profits wasn't enough.

To date his investigation into Riley's stalker had come up empty-handed. If he was going to find her deadly enemy he'd need more resources.

He needed cash.

And Miss Pindar presented his only likely solution. All it would take was a special license and a quick trip to the parson and he'd have enough money to finance the girls' Season and restore Sanborn Abbey and the lands around the estate.

There has to be another way, he thought, sifting through Freddie's investments one more time.

Overhead, the racket rose to a new level of irritation.

"Belton! What is that infernal clamor?"

Mason waited for a response. And waited, and waited a little longer. He rose from his seat and made for the foyer. "Belton?" To his shock and chagrin, the ever-present butler was not at his post.

In fact, no one was about. The entire ground floor was empty, while upstairs in the ballroom, it sounded as if they were entertaining half the *ton*.

Practice, hah! She was throwing some type of bacchanalian revel, by the sound of it.

Well, enough was enough.

He took the stairs two at a time. As he came to the open doors of the ballroom, his anger turned to a stunned silence.

The ballroom had been transformed into a forest of silk trees. In the middle of this fanciful woods stood Louisa, dressed in a simple white gown, her blond hair unbound and falling down to her waist.

"If only my dreams could come true," the girl was saying, "I would see my Geoffroi again."

A young man dressed like a woodcutter came forward out of the trees and fell to his knees. "I am only imagining this. 'Tis some fairy magic or curse. For there is my true love, Aveline. Come to me, if you are real."

"I am, and ever shall be, your Aveline," Louisa said, rushing to the man's open arms.

For a moment there was silence, then the room echoed in a deafening thunder of applause.

The cheers and whistles startled Mason out of his awe-struck reverie for the sights before him, as now he realized that the entire company of the Queen's Gate sat around the edges of their mock stage watching the performance, as well as the bulk of his household staff.

"Excellent! Very good, Louisa," Riley said, coming forward, an open book in her hands. She jotted down a few notes and then looked around. "Now I think we need to go over the pirate scene again. From the top of Act Two."

There were general groans and complaints, but Riley didn't seem to hear them, as she ordered the scenery changed and the players to their feet.

Mason slipped into the room and found himself standing beside none other than Belton.

"Uh, my lord," Belton stuttered. "I was just about to put a halt to this decadence. A shocking display. Hardly appropriate for the girls to be watching, let alone participating in. Shall I make them stop?"

Mason almost laughed, for Belton sounded about as convincing as Cousin Felicity did when she came home with bundles of packages and claims of not having visited her dressmaker—though he did have a point about the propriety of Louisa's practicing with the players.

Mason would have called a halt to the entire charade if it hadn't been for one thing. Louisa's face shone with a smile the likes of which he hadn't seen in years. Not the cattish, sulky turn of her lips he'd grown used to, but a genuine smile. The kind he remembered about her when she'd been a little girl and would rush to his arms for a hug and the required present of candy he always brought her from Oxford when he visited Sanborne Abbey during the holidays.

The center of attention, she wasn't selfishly basking in it, demanding her due; rather, she appeared to be having the time of her life playing the impetuous Aveline, the role Mason knew was Riley's.

"Should I start over here, Riley?" she was asking, placing herself between two actors, one of whom was wearing an eye patch to distinguish him as a pirate.

Riley nodded. "Yes, that is perfect. Now just like you practiced."

Louisa launched into her lines, with an earnest gusto and a surprising amount of talent.

"She's quite good," Mason muttered.

"A rousing performance, my lord," Belton said. "Most convincing."

Yet it wasn't Louisa's performance holding Mason's rapt attention; it was the director. His gaze kept wandering over to the woman pacing along the imaginary border of the stage, script in hand, her steady gaze focused intently on the action before her.

Dressed in a plain muslin gown, she was hardly the silken minx who'd appeared in his study all these days ago. With her hair pulled back in a simple chignon, tendrils slipping down here and there, and a sensible pair of shoes on her feet, she looked more country farm wife than celebrated Cyprian.

What he marveled at was how she seemed to move with each line, pulling the play in and out of the actors as if she were breathing for them.

Nothing slipped past her sharp gaze: the stance of a pirate, Aveline's gown, the way a line should and should not be intoned. She nurtured the story from her company the way a mother coaxed a baby to take its first steps.

Her smile when the scene moved perfectly touched his heart, and he pitied the players who garnered her frown for flubbed lines or disjointed movements. Without even realizing it, he found that he'd whiled away an hour just watching her work.

And work hard, with purpose, he noted with a self-conscious twinge.

When she stepped into the scene and started to play the role of Aveline to demonstrate how it should be done, she took his breath away with her power to transform herself so artlessly. 'Twas a magical moment when Riley faded to the background and the character she played came rising to the surface.

What she did so effortlessly Mason knew came through discipline and intelligence.

This was no woman of leisure, no pampered feline awaiting her lover and her next bauble from Rundell and Bridge; this was a woman whose livelihood and welfare revolved around making this play and these players a success.

Riley worked—worked hard to make her vocation a success.

And it shamed Mason to think that he couldn't say the same about his life.

So lost in his own musings, he didn't notice that Riley had made her way to his side.

"She's very good," she said. "You St. Clairs have a flair for the dramatic."

"What?" Mason asked, realizing that he'd been lost in thought.

"Louisa," Riley said, nodding at his niece, who was even now reciting Aveline's soliloquy from memory. "She's a natural. I hope you don't mind me using her. Ginny usually stands in for me when we do these rehearsals so I can see the play, but she's sick and couldn't make it."

Mason gazed for a moment at his niece. "No, I don't mind."

Riley grinned. "If she weren't the daughter of an earl, I'd cast her as Aveline right this moment."

"But that's your part," Mason said.

"Yes," Riley said, "but look at her. She is Aveline, especially with Roderick playing Geoffroi. Together, they have something very special. As if they were star-crossed lovers."

Mason watched his niece for a moment and realized how right Riley was. It wasn't just Louisa, but Roderick as well. As the two young actors read their lines, they made their audience believe them, as if they truly longed to be together.

Perhaps a little too much.

"Oh, my dearest Aveline," Roderick said, pulling Louisa into his arms. "I swear there is nothing that will keep us apart."

Louisa, playing her role with more enthusiasm than was entirely necessary, clung to Roderick, her body melding to his and her gaze glowing with passion. "I forsake my honor, my family, my duty, everything but you, my love."

Roderick's arms tightened, drawing Louisa even closer. The entire room stilled, as if enthralled and entranced by these mismatched and imperiled lovers. "One kiss, sweet Aveline. A single kiss to seal our destiny."

As the young actor bent his lips to Louisa's, Mason realized that the young man actually meant to kiss her—and Louisa meant to kiss him back.

"Just a minute there," Mason said, feeling for the first time the paternal pangs of watching a daughter grow up. He rushed forward and separated the two. "That's enough for today. You've done an excellent job, Louisa, but I fear Cousin Felicity needs your immediate assistance."

"But Uncle," Louisa protested, her eyes still fixed on her Geoffroi.

"No excuses. You've been a great help to Riley, but now Cousin Felicity needs your assistance."

"No, I don't, Mason," Cousin Felicity piped up.

Mason groaned. How had he missed her? It was easy to see why, for she'd hidden away in the corner of the room, cozied up next to Mr. Pettibone.

Suddenly he realized that perhaps he shouldn't have been avoiding Riley's practices, for it appeared the entire house was finding themselves engaged in rather questionable love affairs.

Especially given the moon-faced expression on Cousin Felicity's face; the lady appeared as lovestruck as Louisa.

Gads, what was he in for now?

"I'm quite fine here, Uncle," Louisa told him, edging closer to Roderick, who stood posed and glowering, just like the frustrated Geoffroi in the play.

"Oh, so am I," Cousin Felicity said, in a show of solidarity.

"No, you are not," Mason said. "Don't you have some embroidery that needs attending, Cousin?"

"I would, but I am out of thread." She turned to her new amour and said, "It is terrible trying to find the right shade of azure."

Mr. Pettibone stepped forward and took Cousin Felicity's hand. Drawing her fingers to his lips, he placed a lingering kiss there, then said, "Just look in a mirror and you'll find the most royal shade of that color I've ever beheld in those glorious eyes of yours, my dearest lady."

Mason shuddered at this overblown gallantry, before he caught Cousin Felicity's elbow and retrieved the rest of her arm from her attentive suitor. "Perhaps you and Louisa can go find the right shade this afternoon," he told her.

"Go shopping?" the delighted lady said. "Oh, Mason, how kind of you. Mr. Pettibone can assist us, Louisa."

"Oh, no, he can't," Riley said, much to Mason's relief. "Aggie has far too much work to do this afternoon."

"But, Riley—" Mr. Pettibone started to say.

"No, Aggie," Riley told him, moving between her partner and Cousin Felicity. "You have a fitting this afternoon with Jane and must wait at the theatre for the playbills to be delivered."

Mr. Pettibone looked exceedingly put out, but he turned to Cousin Felicity and laid his hand on his breast. "We must not think of ourselves as parted, my love, but together always, here in our hearts. Our love is forged so that no one can tear it asunder."

Mason heard Riley muttering something about having to cut those lines as well.

"I don't see why I have to go," Louisa complained. "Riley, tell my uncle you need me here."

Riley glanced at Mason, who in turn shook his head. "We are done with the scenes I needed you for," she said. "So you are free to go with Cousin Felicity."

Louisa frowned, casting one last heartbreaking moue up at Mason, who held firm to his resolve and pointed toward the door.

The last thing he needed was a St. Clair running off with an actor and casting the entire family into shame.

His infatuation and growing admiration for the Queen's Gate leading lady was enough scandal for now.

The waiter at White's leaned over the gaming table and said quietly to Lord Cariston, "There is someone to see you, my lord."

"What does he want?" he grumbled at the fellow.

"Perhaps the rest of your money, Cariston," Colonel Pollard joked. His sturdy fingers tapped the pile of vowels in front of him—all of them the Marquis's.

"That is, if there is anything left!" said a young lordling who'd joined the play early and also held a fair share of Lord Cariston's vouchers.

Everyone but Cariston laughed.

The waiter shifted back and forth. "My lord, he says you asked to meet him regarding *certain matters*."

"Yes, right." Cariston rose from the table, his fellow gamblers complaining about his untimely departure.

"Business, eh, Cariston?" Colonel Pollard asked. "Should I send my man around to collect these now, or will there be anything left in the morning?" He laughed, as did the others.

Lord Cariston steamed at the insult, but hadn't the wherewithal to call the man out. Pollard could as easily put a bullet between his eyes as beat him at cards. The man had the devil's own luck, whereas Cariston seemed to have lost his—for now.

That would soon change, he thought, as he followed the waiter down the hall and through the kitchens.

In a few moments, Nutley would tell him that she was at long last gone from his life, and he would go on receiving the income he needed to maintain his more costly habits.

Stepping out into the alleyway behind the club, he found his hired assassin waiting for him.

Dressed as always in the guise of a gentleman, Nutley appeared bored and insulted at having been made to wait amongst the garbage.

As if he had a right to care where they met, Cariston thought. Looking around to see that there was no one about, he said, "How fares the lady, Nutley? Is she slumbering in the Thames yet?"

"No," the man grumbled. "The little bitch has more lives than a cat."

"You mean she still lives?"

"Just like I said. She ain't dead."

Cariston came eye to eye with his dangerous accomplice. "Why not?"

"I had it all fixed. Then he came along."

"Ashlin." Cariston's hands balled at his sides. How he hated the man. Had since they'd been lads together at school.

"Yeah, that bookish fribble. Who'd have known he'd carry a blade?"

"You idiot," Cariston said. "I told you not to discount the man." He paced a few steps. "Why haven't you gone back and finished the job?"

"I would, but she went and moved in with him. Have you seen that pile of stone?" He shook his head. "It will take a bit more gold to see the job done now."

Lord Cariston turned on him. "You'll do it for the price we agreed on, and you'll do it immediately. I want her dead."

"That's hardly the tone to take with me, milord," Nutley told him, pulling a knife from his jacket and putting it beneath Cariston's neck. The point pressed against the fluttering vein there.

"I could slit you real easy and no one would care," Nutley said. With that, he nicked his employer's neck.

Cariston howled in pain. "How dare you," he managed to sputter. "I'll have the watch on you."

"No, you won't," Nutley told him. "Because if you do, they'll need a bed sheet to mop up what I'll bleed from you."

His guttural laugh echoed down the alley like a banshee's promise, and by the time Cariston had looked up to see where he'd gone to, Nutley had disappeared into the night.

Chapter 14

Mason had never considered himself a coward before, but when it came to facing Riley and the girls now that he continued to remain obstinate about their not attending the Everton masquerade, he thought he might be safer going to a Royal Society meeting than spending another night at home.

Riley had not given up, and spent a part of each day badgering him on one reason or other as to why the girls deserved to go—they were making great strides in their lessons. Bea had gone three entire days without cursing. Maggie had mastered the steps to not one, but three dances.

Yet his pride kept him from explaining that his refusal was more a matter of money than manners.

Someone was buying up Freddie's vowels at an alarming rate—and Mason had no doubts that this unknown creditor would soon be arriving on his doorstep demanding complete reparations.

With this added pressure to their already strained finances, Mason couldn't see how they could spare even a shilling for costumes that would be worn only once.

Still, they needn't be so put out, he thought, after another afternoon tea of sullen looks and steely quiet. He hadn't given up on the idea that the girls would still have their Season, albeit a scaled-down one.

Besides, they were up to something, like cats watching an unsuspecting mouse, and he didn't want to be around when they decided to pounce.

It also didn't help that when it came to refusing Riley, he felt himself the veriest greenling. The lady, in all her guises, touched that part of his heart, that very unrepentant Ashlin core, to which he'd vowed never to succumb to its siren call of vice. And he knew with the right enticement, eventually he would fall prey to her requests and relent.

Much to his chagrin, the scheduled lecture at the Society had been cancelled, and the replacement speaker had been dull and unimaginative.

Throughout the speech he found himself wondering how Riley would be presenting the material—a very distracting notion indeed.

So he'd left at the first break and much to his surprise run into Del's uncle, the Duke of Everton, on the steps of White's.

He'd always liked Everton and looked up to him like a father, since his own dissolute sire had rarely had time for his children, especially a second son with no taste for drinking and gambling.

Glad for the chance for the erudite conversation the Duke always brought to the table, he accepted the man's invitation to join him in a glass of port at their club. The rooms were still relatively quiet at such an early hour, so they could talk without interruption.

Unfortunately, the only subject Duke had wanted to talk about was Riley—where she was from, her lineage, how long Mason had known the girl, and why she'd come to London.

Mason had repeated the lies they'd shared with everyone else, trying to steer the Duke onto another subject, but the man would not be diverted.

Probably the work of Lady Delander, Mason thought. Sending her brother out to do her dirty work. Then again, perhaps the man was being overly cautious about who his nephew married.

Eventually he made his excuses and left, rather than continue to lie to a man he respected. At least at home he could hide in his study and not be interrogated.

His solitary walk home ended when he found Del lounging on his front steps, a wilted flower arrangement in his clenched hand. His friend's horse pranced and snorted impatiently at the post.

"Your demmed butler will not let me in," Del complained.

Mason crossed his arms over his chest. "That is because I told him not to let you have entrance to the house unless I was at home."

Del sat up. "All these years of coming and going from this place as if it were my own and now even Belton is against me. I suppose that is why the poets are so inspired. The anguish. The agony. The pain of unrequited love."

"I think you fell off that beast you insist on riding and hit your head. That might be the real cause of your agonies."

Tossing aside his flowers, Del sighed. "Oh, heartless fiend. Oh, vile interloper. What would you know of my pain? You have hidden away the very angel sent down to cure me. I should have known that practical, cold heart of yours would never understand."

"I understand you should go home and sleep off whatever you've been imbibing tonight."

His horse snorted as if in agreement.

"You think I'm drunk?" Del asked. "Perhaps I am. But it is more from gazing into your cousin's blue eyes . . ."

"Green," Mason corrected.

"No, blue. They are like forget-me-nots in springtime."

"No, they are green."

"Aha!" Del said, staggering to his feet. It was then that Mason smelled the brandy wafting from the man in a thick French cloud. "So you have noticed her. And I suppose you are keeping her locked inside to prevent her from discovering that her heart truly does belong to me and not you?"

"Her heart is hers to give. And I assure you, it doesn't belong to either of us."

Del sighed. "I wouldn't be so sure."

From the smell of the illegal alcohol filling the space between them, Mason would bet that Del had drunk a good portion of his departed father's prized cognac.

"Don't be all that sure," Del repeated. "I've seen the way she looks at you. A lady does not gaze upon a man that way if she isn't inclined." He pounded his fist to his chest, nearly toppling himself over. "We poets know these things."

Mason offered him a steadying arm. "So now you are not only an expert on love, but a poet as well."

Del brightened. "Yes. Might give me an edge with your cousin. Seems a bit of a bluestocking, so I'll court her with verse. That type loves poetry."

"And am I to suppose you have spent the evening composing odes?" Taking his friend by the arm, Mason started to steer him down the steps, and toward the street.

"I have!" Del announced.

"Speak on, Lord Poet," Mason told him.

Grinning from ear to ear, Del began, "There once was a girl from Dover—"

Mason groaned.

"What?" Del came to a wheeling halt. "Not literate enough for you, Lord Professor? I might not have the refined learning you boast, but you must admit it is an imaginative beginning."

"Oh, yes, very imaginative," Mason told him, getting him moving back down the square toward his mother's residence. "However, my cousin isn't from Dover."

"I considered that," Del told him. "Yet it rhymed so nicely with 'rolled over' that I couldn't help taking a bit of a literary leap."

"I'd say you took a large bounding one at that."

Del considered this for a few more steps before it obviously dawned on him that he was being led away from his lovelorn post. "Oh, no, you don't. I intend on staying on your front steps until she consents to be my wife." He swung around and staggered back toward the house. "The bleak of night shall not deter me from true love's path." He tumbled back down on the steps and looked up at Mason. "What the devil is 'bleak of night'?"

"Something I imagine you are going to discover by morning."

Del nodded sagely. " 'Twill probably make me a more perfect tragic poet, anguishing for my art and my lady love, don't you think?"

"Oh, you're something," Mason told him, sitting down beside his friend.

Del whispered in a voice that carried all the way across the square, "After I've written the rest of my cantos or verses or whatever my masterpiece is called, I'll see to my tailor about getting an entirely new wardrobe. Perhaps Mr. Pettibone will recommend me to his tailor. Now there is a man with a Continental sense of style." He sighed and gazed up at the light in the second-story window. "Tell me that is her room. I've seen her gazing down, and it is as if we have been looking into each other's eyes forever. Even now I can feel the true meaning of love welling up inside me, for her face shines like the most brilliant moon, like Venus rising from the sea, like—"

"Oh, Del, leave off. That is Beatrice's room." Mason glanced up and saw the curtains in his niece's room yanked back in place. "And whatever is coming up inside you is probably dinner from your mother's house."

"Well, it is all your fault I had to take dinner with her. She ordered me home this afternoon and started organizing my life, even decreed that the nursery be cleaned out." Del dug around in his jacket and pulled out a large silver flask. "Putting the horse before the cart on that one, but you know my mother." He took a long pull and then offered it to Mason.

Taking it, if only to keep his friend from drinking the rest, Mason took an appreciative sip from the flask and then stowed it in his own pocket.

"I well imagine," Del said, "that she will have my heir's nanny, tutor, and schools planned by the time I get home."

"Your mother is an extraordinary woman," Mason told his friend diplomatically.

Del scuffed his feet against the stones. "I suppose you aren't going to let me in tonight."

"No," Mason told him.

Del got up on his own and staggered over to his horse. Catching the mercurial animal by its reins, he grinned at Mason. "No use then," he said, nodding once again at Beatrice's window. "Bea's room, you say? Should have known my Bea would be looking out for me even when you won't." His horse nuzzled at his pocket, and Del drew out a bit of sugar for it. "If only I could charm your cousin like I can horses."

"I doubt sugar lumps will win the lady's heart."

Del nodded and straightened. For a moment his face became serious and all the vestiges of his cognac binge fell away. "If that were the case I would buy an island in the West Indies for her and bury her in sweet cane. But I doubt even that would turn her heart."

"Why do you say that?"

"Because it's obvious she's in love with you."

Riley eased back from the window and into the darkened room, trying to remember where she'd left off reviewing the scenes she'd brought with her.

She had told herself over and over she hadn't sat up by the window most of the night waiting for Lord Ashlin . . . no, not at all.

And now that he was home, her heart suddenly started thumping about like it was an opening night.

Even worse, after all these hours of practice, she couldn't recall a single line from her play.

All she could hear when she tried to recall her opening monologue as she stood in the middle of the room, surrounded by darkness, was the statement Lord Delander had just pronounced to everyone on Ashlin Square.

It's obvious she's in love with you.

Riley took a deep breath. Well, the only thing that was obvious was that Lord Delander was well into his cups. He had been when he'd arrived at around eleven and been denied entrance to the house.

She'd cracked open the window then and listened half amused as Belton had politely but firmly told the young man he was not welcome in the house.

Even with the door slammed in his face, Lord Delander had taken up his solitary post like a sentry in front of Whitehall.

Riley smiled to herself. The Viscount was persistent, but he wasn't . . .

She stopped herself from finishing that thought.

"Oh, bother," she muttered, creeping back to the window and watching the departing figure of Lord Delander lead his horse down the street. Moments later, the front door closed and she could hear murmured voices in the foyer.

Probably Mason and Belton.

Then the voices ended and the sound of footsteps, strong and commanding, coming up the stairs sent her scurrying into action. She picked up her script and started into Act Two with renewed vigor, even though the room was so dark now she could barely see the page.

Riley didn't care—she'd done everything possible to distract herself from admitting she'd been worried about him.

She was only too aware that Mason's finances had a stranglehold on him. He hadn't said more than a handful of words to any of them in the last few days. She admired his determination to stand on his own two feet, but she also knew that pride alone wouldn't put food in the larders. She'd done what she could do to help—recommending a cheaper grocer and coal supplier to Belton, but these were only salves to keep the household running.

Riley knew what everyone in the house knew—the only way to save the Ashlin name was for Mason to make a marriage of convenience.

The very idea made Riley heartsick, and in her distraction she tripped over a book she'd discarded hours ago and landed in an ignominious heap in the middle of the carpet.

She scrambled to pull herself up into a sitting position, and fumbled around for the offending book.

When Mason had left for the evening without a word to anyone, Riley had assumed he'd gone out to make his fortune—or rather, to court it.

Oh, what the devil had taken him so long? she wondered, as he continued his path up the stairs, his footsteps tolling every ominous image Riley could imagine . . .

Mason asking Miss Pindar to dance. Or fetching the nonpareil a glass of punch. Riley's thoughts ran wild as she saw him in the dark confines of a carriage, the girl's dainty hand tucked into his protective one.

Miss Dahlia, will you do me the honor of becoming my—

Oh, it wasn't fair!

She wanted to be that woman. Like one of the heroines in her plays—a lost heiress, a plucky girl, separated from her family by adverse circumstances only to be rescued by a noble hero who recognized her aristocratic bearing through the grime and rags of her now lowly and humble station.

"As if," she muttered.

Just then the door swung open, the light of a single candle casting a solitary shaft of light across the floor.

"Riley, is that you?" Mason asked.

Her heart skipped a beat. Was it her imagination, or did the man sound hopeful of finding her?

Plain old notorious and dishonorable Riley Fontaine.

Chapter 15

Mason stared at the woman on the floor. "What the devil are you doing down there?" He set the candlestick he'd been holding on the side table beside the door.

Riley flipped her hair out of her face, the strands falling in a tumbled mess from the severe, modest fashion she'd taken to wearing of late. "I was practicing my lines," she said, struggling to right herself.

He held out his hand. "Odd place to practice."

" 'Tis an odd scene," she said, accepting his assistance.

As his fingers entwined with hers and he pulled her to her feet, she came up a little faster than he'd expected. Slamming into his chest, her body connected with his like before.

Magically, intimately, passionately.

Warning bells went off in his mind as she molded to him, her breasts pressed against his chest. Her arms wound around his neck to steady herself. A little sigh fell from her lips as she found her footing, the gentle whisper of it wrapping its wispy tendrils around his heart.

He continued to hold her, even if she didn't need his support.

"Is this part of the scene?" he asked, amazed at the teasing and rakish humor behind his words. It was as if Freddie were speaking for him.

"It could be," she whispered back. "The audience would probably find it quite romantic."

There was a challenge behind her words, as if she dared him not to find the entire situation romantic.

Mason had the feeling even a eunuch would find this situation a trial for his missing sensibilities. All he could think of was kissing her—thoroughly. Like they'd done the other night. He glanced down and found those haunting green eyes of hers staring back up at him, innocent and seductive at the same time. Her lips parted slightly, as if coaxing him to rekindle the fire they both knew smoldered between them.

This time, Mason doubted he could stop the blaze before it consumed them both.

Dammit, he thought. *This isn't right.* He set her aside, more than a little abruptly, and then fled across the room toward the window, leaving what seemed like a boulevard of carpet between them.

A safe and discreet distance. Exactly what the situation called for, he told himself.

Not that it made his desire for her any less. She stood, her figure illuminated in the shaft of light from the hallway, her features in shadows, but only that much more mysterious for it.

A soft breeze rippled in through the open window behind him, tousling her loose hair about her slender shoulders.

Damn his classical education, for all he could see was a vision of Aphrodite standing before him—the only things missing were the Grecian robe, a half shell, and sea foam.

He turned away from the living and breathing temptation before him and went to shut the window—not that the cool breeze wasn't a refreshing change from the heat coursing through his veins, but she'd been shivering when he'd helped her up and he didn't need a bedridden enticement in his house.

In the street below, the night watchman was passing the front door. The man glanced up and gave a quick nod at Mason.

"Good night, sir," the fellow said in a voice that was barely a whisper but carried well in the stillness of the night.

It surprised him that he could hear the man so clearly, but then again, the man knew his job well enough not to raise the dead by calling out and risk losing his post.

For a voice any louder would surely carry . . . carry like Del's, for instance.

Mason stared at the open portal before him, his hands frozen on the window frame, then glanced quickly over his shoulder at the room's occupant.

Obviously Beatrice hadn't been the only one who'd spent her evening eavesdropping on the Viscount's one-act performance.

And if Riley had been standing before the open window, that meant she'd heard everything that idiot Del had been blithering on about.

Mason cringed.

All of Ashlin Square had probably heard his friend's declarations of love and his brandy-soaked theory on the lady's own preference.

When he turned back to Riley, the worst of his suspicions were confirmed, for the hint of blush rising on her cheeks convicted her without his having to ask the question.

Oh, yes, she'd heard everything.

If her blush wasn't enough, her next words only damned her further.

"It is cold in here," she said, shivering in the exaggerated method of an actress. She crossed the room and edged him out of the way, closing the window with an efficient push and then turning and wiping her hands of the entire affair. "I don't know what I was thinking, leaving that window open."

"Yes," he commented. "You never know what the night air will bring in."

It was Riley's turn to cringe, but she recovered well. "Exactly. Can't have the girls catching a fever."

"Yes, quite right," he murmured. He glanced up, trying to find a way to broach the subject properly, but instead, he nodded at the papers and books scattered about. "Hard at work? Don't you ever take an evening off from all this?"

She shook her head. "Not if I'm to make this play a success."

Her words stung him. Here she was, spending every waking moment trying to make her play a stunning success—for herself, her company . . . and him. And how had he spent the evening? Lurking about the Royal Society, avoiding Miss Pindar and his responsibilities to his family.

"Well, it's quiet up here," he said, babbling on like Cousin Felicity. "You probably were able to get quite a bit done—uninterrupted and all. Well, except for Del and that bit of nonsense out there . . ."

She had started to pick up her papers and notes, but stopped her task and glanced up. "Lord Delander? He was here?"

A renowned actress she might be, but even Mason heard the catch in her voice. "Yes. I'm surprised you didn't hear him, what with the window open."

She glanced at the now closed evidence and shrugged. "I am so used to all the comings and goings in the theatre that your discussion with Lord Delander barely registered."

He tipped his head and studied her. "So you didn't hear Lord Delander announce that you'd agreed to marry him?"

She spun around. "He said no such thing! I heard every—" She stopped in mid-sentence. Flopping down in the reading chair next to the table, she swiped at the loose tendrils of her hair. "Oh, bother. Of course I heard every word. The entire house heard him."

He nodded. "This house and every house on the square heard that nattering idiot."

His gaze met hers. To his surprise, he found her eyes alight with mischief, as if she didn't mind at all being caught.

"Was he floored?" she asked. "He sounded as if he could barely stand."

Mason nodded, not too sure that discussing another man's state of inebriation with a lady was entirely proper. But this was Riley, after all, and with her there seemed to be no boundaries or constraints on one's conversation. A notion he found wonderfully freeing. "Stand? Barely. But luckily for him, his horse knows the way to his mother's house."

She covered her mouth to stifle a laugh. "I hope he stops reciting that ridiculous poetry before he gets home. I doubt very much Lady Delander is fond of brandy-inspired poetics."

Mason laughed. "I can't see her as a patroness of Bacchus."

At this, Riley dissolved into a bout of giggles. "Oh, I have a feeling that may be the last we see of Lord Delander—for when he awakens tomorrow morning, if he hasn't forgotten his new vocation as poet laureate, his mother will surely lecture any inclinations toward another display like tonight's right out of him."

"Well, there might be some good to come out of tonight, then, after all," Mason said, settling into the chair next to her, relishing this affable connection between them. He couldn't imagine having such a conversation with Miss Pindar. "A more contrite Del won't be making such outlandish statements for all the neighborhood to hear. Comparing your eyes to forget-me-nots when he should damn well know they are green, not blue."

"When did you start noticing my eyes?" she asked. "Being only tolerably pretty and all, I didn't think my eyes would rate notice."

"I've had them glaring at me for the last week, so I could hardly avoid noticing them."

She laughed at this, and so did he.

"My temper has been up a bit," she conceded.

He cocked a brow at her.

"Fine. It has been in a rare state, but only because I think you are being high-handed about the Everton masquerade and the girls' Season. They deserve all of it."

He held up his hand. "Riley, I wish there was something, anything, I could do about that. You've worked miracles with them. I'm starting to think you replaced them with members of your acting company. But . . ." Mason paused, unwilling to admit his own failing.

He couldn't finance any of it. And he couldn't bring himself to marry Miss Pindar and spend the rest of his life saddled to some irksome featherbrain just to save his family's fortunes.

Not even for his nieces.

He should have known that Riley would see through

his pride and get to the point in her own direct and blunt fashion.

". . . But you don't have the money," Riley finished for him. She sounded truly concerned . . . not like his peers, who viewed the financial crisis of their compatriots as manna for the fodder. "Is it as bad as all that?" she asked.

"Yes, very bad," he told her. For some reason he felt free to confess to her what he couldn't admit even to his family. "The worst of it is that someone has started buying up Freddie's vowels. I don't know who or why, but if they call them due—we'll all be out in the streets. I know you've worked hard to see the girls prepared for their Season, but there is no way I can finance it at this time."

"Oh, bother that. You don't need any money to give the girls their Season. They already have all their dresses ready and waiting for you just to say the word."

He stared at her, wondering if she'd gone as mad as Cousin Felicity. Why, what she was saying would put them on the streets.

He must have looked ready to explode, because she flew to his side. "Oh, don't be mad. It won't cost you a thing! Besides, it was really your idea in the first place."

Mason shook off her wild rush of words like water off a soaking wet dog. And when he opened his mouth to ask the questions, nothing came out of his stunned lips.

How? How could she have done this?

"It was your idea," she repeated. "I knew you couldn't afford new clothes for the girls, so I took the liberty of borrowing from the wealth of clothes you already had."

He eyed her suspiciously. "I have a wealth of women's clothing?"

She nodded, her eyes sparkling again with mischief. "But no one would have guessed that about you."

He laughed a little at this.

"Yes, well," she said, continuing her explanation, "did it ever occur to you while you were reworking Freddie's clothes that the same could be done with your sister-in-law's gowns?"

"Caro," he breathed.

"Now you understand," she said, catching his hand and squeezing it. "You should have seen her clothes press, and the trunk after trunk we uncovered in the attic. All of them filled with gowns that are in perfectly good shape and ready to be made over. Enough so all three girls can make respectable debuts."

Mason sat back in stunned silence. He was starting to believe there wasn't a financial hurdle he couldn't leap with Riley at his side.

Meanwhile, Riley was chewing her bottom lip. "You don't mind, do you? I know I should have asked, but then again, it was *your* idea, so I—"

"—Mind? Hardly. I don't know how to begin to thank you."

"So you'll give your approval for the girls to have their Season?"

He grinned at her. "You can tell them. First thing in the morning."

Riley got up, hands on her hips, and turned an ecstatic little jig.

Mason felt like joining her.

When she whirled to a stop, she studied him for a moment, her eyes full of warmth and something else.

Something not unlike what Del had said.

Love.

Riley in love with him? It was too preposterous to believe. Wasn't it?

She must have been remembering the Viscount's words as well, for she suddenly blushed and then looked away.

"Oh, dear. I've made a mess of your library again," she said, and went to work picking up her littered pages.

Mason stooped down to help her, gathering up a script that looked like it had been annotated to death.

"How goes *The Envious Moon*? Have you determined whether it is to be a comedy or a tragedy?" he asked, starting to leaf through the pages.

"I can't decide," she said, sighing. "I'm having a terrible time with it."

"Maybe I can help," he offered.

"You?" she said, shaking her head at the idea.

"Yes, me." He pulled off his coat and set it over the back of a chair. " 'Tis the least I can do for you."

"I thought you had your own bride to seek, Geoffroi," she teased, nodding at his discarded coat.

"Not tonight," he said, quite relieved to find himself out of the Marriage Mart—at least, for the rest of the night.

"I think you should eliminate that line," Mason suggested, pointing to a piece of Geoffroi's dialogue. "It sounds rather sappy."

They sat, as they had for several hours, side by side at the library table, the candles burning low in front of them, the scattered pages of the script before them.

"No!" she snapped. "Can't you see that line is critical to the next scene?"

"He sounds like Cousin Felicity."

She picked up the page and studied the line in question. "He does not," she protested, though only half-heartedly. She almost regretted having allowed Mason to help her.

Especially when she suspected he had the right of it. Still, she offered one more feeble protest. "I think the line is fine."

"Gracious me?" Mason said, imitating Cousin Felicity's tone and pitch.

She pursed her lips. "Oh, perhaps you are right." She scratched out the line and bit her lip as she considered another phrase. "What would you say?"

"My wish is to have your love," he said.

"Your wish or your command?" she said back, improvising a new line for Aveline. She nodded to him, challenging him to answer back.

He rose to his feet, taking a wide stance, his hand on the hilt of an imaginary sword. "If I must, I command it. But I would rather that you gave it to me freely."

"Now you sound like Geoffroi," she teased. She rose from the table. Taking a step back, she made a low curtsey. "If my lord commands it, then I, the mere daughter of a woodcutter, must humbly comply."

He bowed and accepted her tribute by taking her hand and drawing it to his lips. As he placed a gentle kiss on her fingers, their gazes met.

The easiness that had sprung up between them suddenly grew tense with awareness. For a moment she stilled, and then the clock on the mantel struck three. Instantly she freed her hand.

"I didn't realize it had gotten so late," she said, gathering up her pages and notes. "I shouldn't have kept you. You have your own matters of business to attend to, rather than worrying about lines in my poor comedy." She glanced over her shoulder at him. "You should consider a career as a playwright. You have an able hand for writing."

"Is there any money to be made?" he joked.

She shook her head. "Novelists and diarists do sometimes, but playwrights are a rather sad lot."

She started to leave, but he caught her by the arm. "Don't leave, Riley. Not yet."

His touch melted her heart. She dared not look into his eyes, for she knew she would say something foolish.

Like confirming everything Lord Delander had said.

I do love you, Mason St. Clair. I love your ponderous, stuffy Oxford ways. I love every ordered, honorable, respectable thing about you.

But mostly I love your kiss. I want to spend the rest of my days awaiting the nights so I can while away the dark hours warmed by your embrace.

Somehow Mason must have heard her silent wish, for he did just that, wrapping her into his arms and putting his lips to hers.

His mouth claimed her, commanding her with his very dishonorable intentions.

Suddenly he was every bit the Ashlin rake she'd feared he was when first she'd come to his house. And she was so very glad for that. Oh, he hid it well, what with those spectacles and all, but the man kissing her held her with a masterful skill that she doubted even the most practiced scoundrel could boast.

He pulled back, his hands cradling her face, his gaze heated and devouring. "Riley, I—"

"—Sshh," she told him, raising herself up on her tiptoes and kissing him again.

His hands began to roam over her shoulders, her arms, her hips. His touch held promises she'd never imagined. Promises of passion. Promises that this would not be the last time he took her into his arms.

She moaned, his touch enflaming her need for him just that much more.

Mason must have understood, for he pushed her gown down over her shoulder, his lips trailing kisses from behind her ear, down her neck, and all the way to the top of her breast.

She arched her back, willing to be at his command, his every wish. This time she wouldn't run away from her passions, her need for him.

"Please, Mason—" she whispered in a heady rush.

He granted her plea by taking one of the peaks in his mouth and starting to suckle it with his tongue.

The sensation sent ramparts of pleasure shooting through her limbs, leaving her taut and breathless.

His other hand began gathering up her skirt, roaming up her leg, as if it were searching, frantically seeking its own fantasy. And apparently he found it, as his fingers lovingly explored the garter holding up her stocking.

For once, Riley was glad not to have removed her garters and stockings.

With a deft movement, he untied the red satin and began slowly rolling the garter and stocking down her leg, his fingers stroking a reverent path down her thigh and calf.

He retrieved the other one in the same manner, slowly and deliberately.

But the heat in her body wasn't in her legs, it was higher, and she found that just kissing and being kissed was no longer enough. She wanted him to touch her—there, at her very heart, where her yearning and desire met.

"I have never wanted anyone as I have wanted you," he whispered, as his hands began a renewed ascent up her thigh. "You are so beautiful."

"Tolerable," she whispered back. "I'm tolerable."

His eyes gazed down her with something that hardly resembled toleration. They burned into her with his need and his desire. And in an instant, his lips came crashing down on hers in a claiming that was undeniable.

This was wrong, she tried to tell herself. He didn't love her; he wouldn't marry her; he just wanted her. But already breathless with anticipation, Riley no longer cared what was right or wrong.

Part of her clung to the belief that his feelings for her weren't that far from hers.

That the very proper Earl of Ashlin loved her with a wild abandon.

As if to prove that very notion, he held her with one arm and swept the table clean of their papers. His gesture sent the script and all her notes flying up in the air like confetti.

Including some pieces she'd been keeping well concealed.

One of them fluttered down, landing right side up, right before his eyes. He snatched it up before she could sweep it away.

Did you think you cud hide?

He took a step back from her. Before her eyes she watched his powerful passion turn to outrage.

"When did this arrive?" he demanded, shaking the paper at her. "*When*?" Since she'd given him all the notes her enemy had sent the first day she'd come to live at Ashlin House, he really didn't need to hear her answer.

"Two days ago," Riley whispered, her gaze downcast. Then he realized she wasn't as contrite as she appeared; rather, she was looking around . . .

"This isn't the only one?" His temper exploded. "How many have you received since you came here?"

"Three," she said, leaning over and picking up two more notes.

Three notes? Mason's fury filled the room. "What were you thinking, concealing these?"

"I didn't want you to get hurt," she said, tears welling up in her eyes.

Right now he didn't know if he could trust her—her words or her tears—even though the emotion and fear sounded genuine. His pride was too stung.

"Madame," he said, "I can very well take care of this situation."

She shook her head. "Mason, I've lived in some of the worst neighborhoods of Paris and London, while you've been sheltered—first here, and then at that college of yours. I didn't want you to get hurt . . . or killed. You know nothing about these types of ruffians, or how to—" Her words faltered to a stop.

"How to defend myself?"

"Yes." She didn't even have the decency to look shame-faced about her confession. "You said yourself the day in the alley was nothing more than dumb luck. What if your next meeting with Clyde or someone of his ilk came out differently?"

"I doubt it would."

"You don't know that. If it was Hashim—"

He took a calming breath. "If it was Hashim, you wouldn't worry, is that it?"

She nodded. "If you were good with a sword or even a knife, I wouldn't worry, but Mason . . ."

"A knife, you say?" he asked. "How about this?" In one fluid, swift motion, he leaned over and snatched the dagger he always kept concealed in his boot when he was out about town. Before she could even finish the gasp that came issuing forth from her lips, he sent the blade spinning across the room where it stuck in the portrait of the seventh Earl.

Right in his throat.

Her mouth moved, but no sounds came out. "How did you . . . when did you . . ."

"Choose your weapon, Riley, and you will find I am quite capable with it. I not only taught military history, I studied it. All of it—from planning a siege to cannoneering." He took the other notes from her hands and gave them passing glances. "Where did you find these?"

"In my room."

He let out a blistering curse. Apparently, Riley wasn't safe, even in his house, under his protection. This was his fault. He should never have arrogantly thought her enemy would not seek her within his house.

And if the man could get into his house, he could harm not only Riley, but the rest of his family as well.

He knew the solution to that. He strode toward the door. When he got there, he turned to her. "Tell your maid to pack your belongings. Tomorrow you, the girls, and Cousin Felicity go to the country. You'll remain at San-born Abbey until I can straighten this out."

"But tomorrow is—" She clamped her mouth shut, her eyes opening wide at her own blundered *faux pas*.

Mason didn't need to hear the rest to know how Riley had been about to finish her near confession.

Tomorrow is the Everton Masquerade, she meant to say.

So that was it. She had planned to defy him and take the girls to the Everton masquerade. Well, no longer. He held up his hand to stave off her protest. "Not another word. You will go to the country tomorrow and that is my final answer."

Chapter 16

~~~⟡~~~

Mason was as swift and true to his word as when he'd moved Riley to Ashlin Square. In the morning, over breakfast, he announced that they were returning to Sanborn Abbey, posthaste. Over protests and complaints, he held firm, and to his surprise, it had finally been Riley who had calmed the outbursts and instructed the girls to acquiesce to their uncle's orders.

For some reason her acceptance had left him suspicious, but he needn't worry overly much about her—with Hashim guarding them, he knew his family and Riley were by now safely ensconced in the large rambling pile of stone that made up Sanborn Abbey and far from the harm that had threatened her.

Leaving him free to uncover her enemy, and his as well.

He knew there was only one way to protect Riley, and that would be to send her far away—farther than Sanborn Abbey. But that would take money he didn't have.

But he knew how to acquire it, the special license in his pocket weighing his spirits down as much as the thought of never seeing Riley again.

Yes, he told himself, glancing through the plain black

domino tied over his face toward his companion for the evening. This was the only way to save Riley.

"What do you think of *my* costume, Lord Ashlin?" Miss Dahlia Pindar asked. "I spent weeks preparing it."

He forced himself to smile at her shepherdess guise, the frills and ribbons nearly burying the petite girl in a sea of white and china blue clutter. "Quite nice," he managed to say.

Dahlia beamed, while her mother nodded approvingly.

He knew from the carriage ride over, wherein she'd chattered nonstop, that she had designed the costume herself, instructing her modiste on every detail, right down to her shepherd's crook wrapped in blue silk and decorated with white tassels.

Of course, after fifteen minutes of carrying the ridiculous accessory about, she'd demanded he hold it because it had become too burdensome for her delicate constitution.

This was what he had come to—not only was he wearing this infernal mask, he was carrying a tasseled crook. He only hoped Del didn't see him looking like a complete idiot.

He could well imagine what Riley would say at the sight of him. More likely, she wouldn't be able to say anything through a guaranteed fit of laughter.

Worst of all, he suspected that if he were with Riley he wouldn't find the evening such a bore.

And now that the masquerade was building to a crush, Dahlia's fine costume appeared hardly as novel as she had earlier boasted. The room churned with shepherdesses, all stalking about in search of any wayward bachelor they could hook into marriage with their own tasseled crooks.

As another blue and white country lass passed by, Dahlia sniffed at the girl's costume, fluffing her own ribbons and bows as if they were quite superior. "It is so difficult being an Original. Everyone apes you in such an unseemly manner."

Mason knew now he shouldn't have been so hard on Bea for her less than flattering description of the cit's daughter. His niece had been right: Dahlia had never had an original idea in her life, let alone the fashion sense worthy of copying.

He wondered what Riley would have worn—something daring, something that would have made her an object of desire to every man in the room.

And then he would have escorted her home, jealous of the attentions she'd been paid, and overly proud that she was his and his alone . . .

But she wasn't his—that position now fell to the girl at his side.

And all that was left was for him to make the appropriate offer and the heiress would be there for the rest of his days.

He glanced down at her and found her looking up at him, her gaze and posture expectant.

She was waiting for him to ask that one simple question.

Will you marry me?

He smiled back at her and then looked away. He could silently practice it all he wanted, but forcing himself to say it out loud was another matter.

Truly, it was only one question, albeit a question that would save his family's future.

As he considered how one did condemn oneself to such a fate, Dahlia gossiped on about this and that, interjecting complaints about the hardships of finding the right lace for another new gown. The girl's self-absorbed prattle continued without any sign of abating, laying Mason's future out before him in a long unending whine.

Evenings not spent in the library reading poetry, arguing Shakespeare, or making up outlandish plots for other plays. Making love in the library, as he would have done with Riley last night, if he hadn't seen those notes.

He stopped himself right there. It wasn't fair to compare Dahlia to Riley, since there was no comparison.

He didn't even try to fool himself that Dahlia would ever be capable of such sensual abandon. Especially since Mrs. Pindar had already intimated that she would expect to live with her daughter.

Her presence would go far toward diminishing any man's desire or his sanity.

Miss Pindar, will you marry me?

Mason wondered if any of his ancestors had braved such a frightening prospect, all in the name of securing the Ashlin fortunes, and saving the woman he loved.

"The Ladies Artemis, Athena, and Persephone," the Everton majordomo intoned loudly, announcing the newest arrivals.

A collective gasp stilled the room. The trio paused in a tableau at the top of the stairs, allowing the moment of silence to interrupt the monotone and continuous announcement of guests.

Very quickly a buzz filled the room until it turned into a groundswell of whispered speculation and betting as to who the beauties behind the masks could be.

If that wasn't bad enough, a rush of young blades, dressed as pirates and cavaliers, and a Romeo or two, rushed toward the entrance, elbowing each other out of position so they could be the first to claim the trio's dance cards.

Then as the gossips deemed the night couldn't get any

better, the trio parted as if on cue, and a fourth lady entered their midst.

"The Lady Aphrodite," the majordomo announced.

Mason froze at the sight of her.

Riley!

A simple gold coronet crowned her unbound wheat-colored hair. Her winter white gown was tied together at one shoulder, and bound at the waist by a gilt girdle. The silk clung to her body, revealing the splendid shape beneath, while a slit from the floor to her knees offered an indecent peek at her long legs. Her mask covered her face so effectively that her identity was hidden even from those who rushed forward in unabashed interest to garner a closer look.

Damn her silken hide! All her contrite acceptance about being banished to Sanborn Abbey had been nothing but an act.

Her best performance to date.

"How shocking," Miss Pindar said. "I don't see how they were allowed in."

At the same time Mason stood there wondering how he could get them out without causing a further scene.

The girl's fan fluttered with nervous tidings. "Have you ever seen a lady so . . . so . . . dare I say it? Uncovered?"

"Dahlia!" her mother said, equally shocked at her daughter's loose comment.

"Well, she is! Oh, I wonder who they are?" she whispered, repeating the question on everyone's tongue.

Her mother raised her nose in the air. "Company we won't be keeping. Shameless jades, the entire lot of them. Don't you agree, Lord Ashlin?"

Mason could only nod. This was perfect. If Riley's and the girls' identities were discovered, and surely they would be at the unmasking, not even the chance of having her daughter become a countess would keep Mrs. Pindar placated, given her current state of moral indignation.

The lady sniffed. "The only consolation is that when those harlots are found out, they will no longer be received or invited to any respectable functions. It's beyond me why His Grace hasn't cast them out."

Cast out! Mason could only hope to be that lucky. Then he'd personally see to it the foursome never saw another social function again—for he planned on having them transported to the furthest reach of the Empire.

"What are they supposed to be?" Miss Pindar asked. "Some type of pagans?"

"Goddesses," Mason corrected. "The one with the bow and arrow is Artemis, the goddess of the hunt. The one next to her is Athena, the goddess of wisdom."

"How can you be sure?" Dahlia asked, a hint of annoyance in her voice.

"The lady is holding an olive branch, the symbol of Athena, while the one at the end must be Persephone, the queen of the underworld, for she carries a black scepter."

"Harumph," Mrs. Pindar sniffed. "Sounds suspiciously like some unreadable French novel."

"Look at the way they are parading about," Dahlia was saying. "Lord Ashlin, I can assure you that I would never behave in such an unseemly manner."

Of that Mason was positive. Dahlia would never do anything that turned heads or enlivened a rather dull evening, nor was there any hope in his heart that she ever would.

Glancing once more at the foursome as they continued their parade into the Everton ballroom, it struck him that now that Riley had arrived, the evening was no longer a dead bore.

*   *   *

Cousin Felicity had described to Riley in great detail how the masquerade would proceed—and Riley had plotted accordingly to make the most of each moment.

Like Cinderella, they would be nearly the last guests to arrive, and then before the unmasking at midnight, they would flee—before anyone found out who they were.

Cousin Felicity had secured their invitations by intercepting Mason's refusal and changing it to an acceptance, so each of the girls had the necessary card required for entrance into this exclusive ball.

Though to be honest, Riley hadn't anticipated that their entrance would bring the entire room to a standstill. As she passed the girls and took the lead, she glanced over her shoulder and reminded them, "Remember, no talking, and don't remove your masks for anyone. And avoid your uncle at all costs."

The girls nodded solemnly, their eyes wide behind their elaborate masks at the rush moving toward them.

Taking a deep breath, Riley started their descent into the vast and packed room.

"A dance, miss," a young man called out to Bea. "I claim your first dance."

His friend, dressed as a savage from the Colonies, surged forward, falling to his knees on the marble steps before Louisa. "I worship at your feet, my fair Persephone. Promise me your heart and I will save you from the depths of Hades and bestow upon you all my worldly possessions."

"What? Your vowels at White's?" one of his friends joked.

The bold young man remained nonplussed. He folded his hands in prayer and proclaimed, "Honey, mead, nectar—whatever a goddess demands would be yours."

Louisa took his outrageous display in stride, as if it

were her due. Regally inclining her head, she plucked a rosebud from her headdress and dropped it at his knees.

A murmur of approval ran through the ranks circling them.

"If I could have your name, dear goddess," the grateful young man said, holding up his prize as if it were gold, "I would continue my devotions tomorrow."

With a skill that even Mrs. Siddons would envy, Louisa's gracious smile turned bittersweet, and she shook her head.

After she rejoined her sisters, they continued their descent into the room, now with a train of devoted followers. Given the pointed stares, Riley suspected the attention they were garnering was unprecedented even in the capricious vagaries of the *ton*.

Cousin Felicity had assured Riley that in the guaranteed crush at the Everton masquerade, it was doubtful they'd run into Mason. That was why she'd agreed so readily to his demand they go to Sanborn Abbey while he stayed behind to uncover her enemy.

She'd had no intention of going out of town the day of the Everton ball. Her stalker wouldn't be able to find her here, nor was she about to let the girls down. They'd all worked together, with Jane Gunn's help, to sew these costumes from fabric they'd pilfered from Caro's closets.

Besides, it had taken every bit of her persuasive power, pleading and finally an hour in the carriage with five crying and wailing women to convince Hashim to countermand Mason's orders.

That, and a double dose of Cousin Felicity's sleeping draught Riley had slipped into his tea, finally took effect, leaving the giant man snoring for the rest of the day and unable to stop the ladies's plans.

Now all they had to do was avoid Mason for the evening. Given the press of people, Riley realized that might not be as hard as she'd first assumed. Besides, he'd be occupied with Dahlia and her mother, and certainly not anticipate finding them here.

Yet as crowded as it was, with each step, Riley expected to see a pair of angry blue eyes glaring out at her from behind the plain black domino she knew he wore.

"You have sown a triumph to be envied," she heard Cousin Felicity whisper into her ear. She turned around and found her co-conspirator all aflutter.

"So far," she whispered back, too superstitious to give in to celebration just yet. Even when the first act went over brilliantly on opening night, Riley never celebrated until the final curtain fell and the theatre shook with enthusiastic applause and cheers. "Now remember, we are silent. You don't know who we are. But if you find an eligible gentleman, the type Mason would approve of, then point him out and let me determine if we should allow him a bit of information on how he might seek out his lady love tomorrow."

Cousin Felicity laughed. "Like the proverbial glass slipper."

The musicians, who had been tuning their instruments for the last few moments, paused to announce the first dance.

This Riley knew would be the true test. As scandalous as their costumes were, would anyone be willing to risk the ire of society and dance with the girls?

Just then, their host, the Duke of Everton, crossed the room and stopped right before her.

She held her breath and waited. Was he about to toss them out? She'd heard that suggestion bandied about by more than one spiteful mother since their arrival.

She dropped to a low curtsey, her mind racing with

countless possibilities as to why the Duke had singled her out.

She never considered the obvious one.

"Madame," he said quietly, "you have caused quite a stir and it is not even ten o'clock."

So much for her plan to remain silent. One could hardly ignore a Duke, let alone the host.

"My apologies, Your Grace," she said, using the accented voice she'd affected when she'd played Hélène, a French émigré, in *The Forgotten Daughter*. She could only hope it disguised her identity from the astute gentleman.

"No apologies necessary, Madame Aphrodite. You've made my masquerade an immediate success. I can spend the rest of the evening resting on my laurels." He bowed over her hand. "If you will honor me with the first dance, I think we will set tongues wagging for a better part of the Season."

Riley could only nod mutely at being singled out for such an honor and followed the man to the dance floor.

With their guardian gone, the sisters were instantly deluged with offers.

Very quickly, Bea and Maggie were on the dance floor with their ecstatic partners, while Louisa remained behind. She had her own reasons for holding out. Smiling patiently at the men who continued to seek her favor, shaking her head at the offers to dance, offers for punch, offers of marriage. She held her solitary position until a man all in black, a Hades to her Persephone, approached her.

He didn't even need to ask her—he just extended his hand and she followed, much to the chagrin of her ardent admirers.

Anyone who saw the exchange could tell the pair were deeply in love, for despite her mask, the lady's smile and eyes glowed for all to see.

"Roderick," she whispered. "You shouldn't have come."

He pulled her closer. "And neither should you—dressed like that." Jealousy glowed in his stormy gaze.

She blushed furiously, only too pleased at his response. How could she explain it? All the hours practicing with him, holding his hand, the chaste kiss that was part of Act Three, had led to this . . . this dizzying, unbelievable feeling.

She'd fallen in love. She was in love with Roderick Northard. It was glorious and unthinkable.

He swung her about, his hand on hers possessive in its grasp. She was his, as it should be.

Still, that didn't stop Louisa from worrying. She leaned closer to him. "What if you are caught? You weren't invited."

"I don't need an invitation to be with you. You are my heart, my love, my life."

She sighed. He may not be a Viscount, or even a gentleman, but he did know how to make her head spin. Still . . .

"Riley might recognize you."

"And what if she does?" Roderick smiled. "I don't care. Let her find out."

Louisa wasn't so convinced. If Riley did find out, then her uncle would know . . . and then there would be, as Beatrice would so eloquently put it, hell to pay.

Roderick would be banished from Ashlin Square and she would never see him again. That is, unless they . . .

She tried to shake off that scandalous thought. She'd be ruined, would never be received if she ran off with an actor. The life she'd dreamt of for herself—as a regal lady-about-town—would be lost.

What she needed to do was stop this affair right now,

before she became too entangled to think straight. Even as she struggled to find the resolve she needed, she stole a glance at the man who'd won her heart.

His grin sent her pulse racing.

'Twas a feeling, she knew, that was worth altering one's dreams.

Riley spent most of the evening watching the proceedings from the side of the dance floor, politely and firmly refusing all offers to dance. When several of her would-be suitors became too insistent, she decided to retreat to one of the alcoves set aside for the matrons and chaperones.

Settling down, Riley was only too glad for a respite from the unwanted attentions and spent a well-earned moment basking in her success.

One that was not shared by the marriage-minded mothers of the other girls who now stood in the shadows of the St. Clair sisters. In the next alcove, the occupants were discussing the situation at length.

"If my daughter wasn't spoken for," the plaintive voice complained, "I'd be furious at the Duke for allowing those jades to remain in good company."

"I agree. Look at my Harriet. Completely overlooked! And the fortune I spent on that costume. Utterly wasted." The other lady paused. "Did you just say that Dahlia is spoken for? The Earl has finally made an offer?"

Riley's ears perked. *Dahlia? Offer?*

Egads, was she too late?

"Well, not exactly," Mrs. Pindar confessed. "Let's say I have acquired enough leverage over Ashlin that he will no longer find reluctance financially feasible. My solicitor is slated to call on him tomorrow, so I would say the announcement should be in all the papers by the end of the week."

Riley's mouth gaped open. Mason's unnamed creditor was Mrs. Pindar. And now the woman intended to force Mason into marrying Dahlia.

She raised her chin a notch higher and steeled herself against the crushing heartbreak welling up inside her and threatening to send a maelstrom of tears streaking down her cheeks.

Mason, as proud and honor bound as he was, would not be able to refuse. For if he did, the Ashlin name would be ruined forever.

"There now, I've been looking everywhere for you," an elderly lady said, as she settled down into the chair next to Riley. Dressed in a black gown and an elegant black turban, the regal lady's only adornment was a magnificent emerald necklace. Majestic in her bearing, and from the fawning attentions of those in her wake, Riley guessed the woman to be a person of lofty social consequences.

Riley rose to leave—rude though it was, for she didn't want to speak with anyone, not right now.

"A moment of your time, young lady." The woman put her hand on Riley's arm and stopped her from rising further.

It was a command that Riley didn't know how to get out of, so she sat.

"You've caused quite a stir," the lady commented.

"So it seems," Riley demurred.

"I am the Countess of Marlowe," the lady said, pausing after the introduction as if she awaited Riley's recognition.

"I am pleased to meet you, Lady Marlowe," Riley said. "But now really isn't the best time. I have some matters that—"

"Young lady, I couldn't care less about your matters! I

said I am the Countess of Marlowe, and now I expect your name. We will attend to your matters in due time." Lady Marlowe stared at her, awaiting the introduction that Riley owed in return. When Riley was not forthcoming, she said, "So you fully intend to keep your identity a secret. In my day you would have been cast out, but Everton is an indulgent fool."

"The Duke has been very kind in his attentions," Riley said in the man's defense.

"Kind indeed. He's made you and your companions the talk of the night. Well, at the unmasking you'll find out the price for such forward and unseemly behavior."

Riley would have found such censure rather alarming if it hadn't been for the twinkle in the lady's eyes. So she smiled indulgently at her, saying nothing.

The sharp lady missed nothing. "Oh, I see. You have no intention of being here when all these fools take off their masks and pretend to be surprised when they discover with whom they've spent the evening." She nudged Riley and pointed her fan at a couple on the dance floor. "Lady Kynsley and her lover, Viscount Worthen. As if anyone doesn't recognize the Kynsley diamonds, let alone the mole on her chin."

Riley resisted the urge to laugh.

"And over there," the lady continued. "Even with all these insipid shepherdesses running about, there is no doubt that prancing, simpering miss dancing with your cousin, Lord Ashlin, is anyone but Charlotte Pindar's daughter. She has her mother's unfortunate mannerisms."

Riley's shock must have been evident even behind her mask. "Lord who?" she tried to bluff.

"Don't even try to play coy with me. I pestered it out of Everton five minutes after your entrance, which I must say was better planned than Nelson's recent campaign."

The lady settled back in her seat, a satisfied grin spreading across her face. "As for being a St. Clair, that is another matter. You haven't their coloring nor their height, though you have a presence about you that could give the mistaken impression you actually belong to that hedonistic lot."

Riley didn't know how to answer that.

The lady eyed her. "Oh, don't get missish on me. I have no intention of telling anyone your secret. Now, let's go back to something more enjoyable—discussing this foolishness around us."

For the next half hour, Lady Marlowe regaled Riley with her intimate knowledge of the foibles and follies of the *ton*.

"Now I've kept you from your charges far too long, my dear," Lady Marlowe said. "Look at the time—if you're to get them out of here before the unmasking, you haven't got a moment to spare."

Riley looked up at the clock and then around the room. Not one of the girls was in sight. "Great!" she muttered. "How will I ever find them in this crush?"

Lady Marlowe laughed. "There is one of them there, coming off the dance floor with Lord Betham's son. Drinkers, all of them. Steer her clear of him."

"Thank you," Riley said, rising to intercept Maggie, who was even now blushing at the attentions being paid her by the gallant Cavalier. "Thank you so much for everything," she told the lady. She didn't know what overcame her, but she leaned over and placed a kiss on the cantankerous lady's cheek. "My friends call me Riley. I would be honored if you would do the same."

So intent on finding Bea and Louisa, she didn't see the look of shock on the lady's face, or the one small tear which fell down her wrinkled cheek before the imperious lady swiped it away.

Oh, it was bad enough she'd violated every one of Mason's edicts this evening, if only to prove him wrong, and now it seemed his dire predictions might be coming true.

"Looking for someone?" asked a voice she'd hoped she wouldn't hear all evening.

Mason caught her by the elbow.

Riley shook herself free. "Are you crazy? You'll give us away."

"You wouldn't have to worry about that if you'd done as I'd instructed."

She bristled at his overbearing demeanor. "Since when did you become the commander of my life?"

"When you came under my protection," he whispered back.

Around them, a few curious glances were turning into open stares. Riley could feel the speculation already getting out of hand.

"Gather the girls together and go home," he instructed. "I will meet you there."

"That is exactly what I planned on doing before you got in my way," she shot back.

"Good. At least you are showing some sense," he said back to her. "I will see you there." He smoothly returned to the crowd, mingling into the crush and disappearing from sight.

Then she remembered what Mrs. Pindar had said. Was there any hope that she could warn him before he found himself bound to Dahlia?

If he hadn't done so already.

She glanced nervously at the clock and realized it was now quarter to midnight. Her gaze frantically searched the crowd around her for Maggie. When she spotted the girl, she made her way to her side and asked, "Where are your sisters?"

Maggie looked over the crowded room again, tipping her head this way and that. "Louisa was dancing with Rod—"

The girl's mouth snapped shut and she bit her lip to obviously keep it that way.

"With Roderick?" Riley asked, not really waiting for an answer. Damn his wretched hide. "Where are they?"

Maggie groaned, as if she preferred Riley ask her to lose a limb rather than betray her sister's confidence.

In the end it was the girl's worried gaze flicking back and forth toward one of the open windows which gave away Louisa's hiding spot.

Riley caught Maggie by the hand, towing her charge along. "We'll see about this."

On their way to the gardens, they passed the room set aside for cards. Out of the corner of her eye, and much to her shock, Riley spied Bea at one of the tables.

If that wasn't bad enough, she was surrounded by a large crowd who seemed entranced by the play before them.

As she and Maggie drew closer, Riley's worse fears of discovery came true when she spied Bea's opponent.

Lady Delander.

Eh, gads! What was Bea thinking, playing cards with their gossipy neighbor?

Even worse, Del stood at his mother's side, his gaze fixed on Bea as if there wasn't another woman in the room.

"Look, Riley," Maggie whispered. "Bea's winning."

Indeed she was. Piled up in front of the girl sat a large stack of coins and even one of the Dowager's earrings, the ruby and diamond heirloom winking mischievously amidst the gold.

Oblivious that she'd been caught, Bea played the rest of her cards, smiling in triumph at Lady Delander as she laid down the card necessary to win the game.

Around the table the spectators exchanged shocked glances.

"Well, I never!" Lady Delander sputtered.

"That's the fifth straight hand that gel's won," an older man in a domino remarked to no one in particular.

"I demand a rematch," Lady Delander said. "I will have satisfaction, for there must be something amiss with you, young lady. I'll have you know I am not beaten in piquet. Ever."

"The evidence in front of her begs to differ, Mother," Del said, winking at Bea. "Apparently being a goddess makes the lady impervious to your, shall we say, remarkable skills."

"Oh, do shut up, Allister," Lady Delander snapped. "Now I will have another hand, *Miss Artemis*."

At this moment, Bea glanced up and her gaze met Riley's.

Riley shook her head and nodded slightly at the clock over the mantel, which read quarter to midnight.

"I'm sorry, my lady," Bea murmured, "but I must go." Scooping her winnings into the hunting pouch at her waist, she hastened after Riley before the flabbergasted woman protested further.

Del watched dumbfounded as the beautiful goddess fled the room in the wake of her other appealing companions. Besides besting his mother in piquet, the enchanting huntress had slain his heart with her devilish glances from behind her silver mask.

How had he ever thought himself in love with Riley St. Clair?

The mystery about his newfound love was more intoxicating than his father's entire cache of French brandy, yet there was also something very familiar about her.

As if he'd known her all his life.

Who the devil was she?

For the first time in years, Del ignored his mother's complaints, her demands that the girl be brought back immediately, and a hundred other allegations, and strode back to the ballroom determined to be at this girl's side before midnight.

As he leaned against the doorway and surveyed the crush of the ballroom beyond, he wondered how many times he had stood right next to her and not seen the fire in her eyes or realized that the woman of his dreams was within arm's reach.

Well, he wouldn't make that mistake again.

But first he had to find her and unmask his bride-to-be.

The gardens behind the Duke's residence appeared as crowded as the rest of his house.

But in contrast to the carefully orchestrated notes inside, the refrain filling the air out here was the sounds of soft sighs and ardent kisses. Fine manners and the careful watchful eyes of mothers and chaperones forgotten, the guests outside displayed little reserve.

Couples, tucked away behind statues and rose bushes and cuddled up on benches dotting the gardens, flaunted propriety. Besides, with the combination of masks and darkness, it was hard to discern anyone's identity.

Riley turned to her two unwilling wards. "Find your sister—and find her fast, before anyone sees her."

Bea went in one direction, Maggie the other, while Ri-

ley went down the main path. Not caring a whit for propriety, she started tapping on shoulders.

"Excuse me," she murmured time and again as she interrupted countless couples. Her only relief was not finding Mason and his simpering Dahlia joined in some
passionate embrace.

Just as she was about to give up, she heard Roderick's
all too familiar voice—and his lines.

"Aveline, sweet Aveline, I care not for the disparateness
of our situation or our upbringing, only that we remain
together."

Riley wanted to groan. Mason had been right: the line
did make Geoffroi sound like a simpering fool.

She parted the branches of the foliage before her and
found Louisa enfolded in Roderick's arms.

She caught the errant girl by the back of her gown and
tugged her free. Settling a sputtering Louisa behind her,
she turned to Roderick, who came bounding out of the
greenery looking for a fight.

"I demand satisfaction," he sputtered, before coming
face to face with his employer. "Oh, Riley, it's you."

"Yes, it's me. Remind me to cut that line from the scene
tomorrow—along with all your other ones."

"But Riley—" Louisa began to protest, trying to cut
around her and return to her lover.

Riley was too quick. She held the anxious girl fast.
"That is quite enough out of you! What were you thinking?"

The girl's face told the entire story—one Riley knew
only too well. Louisa's heart had been lost.

She softened her features and smiled at her. "We'll discuss this when we get home." She turned to Roderick.
"As for you—you will stay away from Louisa. If I find
you've done anything that has compromised her beyond

this thoughtless display, then you are fired and I will see you never work in London again."

The young man drew himself up. "Now see here, I mean to offer for Louisa."

Riley shuddered. Oh, this was far worse than she suspected. "And you think your offer would be seriously considered? Roderick, I don't know where you come from, but actors do not marry the daughters of earls." She shook her head and started down the path with a squirming and protesting Louisa in tow.

Roderick glowered as Riley dragged his beloved away. "We'll just see who is so unworthy, Madame Fontaine. We'll just see."

Maggie followed dutifully after Riley and her sisters, more than a little sad to be leaving so early. After years of dreaming about attending fashionable events, she would have liked the evening to last forever.

For the first time in her life she'd been elegant, and best of all, desired. She'd had suitors! Men asking her to dance, asking for an introduction, begging for a hint as to her identity.

She sighed. If only, like Louisa and Bea, she could have found her own true love this night.

Maggie knew exactly what he looked like—dark and mysterious. Perhaps even an eye patch covering an injury he'd suffered in battle or in a duel of honor. She would have danced in his arms, beaten his mother at cards, or done whatever it was Louisa had done in the garden that had her blushing a deep scarlet and Riley looking grim and determined to get them home as quickly as possible.

Lost in this bout of woolgathering, she didn't realize they'd gained the steps down to the street, and she stumbled on the first one.

And into the arms of a stranger.

The book she'd borrowed from her uncle's library and used as part of her costume went clattering down the steps, along with the gentleman's hat.

His steely embrace steadied her and kept her from plunging headlong into the street below. The spicy, tangy scent of cologne, bay rum, she thought, enveloped her.

And when she looked up, she discovered her hero and didn't mind so much her first clumsy step of the evening.

"Are you all right, miss?" he asked. He held her for a moment longer than was proper before setting her on her own feet. "There you are. Are you sure you are well?"

Maggie could only nod, afraid to say anything that might awaken her from this unbelievable dream.

"I fear your book and my hat didn't fare as well," he laughed, taking the steps down two at a time and retrieving her battered book and his flattened hat.

This gave her a moment to study her savior. He wore a naval uniform—not some costume, but his own uniform, of that she was sure from the way it fit his body. And after he picked up their belongings at the bottom of the steps and turned back to her, he paused and stared up at her as if she were the most enchanting creature he'd ever beheld.

Maggie was positive he was the most handsome man she'd ever seen—dark, mysterious, albeit missing a pirate's patch; it was a minor detail she could overlook if it meant she could spend the rest of her life enveloped in his sure embrace.

He made an elegant bow and reached for her hand. "My name is—" he began to say.

She had her hand out in double time but found it taken not by her newfound love, but by Bea.

"Sorry to interrupt, *Athena*," Bea said, shooting an apologetic smile at the man. "But we must leave. Now."

With that, her sister dragged her away.

Maggie tried for a moment to pull out of Bea's grip, but her sister had the advantage of height and a good stone in weight—she might as well be fighting against Mr. Hashim.

Captain Westley Hardy watched the shy little creature be dragged away by the other girl, feeling as if he had just spent eight hours in battle rather than a few short moments in the presence of a mere slip of a thing.

Who was she?

Before he could follow, her party gained their carriage and were off, the horses jumping forward in their traces at the snap of the coachman's whip. The conveyance and its delightful occupants were gone into the night before he could stop them.

Damnation, he didn't even know her name.

Just then, another man came racing past him. The fellow, dressed in some outrageous highwayman's outfit, turned toward him. "Have you seen a quartet of goddesses?"

In any other circumstances, Captain Hardy would have thought the man a complete nodcock, but given what he'd just witnessed, he nodded.

The man cursed. "How ever am I going to find her now?"

Despite the costume and the mask, Hardy recognized the voice. "Delander?"

"Hardy!" Del said back, reaching out and shaking his hand vigorously. "I'd heard you were in town. Glad to see you. The Saint will be beside himself to hear you're about. The three of us, together again."

"St. Clair's in town?" Hardy asked.

"Ashlin now. Inherited his brother's title last year."

"Then one of you must know who those creatures were," Hardy asked. "The ones done up like goddesses."

"You saw them?" Del asked. "You've got the devil's own timing—whyever didn't you order a round fired over that carriage, or whatever it is you do in the Navy to see an enemy ship stopped? You've just lost treasure worth more than any of the prizes I heard tell you've taken in the last few years."

Hardy, though glad to see his boyhood friend, felt a moment of jealousy. "Athena?"

To his relief, Del shook his head. "No, Artemis. Did you see her? Divine."

"Yes, well I had similar thoughts about the other one," Hardy said, holding up the book the girl had left behind.

"At least you have a memento." Del settled down in a dejected heap on the steps, and stared moodily out into the night. "So what is it goddesses are reading these days?" he asked over his shoulder.

Hardy glanced down at his prize, taken aback by the title.

The Battle Tactics of Alexander the Great. He handed it down to Del.

"Not exactly the *Elysian Times*," Del joked, as he glanced over the book. "Who the devil would ever want to read such a boring tome?" He flipped open the first page and stared down at it. Then a wide grin spread over his face.

"Hardy, my good man—how are you at planning a siege?" With that, Del handed him back the book, opened to the first page.

Even in the torchlight, Hardy could read the handwritten note on the first page.

The property of Mason St. Clair, Merton College, Oxford.

Chapter 17

~~~⌒⌒⌒~~~

Mason walked home from the Everton masquerade, each pounding step filled with purpose and anger.

How dare she disobey him and endanger her life just so the girls could go to a foolish party?

Riley! Would she *ever* stop driving him to distraction?

Mason took a deep breath. Much to his chagrin, he had to admit he'd been relieved to see her. She'd stopped him from having to listen to Mrs. Pindar and her daughter's vapid conversation for the entire evening.

As he continued walking the few blocks from Everton's stylish town house to Ashlin Square, he considered the gist of his conversation with Mrs. Pindar, which had been more a series of veiled threats than polite hints.

Marry my daughter, or I will find another down-on-his-luck earl to make her a countess.

With all that, she'd finished by saying her solicitor would call on him in the morning to see if they could settle matters.

He hadn't liked the way the lady's eyes had narrowed, like those of a weasel after a chicken, when she'd smiled and said, "You may find, my lord, that my solicitor is able to offer a convincing argument to ease your reluctance."

Reluctance, indeed! He had no doubts now who'd been buying up Freddie's vowels and for what purpose. And with each step he grew more angry. Nudging loose a stone with his boot, he kicked it into the darkness.

What had he become?

Oh, he was a new kind of Ashlin, all right—just not anything close to the honorable and respected foundation he had envisioned rebuilding for his family.

So where had he gone wrong?

He knew. He'd lost his honor and self-respect when he'd decided on a marriage of convenience rather than one of love.

For when he'd decided to pursue the eminently wealthy Dahlia Pindar, he'd lost his heart.

And he knew who held it.

Riley.

But how could he marry her?

He was penniless—actually, worse than penniless. He'd spent the last seven months going over and over Freddie's investments, the account books, every scrap of paper, trying to find something that might give way to any last coin the family possessed so he could make a better show of it.

And he'd failed. There was nothing to be had. He had nothing but himself to offer the hard-working, dedicated lady.

Exactly the down-on-his-luck earl Mrs. Pindar eyed with such a mercantile gleam.

But Riley didn't look at him like that. She cared not that he was an earl. In fact, he suspected his noble title made him less appealing to the unconventional lady.

As he entered Ashlin Square, he looked across the park to his house, where there glowed a single taper in the library.

She was waiting for him.

Mason knew what had to be done. He could live his life for love and lose everything, or he could see the ones he loved safe and secure by giving up what he wanted.

There really was no choice.

Riley waited in the library for Mason, resisting the urge to peek out the windows and watch for his approach.

She knew if she saw him stomping up the steps, she'd probably lose the nerve to do what she must.

She needed to say good-bye.

She'd done as she'd promised—refashioned the girls into Originals—if the storm of suitors that had plagued them all night was any evidence. And it shouldn't be long before offers of marriage came flooding into Ashlin House.

At least the girls would find happiness, she thought.

And for one night, Riley mused, she too would find her own small piece of that elusive emotion.

Glancing around the room for something to occupy herself until Mason got home, she spied his spectacles sitting atop a book on the library table.

Her curiosity getting the better of her, she looked around to see if anyone was about. Satisfied she was alone, she picked them up and studied them.

They lent him such a stern air, and yet they seemed so innocuous when left by the wayside—still, if he had forgotten them, she wondered how he was to get on without them.

Perhaps he'd proposed to the wrong girl, considering how many shepherdesses had been wandering about tonight. Wouldn't that make Mrs. Pindar see red! And serve the manipulative woman right.

Riley glanced down at the spectacles in her hand and then up at the mirror over the fireplace.

I wonder how he sees the world, she thought . . . carrying them over to the mantel and closing her eyes as she placed them on her face.

When she opened her eyes, she made a startling discovery—the glass inside the frames was just that—glass.

Clear and unground.

She stared at her reflection, wondering why the Earl chose to wear glasses, when he didn't need them.

"Because when you are the son of the *ton*'s most notorious rake and you want to be taken as a serious academic, you try to distance yourself as far as you can from fashionable society," Lord Ashlin said from the doorway, where he stood watching her.

She spun around and faced him. "Pardon?"

"You were wondering why I wear glasses which I don't really need." He stepped into the room. "They do work, though. You look quite the bluestocking."

She plucked the evidence off her face, her cheeks burning at being caught. "I'm sorry," she rushed to say, holding them out. "I saw them here and I don't know what came over me."

"Curiosity, perhaps," he suggested, taking them from her and setting them back down on the table where he'd left them. "I don't know why I still wear them. Habit, perhaps."

Riley felt like the veriest ninny. She'd meant for him to find her like Aphrodite herself, reclined and awaiting her lover, such a seductive sight that he would fall at her feet and profess his undying love, disavowing Dahlia Pindar once and for all.

Instead, he'd come in and found her peering about like an old spinster!

Lost in her own musings, she didn't realize he'd come up behind her until his hands caught her by the shoulders. His touch was different somehow. Stronger. More commanding. Perhaps it was just his anger at her, but she sensed something between them had changed.

"Riley, what were you thinking, disobeying my order?"

She glanced over at him. His mask was gone, but the face that stared at her shone with steely resolve, sending shivers down her spine with the intimacy of his gaze, the intensity of it. "Your order was wrong. I can hardly see what danger, if any, I would be in at the Duke's."

"The least you could have done was choose costumes that didn't stand out. Greek goddesses, indeed!"

Tapping her finger to her lips, she considered this. "Yes, perhaps I should have done them up like shepherdesses, we could have hidden quite nicely with the flock."

"That isn't funny," Mason said, continuing his severe tone, but Riley could see the desire to laugh twinkling in his eyes, at his lips.

"You find something wrong with this costume?" She stepped back from him and slowly turned in a circle. "A man of classical tastes, like yourself, I would think you'd find it quite intriguing."

His jaw worked back and forth. "Yes, very intriguing. Too much so. I know finances are tight around here, but couldn't you have found enough fabric to see that you were all decently clad?"

"Decently?" She smiled, then tipped her sandled foot out, so the slit in her gown fell away, exposing her leg up to her thigh. "I don't see what is so indecent about this. Do you?"

She edged closer to him and took his hands, guiding them down the edge of her body so he could feel the line of her breasts, the curve of her hips.

"You have nothing on beneath this," he said, in a voice filled with need.

"Maybe I do, and maybe I don't," she whispered back. "There really is only one way to find out."

She didn't need to encourage him any further. Mason caught her in his arms and crushed his lips to hers in a hungry kiss.

It made every tense moment since he'd entered the room flare up in a blaze of passion.

She opened her mouth to him, welcoming him.

If only they could kiss like this forever.

Mason seemed determined to give her that wish, for he continued plying her with his lips, teasing her to open up to him, until her senses whirled in a dizzy circle.

When he finally lifted his head, Riley gasped for air.

"Every day you remain in London, you are in danger," he told her.

"Only from you," she whispered back, tipping up on her toes and kissing him anew. She hadn't thought it would be this easy to convince him that propriety and honor had no place in their relationship. She wanted, just for one night, to belong to the man she would never be able to have.

It was a selfish wish—to have this night always in her heart, when by tomorrow, he would be betrothed to someone else.

She didn't blame him—not too much, for Dahlia Pindar's fortune would forge the foundation for the honorable life he so valued.

Something Riley couldn't give him. Her theatre could stave off the worst of his debts, but roofs for tenants and repairs to a tumble-down pile of venerable stones that made up the Abbey would never be possible.

So if there was no place for her to fit into that cozy

future of respectability, for tonight she would pretend that she was his heiress, his convenient bride, rich and in love with him.

Well, at least one part of that was true.

She did love him with all her heart.

He'd started kissing her neck, in that spot right behind her ear, the one that left her knees weak and her breath coming in short, ragged pants.

Her fingers worked open his coat, moving their way over his chest, tracing over the muscles, the strength, the wild, steely cadence of his heart beating beneath her palm.

Mason quickly shrugged off his coat and then his cravat. Riley helped him, pulling his shirt free of his breeches and pushing it up over his head.

Taking a moment just to look at him, she wondered if she'd ever seen a man more magnificently put together. Having grown up in the theatre, she'd seen men—in all states of undress as they switched between costumes in often crowded conditions—so the sight of a bare-chested man didn't alarm her.

What stopped her breath was how beautiful his body was to her. She'd never beheld a man like this, anticipating what was to come, knowing that he would be holding her tightly to him, claiming her with his touch.

She stepped willingly into that irresistible realm.

He reached out and slid the single shoulder of her gown down and along her arm. Her breasts fell free, leaving them exposed to him.

Riley thought she should be embarrassed, but the gleam in his eyes told her not to be—Mason found her desirable. Very much so. He pulled her close, his arm cradling her waist. She arched as his lips trailed a heated path down the nape of her neck. He made the descent with agonizingly deliberate indulgence, tasting each inch of her flesh as if it were his last morsel.

Her stomach tightened as his lips made a tender assault on her breast, touched her with a reverent sigh and whisper.

A soft moan escaped her when he closed his mouth over her nipple, teasing the peak to life. She'd never imagined that it would feel like this, this fluttering, hungry need.

Mason had tossed aside respectability the moment he'd walked in and found her wearing his spectacles.

A goddess in glasses.

He would have Riley in his life and only her—and damn the problems that would ensue. Ashlins forged their own unique path through life, and it was time he blazed his.

He would find a way to pay off Frederick's debts and tell Mrs. Pindar and her greedy plans to go to hell. Then he would marry this woman whom he loved so much. It was easy to believe all that was possible when he stood here claiming Riley with his kiss.

In his arms, she wavered, pressing into his embrace. He glanced about—but there was really no place for them to make love, other than on the hard floor or the poor thin carpet.

That, he decided, would never do. But where to take her? He couldn't very well carry her about the house in this state. There were some bits of propriety he would not shrug off.

"My room," she whispered. "Let's go to my room."

He grinned, for she was right. Her suite was the only other room on this floor that had the one thing he wanted tonight. A bed with Riley in it. So, in a swift motion, he swept her into his arms and carried her down the hall.

Nudging the door open with his knee, he entered her room, and then shouldered the door shut.

Gently he laid her down on the simple bed. Her maid had left a fire kindled in the hearth, which lent the room a cozy, warm glow, but still she shivered.

"Are you cold?" he asked.

Riley shook her head, and caught his face with her hands and pulled him down to her, so she could kiss him again.

"Greedy girl," he told her between languid kisses.

"Perhaps I should have gone as Avarice tonight," she teased.

He laughed. "No, if ever there was an Aphrodite, you are her every embodiment."

"Then I command you to give me your love." She waved her hand with a regal motion.

"As you wish, my lady," he said, happy to comply with her royal demands.

He eased off the rest of her dress. She now lay before him, her hair tousled about her shoulders and torso, the single coronet her only decoration. Her sleek body reclined in a sensual pose, inviting him to come closer.

Tugging off his breeches, he joined her in the bed. They rolled together, tangled in a deep kiss, their bodies growing used to the feel of the other.

Riley couldn't believe this was happening. What was she thinking? She didn't know anything about making love to a man! But at the same time, as her hands wandered over Mason's body, she realized that perhaps she didn't need that much experience, for her touch seemed to excite him.

She followed his lead, touching and kissing and exploring, until her hand brushed against his hardness.

Drawing back for a moment, she wondered what she should do, but as with the rest of the evening, she followed her instincts and reached out for him, curling her fingers along his length.

It must have been the right thing to do, for he sucked in his breath and stilled. When she stopped, he told her in a ragged voice, "No, please keep doing that."

Grinning, she willingly complied.

Not to be left behind, Mason's lips had found one of the rigid peaks of her breasts again and was even then suckling it, teasing it to life. The sensations left her writhing, her legs pressing together at the odd tightness and longing starting to build at the apex.

His fingers began stroking her there, kindling a new need. Her hips rocked back and forth under his touch, answering with a natural response.

Slowly his finger dipped further between her thighs, sliding over a spot so sensitive she gasped in surprise.

He pulled his hand away and gently brushed her tangled hair out of her face, soothing her.

"When you told me you'd never had a lover," Mason said softly, "you meant you'd never done this, didn't you?"

"That is usually what it means when a woman has never had a lover," she snapped back.

"There's that artistic temperament again." He leaned over and kissed her. "I don't care if you have or haven't, but since you haven't, I want you to know this may hurt."

"I fully expect it will."

He glanced down at her in surprise. "Why do you say that?"

"I've lived in close quarters all my life, I've heard people making love before. From all the moaning and screaming, I just assumed it wasn't the most pleasant experience—but you are starting to convince me I might have been wrong on that count." She smiled shyly. "Convince me some more."

He did, most eagerly, kissing her and touching her again until she was reduced to a panting frenzy.

"Oh, Mason," she gasped, her body afire, her fears far flung. "It is so wonderful."

"It gets even better."

Riley didn't know how that could be possible as he covered her body with his, and gently entered her.

At first it was uncomfortable, but Mason took his time, slowly working himself in with gentle strokes, until he came to the barrier that proclaimed her innocence.

Gently, he pressed forward.

She took in a deep breath as the pain subsided and was replaced by his kisses, murmurs of gentle words in her ear.

He continued to move within her and, unbidden, her hips started to match his movements.

Riley knew she was building to something, but what she didn't know until her world grew so fervent, so needy, so intense, it suddenly burst open into an explosion of passion.

She would have let out a triumphant cry if Mason hadn't been kissing her. His own release came fast on the heels of hers, spilling forth and leaving him spent and lost in her arms.

For a time they lay together, quiet in the wonder of what had just happened.

Finally, Riley, his goddess of love, leaned up on one elbow and said to him, "Now I know what all the screaming is about."

Chapter 18

Riley awoke disoriented. The sun streamed in through a crack in the curtains, throwing a telltale shaft of light across the room. She didn't remember when Mason had left, only the delicious memories of the night before.

That is, until she saw the note on the pillow beside her face.

Welcome to your last morning.

The rough letters were only too familiar.

Riley opened her mouth to scream, but a hand clamped down over her lips, preventing her from calling out.

"That wouldn't be very smart," a voice said. "Then your lover would come in here and I'd have to kill him. And I haven't been paid that much. Not yet, that is."

Riley knew that voice—had heard it too many times to count. She twisted around and found Daniel, one of the actors from the company, grinning at her.

Riley watched in horror as Daniel's once friendly expression faded away—his eyes narrowing to a feral gleam, his lips curling back into a mocking sneer—and he began to laugh.

In a flash, he stuffed a rag in her mouth and tied another cloth over it so she couldn't cry out. Then he caught her arms and bound them behind her back. His fingers bit into her skin, until the pain burned across her flesh like white-hot irons.

The man's grip tightened, and then he yarded her into his arms.

She struggled and fought, but the man suddenly seemed as wiry as a terrier and twice as fast. His hand caught her throat and began to cut off her air.

"Who are you?" she struggled to sputter from beneath her gag, staring into the deadliest pair of eyes she'd ever seen.

"Not the poor country actor you so stupidly hired," he mocked. "From here on out, I am Mr. Nutley to you."

A solid pounding on his door woke Mason from a restless sleep.

"What?" he called out, reaching for his dressing gown and glancing at the clock.

Quarter past noon.

Eh, gads, he'd slept away the morning.

That's what happens when you choose not to sleep at night, he could well imagine Freddie saying.

"Uncle," came Bea's anxious plea. "Uncle, I think something is wrong."

He yanked open his door. "I've already spoken to Riley about last night, Beatrice. We will discuss it later." He started to close the door, but Bea shoved her foot into the jamb.

"Uncle, it's Riley I want to talk to you about. Her door

is locked, and when I put my ear to it and listened, I heard—"

Mason shook his head. "Bea, don't you think you are a little bit old to be eavesdropping?"

"Not when it has a purpose," she told him, taking advantage of the slight opening and catching him by the arm. She tugged him into the hallway. "Uncle, Riley's in trouble. I heard a man in her room."

Hot anger and fear tore at his gut, numbing any bit of reason. It didn't take but a second for the shock to register that Riley's stalker had finally gotten to her side.

Mason yanked himself free from Bea's grip and tore down the hallway and to the stairs.

Damnation! Why had he left her? He'd only done it out of some foolish, leftover sense of propriety.

Well, never again.

He tried her door once, but as Bea had said, it was locked. He took a large step back and kicked it open, shattering the frame and sending it flying open to reveal the horrific scene within.

To his amazement, Daniel, an actor from the Queen's Gate, stood next to the bed, his thick hands twisted around Riley's neck, her face bluish, and her mouth covered with a gag.

"Take one step, Ashlin," Daniel warned him, "and I'll snap her neck. Finish her off before your eyes." He twisted his hands tighter, as if to show his deadly intent.

"And then I'll kill you," Mason told him.

Daniel laughed, easing his way toward the open window, dragging Riley along with him. "I don't think so," he said, turning his body to reveal the pistol tucked in his waistband. "I hadn't thought I'd get you both, but this looks to be my lucky day. I'll kill you and your bitch.

Quite a scandal. You murdered your little whore and then took your own life."

"Why?" Mason asked.

"I've got my reasons," he bragged.

Riley's breath rattled, her desperation evident as she clawed at the fingers wound around her throat.

Mason took another step forward, trying to gauge how best to distract the villain.

His help came from an unlikely source. Bea caught up with him just then, and before Mason could stop her, hurled his dagger into the fray, the blade burying itself into the fiend's thigh.

Daniel yelped in pain, releasing Riley as he clutched at the hilt buried in his leg.

Mason could only wonder what his niece was doing with his dagger and where she'd learned to throw it, but her quick thinking gave him the chance he needed.

He plunged forward, pushing Riley away and crashing into Daniel.

The force and power of Mason's attack sent the two men flying into the window. Glass and wood shattered around them, leaving a gaping hole. They continued to struggle, pummeling at each other. Daniel was a dirty fighter, but Mason had left his honor and rules of conduct at the door. He fought like the devil himself, landing one crushing blow into the man's jaw after another, sending him reeling. For a horrible second, Daniel teetered at the edge of the window, his arms flailing about, his eyes wild with fear until he toppled backwards through the opening, crashing to his death on the cobbles two stories below.

Mason slumped to the floor, battered and bleeding.

Bea had managed to free Riley, who now flew to his side. "Are you all right?"

"Yes," he said. His hands smoothed her hair and her tear-soaked cheeks. "Are you?"

She nodded.

He pulled her into his arms and held her, the two of them rocking in shocked silence.

Just then Hashim came rushing in, a guttural warrior's cry coming out of his mouth, his sword drawn. When he looked about, obviously confused, Mason said to him, "It is over," and nodded toward the window where Bea now stood gazing down at the grisly scene.

Bea turned to him. "Uncle?"

"Yes?"

"There's a crowd gathering," she said.

He rose to his feet, pulling Riley along with him, holding her close. They went to the window and stared down at the sight below. "We'd better move the body inside before half of Fleet Street is up here casting about their lurid speculations on the matter." He turned to Hashim. "Can you see to it?"

The Saracen nodded.

After he had left, Riley buried herself in Mason's arms again. "I didn't know. I thought Daniel was just an actor who needed a job. Who would have thought he was capable of such hatred?"

Mason was equally stunned. He'd been unable to find out anything about the man in his investigations, and had finally given up on him as a suspect since he seemed a rather regular sort. "Did he say anything to you? Anything at all that would give you an idea why he would have done this?"

"No, nothing that would explain it," she said. "He changed before my very eyes—as if he were another person and had been playing Daniel all along."

Mason paused. "And he didn't say anything that might give us a clue?"

Riley closed her eyes. "Nutley," she whispered. She looked up. "He wanted me to call him Mr. Nutley."

Mason nodded and filed the name away. For now he needed to find a plausible explanation as to why an actor from the Queen's Gate Theatre had fallen out his window. And then he'd have to see about having the body taken away and buried. "I'll be needed down there," he told her. "Will you be all right?"

She nodded.

Bea moved forward. "I'll stay with her, Uncle."

"Good girl, Bea," he said, ruffling her hair. "By the way, who taught you how to throw a knife?"

Bea blushed. "Viscount Delander. The summer you two came to Sanborn Abbey from school."

Mason shook his head. "Del! Ever the corrupting influence. Remind me to thank him one day."

"Mason," Riley called out. "It is over, isn't it? I mean, with Daniel . . ." She glanced again at the broken window and shuddered. "Now that he's gone, I'm safe—aren't I?"

He smiled at her. "It would seem so. He can't threaten you ever again."

A tear fell down her cheek, and then another.

Mason went to her side, and pulled her close to him again. "There, there. You're safe. You'll not be bothered by any of this again."

"You saved my life. Twice. I'll never forget you." While her appreciation was heartfelt, her gaze spoke even more volumes.

It said the words of love that he dared not say out loud. Not yet. Not until he had the means to make an offer for her.

So when he didn't reply, she turned out of his arms. "You'd best go see to Daniel."

Mason heard the catch in her voice.

The catch in his own heart. But his pride got the better of him. He'd failed her again—as he would if he offered her marriage and condemned her to a life of poverty. Riley deserved so much more.

"Thank you, Mason," he heard her say as he left the room. "Thank you for everything."

He just wished it were true. That he could give her everything.

"Riley, Riley," Cousin Felicity called out. "Come quickly. Oh, dear girl, where are you? Where are you?"

Riley poked her head out the door of her room, where she and Nanette had been packing her belongings. Now that the threat to her life was gone, Riley saw no reason to remain at Ashlin House. Mrs. Pindar's solicitor had arrived not long after Daniel's body had been taken away and made the lady's intentions clear—Mason was to offer for Dahlia immediately, or she would see him in debtor's prison. It seemed Mrs. Pindar did indeed hold the upper hand.

Or at least, that was what Maggie had reported overhearing, and though Riley had made a good show of scolding the girl for eavesdropping, she did so with a heavy heart.

Without the gold to redeem his debts, Riley knew Mason had little choice to save his family. By nightfall, he'd be betrothed to Miss Pindar.

"Oh, Riley, where are you?" Cousin Felicity repeated.

"I am here. Whatever is wrong?"

"Wrong? Why nothing," the lady told her, the lace in her cap awhirl with motion. "You'll never believe who has sent a carriage over!"

Riley sighed. She could see Aggie's wretched influence in the dear lady—she was growing more dramatic with each passing day. "Do tell," she prompted, knowing full well Cousin Felicity wouldn't rest until she had the entire tale out.

Cousin Felicity leaned forward and whispered, "The Countess of Marlowe." She said the name as if it were an event too unbelievable to fathom.

"Lady Marlowe?" Riley recalled the name. "Oh, yes. I met her last night at the ball." She turned around and went back to her packing.

Trailing after Riley, Cousin Felicity followed all in a flutter. "You met *Lady Marlowe*?"

"Why, yes. Is that so odd?" Riley folded a chemise and added it to the trunk.

Cousin Felicity shook her head. "My dear girl, Lady Marlowe does not go out. You couldn't have met her last night."

"I suppose she made an exception for His Grace. We talked for nearly an hour."

"Well, I suppose that explains everything," Cousin Felicity announced.

Riley was almost afraid to ask. "Explains what?"

"Why Lady Marlowe has sent her carriage for you. You are to attend her immediately."

Riley shook her head. "I can't possibly go now. I have to finish packing and then we have rehearsals all afternoon down at the theatre." She picked up another chemise and began folding. "Be a dear, and send the lady my regrets."

Cousin Felicity stared at Riley as if she had just asked her to shop somewhere other than on Oxford Street.

"Is there something else?" Riley asked.

"You can't refuse the Countess. It isn't done."

"I know it was nice of Lady Marlowe to send over her carriage, but I can't just drop everything to go visit some lonely old lady because she wills it."

"Oh, yes, you will," Cousin Felicity said, taking the folded chemise out of Riley's hand and setting it aside. "You will change your gown and march right downstairs and get into that carriage. If not for yourself, then for the girls."

Riley had never heard such a tone in Cousin Felicity's voice. "You make this sound like a royal edict. I hardly think turning down one—"

Cousin Felicity's hands went to her hips. "Lady Marlowe may not go out, but her word is law."

"You said the same thing about Lady Delander, and look at her now."

The lady was not to be persuaded. She lowered her voice and whispered, "Even Lady Delander fears her wrath. 'Tis rumored she had her own daughter committed because the girl was on the verge of ruining the family. You can't refuse."

Riley sighed. Since Lady Marlowe knew she wasn't a St. Clair, she could possibly start rumors to that effect. How the *ton* would view her questionable situation at the Ashlin residence, Riley could well imagine. And guessed it would place enough taint on the girls to ruin their chances of an advantageous match, as well as Mason's with Miss Pindar.

"Perhaps I should go," she acquiesced.

Cousin Felicity brightened immediately. "Of course you should." As Cousin Felicity continued nattering on about how one should dress for a summons from the Countess, Riley reasoned that she could do this one last thing for the girls and Mason before she returned to her old life and spent the rest of her days trying to forget them.

*   *   *

The Marlowe residence surprised Riley with its splendor. She had thought the Ashlin house quite grand, but obviously there was a vast difference in stations even amongst the *ton*. It was a thought that had never occurred to her—she had always thought the high society of London all existed in the same sphere, but obviously this was not so.

Everywhere she looked there was gilt. Gilt frames, gilt curlicues and plasters on the walls, gilt sconces. All of this was set off by brocade wall hangings and rich velvet curtains. The house was, it seemed, as ostentatious as its occupant.

Riley was led up the stairs, down a long gallery of grim paintings and large Chinese vases, and finally into a bright room which overlooked a small garden. The Countess, regal in her black gown, sat at a round table, a chessboard before her.

"Do you play?" she asked, as Riley drew near.

She shook her head.

"Too bad. It is an intelligent game—one of wits and skill. I would guess that you would be quite adept at it." The Countess stared at her this way and that, as if she were measuring her against some unseen composition. "Hmmm," the lady mused. "Well, don't just stand there, child. Sit. I don't bite, though it is a tale told to recalcitrant children to make them behave."

Laughing at this, Riley sat in the chair the Countess bade her to take.

As the lady began to pour the tea, she launched into a dissertation about the prior night's events, commenting quite frankly on the poor choice of costumes, the odd pairings, and the obvious affairs that made the *ton* so diverting. Then out of the blue, she asked, "I'm still quite puzzled about you. I know you aren't a St. Clair, so I must ask, who are you?"

"I fear you would find it quite boring," Riley said. She found her gaze caught by a portrait over the mantel. There, immortalized in oil, was a gentleman, standing beside a pedestal, a hound lounging at his feet. In his hand, he held a sword much as one would a cane, the tip pointed into the ground, the hilt tipped at a jaunty angle. His face smiled out at his audience, a kindly but mischievous tilt to his lips. His eyes, crinkled around the corners, sparkled with a friendly air. In the background rose a great house with a wide lawn before it and graceful trees encircling it in a protective embrace. Across the lawn, swans and other birds dotted the greenery.

Riley could have sworn she'd seen the man before— but where and when she couldn't say. And the house—it was like something out of a dream. "My lady, who is that?" she asked, pointing at the painting.

The Countess glanced over her shoulder. "My late husband. Why do you ask?"

"He seems familiar," Riley mused. "But perhaps it is because he looks so content, so happy there."

"He was. My husband was never happier than when he was in the countryside. That was our estate—Marlowe Manor. He spent nearly all his time there."

Riley glanced over at her. "Was? Isn't it still your home?"

She shook her head. "When my husband died, his title and Marlowe House passed to a cousin."

"I'm sorry," Riley said, not sure why she was, but it seemed sad that such a happy moment should be lost in time.

"Don't be," the Countess said with a wave of her hand.

"Now you evaded my question, and quite well, but I will have an answer. Who are you?"

"No one of consequence, my lady," Riley told her. "Lord Ashlin needed someone to help him with his nieces, and I offered my assistance. That is all there is to it."

The lady reached for Riley's empty cup and began to refill it. "I hear there was a death at Lord Ashlin's this morning," the lady commented, as one might ask about the weather or a visiting relation.

Even with her years of theatrical training, the question stunned Riley, leaving her stuttering and shocked. "Um, yes," she managed to gulp out. "An accident."

"How unfortunate," the lady said, handing her back her cup. "Who was it?"

"A servant," Riley told her, reciting the tale Mason had sworn the house to tell. "Cleaning a window when he accidentally tumbled out it."

"Really." The Countess said the statement more as a question than a comment, and Riley refused to offer any further explanation.

Lady Marlowe shook her head. "I find the entire situation especially odd, considering this servant had a pistol stuck in his waistband. Are all of Lord Ashlin's servants armed?"

A feeling of unease drove Riley to her feet. "I fear I have taken up too much of your time, my lady. Good day to you."

The Countess stopped her. "I haven't finished with you yet. I will know who you are! Who was your mother? Your father, girl? Tell me!" The woman's eyes held a wildness, a desperation.

Riley shook her head and turned to leave, facing the doorway through which she'd entered, seeing now the portrait which had been hidden behind the open door when she'd been announced.

Unlike the man in the bucolic painting on the other side of the room, the figure in this one was more than just vaguely familiar.

She spun around and faced the Countess. "Where is she? Where is Elise?"

Chapter 19

"**O**h, aye, my lord, he was Daniel Nutley all right," Mr. McElliott, the Bow Street Runner Mason had hired, said. The man doffed his hat and took the seat Mason motioned to. "I verified it not an hour ago. There isn't a Runner in town who isn't celebrating that rotter's demise—bad to the core, that one was."

"That still doesn't answer the one remaining question," Mason said. "Why was he after Riley?"

McElliott rubbed his stubbled chin. " 'Twould have to be for gold, milord. Daniel Nutley didn't lift a finger for anything unless he got paid." McElliott wiped his ruddy brow with a less than clean handkerchief. "There's them that say he demanded a farthing from his own mother when she whelped him for the inconvenience it caused him."

"Then you're positive he was paid to carry out these acts."

"Aye," McElliott nodded. "He was paid. Nutley had a reputation for doing a gentleman's less savory business— no questions asked. Heard tell he was braggin' down at the Iron Pig that a toff who was up the River Tick owed him quite a bit for a big job he'd been working for the last year. Claimed he was going to introduce the poor bugger to Mr. Crusher, since it didn't look like the fellow was gunna pay. I'd guess that job must have been your miss."

"Mr. Crusher?" Mason inquired.

McElliott snorted. "Yea, Mr. Crusher." He held up his right hand. "It was what he liked to call his best hand—because he could snap a man's neck with it. Was his trademark, you could say."

Mason shuddered, the memory of arriving in Riley's room and seeing Nutley's hand around her throat leaving him feeling cold. If Bea hadn't heard the noise . . . if he'd been a few moments later . . .

"Then we need to determine who Nutley's employer was," Mason said.

Nodding, McElliott said, "Nutley wasn't one to drop names—part of why he always had work. Had a strict code of discretion—about the only thing he had any morals about."

"And one would assume, since we haven't heard of any member of the *ton* having had their neck cracked," Mason said, "that Nutley was still holding out to collect his bounty."

"That, and he was still working," McElliott pointed out. "He wouldn't have tried to put your miss's light out if he didn't think he was going to get paid."

"Ah, yes. A day's pay for a day's work," Mason said.

"That was Nutley," the Runner said.

"So whoever wanted Riley dead is still out there."

"Must be. Odd, though," McElliott commented. "Nutley had almost a year to kill her, but you said up until she came to you, there were nothing but accidents—only mishaps to drive her out of business and out of England."

"Yes," Mason agreed.

"So," McElliott said, continuing his hypothesis, "why did her moving in with you escalate Nutley's actions? Why did it suddenly become so important for her to die?"

They sat silently, each considering his own theories, when McElliott finally said, "One thing's for sure, Nutley's death won't stop this fellow. In my experience it only makes them more unpredictable. Your miss is still in danger."

Mason got to his feet immediately. He reached over and rang the bell for Belton. Moments later, the butler arrived. "Belton, where is Miss Riley?"

"She is still calling on Lady Marlowe, milord," Belton said.

Mason glanced over at McElliott. "She thinks she's safe. I have to warn her. Get her back here."

"Bringin' her here may not be the best idea, milord," the man pointed out.

"You're right," Mason agreed. "I'll send her away." And this time she wouldn't so easily slip out of his grasp.

He rose and extended his hand to the Runner. "If you'll pardon me, I have a lady to rescue."

"Where is this woman?" Riley repeated. "The one in this painting?"

"So you do remember her," the Countess replied. "Remember my daughter?"

Her daughter? Riley's throat constricted. If Elise was the Countess's daughter, then that would make Riley her . . .

The room started to spin, and she reached out and steadied herself on the back of a nearby chair.

The Countess rushed to her side. " 'Tis quite a bit to take in. I know I felt rather unsteady last night after we met."

"I don't know what you mean," Riley stammered, still unwilling to admit what was happening.

"I think you do," the Countess said. "Everton was right—you have her mannerisms, her way about you, her eyes."

Riley shook her head. "I don't know what you mean, my lady."

"Quit being coy with me, girl. You know exactly what I mean and what I am talking about. Is it so difficult to admit you are my granddaughter?"

Riley continued to shake her head. "How can you be so sure?"

"I wasn't when Everton came here last week to tell me about you."

"The Duke? What has he to do with any of this?"

"If anyone would be able to spot Elise's child, it would be him. Probably easier than his own issue." The Countess paused and glanced at her daughter's portrait. "He loved her very much. I didn't realize how much until after she was gone. He would have protected her . . . and you, if only I hadn't been so stubborn." The Countess laughed. "A trait common on the Fontaine side of the family—one apparently all three of us share."

"*Fontaine*?" Riley whispered, chills tingling down her arms.

"Yes, my maiden name. Elise used it after she went to France. 'Twas how I eventually found her."

"You sent the letter," Riley said, the memory of the liveried servant with the message in hand rising forth in her memory. She glanced back at the portrait of the Marquis—the servant in the background holding the horse—he wore the same colors—the same uniform. "You sent the money and carriage to bring her back here."

The Countess nodded.

Riley took a deep breath and asked the question she'd wanted answered all these years. "Where is she?"

This seemed to take the Countess aback.

"Where is Elise?" Riley persisted, backing away from the Countess and into the middle of the room. "Where is my mother? In Scotland on a hunting trip? Upstairs still sleeping away a late night? Or is she off in Brighton, enjoying the sea air?"

The Countess just stared at her.

"I am not supposed to ask where my mother is?" Riley said. "If you brought me here, surely you knew I would ask where she is."

"You don't know?" Her grandmother's words were but a whisper.

"Know what?"

"Child, your mother isn't here," the Countess said, reaching out her hand to take Riley's.

She shook off the lady's attempt at familiarity. She would have her answers. Now.

"All these years and you didn't know," the Countess whispered, a sad sense of wonder in her voice.

"What is there to know?" Riley asked. "My mother abandoned me."

"No, Riley, she didn't."

Riley shook her head. "You weren't there. Ask her yourself. Ask Elise why she left me behind. Why she abandoned her only child to be sold on the streets of Paris."

"I can't." The Countess's shoulders shook with emotion.

Obviously the lady didn't like to admit that her daughter was capable of such a heartless act.

"You can't, or you won't?" Riley prodded.

The lady turned around, tears shining in her eyes. "I

can't, my dearest girl, because your mother never made it home all those years ago. She died in a carriage accident not an hour after she set foot in England."

It took Riley and the Countess over an hour to put their disparate stories together . . . and make their peace with each other.

"How can you be so sure I'm your granddaughter?"

"Beyond the obvious—your mother's mannerisms and the Fontaine green eyes—your name rather confirms the matter. When you finally introduced yourself last night, it was as if Elise were laughing at me from her grave."

"My name?"

"Yes, *Riley*. 'Twas the name I proposed for her fatherless child. I offered it in spite, and apparently she took it."

Riley still wasn't too clear how her name could be such a clue as to her identity. "Is Riley a family name?"

The Countess laughed. "In a sense." She pointed at the portrait of the Earl. "Do you see that beast there to my husband's left?"

Riley nodded.

" 'Twas his favorite hound . . . and your namesake."

"I was named after a dog?" Riley had never really questioned where her odd name had come from—for it was the only thing she'd ever recalled with any certainty from her childhood.

"Yes, I suppose that is rather odd, but thank your mother she didn't name you after me."

"And that would be worse because . . . ?" Riley asked. The lady leaned over and whispered her name into her ear. "I see. Now I feel much better about my canine namesake."

They both laughed, and for the first time in her life,

Riley felt the warm connection of family. This woman was her grandmother—a link to a past she'd never known.

But the moment of levity was soon replaced by a bittersweet silence.

"I blame myself for all this," the Countess said, shaking her head. "If only I'd acknowledged Elise's marriage—"

"—My mother was married?" Riley sat back from her grandmother.

"Yes," the Countess said. "You didn't know that either, I can see it from your expression. Here you've spent all these years thinking that you were born on the wrong side of the blanket and that your mother left you, and none of it is true."

Her parents had been married. So that meant she was a lady—not just a pretend one on the stage, but a lady as much as Cousin Felicity, the girls, and even more so than the illustrious and oh-so-mercantile Dahlia Pindar.

"I was wrong about your father and his family. I admit that now, though it pains me to say it."

Her father. She tested the word to herself silently. "Who was he? Is he still alive? Does he have other relatives?" Riley asked in a rush.

The Countess held up her hand. "Slow down. The issue of your parents' marriage is a complicated one."

"How can a marriage be complicated?" Riley asked.

"Having never been married, you would ask that," the Countess joked. "Now, back to your questions. Your father's name was Geoffrey Stoppard."

Geoffroi, my dearest Geoffroi . . .

The line whispered through her mind—yet it wasn't from the play, but from her childhood. Her mother had often said those very words in her sleep, and they had stuck in the darkest reaches of Riley's memory until they'd come to life in *The Envious Moon.*

"Why are you smiling?" her grandmother asked.

Riley shook her head. " 'Tis nothing, Grandmother. Pray continue."

The Countess looked unconvinced but went on anyway. "After your parents' elopement to Scotland, they were returning to London when their carriage was attacked by brigands. Your father tried to stop them and was killed for his efforts."

Her father had died protecting her mother—it was more romantic and tragic than one of her plays. Still, that didn't answer a very important question. "But why should that have ruined my mother? They were married, after all."

"Not without proof. The marriage documents were stolen, along with their money and Elise's jewelry."

"There must have been a record somewhere," she insisted. "The church, a clergyman, a witness."

"No, none," the Countess said. "The blacksmith who'd married them was killed in a tavern fight a fortnight after your father's death. With no one to vouch for them and no proof without those documents, only your mother's word that she'd been married to Geoffrey Stoppard remained."

"So my mother was ruined," Riley said.

The Countess nodded. "Utterly. She was already pregnant with you, and with no proof of a marriage, there was nothing to be done but to send her away."

"What about my father's family? Wouldn't they have helped?"

The Countess blanched. "That is where I made my mistake. I believed the Stoppards too far beneath us to consider an alliance with them. I couldn't stomach the idea of Stoppard's father taking control of your mother's inheritance." The lady glanced up at Riley's mother's portrait, as if casting up an apology for the umpteenth time.

"And?"

"And I was wrong. Despite their purchased elevation, the Stoppards are now thought of quite highly. Your grandfather is very much admired in government circles for his economies and reform efforts, while your uncle is an admiral in the Navy. From the accounts I've read of him in the paper, one would think him second only to Nelson in his daring." She paused. "Your relations would have protected your mother and you—whereas I, in my pride and anger, cast you both out to the fates."

Riley glanced up at her mother's portrait. "Where is she buried?" She had wronged her mother all these years—when in truth her mother had loved her and protected her, and had left her life behind to have her child. Perhaps she could make a small atonement to her memory by honoring her grave.

"At Marlowe Manor. We can go there tomorrow. I doubt Stephen will mind, especially since the house is rightfully yours."

"Mine?" Riley asked. "How can it be mine? You said earlier that the title and everything had passed to a cousin."

"Yes, upon Elise's death." The Countess nodded. "But only because I couldn't prove you were her lawful issue or even find you."

"Still, I don't see how it could have passed to my mother or me."

"Because the original Lord Marlowe was a crafty devil—he had helped Good Queen Bess with a number of sticky diplomatic situations and when it came time for him to retire, the Queen granted him a boon: the title of the Earl of Marlowe, the manor, and all the lands surrounding it, as a reward for all his years of unstinting devotion. But the new Lord Marlowe hadn't been a diplomat all those years not to know a thing or two about negotiations. When the Letters Patent were being drafted, he begged Her Majesty to allow the title to pass not only through the paternal line, but also to a daughter." Her grandmother grinned. "He flattered the old girl that she would be a worthy example to his descendants that a daughter could carry on a family's legacy as well as any son." Riley's grandmother laughed. "Besides, his only remaining issue was a daughter, and he wasn't about to see his hard-earned reward revert back to the Crown any time soon."

"So my mother was a Countess."

"Yes, as you would be as well, if I could only prove your mother and father were married."

"It's like something out of one of my plays," Riley murmured.

Her grandmother's hearing was sharper than Riley gave her credit for, as the old girl laughed. "I suppose it is like one of those overreaching tragedies you call art."

Riley tipped her nose in the air and teased. "I'll have you know, my plays are never *overreaching*."

"Bah!" The Countess waved her hand at Riley. "You wouldn't be a success if they weren't. And I take it you are a success?"

"Yes . . . for the most part . . ."

"You hesitated—are you or aren't you?"

Riley shook her head and then told her grandmother about Mason. "So I must make this play a tremendous hit and repay him the money I owe him."

"You'll do no such thing," her grandmother said, her mouth set in a familiar line. "I'll send a draft over to Ashlin this very afternoon. Then you'll move in with me, immediately. I'll hear no more nonsense about you returning to the stage. You are the rightful Countess of Marlowe, and such a public performance is beneath you now."

"It hasn't been beneath me these past years," Riley said, her temper rising. "And I will not take charity from you—even if you are my grandmother. I repay my own debts."

"Stubborn jade," the Countess muttered. "You got that side of your disposition from the Stoppards."

Riley coughed and slanted a skeptical glance at her grandmother.

"Oh, and perhaps a measure of it from the Fontaines," the lady conceded. "A very small part."

Mason lost no time in making his way to the Marlowe town house. As he alighted the hackney Belton had procured, a phaeton came to a stop behind them, and the occupant, Stephen Cheval, the Marquess of Cariston, tossed the reins to the lad who'd sprinted forward from the mews. Hopping down from the driver's seat, the elegantly dressed Cariston gave Mason about as much regard as one might upon finding a beggar on one's front steps.

Mason frowned back. He'd never liked Cariston—not in person or by reputation. They'd been schoolmates years ago—and even then Cariston had held an unholy disdain for those of lesser title and fortune as beneath his contempt or concern.

"Ashlin," he said, bowing only slightly in greeting.

"Cariston," Mason acknowledged.

The other man took a disparaging sniff at the poor hackney as it pulled away. "Surprised to see you out," he said. "Thought you'd have put on the black gloves and headed for the country by now, what with the scandal at your house this morning."

A prickle of unease niggled down Mason's spine. "Hardly a scandal," he said. "Just an accident with one of the servants."

Cariston's eyes narrowed. "An accident, you say. Not

how I heard it. Thought someone said your cousin had been murdered. Strangled, or something like that."

Strangled.

The word stopped him as he recalled the image of Nutley with his hand around Riley's throat.

But how could Cariston have known that or Riley's involvement . . . unless . . .

McElliott's word echoed like a warning.

Nutley had a reputation for doing a gentleman's less savory business.

He looked at Cariston again, this time trying to make sense of all of it. "Hardly anything as dramatic as that," he told the man slowly. Perhaps the vultures from Fleet Street were already spreading wild tales and Cariston had just gotten the story from the usual ill-fed rumor mill.

"And your cousin?" Cariston persisted.

A chill ran down Mason's spine. "My cousin did witness the unfortunate accident, but it didn't frighten her to anything near death. See for yourself. She is here visiting Lady Marlowe."

"Your cousin is *here*?"

Mason didn't miss the slight stumble in Cariston's usually elegant gait, or the tremor behind his question.

When the devil had the Marquess of Cariston begun caring about anything concerning Riley or the Ashlins for that matter? Mason shot him a sideways glance, spying the tense set of the man's jaw.

"Yes," Mason said. "Your aunt was kind enough to invite my cousin over for tea—well, rather demanded her attendance. But you know your aunt."

Cariston shrugged, as if he couldn't care less if his aunt chose to entertain a shipload of sailors or some Ashlin upstart relation, but Mason wasn't fooled a bit.

He hadn't taught first-year students all those years not

to know when someone was feigning indifference—whether it was over a threatened expulsion or something more personal.

Perhaps it wasn't his aunt's association with the Ashlins in general that had Cariston in a knot, he noted.

But someone more specific.

Riley.

Mason shook off his misgivings—he was letting his dislike of the Marquess get the better of him.

At the door, Cariston nodded brusquely to the butler. "Rogers."

"My lord, your aunt is expecting you. Shall I announce you?" Rogers glanced over at Mason, his brow rising slightly. "Yes?"

"I am Lord Ashlin," he said, handing over his card. "I'm here to fetch my cousin. She is visiting with Lady Marlowe."

Rogers nodded and then led the way to the gallery where Riley and Lady Marlowe were surveying the past Marlowe relations lining the hallway.

Lady Marlowe spied them first. "Cariston, you're late."

"My apologies, my lady," he said. "I was delayed by business."

The lady sniffed. "Always business with you young men." She peered at Mason. "Who is that with you? Ashlin, isn't it?"

Riley glanced up at this. She rushed to him, taking his hands and beaming up at him. "Mason, you'll never guess the news."

Mason noticed Cariston had gone almost as white as his starched and spotless cravat.

"Allow me, Riley," Lady Marlowe said, "to tell Lord Ashlin and this no-account relation of mine our good fortune." The lady straightened, and in her most regal manner, announced, "Gentlemen, allow me to introduce you to the Countess of Marlowe, my long lost granddaughter."

Riley, the Countess of Marlowe? What was the old girl talking about? Mason stared at the lady as if she had gone mad, and he noted, so did Cariston.

Then he caught a fleeting glimpse of murder flashing behind Cariston's shocked gaze before it was replaced by an exclamation of surprise.

The news, it seemed, wasn't quite the shock to the Marquess as it should have been.

For while Stephen Chevel, the Marquess of Cariston, Viscount Henley, Baron Walsby turned to his newfound cousin and shook her hand in a hearty greeting, he could hardly be thrilled with the prospect of surrendering his other illustrious title.

The Earl of Marlowe.

Chapter 20

❦❦❦

"**C**an you believe it?" Riley said. "I'm a Countess." She sighed and leaned back in the chair in Mason's study. She held her nose up in the air and waved her hand about in a perfect imitation of Lady Delander.

"Don't let it go to your head," he said, going over to the tray on the cabinet and pouring himself a drink. "You aren't a Countess yet."

"I know, but you heard my grandmother. She is still convinced there is some way to prove my mother's marriage was valid, and then I can make my claim." She sat up. "And my cousin, Lord Cariston, appeared more than willing to help with the matter, which is very kind of him. Grandmother says he rarely goes to Marlowe Manor and has never been overly attentive to the properties, so he probably won't mind in the least giving them back to me." She reached over and squeezed his arm. "I have a family. A grandmother *and* a cousin. It's like a dream come true."

Mason decided against voicing the suspicions that continued to nag at him. Rather, he broached the subject with some careful questioning. "Have you ever met Lord Cariston before?"

She shook her head. "No, but he seemed quite the gentleman, all things considered."

"Yes, quite the gentleman. Perhaps a little too much so," Mason muttered under his breath.

She eyed him. "What are you saying?"

"I met this afternoon with the Runner I hired and he told me Daniel Nutley was a known cutthroat."

She sniffed at this. "Well, yes, we could have surmised that ourselves without your Runner's esteemed opinion."

Mason ignored her barb, knowing she still hadn't forgiven him for firing her investigator without her leave. "McElliott believes Nutley was working for someone, someone in the *ton*."

Riley sat up on the edge of the leather seat. "Are you suggesting my cousin, a man I just met today, and who didn't know I existed until this afternoon, is behind my mishaps?" She waved her hand at him. "It is too ridiculous even to consider. From what my grandmother told me, Lord Cariston is extremely wealthy without the Marlowe holdings. He'll barely miss the income."

What could he say? She was correct on that point, but Mason couldn't shake his skepticism. He'd wager his life Cariston was behind the attempts on her life, and he wouldn't stop until he'd uncovered the identity of Nutley's employer.

Yet how could Cariston have known that Riley was the Marlowe heiress when no one else had?

There had to be some explanation behind all of it, and he intended to get to the bottom of the matter before . . . before Cariston had time to find a replacement for Daniel Nutley.

"I just want you to use some caution for the time being. Until I find out who Nutley was working for, I can't be sure you'll be safe." He tossed back his drink and settled into the seat behind his desk. "At least now you can discontinue your work on the play."

"Why would I do that? We have an agreement. You're the one always nattering on about honor. Well, I intend to complete production of my play and see the girls properly married."

"I won't allow it, and neither will your grandmother."

Riley cocked a brow. "You weren't opposed to my acting a few hours ago. Why is it different now?"

"It is most decidedly different."

"Then I will ask my grandmother for the money I owe you." Riley crossed her arms over her chest. "Surely you can't object to that. Enough to cover the vowels Mrs. Pindar holds." She eyed him. "Yes, I know all about that odious lady's blackmail. Well, you can send her and her solicitor packing." She paused and then frowned at him. "For a man who's been offered his salvation, you don't look overly pleased."

"I won't take Lady Marlowe's money."

"And why not?"

"I don't need it."

"But what about Mrs. Pindar? Maggie said her solicitor demanded—"

He stared at her.

She had the decency to blush. "I told her eavesdropping wasn't proper, but I know you are in a bind." She got up and leaned across his desk. "Please, let me help you."

"You needn't worry about Mrs. Pindar and her threats. I've taken care of her."

"But how?"

He waived off her question. "It is none of your concern."

"Don't you see, Mason? You don't have to marry Miss Pindar. You can marry—" Riley's mouth opened to finish the last of that thought, but she closed it. For a moment she studied him, then her gaze dropped to his desk and she sighed.

Mason was thankful she had stopped short of saying what she had been about to—

—*You can marry me instead.*

Mason was only too aware of that fact.

But how could he ask her to marry him now?

If he went down on bended knee before her, seeking *this* marriage of convenience, he would be the worst type of hypocrite—especially since he'd held his tongue this long.

"If things were different . . ." he started to say. "They aren't—I didn't—"

Riley held up her hand. "Don't say anything more." She looked about ready to burst into tears. She brought her hand to her trembling lips, before turning and fleeing the room.

Mason bounded after her. "What do you think you are doing?"

"I'm leaving. I'll be out of your house as soon as I can collect my papers," she sobbed. "Nanette can finish the rest and come along later." She gathered up her skirt and marched up the steps.

He caught her by the arm. "I don't want you to leave."

"I'm sure you don't," she said. "But I hardly think Miss Pindar or Mrs. Pindar would approve of you keeping your mistress in the house while you are finalizing your arrangements for a respectable union." She turned on one heel, sweeping past Belton.

"I will not allow you to be harmed. Honor requires—"

"Your honor be damned," she shot back. "Where was your honor the other night in the library? Or last night?" She took two steps back down toward him. "I am leaving.

I am no longer your responsibility. Since you do not want my money, there is no reason for me to remain under your protection."

"Riley, this isn't one of your plays."

She laughed, a bitter, angry sound. "A wonderful tragedy, don't you think? You should write it. It might make you rich."

With that she went upstairs. He knew he should try to stop her, but it would only make her that much more determined to leave, and more difficult to follow. As it was, he'd have the Runner McElliott had posted outside the house trail after her and see to her safety. Between Hashim and the other man, it was the best he could do for her.

For the moment.

As he retreated into his study, Riley's final words continued to bedevil him.

Digging through Freddie's papers, he found one of his brother's investments that he'd passed over several times. And as he studied it, he began to smile.

You should write it, she'd said.

Maybe he would do just that.

The Blackened Swan was no place for a peer of the land to be drinking, but this was what Stephen had come to in the two weeks since Lady Marlowe had found her granddaughter. What with Ashlin nosing about and Lady Marlowe renewing her search for evidence of her daughter's marriage to Stoppard, someone was going to lead them back to his father—and then to him.

Plans whirled about in his mind. He had to pay off his creditors before they denounced him publicly. To do that he needed the income from the Marlowe estates.

At least to continue the illusion that the Caristons were still rich and powerful.

Dammit, the money was his right, his due—not hers.

Stephen stared moodily into the barely palatable tankard of ale sitting before him, while all around him the dredges of London drank and plotted in this dark corner of Seven Dials.

"I 'ear you need a new man," a rough voice asked, interrupting Stephen's visions of Cariston glory—all gone because of his father's years of risky investments and costly vendettas. "To fill in for Nutley, now that 'e's been put to bed with a shovel." The man laughed, drawing a few coarse remarks from a few other listeners.

"Quiet, you fool," Stephen told him. "I won't have my business nosed about."

The man reached over and caught Stephen by the throat. The brute's callused fingers wound around his windpipe, starting to crush it. "No one calls me a fool. Not you, not no one."

Stephen nodded, his apology gargling in his throat.

The man smiled and released him.

Gasping for air, Stephen scowled down at the table, but this time kept his distaste for the man and the rest of his loathsome ilk well hidden. "I might be in need of your services."

"*I might be in need of your services*," the man mimicked. He leaned closer until his breath, a combination of rotten mutton and sour ale, washed over Stephen like a cesspool. "Ye sound like a regular Jemmy. Either ye need me services or ye don't." The man started to rise from his chair.

"No, wait," Stephen told him. "I do—if you can provide the same work I had hired Mr. Nutley to complete."

"Mr. Nutley, is it?" The man coughed up a wad of phlegm and spat it at the floor. "Nutley was nuthin' but a filchman, a sorry excuse of a cove who pranced around fancy-like, thinkin' 'e was better than everyone else. If you ask me, 'e got exactly what was comin' to 'im. But me, now I'm a swaddler who ain't afraid to crack what needs to be done." The man pulled a long knife from inside his coat and began picking his teeth with it, his lips spread in an evil grin.

Stephen eyed him. "How do you feel about killing a woman?"

The man leered. "I kills 'em all the time."

A few others around them laughed at this vulgarity, and Stephen chuckled a bit, if only to keep his newfound companion in good spirits.

"There is a woman who I would prefer go aloft."

"Tossed you over, eh? Made you wear the horns, perhaps?"

"Yes, something like that," Stephen said, not caring a whit if this man thought him nothing more than a vengeful cuckold.

"You want to see this bitch gone, but not obvious-like?"

"Yes, exactly," Stephen said. "And quickly. An accident, whatever fits your mood."

The man nodded. "I like the way ye do business, Jemmy. If it's justice ye want done to this bitch, Bean McElliott is your man."

"Riley, do you think this gown would make a good wedding dress?" Bea asked. The girls had been at the theatre for a fitting with Jane Gunn and had come upstairs to have tea with her. "You don't think it's too daring?" She glanced at Maggie, who blushed and busied herself with pouring another round of tea.

"What do you care?" Louisa snapped. "As if either of you two are going to get married. Especially if you keep

wasting every afternoon over at Lady Delander's taking
housekeeping lessons."

"I wouldn't be so sure," Maggie said, rising to Bea's
defense. "I'll have you know that—"

"Maggie!" Bea interrupted.

Riley glanced at both of them and wondered what mischief they'd been up to—not that it could be much if they
were spending all their time at the Delanders'. And she
knew Louisa's ill humor sprang from the fact that Riley
had sent Roderick on a list of errands that would keep him
gone all afternoon.

"Riley, what do you think?" Bea repeated, standing up
and slowly twirling around. "I think this would be a perfect wedding dress."

" 'Tis lovely," she said, truly meaning the compliment.
The pale blue silk might not have been a color Riley
would have chosen for Bea, but leave it to Jane Gunn to
find the perfect hue for the girl. The intricate embroidery,
which Riley knew the lady had done herself, dotted along
the edge of the hem and the neckline in a dainty row of
flowers and curlicues. "I think it is an excellent choice for
Lady Marlowe's ball."

Much to Riley's delight, her grandmother had offered
to sponsor the girls' coming-out ball. Mason had grudg-
ingly agreed to this bit of charity only after the girls had
hounded him nonstop for three days straight, or at least,
that was what Bea had reported with a satisfied smile.

The thought made Riley grin as well. She only wished
she'd been there to see the girls' antics—and perhaps even
lend a hand.

His lenience may also have resulted from the fact that
the girls had finally blossomed into a trio of ladies. The
three of them had flourished all on their own since the
Everton masquerade.

"What do you think of my gown?" Maggie asked. For the brunette girl, Jane Gunn had chosen a primrose muslin, dainty and sprightly, the fabric complimenting Maggie's delicate features. A georgette silk overskirt completed the ensemble, lending it an ethereal quality that made Maggie look like an Eastern princess.

"It's enchanting," Riley told her. "I only hope your uncle approves."

"As if we ever see him anymore," Louisa said. "Since he agreed to our coming out, he has barely been home. Gone all hours and not even taking tea with us. Especially now that the—"

"Louisa, shut up," Bea hissed.

Her sister sat up. "Well, he hasn't been home in days."

Riley drew a deep breath. She knew why Mason wasn't home.

Miss Pindar.

On the day she'd left, when she'd offered to have her grandmother pay off his debts and practically begged him to marry her, she'd seen the evidence that declared he'd already made his decision. For there on his desk had been a special license, granting him the privilege of marrying Miss Dahlia Pindar without a moment's delay.

"I suppose he is making his marriage plans."

"Of course," Louisa told her. "He's—oooof!"

Bea's elbow had landed in her sister's ribs, ending Louisa's disclosure of Mason's wedding plans.

For once Riley was glad for Bea's unreserved manners, because she didn't want to hear about the impending nuptials.

"Cousin Felicity sent her apologies for not coming down," Maggie said. "She's reading that new novel—the one that's all the rage, and she refuses to leave the house until she's finished it so she can be included in the chatter."

Riley smiled. Leave it to Cousin Felicity to put her ability to gossip effectively above all other matters.

"Yes, well, we had best get home," Bea said, rising abruptly, and shooting Maggie a censorious look. "Besides, we'll see you tonight."

"You are coming to the play?" Riley asked. She'd never been so nervous about an opening night in all her life.

"Of course," Louisa said. "It will be a night to remember."

If only Riley had known then that truer words were never spoken.

The Marlowe town house churned with activity. Servants hurried back and forth, while merchants continued to cart in the bottles of champagne, bushels of food, and other necessities for the coming-out ball of the St. Clair sisters.

Mason wove his way through the hubbub to find Lady Marlowe happily ordering about everyone who ventured within earshot. Riley was nowhere in sight—which for now seemed the best.

"Lord Ashlin, if you are not here to help, then you are only in the way," Riley's grandmother complained.

Mason wasn't insulted. He knew his timing was terrible, but it couldn't be helped. What he had discovered this morning confirmed everything he'd suspected. "I came on a matter of some importance, my lady. If you could spare me but a moment of your time."

"A moment is all I can give you," she said, leading him to an alcove in the ballroom and setting herself on a chair tucked inside it. "This will keep us out of the way in case those accursed musicians decide to arrive." She folded her hands in her lap and took a deep breath. "Now tell me what has brought you all the way over here in the middle of the day? Have you finally come to ask for Riley's hand? If you have, I give you my consent. Always liked you Ashlins—your grandfather turned my head with his silvery tongue more than a few times when I was a young thing in my first Season."

"I thank you, my lady. Now that I've turned my finances around, I feel worthy enough to make such an offer."

"Worthy, you say? Bah, shaky finances or not—you've always been the man for her. You love her and she loves you, and that is all that matters."

"And I have every intention of making her my bride before the month is out," Mason said. "But first, I actually came on another matter. How much do you know about Lord Cariston's business?"

She shook her head. "Very little."

"And of his father?"

Her nose wrinkled. "Stephen's father was hardly a favorite around here. A distant cousin of my husband's, and as Lord Marlowe used to say, they were distant for good reasons."

Mason nodded. "Your husband was a wise man." He paused for a second and considered how to ask his next question.

The Countess didn't give him much choice. "Out with it, man. I've never been one to mince words and don't appreciate anyone coating what they say to me. Just have it out."

"How did Riley's mother die?"

She blanched, but only for a moment. "There was an accident. Her carriage overturned, and she was killed."

He nodded. "And her husband?"

"Shot by brigands."

Mason pushed a little further. "And the smith who married them?"

"There was a fight in a pub. He died of a knife wound."

Mason leaned forward. "Did Riley tell you about the attempts on her life?"

Her grandmother shook her head. "The close-mouthed little jade! She spoke not a word."

"Well, the morning you called her over for tea, a man broke into my house and tried to kill her. Luckily, it was prevented."

"The servant who fell out the window," the lady muttered. She glanced up. "I thought there was something odd about that."

"There was," Mason told her. "And I believe they are all connected."

The lady's eyes narrowed. "What are you trying to say?"

"Don't you find it an odd coincidence that all these people died in such violent accidents, or that Riley has been plagued by a long string of murderous threats?"

" 'Tis only fate," the lady said, waving her hand at the matter, but her tone didn't sound all that convinced.

"Fate or careful planning," Mason said. "My lady, I have good reason to believe there was nothing accidental about any of these events."

"You mentioned Cariston." She shook her head. "He couldn't be involved in this, at least not the earlier deaths. He was but a babe."

"But his father wasn't."

Lady Marlowe frowned. "Whyever would my husband's cousin, a Marquess in his own right and one of the wealthiest men in England, go to such lengths to secure the Marlowe lines? My husband's title isn't that old, and certainly the properties offer a good income, but nothing like Cariston's holdings."

"They did when Cariston held them, but the lands you refer to no longer belong to that family. They haven't for years."

"What?" Lady Marlowe's mouth gaped.

"From what I've been able to gather, Cariston is broke."

She sat back. "That can't be."

"It is. Having been a bit up the River Tick myself until recently, I know all the signs. But I've also made some quiet inquiries about town, and your nephew has enough vowels floating around to sink an armada."

"Everyone falls on hard times," she said, shaking her head. "It hardly leads one to murder, as I assume you are suggesting. Cariston is many things, but capable of murder? He hasn't the stomach for it. His father, on the other hand, I could believe him capable of any evil, but not his son."

Mason shrugged. "Not all men think rationally when faced with disgrace—and your nephew is a very proud man." He nodded toward McElliott, who stood waiting in the doorway. "Lady Marlowe, I would like to introduce you to Mr. McElliott, a Runner I hired to help me investigate these matters and the man the Marquess of Cariston engaged yesterday to murder your granddaughter."

"Murder! If that is what is afoot, what in heavens are you doing here?" she asked. "Why aren't you home protecting my granddaughter?"

Mason stared at her. "That is exactly why I'm here. To take her without delay to Sanborn Abbey, where she'll be safe until I can have Cariston arrested and transported so far away, he'll never see England again."

But his words hardly seemed to be reassuring Lady Marlowe, for she frowned at him as if he'd already failed her granddaughter. "But Riley isn't here—she's at your house."

Mason's heart lurched, then his temper flared to life. "That lying, conniving—"

"Go ahead and say it," Lady Marlowe told him. "She's played us both false. I'll wager she's been down at that theatre of hers. Determined she was to pay you back, and on her own terms. Stubborn, impossible girl."

"Determined or not," Mason said, bounding to his feet, "her play is about to have the shortest run in the history of Covent Garden."

Chapter 21

Opening night of any new production found the Queen's Gate fraught with problems, and this one was no different. Riley was being pulled in all directions as squabbles and questions erupted from the deluged box office out front to the prop room in the basement. Much to her delight, tonight's performance had sold out, and even now there was a tremendous crowd outside clamoring for additional tickets.

She'd never seen such excitement surrounding an opening. It was as if the entire city of London wanted to see her production.

If only, her greedy heart wished, she could sell a ticket to all of them this very night. As it was, she'd sold tickets for every spare inch of the floor and added chairs for the patrons who'd begged to be allowed additional guests in their boxes.

Mason would be pleased with his portion of the receipts.

If she could get him to accept the money, she thought with a measure of chagrin. Then again, considering what Louisa had implied today, he didn't need her money. He was probably escorting the ever-perfect and respectable

Miss Pindar somewhere highly exclusive this evening and far from the nefarious reaches of Covent Garden.

Riley shook off her pitiable thoughts. She still had to check with the lighting master, soothe the mutinous orchestra, and get into her costume and makeup.

"Riley, my love," Aggie called out as she scurried past the men's dressing room. "My ensemble is incomplete." He strode out in the coat and breeches Jane Gunn had sewn for his first act role as the King, albeit missing the fur-trimmed robe, crown, and scepter they always kept handy for such parts. "Send that worthless Nanette to fetch my royal accoutrements."

Riley groaned. All actors were responsible for retrieving their costumes from the wardrobe room and their accessories from the prop room. For some unknown reason, Aggie always found it difficult to find either room on opening night, demanding every sort of indulgence before he went on stage.

"Nanette is busy," she told him. "You'll have to do it yourself."

Aggie's look of horror told her only too well he was about to throw a majestic tantrum.

She sighed and made her way through the chaos of sets and props lining the back hall and awaiting their turn on stage. She went downstairs and along the hallway, when she saw the prop room door wedged open. The heavy door had a way of swinging shut and leaving the unhappy occupant trapped inside until someone else came along to free him.

'Twas probably the reason Aggie didn't like the room—he'd spent a rather uncomfortable night down there last winter after he'd sneaked in to borrow a pair of prop pistols.

As she was about to call out to whomever was inside,

she heard a voice that sounded vaguely familiar.

"Say it again," the woman entreated. "Tell me how much you love me, Roderick."

Damn him, Riley cursed.

She should never have hired the man—there was just something about him that didn't play true, and now he was using his role as leading man to romance every female who came within his orbit.

First Louisa, and now some unsuspecting underling was getting her chance to worship him fifteen minutes before the curtain was scheduled to go up.

"Yes, I love you," Roderick was saying. "With all my heart and all I have, I pledge you my troth."

An earthy groan followed, with the sounds of kissing, and the rustle of clothing being displaced.

Riley yanked the door open the rest of the way, only to find a very familiar face glaring back at her.

"Louisa!" Riley said. She caught the girl by her arm and yanked her free of Roderick. Hauling her out of the prop room, she demanded, "What the devil are you doing?"

Louisa straightened, swiping at her tousled hair and flushed cheeks. "I am here to follow my heart. I want to act. To live my life with Roderick. And since I know my uncle will never give his blessing, we plan to elope."

"Louisa!" Roderick groaned and shook his head. But to give him his due, he came out of their hiding spot and took his place beside his intended as if that was his right and due.

"Elope?" Riley repeated. "Have you lost your mind? You can't marry him," she said, pointing at Roderick.

"Now, see here—" he began.

"Oh, stow it!" Riley snapped. "If this wasn't opening

night and your understudy wasn't already too drunk to go on, I'd fire you this very minute."

Roderick straightened up. His stance and demeanor reminded her of Mason when he was being his stuffiest. "Don't bother," he said, in a high-handed, overly *tonnish* voice. "I quit. All I ever wanted was this one chance to act on stage, and I'll have that after tonight. But I won't be alone out there." He took Louisa's hand. "This is my Aveline, or I won't go on."

Louisa? Play Aveline in front of the entire *ton*? Was the pair mad?

Apparently they were—for Riley realized Louisa was wearing Aveline's peasant dress.

"Louisa, go upstairs and get out of that costume," Riley ordered.

Louisa glanced up at Roderick, and then at Riley. She shook her head.

"I am sorry to do this, Madame," Roderick said.

Before Riley could protest, Roderick caught her by the waist and carried her into the prop room, dumping her into a pile of leftover curtain fabric. Riley landed in a whoosh and a thud of old canvas. As she struggled to right herself, her arms and legs flailing about, Roderick and Louisa pushed the door shut.

"Will she be safe in there?" she heard Louisa ask.

"Yes," Roderick told his paramour.

Riley gained her feet and flew across the room, grabbing at the door latch. She twisted and pulled, but it held firm against her. "Let me out," she yelled, pounding on the sturdy oak door. "Louisa, unlatch this door immediately!"

Outside Riley could hear Roderick saying, "Oh, don't look like that, my love. We'll send someone to let her out once we are well on our way to Gretna Green."

Then to Riley's dismay, she heard their departing footsteps. "Louisa, Roderick! Don't do this! Let me out!"

For a time she pounded on the door and screamed until her voice started to crack, but no one came to rescue her. Overhead, she heard the footsteps of the patrons coming in to take their seats. The orchestra first tuned their instruments and then began playing a selection of popular pieces to entertain the audience before the main theatrics began.

And they were about to begin without her.

She looked around for Aggie's props, but found they weren't there. They'd probably been in his dressing room the entire time and he'd found them the minute she'd come to fetch them for him.

Riley put her face in her hands and groaned. This was a disaster.

"I'm sorry, milord, but the curtain is up and the house is full—even with a ticket, I can't let you through."

Mason turned from the doorman in frustration. What if Stephen was inside? There was no telling what the man would do when he found out there was a warrant for his arrest.

Glancing about, Mason considered how he could get inside—then he remembered the side entrance he'd used the day Riley was attacked. Running around the edge of the building, he found that door guarded as well by a fellow just as unwilling to let him in as the man out front.

Discouraged, but nowhere close to giving up, he continued to circle the theatre until he came to a stop in front of a large heap of refuse. There, hidden behind the trash barrels was a small stairwell leading to the basement.

Mason leapt down the steps in a flash, pausing only for a moment to kick the door in.

As his eyes started to adjust to the poor lighting, he spied a staircase down at the end of the hall that he assumed led up to the stage area.

He was halfway down the hall when the sound of someone pounding on a door and calling out caught his attention.

Riley!

He rushed over to the door and pulled it open.

"Mason!" she said.

He rushed inside to wrap her in his arms, but instead of the warm greeting he expected, she cried "No!" and bounded around him, clawing at the door as it swung shut.

As the hinges stopped rattling, she let out a rather salty curse, one equal to any of Bea's best vulgarities.

"You let the door close," she said, standing before it, her head banging against the wood, her fists pounding on the panels.

"I take it, that's a bad thing."

She glanced over her shoulder. "It latches shut on the outside. We are locked in."

Now Mason knew why he wasn't getting his hero's welcome.

Riley settled back down on her perch of canvas and old curtains, her feet swinging back and forth. At least Roderick and Louisa had left the candle lit or she and Mason would have truly been in the dark.

Overhead the audience laughed uproariously, then applauded with great cheer.

She looked up at the ceiling. "End of Act Two, your scene went over better than expected."

"Glad I could be of service," he said from his own spot across the narrow room. "Isn't it rather odd that no one has noticed you missing?"

"Roderick and our new Aveline decided to stage a small revolution tonight. I've been upstaged by my understudy."

"Ginny?"

"No, your niece—Louisa."

Mason bounded to his feet. "Louisa! Why, that little—"

Riley waved aside his comments. "Don't bother. I've already cursed her every way I can think of and even a few Bea probably doesn't know."

Mason crossed his arms over his chest. "This is all your fault. If you hadn't left, Louisa never would have gotten away with this."

Riley's temper flared. She clambered off the canvas and crossed the room to face him. She punctuated her words with her finger, prodding it into his chest. "My fault? I didn't leave because I wanted to! I left because you'd decided to wed Miss Pindar!"

"What would make you think I'd choose her over you? I have no intention of marrying that chit."

"You don't?" She so wanted to believe him.

"Of course not. I made my choice the night of Everton's masquerade. Why would I make love with you and marry another woman? There is only one woman I ever want to share my bed with and that's you."

Riley cocked her head. "But I saw the special license on your desk and Mrs. Pindar was holding Freddie's vowels."

Mason's gaze rolled upwards. "That's why you fled out of my study like you were on fire. Consider that license my last act of propriety." He stepped closer to her. "I couldn't understand why you gave in so easily. And then I thought perhaps you didn't want to live a life of poverty."

"And I would know what to do with riches?" she laughed.

He joined in. "Come to think of it, neither would I."

Their laughter stilled, and when the silence seemed to fill the room, Mason folded her into his arms and kissed her.

"You aren't going to marry Dahlia?" she asked, after several minutes.

Mason shuddered. "Never. I discovered I am not overly fond of shepherdesses or their sheep."

Riley smiled, then laid her head on his chest. "What will you do about Freddie's debts?"

"Don't you worry about those. You should be more concerned about getting us out of here."

Glancing at the door, she said, "Unfortunately, we are stuck here until the end of the play when the stagehands start clearing away the props."

He waggled his brows at her and grinned. "Do you think we have time?"

She cuddled up into his arms. "Are you sure you aren't going to marry Dahlia?"

"Positive."

"Then I think we do," she said.

Mason bent down and kissed her, his lips hungry and firm.

Riley answered back with her own blazing kiss. She'd spent a lot of time in the last few weeks remembering their night together and dreaming of having another chance to be with Mason.

Now that she did, she didn't waste any time. She tugged off his jacket, pulling his shirt free next.

"In a hurry?" he asked.

"You recall those lines you made me cut out? We'd have more time if you'd let me keep Geoffroi's speech."

"Then we'd better not waste another minute." Mason reached over and caught up a velvet cape that lay in a pile of discarded costumes. Shaking it out, he laid it over the canvas pile, grinning at her from the side of their impromptu bed. She climbed into it, looking like a regal cat.

Just before he joined her, he spied a discarded crown, covered in paste jewels. Catching it up, he put it on his head. "You are now mine to command," he said, repeating the King's line from Act Three.

Riley laughed and said her part back. "Oh, command me, my lord." She eased up the edge of her skirt, wiggling her bare leg at him in invitation.

Mason found himself fast becoming a great fan of the theatre. "My first edict is that you make a change of costume." His hands roamed up the length of her bare legs until they reached her hips. He pulled her closer, and continued to undress her. "All my subjects shall go naked henceforth."

"I don't remember that line," Riley teased in a stage whisper, opening his shirt and running her fingers over his chest.

"I'm rewriting the entire script," he told her.

"I like it so far," she purred, her hips writhing back and forth against his groin.

He pushed her gown all the way up over her head, leaving her clad in only her chemise. As his hands cupped her breasts and he went down to suckle the soft flesh, a breathy sigh escaped her lips.

Not to be the only actor in Mason's new play, Riley pulled and unbuttoned his clothing, between fevered kisses and murmured words of endearment, until his jacket, shirt, and breeches landed in a scattered heap on the floor.

Enlivened by his mischievous spirit, Riley caught up a feather duster left on a box beside her. "Your scepter, sire," she said.

Mason grinned, and used his faux royal accoutrement to tease her, along with stroking touches and long, fevered kisses, to ignite her flesh until she was on fire, panting and begging him to give her release.

Her needs, her breathless requests, left him ragged with his own desires, and Riley didn't neglect them. Her hands trailed down his body, where she discovered he was hard and ready.

Unwilling to wait any longer, she wrapped her legs around his hips, urging him to enter her.

He did, and with no barrier to stop him, no need to take it easy, he entered her in a single smooth stroke.

Riley let out a triumphant moan. "Oh, yes. Please, Mason."

All her pent-up fears, her relief at having him back, her heartache over the last few weeks poured into her need for him. Her hips rocked at a frantic pace, urging him, daring him to keep up.

Mason understood her driving need. He'd thought of nothing else—of having Riley forever in his arms—for the last fortnight.

Now she was his, and he pressed into her, stroking her, wanting nothing more than to see the surprise that enveloped her as her release brought her over the edge.

When it did, her mouth sought his as she started to cry out. "Oh, Mason," she gasped.

The quaking of her release pulled him along with her. A ragged cry tore from his lips, but the sound was drowned out by a huge cheer and a large round of applause from the audience overhead. The two of them shuddered together as the entire theatre rocked overhead with thunderous approval.

And as the hue and cry above began to lull, Mason looked down at her and said, "Never had that happen before."

Chapter 22

L ord Cariston lurked about the edge of the crowd pouring from the Queen's Gate Theatre, hating every one of their smiling, excited faces.

He'd been waiting around the theatre most of the afternoon and all through the performance, listening for the alarm to be raised over Riley's demise.

But none had been forthcoming.

He'd seen McElliott enter the place about an hour before the curtain had gone up, but from the outside nothing had seemed amiss since then.

Though much to his delight, he'd also seen Ashlin frantically trying to get in.

"Say good-bye to her," Stephen had whispered as he'd watched the other man disappear down the alleyway. "She would have been your ruin anyway."

Yes, it was better for everyone that she die and be forgotten.

Now, all he needed was confirmation of her death, and he would go to Lady Marlowe's house to console the old girl. He needed to stay in her good graces, for when she died, Stephen wanted to ensure that he was her sole beneficiary.

He hadn't spent all these years toadying up to the old crow not to see his work come to fruition when she cocked up her toes.

He pulled his hat down lower over his brow, considering how he could find out what he needed to know.

Then, as luck would have it, he saw an old friend, Viscount Barnet, filtering through the throng, his toad of a wife a few steps ahead of him.

"Barnet," Stephen called out. "Good to see you, man."

"Cariston." Barnet extended his hand. "Heard you'd gone to the country."

Stephen cringed inwardly and silently cursed the idle tongues of the *ton*. "Nothing of the sort."

"Good. Glad to hear it."

"Barnet," Lady Barnet called out. "Please hurry along. I want to get to Lady Marlowe's presently. I can't find my sister anywhere in this crush and I want to hear if she's finished that book yet. Especially after tonight. Perhaps it will explain what happened."

Barnet nodded to his wife and then turned back to Stephen. "I go to the theatre only when it is that Fontaine creature onstage, and what do you think, she doesn't show up tonight." Barnet blew out a steamy sigh. "But then, why am I telling you—you were inside, weren't you?"

Stephen could barely contain his glee. Riley hadn't appeared onstage—which could mean only one thing.

McElliott had killed the thieving bitch.

"Yes, quite a disappointment," he managed to say.

Barnet leaned forward, his voice lowering to a confidential whisper. "Haven't the vaguest notion who that gel who replaced her was, but she's a tasty little bit. Might perk up my theatrical interests, if you know what I mean." Barnet winked.

"My dear! We must be away or we will never get a

good spot at Lady Marlowe's," his wife complained.

"There now, Cariston, stay away from the parson's mousetrap, or you'll spend your life listening to mandates," Barnet said as an aside. To his wife, he replied, "Yes, my love. We haven't a moment to lose." He bade a hasty farewell and started toward his carriage. Then he turned and asked, "Will I see you at this Marlowe madness later on? Promises to be a terrible crush."

Stephen let himself smile. "Yes," he told his friend. "Should be quite an entertaining evening." As the Barnet carriage rolled away, Stephen said after him, "More interesting than you will ever know, you henpecked fool."

Riley unfolded herself from Mason's embrace. "We'd best get dressed. Our rescue will be coming any moment now."

He grinned at her. "You could order them away and we could spend the night here."

He kissed her anew and Riley felt her blood quicken once again.

"No," she laughed. "You won't persuade me so easily. My grandmother is expecting us, as are the girls."

The girls!

"Oh, no!" she said, rising to her feet. "Louisa! We have to stop her. Now that the play is over, she and Roderick will be off to Scotland." She caught up her chemise and gown and tugged them on. She prodded Mason with her toe. "Get dressed. You have to stop them."

"Perhaps I should call young Roderick out—you know, demand satisfaction, fight a duel for the family honor."

"Oh, honor be damned," she shot back. "Just stop them."

"And what if someone had stopped your parents?" he asked. "I wouldn't be here now, looking at the woman I intend to spend the rest of my life with. Beside, I think Roderick is entirely suitable for Louisa."

"How can you say that?" Riley asked. "You specifically told me you wanted your nieces to marry eligible young men. Roderick is penniless and an actor, and a baseborn, ill-bred, conniving—"

Mason slid his finger over her lips and stopped the sputtering complaints. "—Imposter," he finished for her.

"Yes, an imposter," Riley agreed. "He's the worst kind of fraud."

Mason put his hands behind his back and rocked on his heels. "Truly, for he is hardly baseborn or penniless."

Riley studied him for a moment. "What do you know that you haven't been telling me?"

"Roderick Northard isn't the man you think he is."

"And that would be?"

"Do you remember a few weeks back, when Cousin Felicity was reading in the paper about the Duke of Walford's missing relation and how there were plans to drag the river for his body?"

Riley nodded.

"They should have been dragging Brydge Street instead. Your leading man is the Duke's heir."

She shook her head. "Why didn't you tell me?"

"Because he asked me not to. When I discovered the truth, I confronted him and demanded an explanation."

Outside, the footsteps of stagehands drifted closer. Riley cocked a brow at Mason's state of undress and he quickly pulled on his breeches and continued getting dressed, even as he finished telling his story.

"Your Roderick Northard is more commonly known as Roderick Northard Benton, Viscount Hurley. His father and grandfather have been after him to settle down and marry the Marquess of Rowden's daughter, which he refused to do. His relations, thinking to starve him into submission, cut him off. So when he saw your advertisement for actors, he applied."

Riley still couldn't believe it. "But the stage? If he thought his relations were going to cut him off for not marrying that girl, what did he think they would do when they found out he'd taken to the stage?"

"Actually he hoped they would," Mason said. "At the very least, Lord Rowden would refuse to have his daughter married to someone who'd worked—and on the stage, no less."

She laughed at this. "That explains his ability to play Geoffroi, the embroiled and embittered royal son so well—'tis hardly a stretch for him." Riley still had one last question to ask. "Does Louisa know?"

Mason shook his head. "She'll probably be furious when she finds out. She thinks she is creating the perfect Ashlin scandal, and while tongues will wag, it will hardly be the mismatch she thinks she is making."

"So she'll be a Viscountess?"

Mason smiled. "And eventually a Duchess. Hurley is heir to the Walford duchy. Though it may be years before he ever takes his great-grandfather's title—the Bentons are notoriously long-lived—in time, Louisa may well be the Duchess of Walford."

"She will be furious," Riley agreed. "I think she had plans for a long career on the stage."

"She'll have a long career, that is for certain, but it will be on a different stage," Mason said.

Riley still had some concerns. "Will his family accept her?" This was a question near and dear to Riley's heart. For if the *tonniest* of the *ton* would accept Louisa with her brief appearance on the stage and her scandalous relations, might Mason be able to find it in his heart to take that leap as well?

"They may be a little aghast at first, but she's an Ashlin and our families have always been on very good terms."

The stagehands were close, and Riley almost wished they would never open the door, for what would happen when they did?

As if in answer to her unspoken questions, he folded her into his embrace and said, "You too have a long career ahead of you, Madame—one that begins tonight. I think we need to get you to your grandmother's so you can meet your adoring public." He grinned at her and she wondered for a moment at his odd choice of words, but when his lips bore down on hers, she was lost again in a distracting maze of passion.

They kissed like that until the door swung open.

"Riley!" exclaimed one of the hands.

Mason and Riley pulled apart and she grinned at the men standing in the doorway.

"We wondered where you got to," one of them said. "But Mr. Pettibone wouldn't hear of holding up the curtain to go find you. Glad to see you safe and sound."

In the back of the group, one of the cheekier fellows let out a wolfish whistle, while a few of them chuckled at the sight of their noble patron and leading lady leaving the prop room in such a state of *dishabille*.

"Do you think they know?" Riley asked Mason as they climbed the stairs to the theatre. "Do you think they could tell that we'd . . ."

He plucked a few loose feathers out of the back of her hair. "Whyever would they think something like that?"

The Marlowe residence, as predicted, was a terrible crush. By the time Mason and Riley had made it to her grandmother's house, it was nearly midnight.

They probably would have arrived earlier if Riley hadn't insisted on going upstairs to change and fix her hair—and Mason hadn't insisted on going along to help.

"How will we ever find Bea and Maggie?" she asked, standing on her tiptoes at the entrance of the ballroom and straining to see over the sea of plumes and fancy head-dresses.

"I think I see your grandmother across the room, but I don't see the girls anywhere," Mason said. "Perhaps they are dancing."

"Could be," Riley commented. "Before I venture in there, I am going to go upstairs and get the necklace my grandmother said she wanted me to wear. She told me where it would be if I got here late."

Mason pecked a kiss on her forehead. "Get your treasures and I'll keep an eye out for your cousin."

"Do you really think he would dare come here?"

"Not if he knows what is good for him. By now his house has been searched, and if he was home, he's in custody, but if not—" Mason glanced up the stairs. "Maybe I should come with you—"

She shook her head. "Go find the girls. I'll be up and back before you'll get ten feet in this throng."

Riley dashed up the stairs and into her grandmother's bedchamber. The room was mostly cast in shadows, with only a single taper burning atop the bureau. The drawer where her grandmother kept her jewels was open and the rifled cases were scattered about the floor.

Taking a step further into the room, she nearly tripped over an upended decanter amongst the litter, which explained why the room stank of brandy. Then, to her horror, her cousin stepped out from behind the curtains, a pistol in one hand and a shocked look on his face.

"Riley!" he said, his words slurred with drunkenness. "You're supposed to be—"

"Dead? Yes, Stephen," she said as pleasantly as she could muster. "I so hate to disappoint you, but I am hopelessly alive—and I plan to stay that way."

Stephen didn't even try to deny his part in the attempts on her life. The liquor had obviously provided him with a false sense of bravado. "But I saw McElliott . . . and I heard that you were unable to go onstage . . . and I thought . . ."

Riley shook her head. "You were wrong. As you were to think you wouldn't be discovered in all this." She glanced down at the damage about her feet. "I suppose you thought to make your escape with still more of the Marlowe fortune."

"I wouldn't have to if you hadn't ruined everything. This is all your fault!" he snarled, the pistol waving dangerously in his hand. "You and that do-good Ashlin. He's set the law on me, and for no reason. I'm being hounded like some criminal."

Riley was past the point of caring that the man held a gun on her. The cad actually had the audacity to blame all this on her?

"No reason?" she sputtered. "You hired a man to kill me. Not once, but twice. I think that does make one a criminal in the eyes of the law."

Stephen's bloodshot eyes narrowed. "McElliott—I should have known. He was probably in this with Ashlin the entire time." He cursed roundly. "I should have had Nutley kill you months ago, before Ashlin ever set eyes on you. My father always said the world was better without you Marlowe bitches in it."

"Your father? What has he to do with this?" Though she knew what Mason had told her, she wanted to hear it from Stephen, and in his befuddled and brandy-fueled courage, she suspected he'd tell the entire story.

"Yes," Stephen said, his chest puffing up. He paced a few steps and began to tell the entire horrible truth. "We were broke—he'd invested heavily in the war with the Colonies, and then lost everything else in a foolish plantation venture. We were ruined, so he plotted to kill your mother and thus gain the Marlowe titles and properties."

"But your father failed, just as you have."

Stephen's lip curled. "I haven't failed, not yet." He waved the gun at her before continuing his confession.

"My father never thought the likes of Geoffrey Stoppard man enough to fight back—so when he did, the brigands hired to kill everyone in the carriage fled like a pack of cowards. Though it was disappointing your mother still lived; without the marriage papers *and* pregnant, she was as good as dead." Stephen fished inside his jacket and pulled free a pack of yellowed and wrinkled pages. "My father was a sentimental fool. He saved these as a memento, even when he knew your grandmother searched high and low for them."

Stephen held the papers out to the edge of the candle flame. "I intended to burn these the moment I heard you were dead, but now is as good a time as any."

"No," Riley cried out, seeing her family's title and properties lost forever in this senseless act.

He smiled at her and then pulled the papers away just before they would have ignited. "Perhaps you are right. As long as I possess them, they are of value—to you and me. I suppose you might pay quite a pretty penny for them? If not tonight, then someday." He tucked them back in his coat.

Riley slowly let out the breath she'd been holding.

Her cousin edged over to the window, then pulled the

curtain back to survey the garden and alleyway behind the house. A few seconds later, he yanked the curtain back in place. "He's had the place surrounded." He turned back to Riley, the pistol once again fluttering in his hand as if punctuating every complaining word. "How am I supposed to get out of here now?"

"How could you doubt Mason wouldn't catch you?"

"Mason, is it?" Stephen's lip curled. "Your death will serve as a good reminder to your dear Mason that he is a nuisance. And if he cares for you, your death will ensure that he never interferes again."

He crossed the room and caught her by the arm, his fingers biting into her flesh. When she struggled and started to protest, he laid the muzzle of the gun to her temple and said, "One false move, Cousin, and your grandmother's servants will have a worse mess to clean up than just these empty boxes."

Riley settled down—she didn't trust that he wouldn't pull the trigger, given his state of agitation and drunkenness, and the longer she delayed that unhappy event, the better her chances were of being rescued.

If only she'd let Mason come upstairs with her. He would have been able to disarm Stephen, but now he was probably mired in the crowd, unable to reach her.

"The only way out now," Stephen said, "is the front door. And you, my dearest cousin, are my ticket."

Stephen had his hand on her elbow and the pistol prodding her in the ribs. As a pair, they walked down the stairs and toward the main entrance.

Suddenly the crowd stilled, all eyes watching their descent.

Riley didn't notice it right away, for she was too busy trying to breathe. She had no doubt that once Stephen gained the streets, he would kill her and make his escape in the ensuing confusion—his revenge against her and Mason complete.

" 'Tis her!" someone said.

"No, it couldn't be," another argued.

"But it must be," a third person added to the noisy disagreement. "Look at that hair, those eyes. She is the very image of Régine."

There were murmurs of agreement, then someone in the crowd began to clap his hands, and in moments, the entire foyer was sending up a rousing applause.

Stephen stumbled to a stop at the clamor. "What is this?"

"I haven't the vaguest idea," she said quite honestly.

Prodding her forward, Stephen continued their march toward the door.

The crowd parted and continued to applaud them. Guests from inside the ballroom surged into the foyer, mobbing it even more.

A woman to the right of Riley said to her companion, "Must be part of the book I haven't gotten to yet."

"No, it isn't, for I finished it just this afternoon, and I don't recall this chapter," the lady's friend commented as if she were watching a production at the Queen's Gate and not a woman's life being threatened.

"Maybe there is to be a sequel," the first woman suggested.

"Oh, I do hope!" her companion said. "It looks quite exciting."

Stephen's grip on her arm grew even tighter. "Why are they clapping? What are they doing?"

"I don't know," Riley answered.

"I do," Mason said, stepping out from the crowd to block their path.

The entire room grew silent, except for a few collective sighs from the ladies standing about.

"Get out of my way, Ashlin," Stephen warned. "Or I will kill her as she stands here."

"And then what, Cariston?" Mason asked. "Where will you go? What will you do? I'll tell you—you'll hang. It is over, man. Let her go and you'll only be ruined."

Riley heard Stephen gulp down his next two breaths. What she didn't want to hear was what he had to say next.

"Then if I am to be ruined, you both will share my shame," Stephen said. He waved the pistol in the air. "Ladies and gentlemen, I would like to introduce my cousin, Madame Fontaine."

"No!" Riley protested. "Stephen, don't do this."

"But cousin, I want all the *ton* to know about your illustrious past. Yes, my friends, this young woman is the most notorious whore in all of London—nay, England!"

This announcement was met with disapproving silence, but Riley had the odd sense the crowd's displeasure was pointed not at her, but at Stephen.

A portly gentleman stepped to Mason's side. "That is no way to talk about Régine," he admonished Stephen.

"No, you didn't hear me," Stephen said. "This is *Madame Fontaine*. The illegitimate granddaughter of Lady Marlowe."

Muttered comments followed, and then a brief bit of light applause.

"Please, Stephen," Riley whispered, "say no more."

But Stephen continued, since it appeared he had a rapt audience. "My Haymarket cousin has been living with Lord Ashlin—without the benefit of the parson's blessing."

"How kind it was of Ashlin to take her in," an older

lady standing just a few feet from Stephen commented to her companion.

That woman smiled at Riley as if she were the luckiest girl alive. "The Ashlins always know how to take a stand. To take such a terrible risk on a lady's behalf." Tears glistened in her eyes. "You are so lucky," she told Riley.

"Don't you see," Stephen urged his onlookers, his voice rising to a fevered pitch. "She is a whore, to be reviled. Shunned. Why are you looking at me? Look at *her*—she is nothing but a dirty bit of baggage."

"I think I've heard quite enough, Cariston," a young man Riley recognized from the Everton ball said as he stepped out and joined Mason and the other man. "It would be my honor to assist you, Ashlin."

"Honor?" Stephen snarled, pointing the pistol directly at Mason. "This man has no honor. And he will die like the plaguing dog that he is."

Riley no longer cared what happened to herself, only that Mason was in danger. She spun and knocked Stephen's arm upward, the gun firing wildly, the shot blasting into the ceiling, sending down a rain of plaster.

There was a collective gasp from the crowd.

"My God," the portly man to Mason's left complained. "That pistol was loaded! Demmed fool thing to bring to a party."

Mason surged forward, as did his youthful friend, and they caught Stephen by his arms.

The man struggled and fought wildly, calling out more of his ugly disclosures. "She's an actress, a whore. She isn't fit to serve any one of us, let alone stand amongst us."

Just then, McElliott came dashing through the front door with three members of the watch right behind him.

"I heard the shot, my lord," McElliott said. "Is everyone all right?"

"We're fine," Mason told him. He handed Stephen over to the watch.

As Riley's cousin continued to struggle, jewels started to fall out of his pockets.

"Looks like I'll need to add thievery to the charges," McElliott commented. "Come along, milord. You should find life in Botany Bay quite to your liking."

"Wait," Riley said. She turned to Mason. "He has proof of my parents' marriage. The papers are in his jacket."

A quick search turned up the evidence, which was in turn handed to Riley.

"Those are mine," Stephen protested. "It is all mine!" he continued to say, even as the watch carted him away.

With Stephen gone, Mason caught Riley in his arms and kissed her. This was followed by wild applause. The guests surged around them, congratulating Riley and adding their well-wishes.

"Why do they keep calling me Régine?" she asked Mason, as he pulled her into another embrace—a move which was met with even wilder applause.

"I suppose I should explain," Mason told her. "I tried to tell you earlier—I suppose I should have asked first."

"Asked what?"

Before Mason could answer, a young girl, probably in her first Season, edged forward. She pulled a small, narrow volume out of her reticule. "Lord Ashlin, Madame Fontaine, may I be so bold as to ask you to sign my copy?"

Riley looked down at the title on the book.

The Secret Diaries of Régine, the Illustrious Madame Fontaine.

"What the—" Riley said, having a sneaking suspicion she didn't want to know.

"It was your idea," Mason said, grinning at her. "You told me to write your life story—so I did."

Epilogue

Riley snatched the book out of Mason's hands, as their carriage rolled away from her grandmother's house. "I can't believe you did this," she said.

"I hope you don't mind," he said. "I think you should be honored. I've gone through three printings already, and the fourth is nearly sold out as well."

"That many copies?" Riley took a deep breath.

Mason nodded. "And since Freddie invested heavily in the printing shop, I've made a small fortune."

"A fortune?" Riley liked the sound of that.

"Yes, enough to pay off the worst of my debts. Mrs. Pindar was quite vexed when I came to redeem my vowels." He paused for a second. "You see, I couldn't come to you as a pauper. You worked so hard at everything, you made me realize that I'd fallen into worse habits than my father or Freddie. I needed to follow my industrious ancestors and do something a little more practical if I was to restore our fortunes."

"You prideful, foolish man. I didn't care if you were a pauper or an Earl. I just wanted to spend my life with you."

"I know, but I needed to do this. To pay my own way.

You could say you shamed me into being an honorable man."

"By calling me Régine and selling this exaggerated version of my life story," Riley laughed. "I just wish I'd thought of it first."

"You did. You suggested I write your story the day you left me."

Riley caught his hands and held them. "I don't care how you did it, as long as it means we can—" She didn't care anymore about propriety. "As long as we can be together always."

"I want nothing less," he declared, pulling her into his arms. "I haven't wanted anything else since the first moment I laid eyes on you. And now I have the means to declare my heart." He got down on one knee in the cramped confines of the carriage. "Riley Fontaine, I love you with all my heart. Will you be my wife?"

"Yes," she whispered, almost afraid to say the words too loud and break this magical spell.

He brought his lips to hers and sealed their bargain, this time with more than a handshake.

"Mason, I never sought money or fortune or titles—I only wanted you," she said after some time.

"I know that, and it is exactly why I had to come to you with something in my pockets other than lint."

She shook her head at him. What did she care about his reasons for delaying? He'd finally made his declaration of love.

Yet there remained one other problem—the reason for their hasty return to Ashlin House.

"What do you think happened to the girls?" Riley asked.

"And Cousin Felicity," Mason added. "She told me this morning that Lord Chilton was sending his carriage over for them at half past nine. Given the way Cousin Felicity hounded and hammered me to give the girls their Season, you'd think she'd ensure they made it to their coming-out ball."

The carriage pulled to a stop before the house, every room in the place alight.

Mason bounded down from the carriage and up the steps. Riley followed, hot on his heels.

Inside the foyer, a distraught Belton sat on a chair, his face buried in his hands. "In all my years," he was muttering. "And never have I seen such a disgrace!"

"What is, man? What has happened?" Mason asked the butler.

Belton nodded toward a silver salver resting on the end of the balustrade. Three sealed notes sat atop the tray. "I don't know how this has happened, but this is all that has been found of them."

Riley and Mason exchanged worried glances, and then Mason picked up the first note. He turned it over, where the familiar Delander crest was emblazoned in the wax seal.

"It's from Del," Mason told her, as he broke it open and unfolded the page. "I can't imagine what—" Mason stopped in mid-sentence. "I don't believe this!"

"What?" Riley rose up on the tips of her toes and read the note.

Ashlin,

Sorry to have to break it to you this way, but I have no other choice than to leave a note. Cowardly, this, but 'tis the best I can do right now. Promise me you won't call me out, for I hate arising before dawn, and I'd rather be abed with my wife than facing you

*over a cold lawn. Yes, my friend, my wife. Or soon
to be. I have absconded with your niece Beatrice.
We're off to Scotland to avoid Mother's hullabaloo.
Don't know why I didn't think of it before, but Bea's
a right smart girl and a good hand at piquet, so that
will keep Mother happy. But most of all, I love her.
Suppose I have for years. Should have done this
long ago, but I've never been one to come up with
the right answer the first time around.*

The note was signed with one scrawled word: *Del*.

Riley and Mason just stared at each other.

"Did you know about this?" Mason asked.

Riley blinked and glanced over the note again, trying
to let the shock of it wear off. "I knew Bea was in love
with the Viscount, but I never thought *this* would happen."

First Louisa and her nobleman, and now Bea and Del.

"Oh, there's more, my lord," Belton said, shaking his
head in dismay.

Mason picked up the second note.

Riley looked down at the seal. "Who is it from?"

"Captain Hardy," Mason told her, as he opened the second missive. "Now, why would he leave a—"

This time, Riley didn't wait for Mason to finish; she
leaned over his arm and read along.

Ashlin,

*You know me to be a practical, stable man, but that
was before I fell in love with your niece Margaret.
Love, I suspect you will soon find out, will drive a
man to do things he never thought possible, and so
I find myself composing this note to inform you that
I have carried your niece off to Scotland to be wed.*

I would have made the proper addresses and asked for her hand in a more honorable fashion, but my ship is sailing at the end of the week, so I am marrying Margaret in this hasty fashion so she may accompany me on my new command, the India. *This is her desire as much as mine, and I regret any hardship this may bring between us. But rest assured I will spend every day of my life honoring and protecting and loving your niece with all my heart.*

Captain Hardy

"I don't believe this!" Mason said. "I mean, I don't have any objection to his marrying Maggie, but when did she ever meet Hardy?"

Riley shrugged. For a moment they both considered the possible circumstances, until Riley started to put a few pieces together.

"Oh, dear heavens," Riley said. "The Everton ball. They met on the steps outside. I thought the man's uniform was just a costume, not that he was truly in the Navy!"

"And don't think Del didn't help Hardy along," Mason said. "Those two were always thick as thieves when we were schoolmates, though I'd thought Hardy had grown out of such antics."

Riley started to giggle.

"What is so funny?" Mason asked.

"Well, if the Captain's ship is ever in trouble, they can send Maggie over to the other side. She could sink an entire fleet with just one misstep."

Mason laughed, glancing down at the note again. "I can't begrudge him or Del. If each has found the woman he loves, I understand not wanting to wait even a day to be with her."

Riley put her hand on his arm and smiled up at him.

"There is one more note, my lord," Belton said.

"And so there is," Mason said. "Perhaps it is from Northard, apologizing for his actions."

But the note, they soon discovered, was not from Louisa's beau, but from Lord Chilton.

"What the devil would he want?" Mason asked as he pried open the seal.

Ashlin,

> *It has come to my attention that your cousin, my ever dearest Felicity, is in grave danger. So I have taken the most drastic measure possible to ensure her future safety from that fortune-hunting charlatan Pettibone. As you know, Felicity and I have for some time been engaged in a consideration, which I thought in a few years would result in our union. I have had to change that understanding, by taking your cousin to Gretna Green this night and marrying her forthwith. I would not undertake such a rash course if it were not absolutely necessary, so I hope I have your tolerance in this matter. Felicity's fortune and happiness must be assured, and I know I am the best man to carry out this deed.*

> *Chilton*

The note dropped from Mason's hand, fluttering to the floor. He stared at Riley obviously in as much shock as she.

"He carried her off? Lord Chilton?" Riley started to giggle anew. "Because he feared Aggie was going to abscond with her fortune? Oh, what is he going to say when he finds out Cousin Felicity has no money?"

"I have no idea, but it will be better that Chilton finds out than if Felicity had gone and married Mr. Pettibone," Mason said.

"More than you can know," Riley muttered under her breath.

But it was Belton who spoke up and surprised them both. "What would make you think, my lord, that Lady Felicity is without means?"

"Well, of course she doesn't have any means, Belton. She's lived with the family for as long as I can remember."

"She's lived here only because she didn't want to live alone in her own house."

"Her own house?" Mason asked.

"Yes, sir," Belton told him. "The one she inherited from her husband."

"Cousin Felicity was married?" Riley and Mason both asked at once.

Belton stared at them. "Of course, to Lord Blanden, your mother's cousin. When he died, his will placed Lord Chilton as the trustee of her dower estates and annual income because Lord Blanden didn't trust your father to watch over Felicity's interests. Besides, I doubt Lady Felicity knows the extent of her wealth—which is probably better, given her rather . . . spendthrift nature." Belton studied him for a moment. "I thought you knew."

Mason shook his head. "Obviously not. All this time, and Cousin Felicity chose to live with us in poverty."

"This is her home, milord," Belton said. "I won't be surprised if she tries to convince Lord Chilton to move in."

"It's not as if we don't have the space now," he laughed, settling down on the steps. "Well, I guess I won't have to write my second book—I can get Cousin Felicity to repay me for her clothing bills."

Laughing, Riley couldn't help asking, "And what is your second book going to be?"

"Another bestseller. *The Unabridged Diaries of Freddie St. Clair.*"

"Freddie kept diaries?"

Mason nodded. "Found them when I was looking for some paper to write on. They will probably sell better than the sequel about you I've already drafted."

Riley sat down beside him. It was truly too much to take in all at once. After a few moments she asked, "So what does happen next in my installment?"

Mason grinned at her. "Perhaps you should read it."

"I'd rather you enlightened me."

With that, he rose and swept her up into his arms. "Belton, order my carriage sent around."

"Yes, milord," Belton said. "And the destination?"

"Gretna Green," Mason said, gazing down at Riley with eyes filled with love. "I have a scandal to complete."